THAT
WEEKEND

BOOKS BY KARA THOMAS

THAT
WEEKEND

KARA THOMAS

EMBER

Text copyright © 2021 by Kara Thomas
Cover art used under license from Shutterstock.com and Stocksy.com

All rights reserved. Published in the United States by Ember, an imprint of
Random House Children's Books, a division of Penguin Random House LLC, New York.
Originally published in hardcover in the United States by Delacorte Press,
an imprint of Random House Children's Books, a division of
Penguin Random House LLC, New York, in 2021.

Ember and the E colophon are registered trademarks of Penguin Random House LLC.

Visit us on the Web! GetUnderlined.com

Educators and librarians, for a variety of teaching tools, visit us at RHTeachersLibrarians.com

The Library of Congress has cataloged the hardcover edition of this work as follows:
Names: Thomas, Kara, author.
Title: That weekend / Kara Thomas.
Description: First edition. | New York : Delacorte Press, [2021] |
Audience: Ages 14+ | Audience: Grades 10–12. | Summary: After Claire wakes up
alone on a mountain with no memory of how she got there, she learns
her best friend Kat and Kat's boyfriend are missing and Kat's past is full of secrets.
Identifiers: LCCN 2020025002 (print) | LCCN 2020025003 (ebook) |
ISBN 978-1-5247-1836-7 (hardcover) | ISBN 978-1-5247-1837-4 (library binding) |
ISBN 978-1-5247-1838-1 (ebook)
Subjects: CYAC: Missing persons—Fiction. | Amnesia—Fiction. |
Secrets—Fiction. | Friendship—Fiction.
Classification: LCC PZ7.1.T46 Th 2021 (print) | LCC PZ7.1.T46 (ebook) | DDC [Fic]—dc23

ISBN 978-1-5247-1839-8 (paperback)

Printed in the United States of America
10 9 8 7 6 5 4 3 2 1
First Ember Edition 2022

FOR JAMES

PART ONE

THE MOUNTAIN

CHAPTER ONE

———

NOW

Earth, cold and rocky, pressing against my cheek. Tree roots digging into my body like hardened veins. I open my eyes to an assault of sunlight, wincing at the pain it sends radiating through my skull.

In my ear, panting, presumably what pulled me out of whatever state I was in. Unconsciousness? I don't want to think about that word or what it means because I don't know where I am or whose tongue is an inch from my ear—

I turn my head in the direction of shouting. A woman's voice, annoyed: "Tucker! Get over here!"

I blink until the face of an enormous black Lab, inches from mine, comes into focus. When I prop myself up on my elbows, the dog takes off, barking, running small semicircles in the area around me.

The woman shouts again. "Damn it, Tucker!"

"Help." My voice scrapes my throat, like I haven't used it in some time. I lick my lips, find they're cold as stones.

Footsteps, grinding twigs into the ground. The owner of the voice emerges from a cluster of trees to my right.

"Good Lord." The woman's silver hair falls in curls down

past her shoulders. Tucker gallops over to her and sits at her feet as she sets aside her hiking poles and digs a Poland Spring from her pack.

She uncaps the bottle of water and hands it to me. "What's your name?"

"Claire," I say.

"My name is Sunshine," the woman says. "Are you alone out here?"

"I don't know." I swallow down a knot of dread as my brain orients itself. It's prom weekend. I don't know why this is the detail I latch on to, but it's the one thing I know for sure. "Where are we?"

"Bobcat Mountain," Sunshine says. I hold the water bottle to my lips, watching Sunshine's face cloud with concern. Tucker trots over to me, his nose bumping the back of my hand and leaving a trail of doggy nose drool. I lean on my free hand, pushing myself up to get away from him. Pain shoots from my neck to my eyes.

I roll onto my side and gag up the sip of water. Sunshine's voice cuts through the ringing in my ears. "What hurts?"

"My head." *Hurts* is an understatement. My skull is being cleaved in two. I blink away the spots of light clouding my vision to see Sunshine standing up. She brushes some dirt from the knees of her pants. "You could have a serious injury. I'm going to hike to the ranger station to call an ambulance."

A tsunami of panic rises in me. I don't know where the ranger station is or how long it will take Sunshine to get there and back. "Please don't leave me."

"I promise I'll be back as soon as I can."

She's gone, the crunch of her feet on the trail fading with each passing moment. Tucker nudges my ear with his nose before taking off after Sunshine, and I'm alone again.

I squeeze my eyelids shut until they oscillate with the threat of tears. I don't know where I am or why I'm alone. I know nothing except for the fact it's prom weekend.

4

It's prom weekend. My nails are scarlet to match my dress, a boat neck with a high-low skirt.

I am not on Fire Island, where I told my parents I was going after prom, and I'm hurt. My parents are going to know both of these things very soon.

I will the last few days into focus in my brain. I see my scarlet dress, which cost an entire paycheck. I was honestly relieved when I returned it to Macy's Friday morning and thought of the money going back into my checking account.

I turn a trembling hand over; the past forty-eight hours coming back in a steady *drip-drip*.

It's prom weekend, but I didn't go. I never got my nails done; they shouldn't match the dress I never got to wear.

The cut bisects my right palm, an angry fish gill crusted with blood. It doesn't hurt, except when I flex my hand.

How did it happen? A pulse of pain radiates from my brain. *Too much. Give us a simpler question.*

How did I get here?

I'm in knit shorts, a ribbed tank. My go-to gym-class outfit. I don't remember putting it on, lacing up the sneakers squeezing my throbbing toes. Blisters, probably.

How long have I been here?

I don't know how much time has passed when Sunshine returns with two men. One is old and in a green uniform, the other young and wearing a blue shirt that says EMS. They circle me, murmuring assurances that make my eyes cloud up.

"Can you show us where you're hurt?"

I raise my bloodied left hand and the EMT produces a first-aid kit from a small duffel bag. While he tears open an alcohol wipe to clean my cut, the ranger says into a walkie-talkie, "Young female, possible head injury. Need to evacuate her."

"What does that mean?" I sit up, ignoring the sting of the alcohol on my cut.

Sunshine's hand is on my shoulder. "Claire, it's okay. You can't hike back down in your condition."

The men are gone, out of my line of vision. Tears pool hot in the corners of my eyes. "What are they going to do with me?"

"They're going to have to carry you down on a stretcher."

I'm trembling by the time the men are back with the stretcher. While one straps me in, the other lays a foil blanket over me. My stomach dips as I'm lifted from the ground. I close my eyes, the rocking motion pulling me toward sleep.

"Claire," one of the men says. "We need you to stay awake and answer some questions."

The missive my parents had me memorize every time we went somewhere we could get separated runs through my head.

When they ask my address and I tell them it's 32 Carmen Road, Brookport, the ranger asks, "Where is that?"

"Long Island, right?" the EMT says.

"Yeah." I swallow against the nausea swirling in me.

"You're a long way from home," the older guy says, and for some reason this is the thing that finally makes me cry.

We are at the bottom of the mountain, at the parking lot, which I only know because the ranger announces we're at the bottom of the mountain.

I'm loaded into the back of an ambulance, and the last thing I see before the doors shut in my face is Sunshine, frowning.

When the doors open again, I ask why we've stopped.

"We're at Sunfish Creek Hospital," the EMT says, pulling out the ramp and guiding my stretcher down it.

"Did someone call my parents?" I murmur.

The EMT frowns, pushing my stretcher toward the hospital entrance. "You gave us their number on the ride over. You don't remember me telling you they're on their way?"

I had an entire conversation I can't remember. It's unsettling, but not as much as the fact my parents are coming *here*. I said we were going to Fire Island, which is a short ferry ride from home, and not to my best friend Kat's grandmother's lake house in Sunfish Creek, three hours away, in the Catskill Mountains. I didn't lie because they would have said no; I lied because Kat's parents definitely would have said no.

Kat. I would not have gone hiking on that mountain without Kat—

"Where are they?" I'm shivering, despite the blanket.

"Where are who, Claire?"

"My friends. Kat and Jesse." The EMTs roll me through the hospital entrance; I'm not sure they've even heard me over the sounds of radios blipping, a siren behind us at the curb.

We stop in a white hallway, beneath a sign reading TRIAGE AREA. The older EMT grips my wrists with two fingers, counts my pulse. "You were hiking with friends?"

I close my eyes, reach back in my memory. There is nothing but Sunshine's face in mine, knitted up with concern. Kat, at the lake house last night, stowing hot dogs in the fridge. *For tomorrow.*

"We were supposed to go camping," I say as the EMT clips some sort of meter over my finger. "But I don't remember how we got to the mountain."

"Try to breathe," the EMT says, frowning as the contraption on my finger beeps. "Your heart rate is high."

I close my eyes. It's startling, how long it's been since I've felt pure, undiluted fear like this. I feel like I'm five years old again, wading through the crowd at the county fair, and I've lost my grip on my mother's hand.

"Will someone find them?" I ask.

"I'm going to call the ranger station right now and have them send someone up to the campsite." The EMT pats my shoulder. "It'll be okay. You're gonna be okay."

It's not until he disappears behind the sliding doors that I realize he's not coming back. His job here is done; he's off to rescue the next moron who got lost in the woods.

My stretcher begins to roll again. An orderly wheels me through the emergency room doors, past stretchers docked in every corner and along the walls, occupied by moaning bodies. A spindly woman is handcuffed to the railing of hers, despite her being unconscious. Somewhere in the distance, a man yells that he's shit himself.

As the orderly guides my stretcher behind a curtain, a woman in scrubs trots over to me and plops a plastic-wrapped gown at my feet. "You'll need to change into this."

The orderly disappears; the nurse draws the curtain and turns her attention to the cart she dragged over behind her. "Name and date of birth?"

I rattle off the information she needs and she types it into the machine on the cart; she prints a plastic ID bracelet and fastens it around my wrist, her eyes never meeting mine. My bladder is going to burst any second.

"Where's the bathroom?" I ask.

"Paramedics said you may have a head injury," she says. "You can't be going to the bathroom alone. I'll get an aide to bring you a bedpan."

Horror washes through me. "I have to pee right *here*?"

"Sure do. We need a urine sample anyway. The gown ties in the back." The nurse whisks away.

I peek around the curtain. A man in a hospital gown plods past me, toting an IV drip behind him, a cup of pee in his other hand.

I glance in the opposite direction, where my nurse is now bent over a computer.

The ache in my abdomen is so bad I'm sweating. Another five minutes and I'll probably piss myself.

Screw it. I get out of bed and make a right—the direction the man with the pee-cup came from. There's a bathroom at the end of the row of curtains. I duck in, wriggle my shorts down, and plop on the toilet. The relief is so great I could cry.

I hobble over to the sink, plunge my hands below the tap. The water that swirls the drain is reddish pink. Trembling, I turn my palms up, but all that's left is a streak of dried blood extending from my thumb all the way up my forearm on my left hand.

The sight in the mirror over the sink startles me. I don't recognize that girl, her sunburned cheeks, the scrape on her forehead.

Who are you? I think. *What happened to you?*

CHAPTER TWO

THREE DAYS EARLIER
WEDNESDAY

Eight people are piled into Anna Markey's six-person hot tub. Anna herself, the gracious hostess, made room for number eight by climbing onto my boyfriend's lap.

Ex-boyfriend? I'm not sure exactly. I haven't spoken to him since our statistics final this afternoon. Ben finished the test before me, but promised to wait for me outside the classroom because that's what you do when you've been dating for three months and five days.

Ben did wait for me, but when I finished the test, Anna Markey was with him. Anna Markey, his neighbor since kindergarten. Anna Markey, who calls him *Benny* and puts her head on his shoulder when I'm around, blue doe-eyes on me as if to say *you don't mind, right?*

After the test this afternoon, Anna was propped against Ben's locker, pouting through her signature Clinique Black Cherry lips: "I can't believe you're not coming to my beach house this weekend."

What I hoped he'd say: "There's nowhere I'd rather be than in Sunfish Creek, sexing up my girlfriend at her best friend's grandmother's lake house."

What Ben *did* say: "I know. It sucks."

He hadn't seen me standing in the classroom doorway. He didn't see me stalk off to my car in tears; when he texted *where'd u go??* I'd ignored it, plus his handful of follow-up messages.

Anyway. I came here to apologize, but I'm not sorry anymore.

Anna folds her hands behind her head. Stretches, lithe and catlike. Ben's gaze travels down over her shoulder. Noah McKenna, Ben's best friend, Most Likely to Drop Out of College by Christmas, splashes Shannon DiClemente in the face. Shannon shrieks, because now her flat-ironed hair is wet, and Anna crawls farther up Ben to escape the splash.

They still haven't noticed me, standing at the edge of the patio, trembling hands jammed into the pocket of my SUNY Geneseo hoodie. I am back to how things were pre-Ben. Invisible. His friends, the village kids, only paid attention to me because Ben decided I was someone worth paying attention to.

A tug on my ponytail. Jamie Liu appears at my shoulder and takes a swill from the Solo cup in her hand. "What up, bitch?"

I point at the hot tub, and Jamie says, "Oh. Shit."

Jamie and I stand like that, side by side, watching the scene in the hot tub. She doesn't tell me Ben and Anna are only being playful and that I have nothing to worry about. Since elementary school, Jamie Liu has been the friend I go to when I need someone to be brutally honest about my breath or to talk me out of getting bangs.

After a few moments of silence, Jamie says, "What are you going to do?"

I don't know. I need time to think. "Wanna go inside?"

Jamie glances down into her empty cup. "Sure."

Inside the house is considerably quieter. We wander into the kitchen, where Jamie grabs a bottle of Bacardi from the libations Anna has set out. She pours a few inches of rum into a cup and tops it off with a splash of Coke. Hands it to me. "Let's turn this night around."

Or, more likely, upside down.

We clink rims. The first sip of Jamie's death concoction is so foul I almost gag; there's no choice but to treat it like a shot. I drain the cup in a fluid motion. A shudder passes through me, followed by warmth.

"Woo," I say. "Wow. Make another."

Jamie obeys, more than happy to help me board the train to Sloppy Town. My muscles tighten, and suddenly my head is clearer.

Kat, my best friend, says I hate confrontation. If she were here, she'd remind me just how much I hate confrontation, but she'd still march right up to Ben for me and say something to make him evacuate his bowels in the hot tub.

Kat is not here, though.

I need to be a big girl and not leave without handling this. I knock back another drink, make a third, and follow Jamie into the living room. We nestle into a free corner of the couch; the World Cup soccer match, and reason for this party, is on Anna's television, which is approximately Dad-Owns-a-Chain-of-Ford-Dealerships inches big.

My eyelids feel like they weigh a thousand pounds. During a commercial for Buffalo Wild Wings, Jamie puts a hand on my knee. "Can we go be mean to Ben now?"

When I shake my head, the room does a full tilt. I shut my eyes and chug the rest of my drink.

"I'm going to Mom you now." Jamie reaches over and guides the cup away from my mouth. "No blacking out on me."

"Okay." My body gives a twitch and a shudder. "I'm ready to talk to Ben."

Jamie is at my heels like a cat as I pick my way around the crowd gathering in Anna's living room. Through the kitchen, out the sunroom, and onto the deck, my heartbeat mimicking a terrier's.

I stop short of the hot tub. The spot Anna and Ben had been occupying is empty. Noah McKenna, reaching for a beer on the ledge of the tub, spots Jamie and me. Freezes.

"Where's Ben?" I ask.

"Hey. When did you get here?" His eyes ferret around, avoiding mine. "Uh, I think Ben went to get a refill?"

"Huh. We were just in the kitchen," Jamie says. "It's so weird we didn't see him."

I'm already making my way back toward the house, taking the deck steps two at a time. The patio doorway is jammed with underclassmen—friends of the younger Markeys, there are three—and I lose Jamie to them.

The brief excursion into the hot June night has made my skin clammy; a bead of sweat rolls down my chest, and I can feel the hair at my crown frizzing. I swallow an acidic burp. Scan the kitchen. No Ben.

I step through the dining room, into the living room. *Where the hell are you?*

My gaze locks on the top of the stairs. On Anna, a towel wrapped around her waist. Ben, following her.

I say his name. I don't know how anyone can hear it over the TV, but Anna does.

Her head swivels toward me. She stops short on the stairs. Reaches for Ben's hand and gives it a panicked tug.

He shouts for me to wait, but I'm already halfway to the front door. I stumble on the last step and roll my ankle. *Home. I need to go home.*

I can't drive, obviously. If I call my house, one of my parents will be here in five minutes to pick me up, and even though I won't get in trouble for the drinking, I don't think I can stomach the humiliation of telling them what happened with Ben.

The shame levels me; I sink so I'm sitting on the curb outside Anna's. Stupid, stupid. Stupid for drinking that much—stupid for thinking I could ever fit in with Ben Filipoff's friends. There are only two people who don't make me feel like a fool and they're not here right now because they're together.

I dig out my phone. It slips through my fingers and clatters to the pavement. Someday the screen is going to decide it's had enough and shatter on me. For now, it's intact. I fumble for my favorites.

Kat sounds worried when she answers. "Claire? Are you okay?"

I squeeze my eyes shut. "Are you home?"

"We're at Jesse's."

"Can you come get me?"

A pause. "Where are you?"

"Anna Markey's. I think I'm gonna throw up."

"Okay. Stay where you are. We'll be there in five minutes."

The thought of Jesse Salpietro seeing me like this is the cherry-shaped turd on top of this absolute shit sundae of a day.

"Claire." Ben's voice reaches me, breaking through the clouding in my brain. "Wait."

"Leave me alone." I stand up off the curb.

"Claire." Ben grabs my arm.

I yank it back and slap him across the face with my opposite hand. He blinks at me, stunned. Commotion by Anna's backyard gate—some laughing, Noah bleating, *Damn, wish I got that on video,* followed by a girl shouting, *That's not funny!*

Ben puts his palm to his cheek. "I was just—I didn't want you to step into the road without looking."

Someone says my name. I turn around; Jesse Salpietro is at the foot of Anna's driveway. "What's going on?"

Off to my side, Ben says, "I'm taking Claire home."

"No, you're not," I growl.

"I've got it from here," Jesse says to Ben.

"Of course you do." Ben shakes his head. Tosses his hands up and steps away from me. "Have fun. She's all yours."

Of course you do. What does he mean? By the time I compose myself enough to ask him what the hell he meant, Ben is gone, and Kat Marcotte is standing next to Jesse. She's in a loose denim button-down shirt, crisp white shorts. Gold-streaked, beachy waves that can withstand the swampiest of June nights.

I buckle over and vomit on Anna's lawn.

Kat loops an arm through mine. "Babe, help me get her."

Jesse's familiar smell—grapefruit shampoo, and the hint of Febreze he sprays on his clothes to cover up the cigarette stench from his aunt and uncle's house. I close my eyes, fighting off tears. One hand on the small of my back, Jesse guides me into the backseat of his car. Instead of slamming the door behind me, Kat squeezes in. Lifts my legs and lays them across her lap so we both fit.

"I'm sorry," I say. The adrenaline is gone from my body, and I'm crashing, my anger replaced by the crush of shame.

"Why are you apologizing?" Jesse asks.

"I threw up."

Kat shifts under me. "You missed. You should have aimed for Ben. *Exorcist*-style, right in his stupid face."

"I slapped him," I mumble.

The world around me swirls. I catch pieces of their conversation:

Can't take her home like this—

Can't bring her to my house, my mom will call hers—

"My car," I mumble. "I can't leave it."

"We'll get it in the morning," Kat says.

"I slapped Ben," I repeat.

"Good." Kat strokes a piece of hair off my forehead. "I'm sure he deserved it."

"I love you," I say.

The satisfied smile on her face is the last thing I see before everything spins to a halt.

CHAPTER THREE

**TWO DAYS EARLIER
THURSDAY**

When I wake up, I'm staring at Carlos Santana.

I close my eyes in an attempt to ward off the jackhammering in my brain. *Santana poster, twin bed*. I'm not in my room.

I blink until a black electric guitar propped up in the corner comes into focus; a Les Paul, found on eBay last year after his old Fender strat was stolen from a show. Kat and I pooled our money for his birthday so we could buy him a new guitar.

Jesse is at his desk, his back to me, watching a Marvel movie trailer on YouTube, headphones in.

"Jesse," I say, but he doesn't move. I lob his pillow at him.

He swivels in his chair so he's facing me and tugs out his earbuds. "She lives."

I scramble into an upright position, the back of my skull knocking on the headboard. "What time is it? I have work at noon."

"It's ten-ish. You're good." Jesse moves toward the bed, eyeing me like a dog that might bite. He perches at the edge, leaving a safe two feet of space between us. On his carpet, I spot a pillow and a lump of a blanket.

"You didn't have to sleep on the floor," I say, even though

we both know that's not true. His bed is a twin, and Jesse Salpietro would not leave a drunk girl to sleep on the floor.

"It's fine," he says around a yawn.

I prop myself up against the headboard. When I close my eyes, I see Ben, following Anna Markey up those stairs.

I think I might puke again. "Do you know what happened to my phone?"

Jesse tosses it to me. "We texted your parents saying you were staying at Kat's."

Scrolling through my phone is a brief reprieve from the awkward silence. No calls or texts from Ben. The only new message is a reply from my mom. *Tell Kat hi.*

I set my phone down, swallowing hard and praying I won't cry in front of Jesse.

He is watching me, carefully, as if he wants to say something.

"What?" I ask.

"Nothing." Jesse swivels in his chair so he's facing away from me, a little too quickly. "I can take you to get your car whenever you're ready."

My stomach curls like ash, and a horrifying thought rises up in me. Me, babbling to Kat about how much I love her.

I am not religious, but I say a silent prayer to whoever that after I professed my undying love for Kat, I had the presence of mind to keep my goddamn mouth shut about how I feel about her boyfriend.

Anna Markey's car isn't in her driveway, saving me the humiliation of being spotted picking up my car looking like a sewer rat in last night's clothes. Jesse idles at the curb.

"Thanks." I pause, my hand on the door.

What would it cost me to say it? *I miss you. I miss how things were.*

Jesse moved into town in the sixth grade. The first day of

school, I picked a seat by the front of the bus for the afternoon ride home, squashed to the window and hoping Noah McKenna wouldn't sit next to me, because he sat behind me in social studies the year before and snapped my training bra strap every day.

When he plopped down next to me, Jesse's long, dark eyelashes were clumped together. For a moment, I thought it was the rain outside, but his cheeks were splotchy.

I couldn't remember ever seeing a boy cry at school, in front of people, since kindergarten. "Are you okay?" I'd asked.

He shook his head. "I forgot my key. I have to wait outside until my mom gets home at six."

"Can you go to one of your neighbors? Or call your mom at work?" I asked.

He shook his head—just barely, careful not to disturb the tears welling in the corners of his eyes. I took the hint and stuck in my earbuds. It was hard to look away from him. The birthmark at the corner of his right eye. Soft, brown curls. The Oreo dirt under his fingernails.

The next afternoon, while I was smashed up against the window of the front seat, I saw him getting onto the bus. I held my breath. Scrambled for my headphones, praying I looked convincingly absorbed in untangling the wires.

Someone plopped into the seat next to me. "Hi."

I tamped down the urge to put a hand to my lips, to cover the dopey smile blooming there. "Hi."

"What are you listening to?" Jesse asked.

I handed him one of my earbuds, and we listened together. I'd been listening to "American Girl" by Tom Petty, my favorite song, and I'd been hoping he'd ask because I wanted Jesse Salpietro to know everything about me.

He told me he played the guitar; I'd just watched my favorite movie, *Almost Famous,* for the first time that year, and I told him it was my dream to write for *Rolling Stone* one day.

"Good," he'd said. "You can write about how awesome my band's music is."

We spent the next few years making crazy plans like that. On the bus, at the merry-go-round at the marina playground.

"Claire," Jesse says, bringing me back. "You okay?"

"I'm fine." I unbuckle my seat belt and climb out of the car without looking back at him. "Thanks for the ride."

My parents are at work when I get home. Mom is a psychotherapist who sees patients from an office forty minutes from our house, Dad is a librarian with a rotating schedule, and I work at a restaurant, which means the three of us are rarely home and awake at the same time.

I shower and take a twenty-minute nap that makes me feel even worse before dragging myself to Stellato's Italian Table.

I've had a job there since I was fifteen, first as a busser and then a waitress. Serg, the owner, has been letting me hostess for the past month or so, since the last girl quit and no one inquired about the Help Wanted sign in the door.

No one wants to work these days, he always grumbles. Really, no one wants to work for his wife, who is a nightmare of a human being. The kitchen staff is a revolving door.

Serg's wife has sent me home crying a handful of times, and I think about quitting once every two weeks, but I'm too comfortable to ever go through with it. Comfortable with the regulars, who slip me an extra twenty around the holidays. Comfortable knowing exactly where everything is and never having to ask.

I slip through the kitchen entrance, where Carlos, the chef, is stirring a stock pot of Bolognese. The smell makes bile rise up in my throat. When I cover my mouth, Carlos says something to the dishwasher—a boy I don't know—in Spanish, and they laugh.

"Stop making fun of me," I say.

"How do you know we're making fun of you?"

I scowl. "What does *resaca* mean?"

"Didn't pay attention in Spanish class?" Carlos clicks his tongue, shakes his head.

"All we ever did was watch movies," I tell him. "The only thing I know how to say is '¿Dónde está Nemo?'"

The dishwasher boy laughs again as a girl's voice says to my back: "He's saying you're hungover."

I turn. Kat is standing in the kitchen entrance. Carlos keeps the door propped open to make stepping out for his hourly chain-smoke easier. Kat's golden retriever, Elmo, is tied to the fence post behind her, his nose in the air.

I look at Carlos, then at Kat. "You know Spanish too?"

Kat took French, and she speaks near-perfect Italian, a by-product of living on the Aviano Air Base in Italy for three years.

Kat shrugs. "I mean, it's obvious he's calling you hungover."

"She's right." Carlos whisks past us, headed for the back lot, cigarette between his lips. He gives Elmo a pat on the head; when the dog sees me, he begins to whine and paw at the gravel.

"He misses you," Kat says.

I step forward and rub Elmo's ears with my thumbs. "He just thinks I have food for him."

The Marcottes live around the corner from the restaurant. Kat passes it on her dog-walking route. She knows I could get in trouble for this, so she only ever does it when she sees Serg's truck missing from the back lot. It's been weeks since she's come by.

We both know things are weird, because Kat wouldn't have stopped coming to see me at work unless she knew things were weird.

I guess the weirdness became a tangible thing when college admissions letters went out in April.

Kat got into Boston College and NYU, her dream schools. I was too embarrassed to tell her I got rejected from mine— Northwestern's Medill School of Journalism. So, I lied and told her that I'd changed mine and hadn't bothered applying to Northwestern since I wouldn't get in anyway.

Now, Kat glances at the patio seating area. The empty tables I have to set up before we open at noon. "Want help?"

"Sure," I say. "I'll be right back."

I duck into the linen closet at the back of the kitchen and grab a stack of tablecloths. Kat's waiting on the patio when I return. She watches how I arrange one of the tables before grabbing a tablecloth from the stack.

"Have you talked to Ben?" she asks.

"No," I say, shaking a tablecloth open.

"Are you going to?"

"No."

There's nothing more to say; dating Ben Filipoff was a failed experiment. But that's not why she's really here. This is a recon mission: How will my breakup affect our weekend plans?

I try and fail twice to lay the tablecloth on evenly before Kat is at my side, grabbing the other end.

"I don't know if I should go with you guys," I say, looking up at her when the tablecloth is finally on straight.

Kat's face falls. *"Claire."*

We've had our plans in place for weeks. Unlike the rest of our classmates who will be vomiting Smirnoff slushies into toilets in beach houses in the Hamptons or on Fire Island, Kat, Jesse, Ben, and I were going to spend the weekend upstate, at Kat's grandma's lake house in Sunfish Creek, just the four of us.

I was going to pretend to like all that outdoor shit—hiking, canoeing—so Ben would think I'm cool like Kat, who has skied the Dolomites in Italy and hiked the fjords in Norway. Epcot is the closest I've ever been to leaving the country.

"Ben was supposed to drive me up there," I say.

Kat chews the inside of her lower lip. She and Jesse aren't

going to prom; that's how this all started. They said they *didn't want to,* but it's obvious the real reason is because Jesse can't afford it. The tickets alone were a hundred bucks each this year. I thought about saying screw it too and blowing off the dance to be with Kat and Jesse, but I could tell Ben cared about getting the cheesy pictures and drinking watered-down Diet Cokes and fist-pumping to "Mr. Brightside." So, the two of us were going to go to the dance and then drive up to meet Kat and Jesse after.

"I mean, you could obviously just drive up with Jesse and me tomorrow afternoon," Kat says. "Unless you're still planning to go to prom?"

I stare at Kat. "Alone? That would be even more awkward than being your third wheel."

Kat's face falls. "Claire. You're still coming."

I don't say anything. I have no defense that will betray the real reason I don't want to be alone with Kat and Jesse.

"Please," Kat says. "I want you there."

I nod, a bobblehead, powerless around her as always. It's impossible to win against Kat. The summer before sophomore year, she made a PowerPoint presentation to argue to her mother why our local high school was just as good as the Catholic school she'd gone to for ninth grade.

The world bends the way Kat Marcotte wants it to, and it's not just because she's beautiful.

The fact that she's beautiful is almost an afterthought, a genetic bonus. She has a volleyball spike that makes girls in the next county nervous. Kat makes even the most burned-out, jaded teachers write *amazing job* on her work. She's seen more places in seventeen years than I probably will for the rest of my life. She's been everywhere, while I live only in my head.

So why was I still surprised that Jesse fell in love with *her*?

CHAPTER FOUR

ONE DAY EARLIER
FRIDAY

My mom read an adolescent development book when I was ten about letting kids make their own decisions, even shitty ones. It has been the gospel in my house ever since. The only rules are don't drink too much, don't get into a car with anyone who has been drinking, and don't lie about where I'm going.

The third rule presents a problem for this weekend, because if I'd told my parents about the lake house, they'd want to clear it with the Marcottes, who absolutely do not know we're going to Sunfish Creek. Kat's parents are a thousand times stricter than mine; her mom didn't even want to let her spend the weekend at Anna Markey's beach house on Fire Island.

Anyway, that's why my parents, Kat's parents, and Jesse's aunt and uncle all think we're going to Fire Island.

My parents didn't seem to care when I told them I was skipping the dance. My mom seemed quietly ecstatic I'd finally dumped Ben Filipoff, and when I mentioned returning my prom dress, my dad said something like, "Think of all the books you can buy with that hundred and fifty dollars," because he's a dork.

Kat arrives at my house at 4:00 p.m. in her new Infiniti

SUV, an early graduation gift from her grandmother. We swing by Dolce Vita Bakery to pick up Jesse as he's finishing his shift.

By the time we get to the expressway, Jesse is propped against the backseat window, the Yankees cap he'd tilted to shield his eyes from the setting sun sliding down and covering most of his face.

"Would you rather have tiny sloth claws for hands," Kat says, "or goat hooves for feet?"

It's a game we've played since we were kids; my mom taught it to us on the car ride home from Montauk one summer, Kat and I sunburned and turning crabby as traffic slowed to a stop on Sunrise Highway.

"Hooves," Jesse murmurs, stirring in the backseat.

Kat lifts her eyes to the rear mirror. "Why?"

"I couldn't play the guitar with sloth hands."

"And you already basically have hooves for feet," I say.

Kat snorts and Jesse kicks the back of my seat, and in this moment my universe is realigned. It feels like it used to—the three of us. Not the two of them plus me.

"She's right," Kat says. "I've never seen arches like yours, babe."

And there it is, as fast as an elastic snapping against my skin. The reminder that it can never really be the three of us again.

I humor Kat's insistence on What Would You Rather until we reach the bridges that will take us off Long Island. Jesse hasn't responded to my latest: Would you rather have every hair on your body plucked out with a tweezer, or eat an entire block of moldy cheese?

I glance in the side mirror; behind me, Jesse is slumped against the window, eyes closed, lips parted slightly.

"Claire," Kat says quietly. "We're cool, right?"

I suspect it has nothing to do with what might have happened after I blacked out in her lap the other night, and everything to do with the person in the backseat and the Boston College T-shirt under her hoodie.

"Yeah." I tilt my head to the window, cheek nested in the crook of my seat-belt strap.

"I'm happy you came," she says.

For some reason, I say, "You wanted me here."

I stare at my reflection in the side mirror. Trace a finger over my bottom lip, imagine letting the words slip out. *Sometimes it's hard watching you get everything you want.*

I awake to Kat shaking my arm. I blink the sleep out of my eyes until the time on the dash comes into focus. Eight-forty-five.

"Where are we?" I yawn.

"Technically, we're lost." Kat's voice is sharp with annoyance. "The GPS signal crapped out. Can you get internet on your phone?"

I fish my phone out of my hoodie pocket, swipe a finger across the screen. One bar of cell service, and no internet connection. "No."

"Well, shit," Kat says, pulling over onto the shoulder, the SUV struggling over the rocky, uneven terrain. She throws the car into park, flips on the hazard lights, and covers her face. These are the only times I don't envy being Kat: when something goes wrong. Every event that occurs outside of her control is a mini-crisis.

It's got to be exhausting.

"It's fine," I say lightly. "Let's just stop somewhere and ask for directions."

"There's nowhere *to* stop." Kat inhales, pinches the area between her eyes. "Even if we find somewhere that's open, the house is on a private drive. I doubt anyone has heard of it."

"Okay," I say, my patience beginning to expire. I glance at Jesse, still out cold in the backseat. *Wake up and help me manage her, please?* "Let's just stay on this road—maybe there's a store or something with Wi-Fi and we can look directions up."

I half expect her to argue it's a shitty idea, but Kat puts the car into drive, eases back onto the main road. After five minutes, a gas station appears on the right. She slows and pulls in alongside one of the two pumps. The mini-mart attached to it is dark—the light is coming from the adjacent building, a squat brown box with a sign outside reading THE MERRY MACKEREL.

"There," I say.

"Claire, that place is totally sketchy."

"Yeah," I say, "but unless there's a convent full of friendly nuns nearby, we don't have a choice."

Kat eyes the Merry Mackerel, then her useless cell phone, nestled in the cupholder.

"I'm just asking for directions," I say. "Not looking for a dude to bring home."

Kat sighs. She rolls closer to the building and brakes so I can get out. "Still. Be careful."

I hop out of the car, rubbing my arms at the chill in the mountain air.

The door of the Merry Mackerel is propped open with a rock and I step into a dimly lit, carpeted bar housing a pool table and a single arcade game. My heartbeat picks up as the man and woman playing pool lower their cues and glance at me.

I avoid their eyes and pull out my phone, searching for a Wi-Fi network to join. There's one, password protected and named NOT4CUSTOMERS.

What a charming little establishment. I stuff my phone back in my jeans pocket, step down into the bar area. The woman behind the bar is busy counting singles out of the cash register. I hover at the edge until she notices me and gives me a look: *Well?*

"I'm looking for Quarry View Drive," I say. "My GPS lost signal."

The woman pushes a heavy sigh through her lips. "Give me a minute, okay?"

I move to take out my phone, ready to text Kat that I might be a couple minutes and not to send in the federal guard.

The man at the pool table—red chinstrap beard and thinning hair to match—raises his beer bottle to his lips, his eyes raking over me. He's wearing a shirt with a Confederate flag on the front and a faded pair of jeans that sink low on his bony hips.

I look away, my cheeks hot, before his female companion can catch me staring. She looks like she would crush me like a grape if she thought I were checking her man out.

The bartender returns and hands me a napkin with directions scribbled on it.

"Thank you so much," I say.

"Mm-hmm." Her back is already to me. I don't turn around again, but I can feel the redhead's gaze on me all the way out the door.

In the parking lot, I open the passenger door and fold myself into the Infiniti as Kat asks, "Any luck?"

I pass her the napkin wordlessly, my eyes on the side mirror. Jesse is awake now, his face illuminated by the glow of his phone screen.

Kat holds up the napkin with two fingers. "This probably has hepatitis crawling on it."

I push away the image of the creepy redhead by the pool table, the bartender's withering you're-not-from-here stare. Maybe it's the lingering effects of my hangover or the toll of the emotional whiplash of the last forty-eight hours, but suddenly, I'm sick of being around Kat.

"They were actually really nice in there," I say.

It's a lie, and a pointless one, but it feels good, having power over her for a moment.

Kat clamps her mouth shut and keeps her eyes straight ahead as she starts the engine.

The bartender's directions are solid; we find Quarry View Drive within five minutes of leaving the Merry Mackerel.

Quarry View is a private road, so narrow that only one car can travel it at a time. The houses are all behind iron gates. Even when I was a kid, I found it hard to reconcile the wealth on Quarry View with the shabbiness of the town of Sunfish Creek.

Kat rolls up to the gate and punches in a key code. The doors open; the SUV creeps up the driveway, a motion light springing on.

A cluster of moths hover around the light that springs on over the front door. I sling my backpack over my shoulder and follow Kat and Jesse up the steps.

The first floor is a sprawling open concept living room and kitchen, a full bathroom, and a spare bedroom.

"You guys can go unpack," Kat says, shrugging her duffel bag off her shoulder. "I'm gonna turn the water and AC on."

Kat laid out the sleeping arrangements in the car; I swatted away her offer to take the master suite, jacuzzi tub included, as some sort of consolation prize for getting dumped. I opted for the second bedroom upstairs, which has a queen bed, instead of the one downstairs with two twins where Kat and I used to sleep as kids.

Jesse and I stop at the foot of the stairs; he sweeps his arms in an awkward after-you gesture and I hightail it up the steps like something is chasing me.

I slip into the bedroom next to the master. Fumble for the light switch and toss my backpack onto the bed. I flop onto my back, on top of the comforter, and shut my eyes, press my fingertips to my lids.

We leave Sunday morning. That's less than forty-eight hours of trying to dodge being left in a room alone with Jesse. Tomorrow, when we go hiking and camping on Bobcat Mountain, I won't have to worry about Kat slipping away and leaving me alone with him, even if it means going off to pee in the woods at the same time as her.

I open my eyes at the same moment a peal of laughter sounds from the other side of the wall. I picture her flopping onto the bed next to him, him reaching out to pull her body closer to his—

My skin is itchy, and it's too hot. There's no way I can sleep up here.

I knock on the half-open door to the master suite and call inside: "Hey, I'm gonna take the room downstairs."

I hurry down the staircase, the carpet on the steps absorbing the pounding of my feet. I shut myself in the spare room and deposit my backpack on one of the twin beds, sit down beside it. Cup my hands over my nose and mouth.

Why did I think I could handle being here, with them, without Ben as a distraction? Do I hate myself that much, or had I really deluded myself into thinking I was over Jesse?

I had my chance to tell him. I had several chances. All those late-night chats on Messenger, long before Kat moved home from Italy, before Jesse's mom died and some invisible gate seemed to shut between him and me.

I thought about doing it for real last spring—before Kat started working at Dolce Vita for the summer, before they showed up holding hands at the Fourth of July fireworks show at the marina, both of them smiling sheepishly as if to say, *What did you expect?*

Footsteps in the hall, some cabinet door–banging in the kitchen adjacent my room. I draw my hands away from my face. No way through it but through it, as my mother likes to say. No way out of this except to endure the next forty-eight hours, and with a smile on my face, because if there's one thing that will set Kat off, it's the fear I'm not having fun.

In the kitchen, Kat's back is to me as she empties groceries from a canvas Whole Foods tote. I sidle up to her, root through the bag for something I can stuff my face with while Kat sticks a sleeve of hot dogs in the fridge.

"For tomorrow," she says, resting a bag of buns on the counter.

"How much do I owe you for all this?" I pass over a bottle of Moscato in favor of a block of sharp cheddar.

Kat stretches on the balls of her feet, roots around in the cabinet next to the microwave, and emerges with a cutting board. "Just get dinner tonight."

I know not to press further, even though I don't like feeling like I owe anyone anything. But Kat gets awkward whenever the topic turns to money. Even if Kat's family lives in a small house in the village and Kat shops at American Eagle like the rest of us, she'll never have to worry about money. Her grandmother is paying for her to go to Boston College; Jesse's uncle stole the cash from Jesse's first paycheck in order to pay the cable bill.

"Are we talking about dinner?" Jesse is in the kitchen archway, hair plastered to his forehead. He's in mesh basketball shorts and a white T-shirt.

Kat leans back against the counter, hooks one ankle over her opposite foot. "What do you guys want to order?"

"Anything," Jesse says. "I'm starving."

My own stomach is about to riot; in a bid to prevent Kat from launching into a dissertation about our options, I tug down the Domino's menu stuck to the side of the fridge. "Pizza. Cinnasticks. Done."

"They don't deliver out here," Kat says, and I'm too hungry to engage in further debate. I select a paring knife from the butcher block on the counter and stab open the package of cheddar cheese.

"I'll go pick it up," Jesse says. He looks between Kat and me; I shrug and slice a piece of cheese, popping it into my mouth.

"Are you sure?" Kat says. "I don't mind going."

"Nope. Gives you more girl time." Jesse bends and kisses Kat on the shoulder, grabs Kat's keys from the kitchen island.

Twirls the enamel pineapple key chain over a tanned hand. "I'll be back soon."

My cheeks fill with heat, even though Kat's shoulders are covered, and the kiss was chaste. The way she and Jesse are with each other is the opposite of the hormone-soaked couples making out in the art wing hallways.

It's the most intimate thing I've ever seen.

"There's crackers in here somewhere." Kat bows her head over the tote bag, an attempt to hide the flush in her cheeks.

I keep my eyes on the chef's knife sliding through the cheese block, on the blade that slips dangerously close to my fingers.

Domino's is called in, the cheddar is sliced and arranged on crackers, and our provisions for tomorrow's hiking and camping trip stored in the fridge. I tuck myself into the corner of the enormous leather sectional in the living room, picking at the plate of cheese while I text my parents that I'm alive and well and about to take a moonlit stroll on the beach with Kat and Jesse.

Kat wanders into the living room, carrying two stemless glasses of Moscato. I groan as she moves to set a glass on the coffee table for me.

"Do not make me drink alone, Claire."

"Dude, I threw up in the shower yesterday," I say. "And we're hiking tomorrow."

"It's Moscato. Practically apple juice." Kat pries my hand open, attempting to wrap it around the glass until I relent.

Some hemming and hawing about how to pass the time until Jesse is back with the pizza; we don't want to start a movie without him, and there's no cable for mindless background noise. The silence swells between us until Kat drains her wine glass and announces, "People have probably posted prom pics by now. Let's hate on their outfits."

Kat grabs her phone and pulls up Instagram. I scoot closer to her.

"Ben looks miserable," she says.

I yank the phone out of her hand so I can see for myself. Ben, seated at a table, flipping off the camera, Shannon DiClemente hovering over his shoulder.

Kat grabs the phone back. "Oh my God, look at Shannon's eyeshadow. Did she blend with a broom?"

My cackling halts when Kat scrolls over to the next photo: Anna Markey in floor-length white silk, strawberry-blond hair in a side-swept chignon. A literal goddess.

"Boring." Kat keeps scrolling. "Like her face."

Anna Markey is beautiful—the type of beautiful that caused panicked murmurs among the senior class girls before she even set foot in Brookport High School for the first time— but Kat wants me to feel better.

And this is why, no matter how weird things may have become between us, I am still best friends with Kat Marcotte. Some days I wonder why she even picked me to be her best friend when Kat has a coveted Brookport Village address—the common denominator among the wealthiest, most popular kids at school. But that's never mattered to her. Kat has always chosen me, even when I'm the least appealing option.

No matter how far I stray, I know I'll always have a home to come back to in Kat.

Kat and I are giggly-tipsy by the time Jesse gets back with the pizza.

"I'm not even hungry," I announce as I pour myself into a dining room chair. "I ate half a block of cheese."

Jesse stares at Kat, who is struggling with the chair across from me. "And you?"

"I ate the other half."

"Wow," Jesse says. "Love that I drove all that way for thirty dollars of pizza and Cinnasticks."

Despite his bitching, Jesse winds up eating almost an entire pizza by himself; while I wrap up the leftovers, Kat sets up a movie on Netflix in the living room.

Jesse is asleep by the halfway point, and when the credits are rolling, I realize I have no idea how the movie ended. I blink the sleep out of my eyes until they come into focus on the couch. Kat curled against Jesse, fast asleep on his chest, their hands intertwined.

I get up quietly and brush my teeth before heading into the bedroom.

Kat and I would sleep in this very room when we were kids. Facing each other in the twin beds, staying up late into the night talking about nonsense until Mrs. Marcotte had to knock on the door and tell us to cut it out or we'd be overtired in the morning.

I flip off the light and crawl into one of the beds. Toss and turn for a good bit. The thick quilt is too noisy on my skin. I kick it off; overhead, the blades of the fan rotate with a dull hum, but the air doesn't reach me.

My buzz is wearing off, my wine-warmed veins now thrumming with unrest. When I close my eyes, I can see only them, Kat curled against Jesse's body like she was made to fit there.

Kat and Jesse are in love, and even though they've been together almost a year it's hard for me to look at them and not take a trip to What-If Land, a place I don't like going to.

What if. What if.

Jesse and I were a few weeks away from starting freshman year when he asked if I could meet him at the playground by the marina at the end of my road. I knew something was seriously, horribly wrong when I got there and he was sitting on the merry-go-round, staring at the chain-link fence, hands resting on his knees.

I couldn't even get the words out—*what happened*—before

he grabbed me and threw his shaking arms around me. I patted his back awkwardly. We'd never hugged, ever, and it was the first I'd seen him cry since that day on the bus in sixth grade.

Ovarian cancer. His mom went to the emergency room thinking she had appendicitis and returned home with a prognosis of four months to live.

I told him I was sorry and he put his head on my shoulder and said it in my ear: *I love you.*

My body was still numb with shock when he started sobbing again. I sat there, arms around him, until he pulled away and mumbled that he had to go home.

I've replayed that moment a million times, my skin tingling, trying to convince myself I'd heard him wrong. And then that he hadn't meant it like *that*. Or that he *had* meant it like that and simply regretted the words the second they left his mouth.

Because we never talked about what he said on the merry-go-round ever again. Jesse seemed to want to forget it ever happened, and I played along because I knew he needed me to. He needed a best friend, not a girlfriend.

His mom died six weeks later, despite her prognosis.

Even though we still talked every night on Messenger, high school changed things. Jesse made friends with some of the upperclassmen and started to play guitar in their band, hitching rides home with them instead of taking the afternoon bus with me. When I heard that Jesse had hooked up with some girl from Westhampton Beach after Battle of the Bands, I pretended I didn't care.

Last summer, when he shrugged and said that he and Kat just *kind of happened,* even though I hadn't asked, I pretended I didn't care. But I'm starting to think there's only so much pretending a person can do before it all becomes too much.

I kick the blanket off me and climb out of bed.

The living room couch is empty, the blanket folded neatly where Jesse and Kat had been sleeping just a few hours ago.

The bay window overlooks the lake; the moon, glinting off the surface of the water, lights up the room.

I unlock the back door and tiptoe outside, triggering a motion light.

I follow the light the path carves to the lake. Deposit myself in an Adirondack chair on the dock and draw my knees to my chest. After a beat, the motion light below the deck goes out, leaving me in the glow of the moon.

I need to let it go. He loves her, she loves him, and I love both of them. If I don't let this go, I'll lose them both.

If I'd just asked him, before it was too late, what he meant on the merry-go-round, I would have been able to get over it years ago. Get over *him*.

Wood creaking. Footsteps on the dock behind me. I jolt, nearly tipping my chair backward and into the lake below. A tall, sleepy figure in a white tee and basketball shorts emerges. Jesse scratches the back of his neck, eyeing me curiously.

"Jesus, Jesse," I say. "You scared the shit out of me."

He lowers himself into the Adirondack chair beside me. "What are you doing out here?"

A breeze drifts over us. I rub my bare kneecaps. "I couldn't sleep."

Jesse drags his chair a couple inches closer to mine. "Me neither."

Why? I wonder. He's closing the physical distance between us, but he still can't meet my eyes. I don't have to be a body language expert to be able to tell he's wrestling with something he wants to say to me.

That stab of paranoia is back. Does his not being able to sleep have anything to do with my behavior while I was blackout drunk the other night?

"I would have thought you guys would be taking advantage of that master bed." I slap away a phantom mosquito from my leg so I don't have to look at him as I say it.

"We don't just have sex all the time, Claire."

Hearing my name stings; to Jesse, I am always *dude*. He only ever uses my real name when he's annoyed.

"Sorry," I say. And then, because I can't help myself: "Sore subject?"

Jesse taps his fingers against the arm of his chair, in tempo with a song only he can hear. He's always doing it, and he doesn't even realize it half the time. After a moment, his fingers go still. "We haven't done it."

I draw my knees up to my chest and pull my sweatshirt over them. "Seriously? You've been together a year."

"Why are you so shocked?" There is just enough moonlight for me to see color creep into Jesse's cheeks. "Sex is a big deal."

"It doesn't *have* to be a big deal." I shrug. "Ben turned out to be an asshole, but I don't regret that he was my first."

"*Turned out* to be? I thought the entire reason you liked him was because he was an asshole."

I take off my flip-flop and lob it at him. It bounces off the base of his chair as Jesse laughs. He goes quiet, tilts his head. I have to look away.

"What?" I ask.

"Ben was your first?"

Blood flows to my cheeks. "*Yes*. Who the hell else would I have slept with?"

"I don't know—I thought you and Amos, maybe."

"*No*. Ew, Jesse."

"Really?" He catches himself. "Didn't you have a thing for him?"

"You think I just have sex with every guy I have a thing for?"

"That's not what I said, Claire." Jesse nudges one leg of my chair. "What's your deal?"

"What do you mean?" I hug my knees closer to my chest, against my accelerating heartbeat.

"You're different," Jesse says quietly. "Half the time I feel like you can't stand me."

That's not the problem; it's never been the problem.

If I'd just asked him, I would have been able to get over it.

"Do you remember when you found out your mom was sick?" I ask.

"I mean, I don't love doing that. But yeah."

There's no sound out here; nothing except for the metallic trill of crickets in the distance, and my own heart thwacking violently in my chest.

If I just ask him, I can finally get over it.

I breathe in, out. "Do you remember what you said to me that day, on the merry-go-round?"

Jesse doesn't reply. When I tear my eyes away from him, I can feel that he's looking at me. It hits me that he's not saying anything because what could he possibly say right now that wouldn't crush me?

I stand and swat a gnat away from my ear. "Well. I'm going back to bed."

"Claire," Jesse says.

"Don't. Forget I said anything." I break his gaze, unable to stand the pity in his eyes. "Jesse. Please forget that this conversation ever happened."

CHAPTER FIVE

———

NOW

Someone pounds on the bathroom door as I yank paper towel sheets out of the dispenser.

"Claire? Is Claire Keough in there?"

I hobble from the sink to the door. On the other side, my nurse stares back at me, hand raised, mid-knock, a murderous glint in her eyes.

"I'm sorry," I say. "I was about to pee myself."

"Follow me," she snaps.

The emergency room smells like Purell and burnt popcorn. When we get back to my curtained area, the nurse says, "You need to put that gown on."

I turn my back to her while I strip, shame hot on my skin. Eventually the nurse must get tired of watching me fumble with the strings in the back; she ties them for me before guiding me onto the cot. She picks up my shorts, damp and streaked with dirt, and panic flows through me.

My phone wasn't in my pocket in the bathroom; I have no way of getting in touch with Kat and Jesse and telling them where I am.

"Did those rangers find my phone?" I ask.

"Nope. Whatever you came in with is what you've got."

The nurse kicks the brake up on the bed and wheels me out of the curtained-off area.

"Where are we going?" I ask.

"If you didn't notice, we're swamped today. I don't have the time to babysit you."

I rapid-blink away the sting of tears. The motion sends a fresh wave of pain radiating through my skull. *I just needed to pee.* "Is there any way I can get Tylenol or something? My head is killing me."

"No medication until you're seen by a doctor."

I don't dare ask when that will be. The nurse parks me in front of the nurse's station. She stuffs my clothes into a plastic bag and drops it at the foot of the cot. Panic zips through me: I'm alone, I'm hurt, and I don't have my phone to call Kat and Jesse.

"Wait," I say as my nurse is turning on her heels to disappear.

She folds her arms, bare and freckled, over the chest of her magenta scrubs. "Do you need something?" she says.

I hesitate, my eyes falling to the impatient tap of her neon-pink Nikes. I shake my head. I swallow and make the words disappear. *I'm scared.*

From my spot beside the nurse's station, I can see the TV over the bed in the room opposite me. I focus on the reruns of *Law & Order* while I wait. Someone comes to draw my blood, take a cup of my pee. When my nurse finally returns, she's carrying a bag of fluids. She hooks me up to an IV without making eye contact. Still salty I went to the bathroom without permission, I guess.

I am mustering up the nerve to ask when a doctor will be by to see me when she whisks away again. A man stops her— white short-sleeved shirt, khakis, a clipboard. He says something to my nurse that I can't hear, and she jerks her head toward me. I sit up straighter.

The man approaches; he's clean-shaven, his jaw dotted with razor burn. He looks down at his chart, then at me. His voice gives a post-pubescent crack as he says my name: "Claire?"

"That's me," I say.

He perches at the edge of my cot, his chart balanced against the knees of his khakis. "I'm Eli, a social worker here."

Of course, they'd send a social worker to talk to me. I have no phone, no wallet, no memory of how I wound up alone on that trail.

"Do you want to talk about what happened to you?" Eli's eyes are an unnatural shade of sky blue; he could say he's fifteen or forty and I'd believe either.

"I don't remember. I was supposed to go camping with my friends. . . ."

Eli cocks his head, waiting for me to complete my thought. I try to reach back, to this morning again—waking up, loading our backpacks—but nothing is there. *I was supposed to be with them, so why did I wake up on the mountain alone?*

Eli looks at my chart again. "I see you live on Long Island— what are you doing in Sunfish Creek?"

"My friend Kat's grandma has a lake house here." My chest clenches; I need Kat to get here and take control of this situation. To tell me whatever happened on that mountain, however I wound up hurt and alone, it wasn't my fault. It's not my fault my parents are on their way and we're busted and Kat's parents are absolutely going to kill her—

"Did anyone come here looking for me?" I squirm in my cot so I'm sitting upright. "A girl and a boy—maybe they're in the waiting room?"

Eli rests his chart on his knee. "I don't think so. If you give me their numbers, I could try calling them for you."

"I don't have their numbers memorized." I press the heel of my hand into my brow bone, where a fresh burst of pain threatens to crowd out every other thought in my head. How long has it been since the paramedic said he'd call the ranger station and send someone to the campsite searching for Kat and Jesse? Should they be back by now?

Eli sneezes, nearly sending me jumping out of my gown. "Sorry," he says, nudging his nose with the back of his hand. "Allergies. Do you know the address of the lake house you were staying at?"

I open my mouth, falter. "I don't know—it's on Quarry View Drive, but I'm not sure of the house number."

Eli clicks the top of his pen and drops his gaze to the chart. Below it, his leg is jiggling in a way that makes my pulse tick up. "Claire, any problems with alcohol or other substances?"

"Do *I* have any prob—no." I stare at him, at that jiggling leg, and something in me deflates. "Why are you asking me that?"

Eli pauses mid-scrawl. "It's standard when a patient is experiencing memory loss."

"I wasn't drunk—" I falter, thinking of the blood and pee I handed over, which, for all I know, could prove me a liar. "I don't remember drinking."

Eli makes eye contact with me and lowers his voice. "We do have rape kits here, if you'd like your nurse to perform one."

I don't know what's more horrifying: the thought of that Nurse Ratched shoving a Q-tip inside me, or the idea that something like *that* happened to me during my missing hours. Fear crowds out the air in my lungs. "I don't—I wasn't—"

I don't know why I can't bring myself to say it. Maybe because I can't trust my own memory enough to say it confidently. But I know in my gut that I wasn't raped, and if I was, I wouldn't want to talk about it with a man wearing a tie and a short-sleeved shirt.

Something curdles in my stomach. I feel like I've been hit over the head with a brick. Were we drinking? Could I really have gotten *that* drunk?

No, that doesn't feel right. I've never once had a hangover this bad that didn't involve *Exorcist*-puking the next day.

"I don't need a rape kit," I say. "I need to talk to my friends."

Because they're the only ones who can tell me what the hell happened on that mountain.

I've been in the emergency room for more than two hours, and I still haven't seen a doctor. Thanks to BathroomGate, my nurse is refusing to speak to me, but I got an aide to admit that the doctor is probably waiting for the results of the CT scan I haven't gotten yet.

When a man in scrubs stops by my cot and asks if I'm Claire Keough, I practically leap off the cot. "Yes."

Maybe my parents are here. Maybe Kat and Jesse are here.

The man in scrubs kicks up the brake on my cot. "I'll be taking you to your CT scan."

I close my eyes and swallow a knot of frustration.

The orderly wheels me into a dark room where a small woman in a lab coat is eating a bagel. She sets it down to greet me. "Claire."

I nod, repeat my last name and date of birth while she scans the ID bracelet on my wrist.

"Have you ever had a CT scan before?" she asks as the orderly transfers me to the table beneath the machine.

"Once," I say, prompting a whimper to slip from my mouth. "When I was a kid."

"Try not to move your head," the technician says, flushing something into my IV port. "We don't know the extent of your injuries yet."

My body instantly warms. "I feel funny."

"That's the contrast in your veins. Try to be very still when the machine starts spinning, okay?"

The table moves back, taking me with it. Panic floods me. Somewhere, in the distance, I hear the technician's voice. "Claire, I need you to be very still."

I'm scared.

I don't realize I've said it out loud until the tech says, "Don't be scared. It'll be over in a few minutes."

The machine begins to whir. A few minutes of staying absolutely still feels like an hour. My heart feels like it's going to burst from my chest by the time the table starts moving and the room around me comes into focus.

The orderly wheels me from the radiology unit and back to the ER. My nurse doesn't look up from her computer as she says, "'Move her to 3B." Behind the curtain, my father is sitting in a chair, hunched over, resting on his steepled fingers.

The sight of him sets off a series of mini-explosions in my brain. *How much trouble am I in? Where's Mom? Where are Kat and Jesse? Is he fucking* sleeping?

"Dad?" I croak out as the orderly parks my bed in the empty space next to my father's chair.

Dad lifts himself out of the chair, as if pulled out of a trance.

"Hold on." My father slides his phone from his jeans pocket. "I'd better text your mother that you're back. She's on the phone with Beth Marcotte."

Before I can process this—my mother on the phone with Kat's mom, who knows we were using her mother-in-law's lake house without permission—someone yelps my name.

Mom crosses to me, collapsing into the chair Dad had just been occupying. She opens her mouth, then closes it. Shakes her head and reaches to tuck a sweat-matted lock of hair behind my ear, too angry to speak.

"I'm sorry," I whisper, but still Mom says nothing. I've never seen this look on her face before in my life. It hits me, how badly I've screwed up. This hospital visit is going to cost money, probably a lot of it, and Kat is going to be in more trouble than I can wrap my head around.

"Where are Kat and Jesse?" I croak out.

Mom glances at my father, then back to me. "They'll be fine—what happened, Claire?"

I am fumbling for the words—*I don't know*—when a voice behind the curtain says, "Knock, knock." A pretty dark-haired woman the height of a seventh grader steps inside the room, running her hands under the automated hand sanitizer dispenser.

"Claire?"

"Yes," Mom and I say at the same time. The woman rubs her hands together until the foam disappears. She slips a penlight out of her coat pocket and aims it at my eyes. "My name is Dr. Ashraf. I'm one of the residents here. Can you look up for me?"

I oblige. She sweeps the penlight over my eyes before sitting me up. "Any dizziness, nausea, or vomiting?"

"A little dizzy. My head is absolutely killing me."

Her fingers graze the back of my neck. When they make contact with the base of my skull, I wince.

"Sorry," Dr. Ashraf says, with a pat on my shoulder. "Do you know how you hit your head?"

"No," I say. "I don't remember doing it."

Dr. Ashraf glances down at her chart. "Your CT scan showed a subdural hematoma."

From the corner of the room, my father chimes in: "A what?"

"Basically, a very big bump," Dr. Ashraf says. "I hear you're experiencing memory loss?"

I close my eyes, rewind the tape of what happened today. It grinds to a halt on Bobcat Mountain, waking to the feeling of my skull being cleaved in two. "I don't remember anything that happened earlier today."

Beside me, my mother tenses. In the chart nestled in Dr. Ashraf's arm, I catch a glimpse of a black-and-white scan of what must be my brain. "It's not unheard of with an injury like this for patients to be unable to recall the hours before the trauma."

My father folds his arms across his chest. "What's the treatment?"

"I'm going to have to call in a neurosurgeon for a consult,"

Dr. Ashraf says. "The hematoma might be small enough that it'll go away on its own."

"A neurosurgeon." My mom puts her hands on her cheeks. "She might need *brain surgery*?"

Dr. Ashraf rests her hands on my shoulders and sits me back gently. "The procedure is actually very simple. The surgeon would make a small incision in order to drain the blood from the hematoma. How bad is your pain?"

I close my eyes. "I kind of want to die."

"Have you had morphine before?" Dr. Ashraf asks.

My mother's voice is sharp. "A narcotic?"

"Christine," my dad mutters.

"I'll take it," I tell Dr. Ashraf. She gives my shoulder a squeeze and turns to leave. When she's gone, Mom rounds on Dad. "She can't remember anything and they want to drug her up and make it worse?"

"She doesn't need to remember what happened right now," Dad says. "She needs to rest."

Dad's words stick in my head as I fight the tug of exhaustion. *She doesn't need to remember what happened right now.*

Why would I need to remember at all? Why, when they can just ask Kat and Jesse?

I'm being roused from my morphine coma for more tests. Blood, X-rays, the works.

Before that CT scan, I could barely get the staff to look at me. Now that I'm Scary Head Injury Behind Curtain 3B, I'm as popular as Oprah or something. Around 7:00 p.m., Dr. Ashraf pops back in to tell me I'm going to be moved to intensive care, and yes, she knows it sounds super scary but that's the best place for me right now because the nurses can keep a closer eye on me in case anything scary does happen with my head injury.

An orderly wheels me out of the ER on my cot, my parents

in tow. My heartbeat mimics the rapid beeping of the machines lining the hall.

When I wake up, all the lights in my room are off. The sliding door separating me from the nurse's station is open, and I spy a clock on the wall that claims it's 7:00 p.m.

I sit up straight. Mom is in the chair in the corner, head tilted back. Eyes closed, mouth open, a white blanket falling off her lap that matches the one I'm lying beneath.

"Mom," I say.

Her head flops forward. She steadies herself and blinks at me. "How are you feeling?" she says around a yawn.

"Tired." I rotate to my side so I can see her better, careful not to disturb the IV tube coming from my arm. Dozens of questions surface through the murk in my brain: Where's my father? Where are Kat and Jesse? But only one makes it to my lips: "Can I have water?"

Mom launches out of her chair, makes her way to the wheeled table at my beside. There's a pitcher there, and a stack of plastic cups. She pauses mid-pour, her eyes on the doorway.

My father stands there, a tray of 7-Eleven coffees in his hands. He looks at my mother guiltily. "I was checking in with security and he heard me ask for Claire. We took the elevator up together."

Dad steps aside so "he" can enter my room. A rail-thin man with a white mustache and shock of matching hair combed to one side. Judging from his brown leather jacket, he's not a doctor.

The man extends a gnarled hand to me. There's an arthritic tilt to his posture. He looks like he would collapse if someone sneezed next to him. "Sheriff Dave McAuliffe," he says. "Are you up to talking for a bit?"

Sheriff. Why would the *sheriff* need to talk to a dumbass kid that got lost in the woods? Am I—are we—in trouble?

I shift in my cot so I can accept McAuliffe's handshake. "I— Sure."

The sheriff tucks his hands in his armpits. "You're a tough girl to get a hold of."

I'm about to point out that I haven't moved from my cot in hours when my mother speaks up. "Claire's doctors wanted to limit visitors."

McAuliffe's mustache, toothbrush-stiff, twitches. "I understand, as I'm sure you understand time is also of the essence."

The dull tick of dread in my ears reaches a crescendo. "What are you talking about?" I ask.

McAuliffe's mouth slips into a frown; he glances at my parents, who are sharing a panicked look.

"What's he talking about?" I say, louder. "Are Kat and Jesse okay?"

The sheriff blinks at me. "Well, we don't know. We haven't located them yet."

"What? I thought—" I stop short of saying it, direct my stare to my mother. *You told me they'd be fine.* Those were the exact words she'd used. *They'll be fine.*

Mom's expression morphs with panic as she turns to the sheriff. "We hadn't gotten the chance to tell her. It's been a very stressful day."

"I can imagine." McAuliffe studies me now, still frowning. The silence prompts my father to speak up from the corner of the room.

"Why don't you sit, Sheriff?" Dad gestures toward the open chair at my bedside. McAuliffe shakes his head. "No, no, I'm fine standing." What ensues is an awkward dance wherein my parents both pass over the chair, and all three of them wind up gathered around my cot in a semicircle.

"I don't understand," I say, the walls of my throat thickening. "Are Kat and Jesse lost?"

McAuliffe thinks about this question for a beat before saying, "We're not sure where they are." The very definition of *lost*.

The sheriff cocks his head at me. "When did you last see them?"

"It was last night," I say, my stomach buckling. "I don't remember what happened after I went to bed."

This admission prompts my mother to grab my hand and squeeze.

"Do you remember going to Bobcat Mountain?" McAuliffe's eyebrows, thick and white, lift so high they practically disappear beneath the brim of his hat.

"No—Kat had talked about going there and camping at Devil's Peak."

"Devil's Peak." McAuliffe blinks. "You didn't tell the paramedic you were camping at Poet's Lookout? That's the only designated camping area on the mountain."

"I've never heard of Poet's Lookout," I say. "All I said was we were camping on the mountain."

McAuliffe's expression grows grim. This detail obviously changes things. "When you say you saw Kat and Jesse last night, do you mean you saw them at your campsite at Devil's Peak?"

"No—we were at the lake house last night," I say.

My mom's hand slips from mine. She covers her mouth; my father steps closer to her, puts an arm around her shoulder at the same moment the sheriff says, "Claire, do you know what day it is?"

My heartbeat quickens. I hate the way they're looking at me, like I've somehow failed a test I haven't even sat down for yet. "Saturday," I say. "Right?"

My mother slumps into the empty chair.

CHAPTER SIX

———

NOW

It's Sunday. The idea is so incomprehensible, so *out there,* that my mother may as well have told me that my CT scan showed an alien tracking device implanted in my brain.

It's Sunday, and the last thing I remember is Friday night. Between that awful, humiliating conversation with Jesse on the dock and waking up on Bobcat Mountain, there are thirty-six missing hours during which everything went wrong.

Did I get hurt, and did they leave me to find help? Why wouldn't they have made it down the mountain? I shut my eyes, reach back in my memory for an answer to McAuliffe's question. No matter which direction I stretch, I keep landing on the dock.

The sheriff moves to questions I'm able to answer. What time did we get to the lake house? What did we do? When did we go to bed? I respond dutifully, even though the look on his face says the answers aren't helpful.

All that matters is what happened on that mountain. The only important information is what I can't remember.

When the sheriff leaves, an aide immediately ducks into the room in his wake, squeaking about needing to change the bathroom trash can. When she's out of earshot, Mom looks at me and says, "You don't remember *anything* that happened yesterday?"

"I actually remember everything," I snap. "This is all just an elaborate ploy for attention."

Mom makes a face like she's sucking her teeth, which means I'm in for it once the aide finishes cleaning the bathroom. I don't care that I'm being a little bitch—Kat and Jesse are missing, which my parents have known all day. Not only did they *not fucking tell me,* they kept me from talking to the sheriff right away.

"You should have let me talk to him," I say. "If they'd known to look for Kat and Jesse at Devil's Peak hours ago—"

"Your doctors said that being interviewed would stress you out and interfere with your test results." Mom sets a bag of clothes down on the chair. "And I agreed with them. You obviously have post-traumatic amnesia."

"Can you let the real doctors diagnose me, please?" The words slip out. The look on Mom's face makes me want to stuff them back in my mouth until I choke.

This isn't *me.* I argue with my mom, sure. But it's always about stupid shit like a wet towel left on my bedroom carpet. I am never nasty for no reason.

I want to bury my face in her shoulder and cry. *What is happening to me?*

"Teenie," Dad says. "Why don't you grab dinner?"

"I'm fine," Mom snarls.

Dad puts a hand on her arm. "Please. Grab something from the cafeteria for yourself, and bring something back for me, okay?"

I shut my eyes so I don't have to see her leave. I want her here, but I don't, because it's her fault the rangers have been searching the wrong part of the mountain for Kat and Jesse. I can't even begin to think about what that might mean or how I'll ever forgive my parents if those wasted hours wind up mattering.

When I open my eyes, Dad and I are alone. He looks at me, rubbing the stubble cropping up on his chin. "That was a low blow, Claire."

"I know," I murmur.

"You have no idea how terrifying it was to get the phone call we got. How terrified Kat's parents and Jesse's aunt were when we called them"

"I *know*," I say, bringing my voice to its full volume.

It doesn't feel worth pointing out that no one regrets this stupid trip more than I do right now, that no one wishes I hadn't lied and come to Sunfish Creek this weekend more than I do.

"They could still be lost somewhere, right? There's no way they searched the whole mountain today." My voice quavers. I know what I'm really asking is for him to lie to me, even though that's the most important rule in this family. Don't lie.

The sad look on Dad's face says he won't, or can't. Maybe because I've already lied enough this week for all of us.

A nurse knocks at the door to take my vitals around eleven. He's beefy with gym-addict arms, and the badge on the lanyard around his neck says SCOTT MILLIGAN, RN.

"Well," he says, coming at me with a blood pressure cuff. "Aren't we all smiles in here?"

Mom looks at him as if she wants to punt his balls into his throat. "My daughter has a serious injury."

"Yeah, but everything's gonna be all right," Scott says, pumping air into my blood pressure cuff. "That's what they say in Jamaica. I was just there; that's why I'm so tan."

I turn until my father's face comes into focus. "You guys should really go back to the lake house. It's late."

"We're staying here with you," my mom snipes.

Scott records my blood pressure. "Visiting hours actually ended at eight."

Scott takes a step back so my parents can give me a proper goodbye. Dad brushes his lips against my forehead. My mother collects my bag of dirty clothes from the chair, her back to me. Her shoulders rise for a beat before she turns to me. "We'll see you in the morning. I'll bring a change of clothes."

When they're gone, Scott says, "Hope you don't mind. You seemed like you could use a reprieve from them."

"Thank you."

"Try to get some sleep. Rest is the key to recovery."

In the hall, a machine beeps like a gong. I shift in my cot. "I don't think I'll be able to sleep here at all."

"Too loud?"

I think of Kat, curled into the couch Friday night, feet tucked under her. The thought of not being able to call her a thousand times to see if she's okay makes pressure mount in my head. I shake my head, knocking a tear loose.

Scott looks at me. "Oh, sweetie. Do you want me to see if the doctor will prescribe you something to help?"

"Yes please," I whisper.

He nods.

When he returns with a pitcher of water and pill in a paper cup, I knock it back, folding the thought of Jesse and Kat like an origami triangle in my brain, letting it shrink until it's small enough to tuck away for tonight.

Scott flicks off the light on his way out of the room. I turn on my side and close my eyes. The hospital blanket is scratchy on my bare legs, and it's too warm in here.

Friday night, at the lake house. I couldn't sleep. I can feel the quilt on my bare legs, my feet carrying me outside, following the light of the moon to the dock—

A scream splits the quiet. I'm running, my chest about to burst with panic.

The scream came from me.

I stumble, lurch forward, elbows and knees hitting the

floor. Warmth trickles down my hand. A flash of the drain in the emergency room, the water swirling pink, my hands furiously scrubbing.

"Whoa! What is going on?"

Hands, grabbing me. Cold tile beneath my palms. A chorus of machines beeping. I'm not in the Marcotte lake house, or the emergency room bathroom—I'm in a hospital hallway.

I stumble and blink until my forearm, streaked with blood, comes into focus.

The woman holding me shouts: "Someone get me a towel. She ripped her damn IV out."

My heart is hammering. Nurse Scott's face is in mine. "Claire, I need you to breathe."

"I heard screaming," I say.

"No, honey, *you* were screaming." Scott presses a towel to my bleeding arm. "Very loudly, while people are trying to sleep."

A small crowd of nurses have gathered to gawk. Muttering: *head injury*. Scott extends an arm like we're going to cotillion and walks me back to my room.

Once I'm in bed, Scott holds my arm down, wiping away the blood with an alcohol pad. "Oh dear," he clucks. "Look what you did."

I close my eyes as he tears a fresh needle from its packaging and guides it under my skin.

Look what you did.

Someone is rustling me awake. The clock overhead says it's 7:45 a.m. Scott is hovering over me, holding a blood pressure cuff.

"Good morning, Starshine." He hooks the blood pressure cuff around my arm. "Nurse Scott says hello. You're not going to run off on me again, are you?"

Last night wasn't a fever dream; I really did tear my IV out of my arm and take off running down the hall, screaming. "I'm sorry," I say. "I don't know what happened."

He sticks the tip of a thermometer in my ear. "Ambien happened."

Scott enters my temperature into the laptop on his cart. I wriggle so I'm sitting up slightly. "Ambien makes people freak out like that?"

"Does a bear crap in the woods? Hold still," Scott says, hitting a button that makes the blood pressure cuff tighten around my arm. The machine displays numbers that mean nothing to me. While he's putting the numbers into the computer, I sit back. "Are my parents here?"

"You were sleeping when they got here, so I sent them on a coffee run so they wouldn't wake you," Scott says. "They're very loud."

"I know."

He unwraps the blood pressure cuff from my arm. "There's a lady outside who wants to see you, though."

"Who?"

"I think your grandma? She's short and dressed real fancy," Scott says. "Wasn't happy I told her she'd have to wait outside until I checked if you wanted to see her."

My nana has been dead for three years. Her fanciest clothes came from Chico's and she sometimes left the house with parakeet crap on her shoulder. There's only one person who could be waiting outside the room, and I cringe at the thought of Scott telling *Marian Sullivan-Marcotte* she had to wait.

"You can send her in." I shift in my cot so I'm sitting up as straight as possible.

Scott leaves, dragging the cart behind him. Some murmuring outside the door, and Kat's grandmother steps into the room, holding a Louis Vuitton bag in front of her chest.

"Claire." Marian sets her bag down on the chair by my

bedside and clasps her hands around mine. She smells like Chanel No. 5; I only know what it is because Marian is the only woman I've ever known who wears Chanel No. 5. The smell makes my stomach clench because whenever Marian is around, Kat is close by.

Kat's grandmother is here and Kat isn't and this is all so wrong.

I swallow. "Hi."

Marian sits in the chair and crosses her legs, as if sitting down for an interview. She looks prepped for one: Her blond bob looks like it was styled in a salon, and her arms are toned and tan beneath a sleeveless white silk blouse. She must be nearing seventy now, but there's barely a line detectable on her face.

It occurs to me that maybe she *is* prepping for an interview. Marian was always on CNN or something when we were kids, ripping apart some bill or sparring with her opponents. If her granddaughter is missing, Marian Sullivan-Marcotte will burn the world down to get her back. The look in her eyes reminds me of Kat, furiously focused during an exam, as if her life depends on it.

"I haven't seen your parents yet," Marian says. "They'd already left the lake house when I arrived this morning."

My stomach does an accordion fold at the mention of the lake house. "I'm so sorry we used the house without permission."

"Oh, Claire, that is the last thing on my mind." Marian's forehead knits with concern as she takes me in. "I hear they're considering operating on your brain?"

I nod. "If the swelling doesn't go down they have to drain it somehow."

"My God. Do they know how a procedure like that would affect your memory?"

My throat tightens. I hadn't even considered that. "I don't know. I—I'm trying so hard to remember what happened."

"Claire. That's not why I'm here. I know how badly you want to help." Marian averts her eyes. "My son and daughter-in-law wanted to come with me. They feel terrible they haven't been here yet—Johnathan went straight to the mountain this morning to help with the search."

"How long do they think it'll take to search Devil's Peak?"

"Some parts of the terrain are too dangerous to search," she says. "Most of the volunteers aren't experienced hikers." Marian's eyes lock with mine; something shifts in her expression, as if she were seeing me for the first time, remembering who I am. Deciding that I deserve more than a politician's non-answer. "It could take weeks to search the whole mountain, I'm afraid, and that's *if* the sheriff gets FAA approval to use a drone in the search."

I don't know what to say; I can't wrap my head around the chaos we've caused with one simple decision. Blow off prom. Spend the night in the woods.

Marian moves her hand toward mine. "I don't want you to blame yourself, Claire. I know my granddaughter, and as responsible as she is, she thinks she can evade the rules."

Unease creeps over me. Did I say I blamed myself? And why hasn't she mentioned Jesse? Her granddaughter isn't the only one who's missing.

"Is Jesse's aunt in town?" I ask.

Marian's gaze drops to my bed. She smooths a hand over the blanket, careful to avoid the tubing sending fluids to my IV. "I only saw her briefly at the sheriff's station. She's staying at the Motel Six across the street."

"From the hospital?" I ask. The lake house is almost forty minutes away from Sunfish Creek Hospital; when Dad mentioned how long they had to drive to see me every day I added it to the list of things to feel guilty about for the rest of my life. The thought of Jesse's aunt only being able to afford a budget motel forty minutes away from Bobcat Mountain makes me incredibly sad.

"I offered her to stay at the lake house, but I think she felt like it would be too crowded," Marian says.

I'm about to say that I hope my own parents aren't imposing by staying at the lake house when my IV makes its gong sound, signaling that my bag of fluids is empty.

"Claire," she says, a sudden urgency to her voice. She touches her fingertips to mine. "You are so important to my granddaughter."

I don't know what to say. What can I say that won't sound insincere? There are no words to describe what Kat is to me. She showed me how to use a tampon. She made me laugh so hard once I pissed myself in her pool because I couldn't get out in time. She's allergic to bananas and she would die for her dog.

I can't think about what will happen if she doesn't come home.

Marian takes my hand again. "I know you and Katherine trust each other with everything, and well—it's important to me that you feel as if you can trust me as much as you trust her."

I nod, too startled to process, unable to think around the *bong-bong* of my IV machine.

She gives my hand a quick squeeze before whisking out of the room, calling out, "Excuse me? This machine has been going off for several minutes and no one has come to check."

Time moves slowly in the hospital. There's no TV in my room, and as far as I know, the searchers haven't found my phone. My only link to the outside world is my parents, who try to keep me occupied with mindless reading material. Only magazines filled with overpriced designer dresses and celebrity gossip, never newspapers. They say too much stimulation can put stress on my brain and slow my recovery, but I have to wonder if they're trying to shield me from whatever the news is reporting about Kat and Jesse.

I wake in a tangle of IV tubing, sensing someone in the

room with me. A brown hand is by mine, the ring finger occupied by a thin gold band with a small ruby in the center.

My gaze travels up to the owner's face. It takes me a beat to recognize her: Dr. Ashraf, from the ER.

"Hi, honey," she says. "How are you feeling?"

I blink the sleep from my eyes, unsure if it's day or night. The clock over the sink in my room reads 6:10. The whiteboard on the adjacent wall reads TODAY IS TUESDAY.

"Tired," I say as Dr. Ashraf's face comes into focus. "They wake me up for my vitals every half-hour."

"I know. It sucks." Dr. Ashraf rifles through the file in her hands. "I've got your most recent scans. Your swelling has gone down significantly."

"So no surgery, then?"

"No surgery. The neurologist agrees that you're healing nicely. You're not experiencing dizziness, confusion, loss of consciousness?"

I swallow, thinking of the Ambien incident Sunday night. "Not recently."

Dr. Ashraf sits me up. "How's the pain?"

"Not bad."

"As long as you're feeling all right, I think you can probably go home soon."

My pulse quickens at the thought of busting out of this hellhole—taking a shower, getting a real night's sleep, and finally, being able to get cable news. "How soon?"

Dr. Ashraf looks at the clock. "How does by lunch sound?"

She gives my knee a squeeze. Instead of running out of the room, like all the doctors do as soon as they have nothing left to say to me, Dr. Ashraf sits at the edge of my bed and folds her hands over her knee. "How are you doing mentally?"

I shrug, pressure mounting behind my eyes. I'm missing the most crucial thirty-six hours of my life, and I've been lying in a hospital bed for the past two days while a search party combs Bobcat Mountain for my friends' bodies.

Dr. Ashraf cocks her head, so I say, "I'm having some anxiety."

"I can prescribe you something called Ativan," she says. "You can take it as needed, especially if you can't sleep."

"Thank you."

Dr. Ashraf sits at the edge of my bed, crosses her legs at the ankle of her black leather boots. "How about your memory?"

"I still can't remember anything that happened Saturday."

Dr. Ashraf's forehead knits up. "Nothing at all about how you got hurt?"

I shake my head. "Is it weird I still can't remember?"

"No. Even when people heal completely from an injury like yours, sometimes they can't remember the accident. It's your brain's way of protecting you from the trauma." Dr. Ashraf forces her mouth into a smile. "I didn't mean to worry you, Claire."

She stands, adjusts the lapel of her lab coat. "I'll go get that discharge paperwork started."

On the way out, she glances down at the scan of my brain, the smile completely wiped from her face, but I don't let it worry me. Because I'm going home.

As it turns out, I am not going home.

Mom is; she is already on a bus to Long Island by the time I'm officially discharged. She has two patients in crisis and even though not everything is always about me, I wonder if maybe it's about me. I still haven't apologized for being such a bitch to her the other day, but she still won't apologize for not letting me speak to the sheriff until Sunday night.

Sheriff McAuliffe is the reason I am not going home, even if Dad won't come out and say it. Despite Dr. Ashraf's promise to have me discharged by lunch, it's almost four thirty by the time we arrive at the lake house.

The sight of Kat's parents' Ford Escape nestled in the curve of the driveway sucks the air out of my body. What am I supposed to say? Sorry I made it back and she didn't?

"It'll only be a few days," Dad says. "In case your memory comes back, it'll be better if we're close by. It's the right thing to do, Claire."

I command myself to unbuckle my seat belt, follow Dad up the driveway to the house, even though I'm debating shutting my head in the car door just to get sent back to the safety of the hospital.

I can't do this. I'm afraid of people I've known almost my whole life. Mrs. Marcotte, who has clipped and saved interesting *New York Times* articles for me since the seventh grade, when I announced I wanted to be a journalist. Mr. Marcotte, who dutifully sat beside his wife and watched the plays Kat and I put on as children, even though there were probably a thousand other things he'd have rather been doing with his precious time at home on leave from the air force.

Dad waits for me by the front door. He holds a hand out to me, unsmiling. I grab it as the door swings open.

Elizabeth Marcotte stands in the foyer, cell phone propped between her ear and shoulder. She gestures for us to come inside, says into the phone: "Tell him it doesn't matter how late it is—listen, can I call you back?"

Mrs. Marcotte lowers her phone with one hand, clasps a hand over her mouth with the other. "Oh. Sweetheart."

Dad clears his throat. "We didn't mean to interrupt your call—do you need us to give you some privacy?"

Kat's mother's fingers move to the chain on her necklace—a delicate diamond infinity loop she's worn since we were kids. She shakes her head. "Oh no, that was just my sister-in-law. I can call her back—come on in, Johnathan is in the kitchen."

Dad still has me by the hand; he tugs me into the kitchen, my pulse in my ears.

"Can I get you guys coffee?" Mrs. Marcotte is saying. "I just made a pot—"

A man's voice cuts through Kat's mother's chattering. "Claire Bear?"

Mr. Marcotte is in jeans and a white T-shirt, a fleck of shaving cream on his tanned jaw. Like Kat, he's tall, his skin golden in the summer months, nose dotted with freckles.

Mr. Marcotte retired from the air force last summer and took a job with United Airlines. The last time I saw him was months ago, sneaking through the door in his pilot's uniform.

He stands from the table and pulls me into a hug. "How are you, sweetheart?"

My throat seals up. Over his shoulder, I catch a glimpse of his wife, watching me, her fingers working the chain on her necklace. Last year, when my nana died, Kat and her mom were on our doorstep with a card and a homemade meal within a few hours. How am I so bad at this? How do I still have no clue what to say to Kat's parents when I've had days to think it over?

"I'm sorry," I choke out.

Mr. Marcotte plants his hands on my shoulders. His eyes—steel gray, like Kat's—meet mine. "What are you apologizing for?"

I wipe my eyes with the back of my hand, almost scratching myself with the hospital ID bracelet I'd forgotten was there. "I still can't remember what happened."

Mrs. Marcotte's composed expression collapses. She turns to the coffee maker, hands trembling, as it gurgles and spits into the pot.

Kat's father steps back from me as Dad considers him, almost as if he's surprised to see him here. "Are you headed back to the mountain?"

"They called off the search for the day. Thunderstorms expected for tonight." Mr. Marcotte sighs, runs a hand through his curls, the same shade of dark blond as Kat's. The skin under his eyes is a sickly shade of gray.

Fear pulls at me. A few months ago, I'd mentioned around Mr. Marcotte that I was terrified of flying; he winked and said he gave every nervous flier the same advice: *Look at the flight's crew, how calm they always are. You don't need to be scared until they look scared.*

For the first time I can remember, Kat's father looks scared.

A low rumble outside. Not thunder—tires crunching gravel, the slam of a car door shutting. From the way Mr. Marcotte's expression darkens, it's obvious they hadn't been expecting anyone.

My gaze moves from Mrs. Marcotte, her hand trembling around the handle of the coffeepot, to my father, still standing in the kitchen archway, arms crossed in front of his chest, to the back door, where Sheriff McAuliffe appears behind the pane of glass.

Mrs. Marcotte yelps, jumping back to avoid a tidal wave of scalding coffee. The pot hits the tile and shatters.

"I'm so sorry," Kat's mother blurts. McAuliffe stands, watching from the other side of the door, his hand frozen mid-knock.

My dad is at my side, murmuring into my ear: "Claire, let's give them some privacy."

I stare at McAuliffe, still on the other side of the door. Mr. Marcotte doesn't seem to register his presence; he watches as his wife scrambles for the glass shards with trembling fingers. His eyes dart back and forth until he can't take it anymore, snaps: "Beth. Let me take care of that."

Mrs. Marcotte straightens, her eyes welling with tears. "It's everywhere."

"Beth." Mr. Marcotte's voice is sharp. "Leave it."

My father makes a strangled sound that's half-sigh, half-throat clearing. He sidesteps me and opens the door for the sheriff. The second he crosses the threshold into the kitchen, Kat's parents snap to attention.

"Sheriff," Mr. Marcotte says, pink blooming up and down his neck. "Did you call?"

McAuliffe slips his hands into the front pockets of his pants, rocks back on his heels. "No—sorry, folks, I didn't mean to alarm you. I'm afraid I don't have any news."

I allow myself the smallest of exhales. No news means no bodies.

"No apologies necessary." Mr. Marcotte waves the sheriff, who is still lingering in the doorway, inside. "Come, sit. I'd offer you coffee, but . . ."

The weak joke seems to recharge Mr. Marcotte. He pulls out a chair at the kitchen table for the sheriff, who glances over at me. "Actually . . . I'd like to talk to Claire, if she's feeling up to it."

I knew this was coming, that I would eventually have to talk to the sheriff again, but I still feel like I'm standing in the middle of the street, staring down a bus barreling toward me.

"Of course." Mr. Marcotte grips the back of the kitchen chair, gestures a hand to me. "For you."

McAuliffe takes his hat off, crushes it between his hands. "Actually—is there somewhere I could speak with Claire in private?"

Mr. Marcotte pauses. "Of course. Maybe the patio—"

My heartbeat rises to a steady gallop as Mr. Marcotte moves to the patio door at the rear of the kitchen, sliding it open. The sheriff is the first to step outside, his body pitching slightly to one side.

My feet are rooted to the kitchen floor; Dad nods for me to follow him.

Mr. Marcotte stands by the door like a sentry as we file out. He gives me an encouraging smile as he shuts the door, closing us on the patio. I picture the smile dissolving from his face once he is alone inside with his wife, cut off from whatever is about to go down out here.

McAuliffe deposits himself into one of the chairs at the patio table. Dad and I arrange ourselves so I'm across from the sheriff, the sun-warmed metal chair searing into my bare thighs.

"I hope it's all right I sit in," Dad says. His tone is crisp, aimed at McAuliffe.

"I—yes." McAuliffe lifts his hat from his head, scratches a spot on his brow before replacing it. "That should not be a problem."

I wedge my trembling hands between my thighs to calm them. McAuliffe is obviously not here with an update, because he would have asked to speak to Kat's parents; whatever he is here to ask me about can't be good if he doesn't want the Marcottes to hear it.

"Well, best get to it. We found this not far from where you were found." McAuliffe sets my phone on the patio table, a slight tremor in his hand. "I'm sorry we couldn't return it to you sooner. We needed to determine if it held any information relevant to the search."

Dad frowns. "Can you do that without her permission?"

"We were only interested in the GPS data," McAuliffe says.

"How were you able to bypass her security code?" he asks.

"I don't have one," I say as a sigh sneaks from my dad's lips.

"Did you get the GPS data?" I ask, throwing my father a nasty look, cutting off the lecture I know he's dying to give me about personal security.

"Some," McAuliffe says, his voice even. "There's no service on the trails, but there's a bit in the parking lot and at Devil's Peak. We were able to determine some things based on when your phone made and lost contact with the cell tower near Bobcat Mountain."

McAuliffe pauses, as if giving me a moment to remember *some things*. But my memory of Saturday is as blank as it was when I woke up on Bobcat Mountain.

The air is thick with the impending storm, the gentle breeze through the trees the only thing making sitting under the late-afternoon sun tolerable. There's sweat pooling under the arms of the sheriff's white shirt. "The times are all approximate, but it would appear you got to the mountain at one and reached Devil's Peak around three. Your phone lost contact with the nearby tower around four Saturday afternoon."

McAuliffe is quiet, his fingers working the troublesome spot on his leg beneath the table, as I process this information. We didn't get lost on our way up the mountain. We made it to Devil's Peak.

We made it all the way there just to turn back an hour later?

I glance at Dad; one hand is tucked in his opposite armpit, the other covering his mouth, as he studies McAuliffe.

My voice cracks when I finally speak. "I don't know why we would have turned around. I don't even remember *being* there—"

Dad reaches and covers my hand with his. I blink away tears.

McAuliffe clears his throat. "I think we should take a step back. Focus on what you do remember. Did you three stop anywhere else on the way to the lake house Friday?"

"Anywhere besides the bar where I asked for directions? No."

McAuliffe's gaze flicks to my father, then back to me. "You're sure you came straight to the lake house after the Merry Mackerel?"

"Yeah. Where else would we have gone at eight o'clock at night in a strange town?"

My dad gives me a warning glance while McAuliffe produces a handkerchief from his shirt pocket, mops his head. "Claire, we found an empty bottle of vodka at Devil's Peak."

I don't know what to say. What does he expect me to say? If we were drinking, it's not like I would even remember.

Were we drinking? That makes no sense. Drinking is not something the three of us ever really did together. I did my fair share of it with Ben and his friends, and sometimes Kat and I managed to get our hands on a bottle of wine from one of the chefs at Stellato's. But Jesse didn't drink, and out of fear it would make me get too honest, I didn't drink around Jesse.

"Are you sure you didn't perhaps stop at a liquor store at some point?" McAuliffe's voice is prodding, as if my silence were some sort of admission.

"No," I say. "None of us even has a fake ID. Kat and Jesse don't really drink."

McAuliffe clears his throat. "Claire, there was also an empty bottle of wine in Kat's trunk."

"Kat brought that. She and I drank it Friday night." I avoid my father's eyes. "We didn't get drunk or anything—it was practically apple—"

Dad cuts in: "I don't mean to be rude, but what does the girls having wine Friday night have to do with what happened Saturday? The emergency room doctor said Claire's blood alcohol content was completely normal when she arrived."

I can't help tossing Dad an irritated glare, for knowing something about me that I didn't even know myself.

McAuliffe looks at me. "It's not uncommon for teenagers to conceal drinking problems, even from their closest friends."

"I'm sorry, which one of us are you saying has a secret drinking problem?" As the words leave my mouth, Dad's body tenses next to mine, his eyelids fluttering shut.

"I understand that alcoholism runs in Jesse's family," McAuliffe says.

"His uncle's side," I say. "But it's not his biological uncle."

McAuliffe shifts in his chair. "Claire—when I spoke with Jesse's aunt, she seemed concerned that he was depressed."

Something about McAuliffe's tone makes my heartbeat stall. I know how other people see Jesse; head always bent over a guitar, average-to-less-than-average grades, no interest in college. On the surface, he's the opposite of Kat in every single way, but it doesn't mean he has no ambition of his own. As much as he loves playing music, his dream is to write it.

Jesse's aunt might look at him and see someone who has withdrawn from life; I know Jesse Salpietro, though, and it's only because he's imagining a better one. "He's not depressed," I say.

"She said he was sleeping more than usual during the day," McAuliffe says. "And he was on the phone until very late each night."

"He naps when he gets home from work because his job is tiring. He has to wake up at four thirty, and he's on his feet all day."

McAuliffe frowns. "Are you aware his band broke up last month?"

Jesse was one of my best friends and he hadn't told me Salt Lyfe broke up? I think of waking up in Jesse's bed the other morning. How he'd been at his computer, headphones in, dead to the world. Whenever he was around that Fender, it was in his arms, calloused fingers working the strings, but he hadn't been playing.

"He hadn't mentioned it," I say, deflating.

Dad is searching my gaze, his forehead creasing. McAuliffe, on the other hand, looks as if he's about to tell me he ran over my beloved pet with his pickup truck. "Did Kat ever express concern about Jesse's behavior? Any issues with jealousy, maybe?"

"No," I say. "Why are you asking this? Jesse is missing too, but you're acting like he's a suspect or something."

I look over at my dad for some reassurance that I have it wrong—that McAuliffe's focus on Jesse's state of mind is totally innocuous—but he's watching the sheriff, worry in his eyes.

McAuliffe's voice is gentle when he finally speaks. "Claire, partner violence can happen even among teenagers. I wouldn't be doing my job if I didn't consider that whatever happened at Devil's Peak was a domestic incident."

Domestic incident. Like, a murder-suicide? The thought

zaps all the oxygen from my blood. I lean forward, rest my elbows on the patio table, bury my face in my hands.

"Claire?" Dad has me by the shoulders. "Honey, are you with us?"

I blink until Dad's face comes into focus; the sheriff is on his feet, crossing over to us.

"Yeah," I mumble through the prickly feeling of my blood returning to my lips. "I'm fine."

"Is there anything else you need from us, Sheriff?" Dad asks.

"I, well, there's just one more thing I need to do right away." McAuliffe looks flustered at the interview being cut short. "It won't take long."

McAuliffe reaches in the pocket of his khakis. My insides frost over as I see what he's holding—a digital camera.

"I'll need to take photographs of Claire's injuries," he says. "It's protocol."

Dad blinks at McAuliffe. "Why wasn't this done in the hospital?"

McAuliffe's face flushes. "Well, truthfully, when Claire was brought in, the rangers didn't realize they were dealing with a potential crime."

The word lands like a kick to my stomach. I think of the girl in the emergency room mirror. It was as if I had woken up in someone else's body. Covered in scratches, bruises, that cut I had no memory of getting.

McAuliffe turns the camera over in his hands. A troubled *hmm* leaves his lips. "Er, one moment—"

He doesn't know how to turn the damn thing on. After some fiddling, the camera chirps to life; McAuliffe uses his free hand to dig out his handkerchief and mop the sweat from his forehead. "Claire, if you wouldn't mind standing."

I ignore the steady thump in my chest and move against the side of the house. Obey all of McAuliffe's directions. *Tilt your head,* snap. *Turn this way,* snap.

"If you could turn your hands up, please."

I close my eyes, feel McAuliffe's gaze lingering over my cut, now reduced to a thin pink scab. When I force myself to look at him, the sheriff is holding his camera to his chest. His cheeks have gone pink. "If you wouldn't mind—your legs—could you turn a bit for me?"

"Yeah. Sure."

I glance down while McAuliffe scans my bare legs. Shut my eyes until he speaks.

"I think I have all I need. Thank you both, for your time."

I'm not sure how I'm supposed to respond, so I stay silent as Dad puts an arm around my shoulder and moves me aside so McAuliffe can slide open the back door to the kitchen.

In the window overlooking the patio, the curtains rustle. Dad's arm tenses around me; I know he saw it too. Someone— one of Kat's parents—watching us, maybe, studying the words forming on our lips.

But when we make our way into the kitchen, it's empty, silent except for the hum of the fridge. The floor tiles are gleaming white, not a trace of the mess that was there earlier.

Dad shuts me in the bedroom with a command to nap while he picks up my painkillers and Ativan from the pharmacy in town. I close my eyes, listen for the slam of his car door in the driveway outside the window over my bed. Moments ago, Mr. Marcotte left to return to the mountain. I don't know where Mrs. Marcotte has disappeared to or where Kat's grandmother is. I haven't seen Marian at all since she visited me in the hospital.

I curl up on my side, away from the window. My phone is charging on the nightstand beside me. For the past several days, I felt untethered without it. Now, I'm avoiding it like it's a grenade.

I can't bring myself to listen to the panicked voice mails my parents must have left when I didn't check in Saturday night. Or read the texts from people at school, who have no doubt heard by now that something happened to the three of us this weekend. How do I even begin to explain myself?

Yes, I was there. No, I have no idea what happened, because I have post-traumatic amnesia. No, I'm not full of shit, I swear.

I shut my eyes against the ache brewing behind them. Even more than the prescription-strength ibuprofen waiting for me at the pharmacy, I want the Ativan. I want to slip away into numbness, to sleep until this nightmare is over.

My heartbeat picks up, the memory of my Ambien trip sending gooseflesh rippling across my body. The nurse had said Ambien can make people hallucinate.

But what if the hallucination had grown from some seed of truth? Had I actually remembered something while I was unconscious? What—or who—was I running from? I'd thought maybe I got separated from Jesse and Kat after I hit my head; Kat was an experienced hiker. She would have known it was too dangerous for me to hike down with a head injury. Had she and Jesse left to get help, only for something worse to happen to them on the way down?

The only problem with that theory is that neither Kat nor Jesse would leave me alone, hurt and without cell service, on the side of a mountain.

So then, what—had I gotten hurt after we got separated? According to the sheriff, the data on my phone revealed that we made it to Devil's Peak in the afternoon. We were supposed to camp overnight, and yet, by four, my phone was so far deep in the wood, it stopped pinging the nearby tower completely.

Why would we hike all the way there just to turn around?

For *me* to turn around. There's nothing to suggest Kat and Jesse were with me, that they left the campsite at all.

I move my hand up to my neck, let my fingers find the

bump at the base of my head. If I was running through the woods, I could have tripped on a rock or one of the gnarled tree roots jutting from the trail. If I was running, terrified and distracted, I could have fallen hard enough to knock myself out.

But *why* was I running? Why was I so terrified? Because of something I'd seen at Devil's Peak?

I lie back on my pillow, press the heels of my hands to my eyes.

No. Jesse wouldn't hurt Kat or me. I've never even seen him get *angry*. Even in freshman year, when he got into a fight in the hallway with some asshole sophomore who'd been teasing him, Jesse was white in the face when a teacher pulled the other kid off him. When Jesse looked down at his hands, drenched in the blood spurting from his nose, he'd started to tremble, completely unaware of me shoving a maxi pad from my bag at him to stem the flow of blood.

No. Jesse wouldn't kill his girlfriend. He wouldn't kill his girlfriend and then kill *himself*.

But that's what McAuliffe thinks happened, right? He thinks Jesse was depressed.

I think of my best friends as I last remember them: curled into each other on the couch, asleep. It had been almost unbearable to watch—how happy and in love they were—unbearable because he wasn't in love with me.

Now, though, I would do anything to have them back.

I wasn't raised with religion, but I don't know if I accept that it's all random, that we're not accountable to anyone. I make a silent bargain with whoever is listening: *Please. I'll get over him. I'll accept them, I'll be a better friend, if only they can come home and be okay.*

I use my shoulder to nudge away the tears trickling down my cheek. Inhale, and grab my phone. I skip over everything—missed calls, a handful of texts and voice mails—and find Kat's number in my contacts.

Kat never set up a voice greeting. An automated voice tells me the user I have reached is not available, to leave a message after the tone.

I end the call and hold my phone to my chest, my heart thumping like a jackrabbit's. I know what I'll hear if I call him and I know what it'll do to me but I can't help myself. Because if I can hear his voice, it means he's still *here,* doesn't it?

I find Jesse's number, press call.

Hey, it's Jesse—you should probably just text me instead of leaving me a long-ass voice mail I probably won't listen to . . .

The bedroom door hinge creaks open. I flip my phone upside down to hide the light. Squeeze my eyes shut, my pillow wet under my cheek.

"Claire?" Dad whispers, the crinkle of a paper bag at his side.

I say nothing, letting my chest rise and fall steadily, as if I were asleep.

CHAPTER SEVEN

———

NOW

Dad left my prescriptions on the nightstand before sneaking out to help Mrs. Marcotte with dinner. As soon as his footsteps fade down the hall, I fumble for the bottle of water next to the medication. The dregs of water in it are enough to swallow an Ativan and two ibuprofen. I shut my eyes, my veins warming from the Ativan, and block out everything but the steady plink of raindrops on the bedroom window.

I'm powerless against the riptide of exhaustion. I picture storm clouds rolling over the mountain, the trails turning to rivers as the ground is battered by rain. I think of the blood swirling down the drain in the emergency room bathroom, my fingers tracing the cut on my palm until I fall asleep.

When I wake, it's too quiet. I realize I'm listening for the sound of my IV machine beeping, the nurses chatting in the hall outside my room.

I blink the sleep from my eyes. Sunlight streams through the cracks in the blinds above the twin bed across the room. The bed is empty and made, the corners of the quilt tucked in. My father's things litter the shared nightstand between our beds: some spare change, his wallet, a receipt from the hospital cafeteria.

Dad can't be far if his wallet's here, but I'm afraid to get out of bed, to move through the house without him as a buffer between Kat's family and me.

I sit up and crack my neck. In the mirror over the dresser, I catch a glimpse of myself.

I slept straight through the night, through a storm, but the full-length mirror in the room shows me the area under my eyes is so gray it looks bruised. The one shower I took in the hospital made me feel even dirtier; my hair is matted in an osprey nest atop my head.

I head for the bathroom across the hall, the bedroom door groaning when I push it open. From the kitchen, Mrs. Marcotte calls my name. So much for sneaking into the shower. I pad down the hall, praying that my father is in the kitchen with Kat's mother.

Mrs. Marcotte is at the sink. The time on the stove says it's seven forty-five, but she's already fully dressed in a crisp white-and-blue-striped blouse and beige slacks. Her honey-blond hair is in a neat bun. The only thing out of place is a smudge of pale concealer on the inside of her nose.

"I hope we didn't wake you," Mrs. Marcotte says.

My gaze locks on the kitchen table at the corner of the room, where the rest of *we* is seated.

Amos Fornier, Kat's cousin. He sets down the croissant he's eating and offers me a grim smile. "Hey."

My insides feel like they've been vacuumed up. I can't reply, can't crack through the icy grip of panic to even muster a simple *hello.*

What the fuck is he doing here?

But then, Amos is family. He has more of a reason to be here than I do.

Mrs. Marcotte wipes her hands on a dish rag. "Claire, you remember Amos, right?"

Amos brushes a flake of dough from his lip with his thumb. He looks the same as he did two and a half years ago—same gray-blue eyes, sun-streaked hair that falls just behind his ears. He looks the same, but *better,* while I'm braless under a ratty T-shirt and haven't showered in three days.

"It's been a while," he says. He continues to pick at his croissant, giving off no indication he's thinking of exactly what happened the last time we saw each other.

I swallow against the bile rising in my stomach. "When did you get here?"

"Late last night." Amos leans back in his seat, drapes an arm around the empty chair next to him. He's in a salmon hoodie with a sailboat on the pocket. In spite of myself, my gaze travels down his legs, tanned and golden-haired.

"Amos is my knight in shining armor," Mrs. Marcotte says. "He brought a bunch of things I needed from home, including this."

She's holding up a full pot of coffee. It takes me a beat to remember the incident with the coffeepot yesterday, to reconcile this frenetic, smiling Mrs. Marcotte with the mess she was yesterday.

"Would you like a cup, Claire?" she says, already opening the cupboard where the mugs are kept. I'm only half listening, my attention on the stack of papers next to Amos on the kitchen table.

"Sure," I say, and while Mrs. Marcotte's back is turned, I edge closer so I can read the flyer at the top of the stack.

Missing: Katherine Marian Marcotte

Kat stares back at me, golden hair radiant even in a laser-printed photo. She's bent over the counter at Dolce Vita Bakery, her hair piled into a bun atop her head, smiling with her lips closed.

Katherine was last seen on Bobcat Mountain Saturday, June 26.

Kat is 5'5", one hundred and five pounds, and has a small scar over her right eyebrow. She may have been wearing a hot-pink bandana and a gray tank top at the time of her disappearance.

At the bottom, almost an afterthought: KAT WAS LAST SEEN WITH JESSE SALPIETRO.

Quietly, from the table, Amos says softly: "Fucked up, right?"

I look over the flyer, pulse pounding in my neck. Amos drops his gaze from me to the phone on the table in front of him as Mrs. Marcotte returns with a cup of coffee for me.

"Thank you." I bring the mug to my lips. "Do you know where my dad is?"

"He got up a little while ago," Kat's mother says. "He said he was going for a quick jog. Do you take cream and sugar?"

My best friends are missing, we're basically being held captive in this lake house, and my father went for a run like we're on a freaking cruise?

"Amos brought some pastries for breakfast, but I could also cut you some fruit. . . ." Mrs. Marcotte flits back to the counter and grabs the dish towel absently. I should sit and tell her not to worry about me, I can fend for myself, but she has been this way as long as I've known her.

In any case, though, I am not sitting down to have breakfast with Amos Fornier. I glance at Amos, but he's already scrolling CNN's home page on his phone, checked out of the conversation.

"Mrs. Marcotte—I, um—actually, do you mind if I take a shower?"

"Of course not," Mrs. Marcotte says. "Did Kat explain how to adjust the new faucet in the guest bath?"

Her voice cracks on her daughter's name. I shake my head, my throat tight.

Mrs. Marcotte forces a smile. "I'll show you, then—it's tricky."

I follow Kat's mother out of the kitchen, probably a little

too eagerly. I would do anything right now to put as much distance as possible between Amos and me. I would submerge my body in drain cleaner and dissolve down the tub drain, Russian mafia-style, if it meant I wouldn't have to spend another second under the same roof as him.

When we get to the bathroom, my heartbeat is so wild I barely hear Mrs. Marcotte as she bends over the clawfoot tub. "There are two controls—you have to put the tub one on first—"

I hang by the vanity awkwardly, as Mrs. Marcotte adjusts the tap until water begins to flow from the showerhead. "Thank you."

"Of course. The towels are—"

Mrs. Marcotte turns from the tub, pauses. Watches me open the closet door to the right of the vanity.

"In there," she says, her hand moving to the infinity loop at her neck. A question flickers in her eyes. How did I know where the towels were, if I didn't take a shower here last weekend?

"Thank you," I repeat stupidly, even though I feel like I owe her an explanation.

"Of course," Mrs. Marcotte says, her smile slipping. "Let me know if you need anything else."

I have been standing under the blast of the showerhead for almost ten minutes, working out the knots in my hair with conditioner that smells like violets and probably costs more by the ounce than white powder heroin.

My thoughts are forming a squall in my head. There are only two closets in this bathroom; the odds were pretty good I'd pick the one that houses the towels.

But I'd opened that closet without even thinking what I was doing. Almost like I knew the towels were there because I'd taken a shower Saturday morning before we went hiking.

I close my eyes against the blast. How is it possible I can remember a piece of information—where the guest towels are kept—but not the act of standing *right here* in this tub?

Does it mean that my memories from Saturday are in a locked drawer in my brain somewhere? The hospital neurologist told me it could take weeks or months to get my memory back, if I do at all. He'd been careful to work that part in: that some people with head injuries like mine never get their memory back at all.

The thought makes me want to crawl out of my skin. I rinse my body, climb out of the tub, and wrap myself in the towel. When I get back to the bedroom, Dad is perched on the edge of his bed, panting, shirt soaked.

"You went for a run?" I hiss, closing the door behind me. "Doesn't that seem a little *insensitive*?"

Dad blinks, face pink and sweaty. "Claire, did something happen while I was gone?"

I sit on my bed, opposite him, pulling the towel tight around my body. I'm projecting onto my dad because I'm scared—scared that my friends might be dead, scared I'm missing thirty-six hours of my life, and now, scared that maybe Mrs. Marcotte doesn't trust I'm telling the truth about what I remember.

Dad wipes sweat from his brow, waiting for me to answer his question.

"I just don't want to be here," I whisper. I don't want to be here without Kat and Jesse; I don't want to be here when they're found.

It's been more than seventy-two hours. I watch *Dateline*. I know what their odds of being found alive are.

"Oh, baby doll." Dad puts his hands on his knees, but doesn't motion to cross to my bed to comfort me. Probably because I'm in nothing but a towel so it might be weird so I just sit there, practically naked in front of my dad, crying.

I fan my eyes with the hand that isn't holding up my towel,

even though it's too late. I'm probably a splotchy mess. Mrs. Marcotte and Amos will see and wonder what the hell *I'm* crying about when I'm the one who made it off that mountain alive.

"Can we do something to help today?" I sniff.

"Like what?" Dad frowns. "You're supposed to be resting."

"I don't know, but I can't go another day being completely useless." In the hospital, I had a purpose, even if that was just existing as a body for the nurses and orderlies to draw blood from, usher from test to test.

"What about the flyers?" I ask. "Do they need help hanging them or something?"

"They were going to go door-to-door in town with them," Dad says, watching me stand and paw through my backpack for the spare bra I packed.

"Great, we can help cover more ground then." I grab the plastic Walmart bag of clothes my mother picked up for me while I was in the hospital. A package of granny panties, black yoga pants, and a cotton T-shirt emblazoned with a peace sign. I step behind the closet door so Dad can't see me drop my towel and wiggle into my bra.

When Dad speaks, his voice is flat, defeated, as if he knows he's not keeping me in this house all day. "Are you sure you're up for all that driving around?"

"Positive."

Dad sighs. "I'll go tell Beth and grab a stack of flyers."

When I'm cleaned up and dressed, Dad already has the car running outside. This is the first time we've been truly alone since McAuliffe's visit yesterday afternoon.

I feel like I need to defend myself. Defend Jesse. All the words wither and die on my lips. Finally, Dad breaks the silence by saying, "Want to try to find NPR?"

I fiddle with the seek buttons on the radio, even though it's useless; there's barely a signal up here. I skip over the twang of a banjo, a garbled Aerosmith song, before we opt for total quiet instead.

Dad follows the signs directing us toward Grist Mill, a town south of Sunfish Creek. The roads are winding, prompting me to shut my eyes against the swell of nausea.

"This looks like a good place to start," he says.

I open my eyes as Dad coasts to the curb and cuts the engine. We're on a residential street lined with squat single-story houses in various stages of decay. There is no movement around the home we're parked in front of; on the lawn is a sun-faded kiddie pool, the surface of the browning water strewn with debris from last night's storm.

Dad plucks a flyer from the top of the stack in my lap. I watch him head to the house. Ring the doorbell, knock. Repeat. Eventually he slips the flyer inside the mailbox beside the door and heads back to the car.

The houses are far enough apart that we have to drive to the next house and gradually we fall into a rhythm that thankfully requires little talking: I hand him a flyer as he gets out of the car, and he knocks on the front door. If no one answers, he sticks a flyer in the mailbox and we move on. I count how many we hit because I think this entire exercise will drive me crazy if I don't.

Dad climbs back into the car after house number twenty-eight and creeps up to twenty-nine, a ranch with faded brown siding. In the driveway, there's a pickup truck, its back window plastered with so many decals it's a miracle the driver can see to back out. Among them: a skeleton giving the middle finger, a Confederate flag, and an assault rifle with the words COME AND TAKE IT.

"I don't think you should knock on the door," I say, eyeing the house uneasily. A dark bedsheet is tacked over the front windows.

Dad puts the car in park. "Why?"

I point at the back window of the truck. "I don't exactly get a welcoming vibe."

"Don't be silly," Dad says, but when he climbs out of the car I notice him glance at the decals, frowning.

I track Dad up the front porch of the house, my heart rocketing in my chest. Watch him knock, wait a beat.

A man steps out, shutting the screen door behind him. He's wearing jeans with oil stains on the shins and a black T-shirt. When Dad holds up the flyer, the man rests his hands on his hips, head tilted slightly. Listening. He grabs the flyer and nods to Dad.

The entire transaction occupies less time than it takes for me to evict the sneeze lodged in my nose. When Dad starts heading back for the car, the man doesn't go back inside his house.

I can't tear my eyes away from him. His hair is reddish blond and he has a scrubby beard shaved low to his jawline. My pulse begins to race.

I *know* him. But that's impossible, because I don't know anyone in this town.

The man's gaze lands on me. He drops his hand from his beard and cocks his head. Stares back at me in a way that sends gooseflesh rippling over my arms.

He recognizes me too.

He frowns. I tear my eyes away from him and stare straight ahead, heart hammering. When I steal a glance back at the house, the man is gone, and Dad is opening the driver's side door.

A slick of sweat coats the back of my neck. I fumble for the control to lower the window. It's too damn hot in here, I need air—

Dad's hand is on my shoulder. "Claire. Are you okay?"

I don't know. "What did that man say to you?"

Dad gapes at me. "He didn't really say anything. Claire—what's going on?"

"Do you have the sheriff's number?" I ask. "I need to talk to him."

CHAPTER EIGHT

———

NOW

The parking lot of the Sunfish Creek's sheriff office is worse than a Target's on Christmas Eve. Reporters, tailgating.

A uniformed sheriff's deputy flags us down. Dad tells him we have an appointment, and the deputy directs us around a blockade.

"Park in the back lot," he tells us. "Someone will let you in the back to avoid the vultures."

As Dad parks, I swallow to clear my throat of the rising panic. They're not here for me; the articles I found online about Kat and Jesse's disappearance didn't mention me at all.

Kat is the reason the story is blowing up. An attractive missing teenage girl, the granddaughter of a prominent former congresswoman? It's their Super Bowl.

"Marian was on the *Today Show* this morning," Dad says quietly as we climb out of the car. "She left for her apartment in the city last night."

The back door to the sheriff's station is propped open. Dad and I head through it, where Dave McAuliffe waits in the hallway, his fingers working at his belt buckle. "Thanks for coming in," he says, as if we're doing him a favor, and I hadn't grabbed the phone and demanded to talk to him when the receptionist told us the sheriff was at the mountain and she didn't know when he'd return.

Behind the front desk is an empty chair and a handwritten sign that reads RING BELL FOR DEE. McAuliffe ushers us past a row of empty cubicles and through a door with a frosted-glass pane.

McAuliffe lifts the phone on his desk from its cradle before he even sits. He tucks it between his ear and shoulder and says into the mouthpiece: "Hello, Dee? Please, for the love of God, tell them they've got to wait at the street."

In the corner, propped on the windowsill, is a fan blowing warm air at us. There's barely room for the two chairs squashed opposite McAuliffe's desk. My father and I stuff ourselves into them, our elbows knocking into each other's.

"These reporters," McAuliffe says, his voice deflating. He shakes his head, as if finishing the thought is too exhausting. I almost feel sorry for the poor bastard. He looks like he should be in a pool in some retirement community in Florida by now.

McAuliffe leans forward and props his elbows on his desk. He raps a pen against the knuckles on his opposite hand. "I hear you believe you have important information?"

I swallow, my nerves clogging my throat. "I saw a man this morning, in Grist Mill. I recognized him."

The pen in McAuliffe's fingers goes still. "Your memory's come back?"

"No—my dad and I were passing out flyers this morning and this man opened the door at one of the houses. I don't know where I've seen him before, but I knew him, and he was looking at me funny. Like he recognized me too."

McAuliffe frowns. Shifts his gaze sideways to my father, as if to say, *You dragged me away from the search because someone looked at her funny?*

"I'd seen him before," I say, sure of it. "I just can't remember where. Maybe it means we ran into him on Saturday."

No one speaks; the purr of the fan in the corner is the only sound in the room.

"All right," the sheriff says. "Perhaps you could give me some more information on this man?"

I don't like McAuliffe's tone; he sounds like my parents when I was a small child, after I'd crawled into bed with them after waking from a nightmare. *And then what did the scary man do to you?*

The words are on my tongue when my father cuts in. "He lives on the corner of Phoenicia Road." I feel a surge of gratitude for my father for thinking to note the house number.

Something clicks into place in McAuliffe's expression when he hears the address. He holds up a finger—*hold, please*—and fumbles through the pages in the filing folder in front of him.

"What is it?" I ask, my heart stalling.

The sheriff sets the folder down, looking from me to my father, without really looking at either of us. "I spoke with a man who lives there yesterday. He was on Bobcat Mountain on Saturday and came forward with some information."

My pulse floods my ears, my thoughts piling up in my brain, chaotic as a highway wreck. *I did see that man. I remembered something.*

I will the man's face into focus, dive deeper into the black hole of my memory. I saw him, while we were hiking, or maybe at the campsite. I couldn't have just *seen* him, though—I remembered his face, and he remembered me.

Did we talk to him?

It's Dad who finally breaks the silence. "Did the man have any helpful information?"

"I'm afraid I can't tell you that," McAuliffe says.

"Why not?" The bubble of hope building in me that I might finally get an answer about what happened Saturday. "I was *there*—I just don't remember."

McAuliffe's upper lip twitches. "I can't share details of an interview with a witness."

"So I don't have a right to know something I said or did just because I can't remember?" Anger floods my voice, despite how hard I'm trying not to leap across the desk and rip McAuliffe's mustache off his face. He has a piece of my memory, and he's holding it hostage. Why?

Dad puts a hand on the armrest of my chair, a warning.

"Quite frankly, my department is concerned about the level of media attention this case is attracting." McAuliffe's gaze shifts to the window at the rear of his office, a few feet from the circus in the parking lot. "Any leaks could compromise the integrity of this investigation."

Dad's mouth falls open. "Claire's not going to speak to the press."

"I appreciate your reassurance, Mr. Keough, but we're talking about a very sensitive investigation here." The sheriff stands, knocking a bony knee on the metal edge of his desk. He winces as he gathers the papers on his desk into a filing folder, a tremor in the knobby fingers on his right hand. "Is there anything else? I need to get back to the mountain."

I shake my head, my veins humming with anger. In the doorway, McAuliffe uses the folder in his hand to gesture to the direction of the exit.

"Claire," he says wearily. The area under the sheriff's eyes sags with exhaustion. "Please don't tell anyone what we discussed here today."

"I won't," I say stiffly as my father comes up next to me, resting a hand on my shoulder.

"In fact"—McAuliffe glances between me and my father, frowning—"if I were you, I might not tell anyone beyond your immediate family that you were on Bobcat Mountain at all."

Neither of us says much on the ride back to the lake house. My head is killing me, so Dad uses it as an excuse to end our flyer-distributing mission, even though neither of us is in the mood to continue anyway after that shitshow in McAuliffe's office.

When we pull into the lake house driveway, Dad cuts the

engine of the Civic. "Claire—don't tell anyone about what you just told McAuliffe, okay?"

He's not looking at me. He stares through the windshield, at the cars lined up in the driveway. Amos's silver BMW sedan, Mr. Marcotte's black Highlander. Don't tell *them,* he means.

My mouth goes dry. I don't think it's the leaks to the press that he's worried about; he doesn't want Kat's family to know I remember something.

Dad's cell begins to trill with "And I Love Her" by the Beatles, his ringtone for Mom.

"Maybe she heard from the neurologist," Dad says, scrambling to fish his phone out of the debris building up in his cupholder—a receipt from the local pharmacy, a Taco Bell cup.

"Teenie." Dad puts a finger in one ear. "What's up?"

"I'll see you inside," I say, unbuckling my belt. I don't need to hear Dad recap what happened inside McAuliffe's office to Mom. Living it once was bad enough.

I pull my phone out on the walk to the front door, swallowing a grunt of frustration at the sight of the blank search page, trying in vain to connect to the spotty 3G.

Friday night, Kat had said the Wi-Fi password is on the router in Marian's office upstairs. I had been too lazy to go get it then, and apparently Saturday Claire was too lazy as well.

The front door is open, but no one seems to be downstairs. The kitchen, Mrs. Marcotte's home base, is quiet, save for the whir of the water cycling through the dishwasher. I head up the stairs, startled at how my legs resist each step. My muscles are heavy from lying in a hospital bed for three days.

The sound of voices at the top of the stairs makes me slow my pace. The door to the master suite is cracked open. A figure paces back and forth, and instinctively I flatten myself against the bannister, even though there's no way they can see me from here.

"He needs to push her harder." Mr. Marcotte's voice is urgent, clipped.

"She needs time, Johnathan," Kat's mother says.

"Our daughter doesn't *have* time."

My insides frost over. They're talking about *me*. I know I shouldn't be listening to this, but I can't tear myself away from the bannister.

"She's traumatized," Mrs. Marcotte says. "The doctors said the stress of questioning could make it worse."

Mr. Marcotte is quiet when he speaks. "And you believe that?"

A tremor in my right knee. I grab the bannister, my legs threatening to give out underneath me.

Humming inside my ears as I wait for Mrs. Marcotte to defend me. I think of her face in the bathroom yesterday, my heart sinking. More pacing, floorboards groaning.

"Claire's always been protective of him," Mr. Marcotte finally says. "You said it yourself."

Mrs. Marcotte's voice is hushed; I only catch part of what she says next. "—but with what's at stake—"

Her response is drowned out by the sound of a phone ringing, echoing off the vaulted ceilings. A crush of panic as I realize the ringing is coming from downstairs.

Mr. Marcotte snaps, "How could you not have your phone on you—"

Get away. The thought cracks through me like lightning. I'll never make it downstairs in time; I dart toward the spare bedroom next to the master. Throw a hand over my mouth to muffle a yelp at the sight of Amos Fornier, seated on the edge of the queen bed.

He tilts his head slightly, the look on his face saying he's been watching me—and listening to his aunt and uncle—this whole time.

He lifts a finger to his mouth. Jerks his head to the door.

I shut it quietly and press myself against the wall, as the master door screeches open. Footsteps, storming down the stairs.

Amos watches me from the bed. The look on his face launches me back to the last place I want to be.

His bedroom. I'm fifteen, my legs shaved with surgical precision, quaking as Amos runs his hands down my sides, tugs at the waist of my jeans. I'm in my brand-new red bra, because I'd read in some stupid magazine that the color red triggers lustful feelings in men. Back then, Amos, at seventeen, *was* practically a man to me.

I was fifteen and that felt like a perfectly acceptable age to lose my virginity; my best friend's hot older cousin a more-than-acceptable person to lose it to.

Now: Amos stands, crosses to the bedroom door. Mr. Marcotte's voice carries up the stairs, pinning us in this room.

Then: I'd planned it, *wanted* it, pushed for Kat and me to go to the party she mentioned her cousin was having while his mother was in Paris. Amos unhooked my bra, wrapped his hands around my bare back, and pulled me to his body. His tongue, parting my lips, tasted like Captain Morgan.

Now: I swallow, cross to the door. Amos shakes his head. "You don't want my uncle knowing you were up here. Trust me."

Then: Amos flipped me onto his bed. The Captain Morgan shots roiled in my gut; his sheets, too cool, too foreign on my back, prompted a single thought: *I want to go home.* When Amos's fingers moved to the zipper on my jeans, I covered his hand with mine.

Now: Amos turns, crosses to the sliding door at the rear of the bedroom.

Then: *Are you serious?* His words were sour against my neck. I scrambled until I was sitting up against his headboard, my heart jackhammering. Slurred excuses tumbled out of me: *I think I drank too much, maybe some other time—*

Now: Amos slides the balcony door open. *Follow me.*

Then: He scooted so he was sitting up. Shook his head, laughed as he shrugged himself back into his T-shirt. He was gone from the bedroom before I could even gather all my clothes, my throat sealed with humiliation.

Now: I have no choice. I follow Amos onto the balcony.

There is a single Adirondack chair on the balcony. Amos steps past it, leans over the railing dividing his bedroom's balcony from the master balcony.

He swings a leg over the railing, effortlessly launching himself onto the master balcony.

"What are you doing?" I hiss.

Amos extends his arms to me. *Trust me.*

I swallow, grab his wrists. Hoist a leg over the railing and let Amos pull me over to the other side. He helps steady me, his hands at my waist, close enough that I can smell the weed lingering under the linen spray he must have doused his clothes with.

"Sorry." Amos drops his hands to his sides.

I straighten, glance around the master bedroom balcony to avoid his eyes. Behind Amos are the glass sliding doors leading to the master suite; inside them, white curtains are drawn tight. To our right, a set of stairs leads down to the patio and grill area.

I follow Amos down the stairs, panic needling me as I take in the proximity of the balcony to the patio. The outdoor seating area offers a poor view of the balcony; anyone could have been up there, listening to my conversation with Sheriff McAuliffe yesterday.

Amos hops down, skipping the last step, and continues toward the lake. He turns around, eyebrows lifting when he sees I haven't moved from the patio. "You coming?"

"Where?" I ask.

He thinks for a moment before saying, "Away."

I glance back at the house; I can't stomach the thought of going in there and looking Kat's parents in the eye after what I overheard. I never heard Dad come inside the house, nor do I expect him to for another fifteen minutes. Most phone calls with my mother are akin to a hostage situation.

Amos waits for me to catch up. We head down the back of

the property, which slopes to the lake. A chipmunk skitters across our path and disappears through a crack in the stones encircling the firepit.

The sounds around the lake dissolve as the dock comes into focus. I see Jesse, leaning forward in that Adirondack chair. I banish the image from my brain because I can't handle the idea that it's the last memory I'll have of him.

To the right of the dock is a shed; Amos spins the combination into the padlock holding the doors shut. He opens them, ducks inside. Emerges a moment later dragging a red canoe by its hull.

He pivots, pushes the boat toward the lake. A sliver of tanned, toned lower back peeks out as his polo rides up. He uses one of his Sperrys to nudge the canoe into the lake. Once the boat is afloat, he turns to me. "Hop in."

I meet him at the water's edge and glance inside the body of the canoe. A daddy longlegs hobbles out from under the rear seat as I lower myself onto it. We pitch to the right; Amos leans forward, hands on both sides to anchor the boat.

He hops onto the opposite seat, facing me, and picks up the oars lying between us. Overhead, the sky is brilliant blue and cloudless. I close my eyes to block out the afternoon sun, listening to the steady drip of water from the oars between Amos's rows.

When I open my eyes, we're in the middle of the lake. Amos has taken a break from rowing, his face tilted back to the sun. I can make out a small smattering of freckles on his nose. "I got Kat in trouble all the time for this when we were kids," he says. "Convincing her to take the canoe out without asking."

Humming overhead draws Amos's attention away from the sky. A dragonfly dips down and lands on the edge of the canoe. "My uncle always thought I was a corrupting influence."

I don't know why he's telling me this. Maybe he wants me to feel less shitty about what Mr. Marcotte said. I swallow to clear my throat. "You heard everything?"

Amos nods. "Yep."

I inhale through my nose, the smoky scent in the air making my eyes water. Somewhere, someone is grilling.

"I'm not making it up," I say. "I have no idea what happened on that mountain."

"I know." Amos leans back, slices the oars through the water. The dragonfly, startled, lifts off and flies away. Something feels significant about how he's chosen to word it: *I know*. Not *I believe you*.

I look at him. *Why?*

"My buddy got into a car accident last year," Amos says. "He dropped his car off at a repair place, called his girlfriend to come pick him up, got home, and went to sleep. Said when he woke up, he asked his girlfriend what happened to the car. He didn't remember waking up that morning . . . didn't remember the accident or anything that happened after."

My toes curl in my flip-flops. What he's describing is exactly what happened to me.

Amos pauses, hands on the oars, as the canoe drifts. "Claire . . . you don't just fall and hit your head hard enough to forget an entire weekend."

The troubled look in his eyes makes my stomach somersault. It's the look of someone who is staring down a person who is failing to see what's right in front of them. It reminds me of Dr. Ashraf, right before I was discharged.

My brain hums. "Jesse didn't hit me on the head."

I lean forward and let my knees rest on my elbows. That's what everyone is thinking, right? That Jesse was drunk and angry at that ledge and lost control. Angry at his girlfriend, and somehow I got in the way—

I sit up abruptly, rocking the canoe so that Amos has to shift on his seat to rebalance it. "Do Kat's parents think Jesse killed her?"

"They haven't come out and said it," Amos says. "My aunt Beth has always thought Jesse is too serious about Kat. She said they'd been fighting a lot lately, and she was worried Kat might have been too afraid to break up with Jesse before she left for BC."

"That's insane," I say, my throat thick with anger. "Jesse's not violent."

My fingers itch to find the bump at the base of my skull. I can't explain Jesse to someone who doesn't know him. Last summer, I went to Alive After Five in the village with him so he could see his favorite local band; right before they began to play, I tripped on the curb, split my kneecap open. Jesse insisted on accompanying me to the CVS down the road, helped me clean and bandage my cut, even if it meant missing half the band's set.

"He would never hurt Kat," I say. *Or me.* I know it's weak, it's not even an argument. But Amos doesn't look interested in arguing.

"I know," he says, lifting the oars. He dips them back down, propelling us farther away from the lake house. "I've seen them together. It's pretty obvious he'd die for her."

The dragonfly that has been circling us floats down and lands on the surface of the lake. The hair on the back of my neck lifts as the dragonfly begins to devour one of the mosquitos buzzing on the lake's surface.

I'm silent as Amos rows. Someone else believes me; someone else doesn't believe Jesse hurt me and made Kat disappear.

But if not Jesse, who? The redheaded man?

Amos nudges his knee with mine. "Claaa-ire. Care to share what you're thinking?"

The zip of electricity that passes from his bare skin to mine startles me. The current moves to my thighs as Amos brushes his hair, unruly and sun-streaked, behind an ear.

I'm so disgusted with myself, it prompts me to look away, say, "With you? Not really."

The silence that follows feels like a door slamming between us. I half expect Amos to begin rowing us back to shore. Instead, he says, "I get it."

I pin him with my gaze. "Do you?"

"I was a stupid kid. I'd like to think I've since learned some things about how to treat women."

My heartbeat gathers momentum. At the thought of me, in that red bra, Amos's fingers finding the clasp. At the thought that Amos, of all people, might be the only person in Kat's family that believes me, maybe even trusts me.

I'm not sure it's a good enough reason to trust him, but someone else needs to know what happened in that office at the police station. How McAuliffe completely dismissed me, refused to tell me what he knows about what happened between me and the redheaded man on the mountain.

If the sheriff is going to keep shit from me, I don't have to keep my half-assed promise not to tell anyone about the hiker.

"Something weird happened earlier," I say, my voice barely above a whisper, even though we're several hundred feet away from the house.

As I describe what happened outside 84 Phoenicia Road, the conversation in the sheriff's office, Amos freezes, oars hovering above the surface of the lake. "Wait. What did the guy look like?"

"Red hair, beard, mid-thirties probably."

"You saw him while you were hiking?" Amos asks.

"I don't remember where I saw him, but McAuliffe said he was on Bobcat Mountain too and he saw us."

I close my eyes, the sun turning the inside of my lids orange. I let the tape from Friday night roll in my memory: that humiliating conversation with Jesse on the dock, retreating to the house in shame. Everything after that is a darkened tunnel, and the redheaded man's face is already disappearing down it.

I open my eyes to Amos's probing stare. "You're sure you didn't know him? Or maybe you'd seen him before you got to the mountain?"

"I don't know. I don't remember anything that happened Saturday morning. Unless maybe I saw him Friday—" I stop short, a memory clawing its way to the surface of my brain.

The redheaded man in the Merry Mackerel—the one in the Confederate flag T-shirt. The man outside the house in Grist Mill had a Confederate flag decal in the back of his truck.

"Oh God." I lean forward and cover my mouth. Had the man in the Merry Mackerel had a beard?

Yes—maybe? No, he definitely *did* have a beard. I can see him now, chalking the tip of his pool cue, listening as I gave the bartender the address of the lake house.

Kat hadn't wanted me to go inside and ask for directions. I swallow down the anxiety clogging my throat, push away the idea that all of this could be my fault because I was loud and careless.

"Claire." Amos leans in. "What's the matter?"

"We stopped for directions Friday night—there was this guy in the bar, watching me. What if he was the same guy who was on Bobcat Mountain?" I say. "He could have followed us—I have to tell McAuliffe."

Amos scratches the corner of his mouth. His voice is quiet when he finally responds. "If I tell you something, promise not to spread it around?"

I nod.

"When I was handing out flyers this morning, some guy at the deli kind of bugged out when he heard me say Bobcat Mountain." Amos lets the tips of the oars drag across the surface of the lake until the canoe slows to a coast. "He said last fall, his daughter and her friends were camping at Devil's Peak when some crackhead with a knife tried to rob them."

I swallow. "Were they hurt?"

"The guy didn't get the chance. Some hikers were passing through and scared him off."

"Did they ever get the guy?"

"That's the fucked-up part," Amos says. "The girl's father told me that he doesn't think the sheriff's department ever even looked for the guy."

"What the hell? Why not?"

Amos shrugs. "I mean, he gave me an earful, but the gist of it is, he thinks McAuliffe only cares about being able to brag about how safe Sunfish Creek is so he can keep getting reelected."

Fear flips my stomach; of course McAuliffe wants to believe Jesse is responsible for whatever happened on that mountain. An out-of-towner killing his girlfriend and himself with a tragic tumble off Devil's Peak is much easier for his constituents to swallow than the idea of some bogeyman lurking in the woods.

"Claire!"

My name echoes through the trees circling the lake. Frantic, angry. I follow the sound to my dad, standing at the end of the lake house dock.

"Fuck," I say.

Amos rows us over to the dock, his strokes urgent. My dad is watching us, arms folded across his chest, looking on the verge of having an aneurism.

When the canoe is close enough to the dock that he doesn't have to shout for us to hear him, Dad says, "Where the hell were you?"

My heartbeat picks up. I've never heard my father utter anything more severe than a *heck* or a *gosh dangit*.

"We've been right here, on the lake," I say as Amos hops out of the canoe. He grabs the front and drags the boat onto the shore so I can scramble out.

Dad stares at me, the tips of his ears red. "You left your phone in the house. Do you have *any idea*—"

Amos steps into my dad's view. "I'm sorry, Mr. Keough. It was my idea."

Dad stares at Amos, his face softening a bit. He's not going to rip me a new one in front of an audience. "I—I would have appreciated you letting me know where you were going."

"I'm sorry," I say. "I just needed to get out of the house."

I look from Dad's strained expression to the space in the

driveway where Mr. Marcotte's car was fifteen minutes ago. Why was my dad so anxious to find me? My blood drains to my toes, and the words spill out of me: "Did they find something?"

"No—Kat's parents had to go to the sheriff's station to identify some things," Dad says, watching Amos head back up to the lake house, throwing an apologetic glance at me over his shoulder.

When Amos is out of earshot, Dad exhales. "Go to the car. I'll go get our stuff and meet you there."

"What?"

"We're going home, Claire."

"Is this all because I left the house for like ten minutes?"

"No, of course not." Dad exhales. "Mom got you a neurologist appointment for tomorrow afternoon."

Tomorrow afternoon. Twenty-four hours from now. It doesn't explain why he's so urgent to leave Sunfish Creek *this second*.

No—this is about what happened in McAuliffe's office.

"The sheriff said not to leave," I croak.

"He has no reason to keep us here. You've told him everything you know. I just want us home," Dad says, his voice soft.

Home is Jesse tucked into the corner of my basement couch, Twizzler hanging out of his mouth, arguing with me about whether it's an unfair advantage for me to use Kirby in every Smash Bros. match. Home is Kat surprising me at work with a rainbow Italian ice on her walk home from Nina's Sweets, the kids she babysits over the summer in tow.

I don't want to go home if they're not there. But I can't be here, either.

I look up, see my father's outstretched hand. I slip mine in it, let him lead me to the driveway.

He opens the passenger door of the Civic and I duck in. There are dozens of questions on the tip of my tongue; questions I don't really want the answer to. Does he know Kat's father thinks I'm lying? Are we leaving because of what McAuliffe said about the man on the mountain? Why does it feel like we're running away?

I buckle my seat belt, my heart battering my ribs beneath the strap. When I look up, I spot Amos in the bay window.

He nods at me as if to say *Get out while you have the chance.*

CHAPTER NINE

———

NOW

We get caught up in the summer traffic funneling through New York City. I spend the trip on my phone, waiting for an update about how today's search of Bobcat Mountain went. The Sunfish Creek sheriff's department is holding a press conference, but I can't get a strong enough connection to stream it.

I refresh CNN's live blog of the search coverage, now updated with bullet points from McAuliffe's press conference.

- No sign of missing teenaged couple as search stretches into fourth day
- Forensic examination of Kat Marcotte's car underway
- Former US Representative Marian Sullivan-Marcotte announces $100,000 reward for information regarding granddaughter's disappearance

Eventually, the sight of the words on my screen make me so carsick I have to put it away and recline my seat.

I wake to the Civic rolling to a stop, and blink until our

house comes into focus, my mother standing behind the glass door. The sky is swirling blue and gray; the time on my dad's dash reads 7:17.

P.M., I remind myself. It doesn't feel possible I was in Sunfish Creek earlier today. Sitting in the sheriff's office, out on the lake with Amos. There is a heaviness in my limbs, my eyelids, as if I'd lived a hundred days since waking up this morning.

I weakly return my mother's hug and slip into the bathroom. Scroll through my phone while I pee, eyes still bleary from my car snooze.

Seeing Ben Filipoff's name in my text inbox nearly makes me fall off the toilet.

> Hey . . . I know I'm the last person you probably want to hear from right now, but I wanted to see how you're holding up. I guess you're not coming tn.

I glance at the time on my phone. The graduation ceremony began over an hour ago. A shudder moves through me, to the tips of my toes. With no school this week, no one would have noticed that I've been MIA since Kat and Jesse went missing. But tonight—my empty chair at graduation—of course, Ben wants to know why.

I think about what I want to say. *I am not okay at all. Everything is so fucked up and I'm not supposed to talk about it.*

I swallow, type, send:

> I'm okay.

Ben starts typing, stops. Just when I think the conversation is going to end there, he replies.

> Where have you been? I stopped by your house a
> couple times Monday but no one was home.

A knock at the bathroom door, followed by my mother's voice. "Claire? You okay?"

"Yeah." I flush, turn on the tap in the bathroom sink with trembling hands. Sometimes I think there is a third testicle where Ben's brain should be, but he's not *stupid*. It's only a matter of time before the gossip starts and he figures out I wasn't here last weekend because I was in Sunfish Creek.

Maybe Ben's already figured it out. He knew about the trip, because he was supposed to come with us. For all he knows, I went anyway, despite our breakup.

I inhale, type out a response.

> I went with Kat and Jesse to Sunfish Creek.

> What???

> Yeah.

> I don't remember Saturday. We were hiking and
> I hit my head bad . . . I just got out of the hospital
> yesterday.

I slip across the hall, into my room, shutting out the sounds of my parents murmuring in the kitchen. I kick off my shoes, plop down on my bed as Ben replies to my message.

> Jesus, Claire.

> So you have no idea what happened to them??

I burrow under my covers, I swallow the anxiety knotting up in my throat. I think of the reporters packing the parking lot at the sheriff's office when Dad and I got there . . . the gossip that must have been flowing through Stellato's when I didn't show up for work. . . . Brookport is a small town, and there are no secrets.

Soon everyone will know I was with them on the mountain. They'll want the answer to the question I can't answer, the only question that matters now.

Why did I make it back, and they didn't?

A knock on my door yanks me to consciousness.

My curtains. *My* bed. The comfort that it brings me dissolves immediately.

I'm home. I came home from Sunfish Creek without Kat and Jesse.

Another knock before my mother steps into my room, struggling with the clasp on her bracelet. "How did you sleep?"

If Mom is getting ready to leave for work, it must be around eight in the morning, which means I slept for thirteen straight hours. I sit up and crack my neck. "Have you heard anything?" I ask.

Mom shakes her head; the bracelet slips off her wrist. She bends to peel it from my carpet and sighs. "I don't think you should be alone today. Are you sure you don't want Dad to stay home from work?"

"Dad's already missed enough work for me."

I didn't mean it like that, but Mom looks hurt.

"Well, try to keep busy," she says. "Maybe clean up this disaster of a room. Dad will be home a little early to take you to Dr. Wen's."

She closes the door and I roll over, away from the sunlight streaming in my window. The thought of having the same conversation with my father before he leaves for work is so exhausting that I pretend to be asleep when his knock at my door comes half an hour later.

When I hear the purr of his engine leaving the driveway, I grab my phone and head into the kitchen.

Dad left out a mug of coffee for me; I nuke it in the microwave before making my way to the living room. I dump my phone and mug onto the coffee table, kneel before the couch in order to excavate the television remote from between the cushions.

I flip through the channels, the caffeine hitting my bloodstream only making the edge to my mood worse. All week, I wanted nothing more than to be alone—away from prodding doctors and nurses, to sleep without my father hovering over me, able to read the news without Kat's parents lurking nearby—but now that I'm by myself, I feel ready to jump out of my skin at every noise around me.

A doorbell in a commercial. The rumble of the garbage truck outside.

I hold one hand over my rapidly beating heart, lower the volume on the TV with the other. My mother watches everything with the sound blasting; I picture her in this exact spot, alone each night while Dad and I were in Sunfish Creek, with a nudge of guilt.

My heartbeat goes still when the news program returns from the commercial break.

It's them.

Of course, it's them—this is the local news, and nothing fucking happens around here. The granddaughter of our former congresswoman going missing definitely ranks higher than a drunken crash on the LIE or an upcoming pet adoption drive.

There they are—a photo of Kat and Jesse, hovering next to the face of Deanna Demarco, our local news anchor. I have to turn the volume back up in order to hear over the thrum of adrenaline in my ears.

"In Sunfish Creek, the search for two teens from Brookport is entering its *fifth* day—"

Deanna Demarco and the News 12 studio give way to a video montage. A chopper view of Bobcat Mountain, emergency vehicles blocking off a parking lot. The camera pans to a man standing in the lot, arms crossed over his chest.

Mr. Marcotte.

"Earlier this morning, News Twelve spoke with the father of missing teen Katherine Marcotte, who has been on the ground with searchers every day since his daughter and her boyfriend, Jesse Salpietro, did not return from a camping trip at Devil's Peak."

A male voice offscreen says, *"Mr. Marcotte, what can you tell us about the search?"* The chyron at the bottom of the screen reads: JOHNATHAN MARCOTTE—MISSING TEEN'S FATHER AND SON OF CONGRESSWOMAN MARIAN SULLIVAN-MARCOTTE.

Mr. Marcotte leans into the News 12 microphone jammed in his face, wipes sweat off his brow. "There's still a lot of ground to cover. A lot of it is unsearchable by foot. But I'm not giving up hope."

"But what about the time that has passed—do you think, if Kat is hurt and lost somewhere, the odds just simply aren't in her favor?"

Mr. Marcotte lifts his eyes to the camera. He blinks back tears, swallows. "If anyone can beat impossible odds, it's my daughter."

The screen cuts to the scene in the parking lot of Bobcat Mountain. Emergency vehicles, lights flashing: Sheriff McAuliffe is standing outside one, hands on his hips, defiantly staring down the camera crew crowding him. In the distance, the sun is rising into a pink-and-orange sky over the mountain.

Deanna Demarco's voice-over informs us: "This morning, the Sunfish Creek sheriff addressed reporters prior to the search."

McAuliffe clears his throat. "I've been asked to provide an update—all I can reveal about today's agenda is that we will be focusing on the area below Devil's Peak."

My head goes hollow. *Below* Devil's Peak—he means the bottom of the ledge.

I was right. He thinks Kat and Jesse went tumbling over it.

On the coffee table, my phone rattles. I lunge for it, open the text with trembling fingers.

The sender isn't in my contacts, and I don't recognize their number.

hey

Another message sprouts under it:

It's Amos

My heart knocks around in my chest as I absorb this. Amos Fornier, casually texting me *hey*. I let my thumb hover over the keys for a moment before I type back hey, hit send. I drum my fingertips against my lips, waiting for Amos's response.

On the TV, Deanna Demarco has moved onto something other than Kat and Jesse. Her chattering in my head is too much; I turn the TV off as Amos texts me back.

just wanted to see how ur doing

I pull my feet up onto the couch, tuck them under my body.

Okay, I guess

I want to ask how he got my number, or if he's heard anything. But the ellipsis appears, signaling that Amos is typing. My fingers go still; I watch the screen, letting him steer the conversation.

did u leave because of what my uncle said?

> It wasn't that,

I type back, probably too quickly.

> I'm seeing a neurologist today. Here on LI

I'm anxious to move the conversation away from my busted-up head. Before Amos can begin responding, I fire off another text:

> Do you think I should call the sheriff's office and tell them about the guy in the Merry Mackerel who was watching me?

The conversation window goes static; Amos has read the message but isn't responding. Finally, he replies:

> Can you keep another secret?

> of course

> There were FBI agents here last night

> Seriously??

> yep. theyre "assisting w the investigation"
> between u and me ... I think Marian called in a favor

I swallow.

> Why are you telling me all this?

Amos is typing. The ellipsis disappears, then reappears. When he finally sends the message through, I'm surprised it's so short.

I squeeze my eyes shut against the threat of tears. Amos is talking about Kat like she's still alive. It doesn't mean anything—Amos having hope doesn't change the odds they're *not* alive—but it's enough to propel me off the couch. Maybe, it'll even be enough to get me through the day.

I scrape my hair into a bun, survey the wreckage of my room. My gaze lands on the clear plastic bag resting beside my basket of unwashed laundry.

The sight of it immobilizes me. I'd assumed the sheriff took the clothes I was wearing on the mountain as potential evidence, but Mom must have brought them home with her. My heart batters my rib cage as I loosen the string on the bag.

I pull out the ribbed gray tank top first and turn it over, realizing I'm looking for blood.

I toss the tank into my laundry basket and move on to my shorts. The thighs and butt are smeared with dirt. I close my eyes, attempt to quiet my mind long enough to picture the area off the trail where I woke up.

I chuck the shorts. The jangling sound they make when they hit the pile of dirty clothes roots me to where I'm sitting.

There's something in the pocket.

I stick my hand inside. Produce a set of keys, a silver Infiniti logo imprinted on the fob. I swallow my heartbeat, close my eyes, fingers closing around the shape of an enamel pineapple.

Outside my room, the doorbell rings.

CHAPTER TEN

NOW

Why did I have Kat's car keys in my pocket?

The doorbell rings again, cutting through the thoughts forming a squall in my brain. I say a silent prayer that whoever is at my front door is selling something and jam the keys into the top drawer of my desk.

When I open the front door a slender black woman and a stocky white man are standing on my porch. Her face is wrinkle-free, while the man's face is scarred and plagued by rosacea. When he sticks a hand in his pants pocket, his suit jacket moves to reveal a gun.

I'm pretty sure they don't have Thin Mints with them.

"Claire Keough?" the woman says through lips slick with raisin-colored gloss. Her hair is in a bun and she's wearing silver hoop earrings.

"That's me." My voice cracks guiltily, as if I'm doing something wrong by existing. My thoughts drift to Kat's car keys; I have to balance a palm against the doorway to steady myself.

"We're with the FBI's Long Island office," the woman says. "Is now an okay time to talk about what happened last weekend?"

I pause, my arm still outstretched, holding the door open. I will the tremor in the crook of my arm to go away. "Can I just, see your badges or something?"

The man shoots the woman an amused look, but he opens his jacket and removes his wallet. She follows suit. I examine each ID card and badge with shaking hands. Her name is Nicole Cummings. His is William Novak.

I step aside to let them in; as I shut the front door behind them, Agent Cummings retrieves an Altoids tin from inside her jacket and pops one as she considers the living room. Agent Novak crosses to the fireplace, enormous Popeye arms folded across his chest.

He's eye-level with a frame on the mantel, examining the picture in it. Kat and Jamie Liu and me, dressed as the Three Musketeers for the tenth grade Halloween dance.

There are FBI agents in my living room. I don't know why I didn't see this coming—Amos had told me they were assisting with the case.

"We'll be working closely with our counterparts upstate," Cummings says.

"Okay." I sit on the chaise portion of our sectional couch, feet planted firmly next to each other on the carpet, hands on my knees.

"How are you feeling?" Agent Cummings asks. "The ER doctor we spoke with said you came in pretty banged up."

"All right, I guess," I say. "I'm seeing a neurologist this afternoon."

I glance over at the mantel, where Agent Novak is holding the framed photo of Jamie Liu, Kat, and me. On the couch, Cummings takes off her jacket, revealing sculpted bronze shoulders.

"I can turn the AC on," I say.

"Don't," Novak says, replacing the photo.

I stare at him; he nods to the living room wall where our Nest is located. "Not worth your dad throwing a fit about someone messing with the thermostat."

"It's my mom." I swallow. "How did you know?"

Novak shrugs. "No AC cranking on a day like today—someone's a stickler about the bill."

Cummings raises her eyebrows at her partner as he moves from the mantel and sits on the arm of the love seat adjacent to the couch. "Agent Novak tortures his daughters the same way."

I try to return her friendly smile, but the whole interaction has frayed what's left of my nerves. It has everything to do with Kat's car keys, tucked in my desk drawer. How long will it take Agent Novak to sniff out I'm hiding something?

"Claire." Agent Cummings's voice draws me back. There's a question at the end of my name, as if it's not the first time she's said it.

I blink until my vision returns. "Sorry. I still get headaches."

Novak shifts on the arm of the seat, pulls his ankle up and rests it on his opposite thigh. Cummings fishes the Altoids tin from the balled-up jacket beside her. "We'll try to make this quick so you can get back to resting."

I nod, then shake my head when Cummings offers me an Altoid. She pops a mint in her mouth and says, "We know the sheriff in Sunfish Creek already interviewed you—we'll try not to make you repeat yourself too much. Can we go back a bit further? When did Kat and Jesse tell you they weren't going to prom?"

"Um, April, I guess? I asked Kat if she wanted to go dress shopping and she told me she didn't think they were going to go."

"When did they decide for sure they weren't going?"

"I don't know exactly." A slick of sweat comes to the back of my neck. "Two weeks before prom, when I asked Kat what they were doing after the dance, she said she and Jesse were going up to the lake house instead. She said Ben and I should come too."

"She waited until two weeks before prom to tell you they weren't going?" Novak peers at me. "You two didn't talk dresses, hair and nail appointments or whatever, before that?"

The implication is clear: prom minutiae is something best friends discuss.

I shrug. "I guess she was embarrassed to talk about why they weren't going. It was too expensive for Jesse—the tux, the ticket, and whatever."

Novak blinks. "Marian Sullivan-Marcotte's granddaughter skipped prom because of money?"

I press the heel of my hand to my brow bone; now I really do have a headache. "Jesse would sooner die than let Kat pay for everything."

I don't realize what I've said until the silence balloons to something tangible. I drop my hand to my lap. "I didn't mean that literally—I'm just saying he's sensitive about being broke."

Cummings pops another Altoid, as if she hadn't heard me. "Who is Ben, and why didn't he go to Sunfish Creek with you all as planned?"

I hook an arm around my neck, my skin warming with embarrassment. "My ex-boyfriend."

Novak's eyes lift; I am terrified he's going to make me explain catching Ben about to play *oops I dropped my towel* with Anna Markey, but he clears his throat. "So, you and Ben were supposed to drive up to Sunfish Creek after prom. Instead, you hitched a ride with Kat and Jesse."

I see myself in the passenger seat of Kat's Infiniti, slunk low and dozing off, the enamel pineapple on her key chain swinging like a hypnotist's pendulum. I nod, swallow to clear my throat. "Um, about Friday night—something happened and I'm not sure it's important."

Novak and Cummings stare at me.

"We lost signal on the GPS and had to stop at this place called the Merry Mackerel to get directions," I say. "Inside, there was a man by the pool table. He was definitely listening to me when I gave the address for the lake house."

Cummings's fingers go still around her Altoids tin. "You remember what this man looked like? What he was wearing?"

"He had red hair and a beard. He was wearing a Confederate flag T-shirt." I lean forward, knot my hands together and rest my forehead on them. "My dad and I saw this man yesterday when we were distributing fliers—I recognized him—"

"Yes, the sheriff brought us up to speed on that," Novak says. "Now, what about this man you saw at the Merry Mackerel?"

I look up a bit thrown by Novak's abruptness. "I was getting to that—the guy I saw on Bobcat Mountain has a Confederate flag sticker in his truck window, and he has red hair too."

"You think the man you saw Friday night in the bar was the same man you saw Saturday on the mountain?" Cummings asks, her expression inscrutable.

I move my palms to my knees. "What if he saw Kat's car Friday night and thought we had money. He could have been following us the whole weekend."

Novak tilts his head. Surveys me a bit before saying, "It's an interesting theory, but the man from the mountain couldn't have been the same man you saw in the Merry Mackerel Friday evening."

I swallow. "How do you know?"

"Because he was camping on Bobcat Mountain Friday night," Novak says. "He couldn't have been in two places at once."

I sink back into the couch cushions, the blood draining from my head. It takes me a beat to recover my voice. "What about the other people who might have been hiking or camping? Did anyone else come forward?"

"We don't believe anyone else was camping on the mountain Saturday night." Novak props his fist under his chin, studies me for a reaction. I break eye contact, catch a glimpse of the TV over his shoulder. I picture McAuliffe's face on the screen, that brief sound bite for reporters. *We will be focusing on the area below Devil's Peak.*

My breathing goes shallow. "But still—someone else could have been there, right? Besides the man I remember. Someone else could have . . ."

My voice falters. Agent Cummings slips her Altoids tin inside her jacket pocket, her eyes never leaving mine. "Someone else could have what, Claire?"

Have done this. Someone else besides Jesse could have done this. I glance at Novak, a statue on the edge of that armchair.

"The sheriff was asking me all of this stuff about Jesse," I say. "Whether he was depressed or jealous—it's like he thinks Jesse pushed Kat off the ledge."

I wedge my hands, now trembling, between my knees, and watch Cummings and Novak for a reaction. Anything to indicate that *they* think Jesse pushed Kat off the ledge.

"You don't think that's what happened," Agent Novak says evenly. "Why?"

Because I know Jesse. It sounds so stupid—it's exactly what every woman says that I've rolled my eyes at while watching *Dateline,* the deluded sisters, mothers, wives. *He'd never hurt anyone—I know him.*

But this isn't a TV show—this is my life. These are my best friends. And they were in love. And not the hormone-fueled, all-consuming type of love that ends with an argument and mangled bodies at the base of a cliff.

No—Kat and Jesse's was the type of love that was difficult to witness. The type of couple you'd see kissing in public and lose your breath and think, *What if I never have that?* Jesse was not a jealous boyfriend, depressed that his girlfriend was departing for Boston College and leaving him behind. For Kat, there *was* no leaving Jesse behind; he'd wait for her or he'd follow.

It makes no sense Jesse would throw that all away—that he would kill the person he loved most in the world, and then himself.

It had to be someone else.

I close my eyes, and I'm back in the Sunfish Creek emergency room. Running a finger over the streak of blood on my arm. Why was there so much blood on my arm when the cut was on my palm?

"Claire?" Cummings's voice draws me back.

I tug at the neck of the T-shirt I slept in, letting some ventilation in. I can't help but let my gaze wander to my bedroom door.

"Everything all right?" Novak asks.

I crane my neck toward the living room TV, as if I'd really been trying to catch a glimpse of the time displayed on the cable box. "I—yeah, I just have to get ready to go to the neurologist soon."

"Of course," Cummings says. "Just one more thing and we'll get out of your hair. By any chance, do you know your blood type?"

My stomach turns over. "Not off the top of my head—why?"

"Purely for elimination purposes at this point," Novak says.

To eliminate my blood from someone *else's* blood. Which means they *have* blood. They found blood and obviously they need to know who it came from. I tamp down the panic flaring in my chest. "I, um, donated blood last spring. I think I have the donor card in my room. Lemme check."

"That would be great." Cummings smiles. There is something carefully placating about her tone that wasn't there before. *You're so helpful. You have nothing to be afraid of.*

I duck into my room, yank open the top drawer of my desk with shaking hands. I'm half hoping I'd hallucinated finding Kat's car keys in my shorts, but there they are, sunlight from the window over my desk glinting off the enamel pineapple key chain.

Why would she give me her keys?

To escape? If not from the redheaded hiker, maybe another stranger. We were three out-of-town kids, parking an expensive car in the lot, camping out in a top-of-the-line tent. A prime robbery target.

Why did I escape and they didn't?

It doesn't make any sense. Kat was a star athlete, and I would fake my own death to get out of running the mile in gym. How did I get away from our attacker—whether it was a stranger or Jesse—and she didn't?

Why would I have her keys?

I push the keys to the back of the drawer and root through the junk inside. A Metro card, some stamps, an oily squeeze-tube of Carmex.

I move aside an expired library card to reveal the blood donor card.

My blood type is A negative.

I collapse into my desk chair, holding the card to my chest. I could just say I couldn't find it, but then what? If they don't get the answer from me, they'll get it from someone else, like the Sunfish Creek hospital.

I stand up, push my chair in, and head back out into the living room.

"A negative," I say, handing Cummings the card.

She looks it over and hands it back to me. "You're tougher than me. I can't give blood. I just pass out."

Cummings's eyes flick to her partner. "Well, I think we covered what we needed to, right, Bill?"

"For now."

Cummings hands me a business card with her contact info. "If you think of anything else and need to reach us."

"Okay," I say. It must come out a little too slowly, because Novak pauses in the doorway, jacket tossed over his shoulder.

"*Is* there anything else?" he asks.

I shake my head, slowly, walk them to the front door.

The second the lock clicks into place behind them, I run to the bathroom and throw up.

I am at my desk, my hand trembling under the Ativan pill I'm tipping into my palm.

Mom told me I should only take them to sleep, but my anxiety level is beyond an emergency right now. It's at DEFCON 1, can't-breathe-through-the-crushing-panic anxiety.

My brain pulsates as I pick over the conversation with Cummings and Novak. They hadn't answered my question, about other people besides the redheaded hiker being on the mountain last Saturday. It was a warm weekend day, a clear night by all accounts—that man and Kat and Jesse and me couldn't have been the only people who decided to go for a hike. We had to have encountered some other person. The *wrong* person.

Because if we didn't, and the redheaded hiker has been ruled out . . . that only leaves the three of us.

I'm pacing my room; I'm not sure when I made the transition from sitting at my desk to standing. My fingers move to the base of my neck, thinking of Amos's story about his friend's car accident.

He said his friend had dropped his car off, gone home, had dinner with his girlfriend, only to wake up in the morning not remembering a single thing.

What if my assumption is wrong—that whether by falling, or being attacked, I'd been knocked unconscious in the place where Sunshine found me, almost two miles from Devil's Peak? What if I'd gotten hurt at our campsite and tried to hike back to get help, only to wind up lost and disoriented? Maybe I'd given up when it got dark and went to sleep, only to wake up with the memory of the past thirty-six hours gone.

But why would Kat and Jesse let me hike back hurt, alone?

They wouldn't have. Whatever happened to incapacitate them, to stop them from making it down the mountain, had to have happened before I fled.

I sit at the edge of my bed, cover my face with my hands. The Ativan has started to slow the panic zipping through my veins; I relax my shoulders, reach for my phone.

No new texts; my conversation with Amos is at the top of my inbox. Unease settles over me.

Amos and Ben are the only people who've reached out to me this week. I'd dismissed the silence as the hazards of senior year—I'd let my social circle shrink to my two best friends and my boyfriend, and I'd lost all three of them in a manner of days.

But what if there's another reason no one has contacted me to see how I'm coping with the news about Kat and Jesse?

You should check Facebook.

The thought comes out of nowhere. I know it's a terrible idea, and clearly the Ativan talking, but I stumble over to my desk, open my laptop. With quaking fingers, I scroll past prom dresses in every shade of pastel, hat-toss photos from graduation. Glimpses of the life I'd be living if I hadn't gone to Sunfish Creek with Kat and Jesse.

Graduation was last night. While Dad and I were driving home from Sunfish Creek, my classmates congregated on the soccer field to collect their diplomas. Three hundred brains, at once thrumming with their own theories regarding the three people missing.

Even if Ben didn't tell anyone that I was with Kat and Jesse, there's no way around my empty chair. People are probably talking.

I want to know what they're saying.

I halt at a post Anna Markey made last night. Two pictures: One of Anna and Shannon, robed arms wrapped around each other, cheek to cheek and beaming. The other, an empty folding chair covered in flowers.

It takes me a moment to process what I'm looking at. Marcotte, Markey. Kat was supposed to sit next to Anna at graduation. The chair is hers.

> This evening two bright souls were missing from the graduation stage, but they were in our hearts and on our minds. Hoping Kat and Jesse will be home soon to celebrate with all of us ♥

I picture Anna grinding her teeth while typing those words. Anna Markey, who talked shit about Kat behind her back because she's a better volleyball and lacrosse player than Anna is.

There are over two dozen comments on Anna's post.

> Praying! **Written by Samantha Kellog at 10:35 p.m.**
> ♥ ♥ ♥ ♥ ♥ **Priya Viswanathan at 10:39 p.m.**

I scroll through the well-wishes, feeling a stab of fear when I see Shannon DiClemente's name.

> Anyone else wondering where CK was last night?

CK. Claire Keough.

> **Noah McKenna:** looney bin maybe
> **Noah McKenna:** she was with them but she can't remember anything
>
> Oh, please. She's setting herself up for an insanity defense

Written by Shannon DiClemente, three hours ago. Five people have liked her comment.

My fingers move to my lips, searching for feeling as the blood drains from them. I keep scrolling through the direct replies to Shannon.

> Um, this is a really shitty thing to accuse Claire of??
> What she ever do to any of you?

Katy O'Connor, a junior from the newspaper staff, a girl I barely spoke to outside of meetings.

Five minutes later, Anna Markey replied to Katy:

Um, maybe you want to ask Ben Filipoff? She bitch
slapped him bc I brought him to my room to get him a
clean T-shirt. Girl is psychotic.

Four likes.

Noah McKenna, replying to Shannon, Katy, and Anna all
at once:

Keough would never kill Salpietro . . . she's in love w him.

Three likes.

My body is numb with the shock of seeing the words.
Something I thought was a secret, blasted on Facebook for the
past six hours without anyone bringing it to my attention.

Because they all think you *did it.*

I've never even been in a fight. Do they really think I have
it in me to push my best friends off a cliff? Or are they being
cruel just because they can?

Shannon and Anna . . . Ben's friends. People I ate lunch
with every day for the past four months. I knew they didn't
like me; they humored me, waited for Ben to get me out of his
system.

But still. To accuse me of something like this, where they
knew I might see it? I thought I was liked at school. I wasn't
popular by any stretch, but I thought people liked me enough
that if they suspected I was involved in something as serious as
a potential double murder, they'd whisper about it in private.

I swallow against the tsunami of panic rising in me. When
my vision returns, I realize I have been tracing the scabbed-
over cut on my right palm.

I picture the blood streaking my arm; the blood I washed
away in the emergency room bathroom; the blood that deep
down, I know, did not come from me.

CHAPTER ELEVEN

NOW

Dr. Peter Wen is supposed to be the best neurologist in Suffolk County, but he looks like he graduated from high school yesterday. I can tell Dad thinks so too by the way his eyebrows shot to the rim of his glasses when Dr. Wen walked into the room.

"So," he's saying. "Your scans show significant reduction in the size of the hematoma."

"That's great news," he adds when I don't react.

My mind is not in this room; I left it at home, with my laptop, with Kat's car keys. The second Ativan I snuck before Dad picked me up was the only reason I could stay still throughout the MRI administered upon my arrival here.

I've heard and processed maybe about twenty percent of what Dr. Wen has said since we sat down in his office, a leather-and-mahogany prison.

How could they be saying that shit about me? How much worse would it be if they heard Dr. Wen say I'm fine?

"So it's just going away on its own?" I ask.

"That's usually the case with young and healthy patients." Dr. Wen twirls a pen between his fingers. "We'll do another scan in six weeks, but you aced the cognitive and short-term-memory tests. Do you have any questions?"

I grip the armrest. "Dad, I want to talk to Dr. Wen alone for a second."

Dad gapes at me. "I—all right. I'll go make your follow-up appointment."

When Dad is gone, Dr. Wen cocks his head. "Everything all right, Claire?"

"Anything I say to you stays between us, right? Doctor-patient confidentiality or whatever?"

The pen Dr. Wen is twirling between his fingers slips and clatters to the desk. "Well, yes, unless you tell me you're thinking of hurting yourself or someone else."

I inhale, exhale. "Is there a way to tell from my scan if someone hit me in the head?"

Dr. Wen's lips purse. I can make out the ghost of a mustache he's probably been trying to grow since medical school.

"Physical force or an assault could result in a hematoma, yes." Dr. Wen looks uncomfortable. "Do you feel unsafe at home, Claire?"

I swallow down the knob forming in my throat. "No, it's nothing like that—I just need to know if someone hit me. Or if I was running and tripped and fell."

"Unless your memory returns, there's no definitive way—"

"Could it come back?" I ask. "Could I remember everything?"

"There's no way to know—every head injury is different," Dr. Wen says carefully. "You have to keep in mind the brain is incredibly complicated."

I inhale around the quaking in my chest. "How complicated? If I hit my head—is it possible the head injury could have made me do something I wouldn't normally have done?"

Dr. Wen blinks. "I'm not sure what you mean."

"I don't know," I whisper.

I need to know. *Did I hurt them? Why would I hurt them?*

Dr. Wen is still blinking rapid-fire at me as I stand, so forcefully the chair legs snag on the carpet, nearly sending the chair toppling.

Dad is standing by the exit door in the waiting room, but he doesn't say anything to me until we get to the car.

"Want to tell me what that was about?"

My heart is still speed-bagging in my chest. I'm afraid if I open my mouth all the fears I've been holding in will fly out like projectile vomit.

What if I hurt them?

There's no turning back from telling my father about the car keys in my pocket, the amount of blood on my hand in the emergency room. He will tell Mom and they'll argue about whether we should tell the FBI and it'll just be *out there* that I destroyed possible evidence, even if there was a totally innocent reason for my hand to be covered in blood.

Maybe Kat or Jesse got hurt. One would have stayed with the other one while I ran to get help. The blood got on me because I was trying to *help*.

There's no other option.

I love them both.

Hurting people—that's not *me*.

But I wasn't myself, was I? Whatever memories I have of Saturday don't belong to me. They belong to some other girl, wandering a trail, bloodied and confused.

That girl wasn't me. And I don't know what she was capable of.

"Claire," Dad says, an edge to his voice that cuts me off at the knees. "I think you need to talk to someone about all of this. Maybe someone at Mom's office."

I tilt my head against the window, the glass cool on my temple. "That's probably a good idea," I admit.

Dad says nothing; obviously he'd been preparing for a

fight, but I don't have it in me. I just need to survive this car ride, the walk from the driveway to the house, from my front door to my bedroom. I'm counting the steps until I can disappear under my covers.

When Dad turns onto our street, it becomes clear I'm not sneaking anywhere.

There's a car parked in front of our house. The back door on the driver's side is dented.

Dad pulls into our driveway and cuts the engine. "Go right inside, Claire."

His voice says he's thinking the same thing I am—whoever is in that car is probably someone I want to see even less than another cop or FBI agent.

Dad slams his door and strides over to the man getting out of the car. I trail behind; I have no intention of heading inside the house as Dad directed.

The guy extends a hand to my father. "Oliver Fucillo. I'm a reporter with the *Long Island Register*."

Oliver Fucillo is in too-tight jeans and a dress shirt rolled up to his elbows. His hair is gelled to the side, and his glasses make him look like a serial killer.

Dad accepts his handshake and promptly folds his arms across his chest. "What can I do for you?"

"I'm covering the Marcotte-Salpietro case for the *Register*," Oliver says. "Does Claire have a moment to chat?"

"Surely you could have called first?" Dad says.

"I did—no one answered." Oliver Fucillo's jaw is dotted with acne. He's probably a fresh-out-of-college hire desperate for a big story that will bring him one step closer to his dream of being an NPR host.

"Claire, why don't you go inside?" Dad says over his shoulder, eyes not leaving Oliver.

My feet are rooted to the driveway.

Oliver waves at me. "I was hoping for a comment on the potential person of interest in the case?"

My heartbeat goes still; Dad's mouth hangs open. "We weren't aware there *was* a person of interest. Off the record, of course."

"Paul Santangelo," Oliver says. "The man Claire accused of being involved in Kat and Jesse's disappearance."

The redheaded man. He has a name. I stare at Oliver. "I didn't accuse anyone of anything."

"Claire. Don't say anything else." Dad takes a step toward Oliver. "Please leave before I call the police."

Oliver pales. His eyes flick to me. "Maybe I could give Claire my card—"

The look Dad gives him nearly gives me organ failure. I've never seen him this angry—I turn and hurry into the house without looking back.

Dad isn't far behind me. He pulls the front door shut behind him, his face suddenly scarily serene.

"What did you say to him?" I ask.

"I told him I'm calling the *Register* and letting his boss know about his inappropriate conduct." Dad massages his temple with his thumb and his forefinger. He freezes as we both hear it—the phone ringing in the kitchen.

I dart ahead to get it, but Dad is faster. He snatches the phone out of the cradle, lips forming a line at the voice on the other end.

"No," Dad says tartly. "She's not home. Please don't call again."

"What is happening?" I whisper.

"I don't know." Dad replaces the phone in the cradle as it begins to ring again.

With Dad occupied by the phone blitzkrieg, I slip into my room and sit at my desk.

I pull up Google, commanding myself to breathe. That reporter, Oliver or whatever, had said I'd accused the hiker of killing Kat and Jesse. He has a name: Paul Santangelo.

And apparently, he's trending, thanks to a story in the *Daily News*.

FRIEND OF MISSING TEENAGERS IDENTIFIES POSSIBLE SUSPECT

"Oh, shit." I cover my mouth and check the time stamp on the story. It went up about two hours ago, when I was in Dr. Wen's office.

> The *Daily News* has learned that Paul A. Santangelo, 37, of Sunfish Creek, has been interviewed in the investigation into the disappearance of two teenagers from Bobcat Mountain. The Sunfish Creek sheriff's department declined to confirm whether Mr. Santangelo was interviewed.
>
> However, sources familiar with the investigation tell us that the friend who accompanied Katherine Marcotte and Jesse Salpietro on the ill-fated camping trip made statements to the sheriff suggesting that Mr. Santangelo may be responsible for the missing couple's disappearance. The sheriff's office would not comment on the nature of these statements.
>
> The identity of the young woman has not been independently confirmed, but an individual familiar with the parties involved tells the *Daily News* she is a friend of Marcotte and Salpietro. According to sources close to the Marcotte family, the young woman was found on Bobcat Mountain with an unspecified head injury. While she is cooperating with the investigation, she claims she has no memory of the hours preceding Marcotte and Salpietro's disappearance.
>
> The FBI has taken control of the investigation and declined to comment for this story.

They didn't name me.

But the reporter from the *Register* and whoever the hell else is calling our house know I was on the mountain.

Everyone knows. How?

Do not Google yourself.

I have to Google myself.

WHO IS CLAIRE KEOUGH? 5 FACTS YOU NEED TO KNOW ABOUT MISSING TEEN KAT MARCOTTE'S BEST FRIEND

I press a fist into the sharp pain in my abdomen as I click through to the article. I am not sure I could even come up with five facts about myself, but whoever operates Heavy.com did.

1. Claire Keough is attending SUNY Geneseo in the fall.
2. Claire Keough was released from Sunfish Creek Hospital Thursday morning.
3. Claire Keough was editor-in-chief at the *Rookery*, Brookport High School's newspaper.

I don't get to the last two facts about me because I'm too distracted by the pictures, obviously ripped from my Facebook page.

My page is private and my name is listed as Claire Margaret, but they found it anyway. They found someone with loose privacy settings who posted these pictures—why, oh God, would someone post these—

"Oh God," I whisper.

Jamie Liu and I knocking back shots. My eyes are glazed, my head tilted back. Jamie is laughing at me and the photo is positioned in a way that suggests the actual subject of the picture was cropped out. Lucky shot.

I barely recognize the girl in the picture. She looks like the sloppy chick at the party you never talk to, who hangs on your neck like a spider monkey, crooning into your ear that she's soooo wasted.

That girl looks like she's totally lost control.

People are going to see this. The thought lands like a thumb mashed into the panic center of my brain.

My parents. My future professors at Geneseo. Anyone who Googles me in the next fifty years. All of them are going to see the worst version of me.

My panic quickly morphs into anger and my anger turns into a heat-seeking missile. I need someone to blame for my conversation with the sheriff about the hiker being leaked to the press.

Someone in the sheriff's department? No, the building was a ghost town when we arrived, and McAuliffe's office door was closed when we spoke. Sheriff Sanctimonious would never leak sensitive information to the press himself.

So who else knew? My dad, obviously, but he looked like he wanted to drop-kick Oliver Fucillo into oncoming traffic. He'd never do anything to bring reporters to our doorstep, which leaves one person—

"You fucking asshole," I whisper. I say it over and over under my breath as I find my phone and fire off a text to Amos Fornier.

> Thanks, asshole.

His response is instantaneous.

> What did I do?

> You're the only person besides my dad who knew I talked to the sheriff about the redheaded guy, and now it's in the *Daily News.*

My phone vibrates in my hand; Amos is calling me.

I accept the call, lift my phone to my ear. Amos speaks before I have the chance to open my mouth.

"Sorry, I actually hate texting." Amos's voice is low, quiet. "I didn't speak to the *Daily News*. Or any news, for that matter."

"Then you told someone what we talked about," I hiss. "McAuliffe's office wouldn't have leaked that conversation—"

"I did tell someone," Amos says, cutting me off. "I'm sorry. I had to."

I sink into my desk chair, heart hammering. "Who?"

"There are no secrets in my family, Claire. When my grandma got back to the lake house this morning, she wanted to know everything you and I talked about," Amos says. "You remembering seeing that man is huge. She would have pried it out of me even if I wasn't willing to tell her."

I don't say anything; beyond my door, the house phone rings again, setting my skin crawling.

"Claire," Amos says. "We all just want to find Kat."

"Then why would she leak sensitive information?" I ask. "The sheriff said it could hurt the investigation."

"We don't know it *was* my grandma who talked to the *Daily News*," Amos says. "She may have trusted the wrong person and they leaked the story—hell, it wouldn't be the first time a reporter hacked the phone of a missing girl's family."

"My name is all over the internet," I whisper. "Who would name me to the press?"

"Claire," Amos says softly. "Did anyone outside of my family and yours know that you went with Kat and Jesse last weekend?"

My insides go cold. Noah had blasted it all over Facebook: I was with Kat and Jesse last weekend. But there's only one way Noah would have known that I'd gone with Kat and Jesse on the trip after all, even though Ben and I had broken up—

"Claire?" Amos asks. "Are you okay?"

"I've got to go," I say. *I need to murder my ex-boyfriend.*

The only thing that stops me from texting Ben, tearing him a new asshole for blabbing to his friends about my being on

Bobcat Mountain and having memory loss, is the thought of my messages being blasted all over Heavy.com or some other trash site.

I don't know how to deal with a violation like this. Even if the public shaming hasn't really begun, I can't escape my own shame. At those pictures of me, wasted, being on the internet. At those ugly things Ben's friends said about me, my feelings for Jesse.

I need to do damage control.

No, damage control is what you attempt if you're caught making fun of your gym teacher in the locker room; not if pictures of you wasted are being blasted over the internet and your classmates are low-key accusing you of murder.

What I have to do is the equivalent of trying to scoop shit back into an overflowing toilet.

I massage my eyelids, haunted by those pictures. Who was in the kitchen with Jamie and me? There were a handful of the younger Markey siblings' serfs hanging around, iPhones out. It's not my fault one of them snapped those pictures and put them online, but guilt surges through me at the thought of Jamie's parents seeing them.

I pick my phone back up and start composing a text to Jamie.

> Hey . . . I hope you didn't get in too much trouble for those pics.

Something stops me from pressing send. Why hasn't Jamie sent a single message checking in with me? She and I have always had the type of friendship where we could go weeks without talking or hanging out and it's not weird, but her silence now is definitely weird.

I think of the picture of Jamie and Kat and me on the fireplace mantel, the one Agent Novak had seemed so interested in. When Kat moved home from Italy at the end of freshman year, she, Jamie, and I were basically inseparable. Then, around the end of junior year, things started to get awkward between Jamie and Kat. They were both circling valedictorian, even applying to some of the same colleges. Eventually Jamie stopped accepting our invitations to hang out, citing that she had to work at her parents' restaurant, or study.

At the end of last August, Jamie said she couldn't come to the beach for Kat's birthday because she was taking an SAT prep course. When we stopped to grab sandwiches from the deli, I spotted Jamie leaving the village CVS with Shannon DiClemente and Anna Markey.

Kat never confronted Jamie, swearing that she didn't care what Jamie did or who she hung out with. But by February break, the two of them were barely speaking at all.

Maybe Jamie hasn't texted me because she's busy working through her own shit. Kat going missing has to be bringing up some complicated feelings for her, maybe even guilt at how they left things off.

You are deluding yourself. You know why she hasn't texted you.

I swallow the anger building in my throat, send off the message.

Outside my room, a war is raging.

Mom's voice is slightly raised; I only catch her say *don't call again* before I find her alone, at the kitchen table, cradling a glass of seltzer that I'd wager has vodka in it.

"Who were you just talking to?" I ask.

"No one important."

A chill climbs my spine. "Mom. Who was it?"

Mom sets her glass down. "It was a producer from Brenda Dean's show."

I have to sit down. Brenda Dean is quite possibly higher than the FBI on the list of people I don't want up my ass right now.

Twenty years ago, Brenda Dean's younger sister was abducted off her bike and murdered, the killer never caught. Brenda dedicated her life to justice—first as a lawyer, then with her own cable show—lambasting suspects in high-profile murders. The cases always involve children—the younger the better—or pretty women abducted while jogging.

Lately she's been obsessed with this man, Lawrence Cowen, who left his two-year-old in the car on a hot summer day. Mom and I are both guilty of flipping to Brenda's rage-fueled coverage of the trial on weeknights when nothing else is on.

"She wants to interview me," I guess.

"It's absolutely out of the question." Mom lifts her glass to her lips, cutting herself off.

Years ago, Brenda Dean interviewed the mother of a missing toddler on air. She accused the mom of knowing more than she was saying about what happened to the baby; the woman left the set a sobbing mess, and went home to slit her wrists in the bathtub.

I stare at my mother. "You weren't even going to ask my opinion?"

"Your opinion is irrelevant. It's not happening."

I shoot up from the table, nearly startling the glass out of Mom's hand. When I turn away, she says my name sharply. "You don't want that vulture pegging you with questions you can't answer."

I feel all my chill slipping away from me. I want her to tell me I don't have to be afraid of Brenda Dean because only guilty people should be afraid of Brenda Dean.

I want her to tell me I'm not guilty, even if I don't know it myself, because she's my mother and it's her job to make things better.

My heart sinks to my feet. "Do you think I did something to them?"

"Of course not," she says. "But I can't control what everyone else thinks."

"Then maybe you should let me defend myself," I snap.

Mom buries her face in her hands. After a long pause, she looks up, eyes red, cheeks blooming to match. When she speaks again, her voice is barely a whisper. "I found a lawyer—I want you to meet with her. She can get us in tomorrow morning."

"*What?* When did you call a *lawyer?*"

The shame on her face, the way she avoids looking at me, makes it clear this was not a reaction to the reporters or to the Brenda Dean producer calling.

She's had the appointment for longer than that. Maybe since yesterday, when my dad called and told her about what happened in Sheriff McAuliffe's office, how he refused to tell me what the man on the mountain saw or what we said to each other. Maybe she's had the lawyer on call since she set foot in that hospital and realized my friends weren't coming back and I was the only one who had answers.

"No." I stand up violently. Cross to my room, blocking out her shouting *Claire,* and slam my door so hard it rattles every bone in my body.

CHAPTER TWELVE

NOW

The fight with my mother sends me to the bottle of Ativan. Sometime later, I wake in a pool of sweat. I sit up, rub my eyes until I can make out the time on the clock over my desk. It's after seven.

The *Hard Line on Crime with Brenda Dean* airs at eight every night. I've never had a TV in my room; even if I were willing to venture out of bed and face my mother, I would sooner stream porn with my parents than watch tonight's episode of Brenda Dean's show with them on the living room couch.

I lean back against my headboard while my body adjusts to being awake. The pulsing behind my eyes is a different type than the ache I've been waking with the past few days. The Ativan, maybe.

A surge of fear as my brain reboots reminds me of the hell today has unleashed.

Kat's car keys in my pocket. A reporter outside my house. FBI *inside* my house. The things Shannon and Anna and Noah said about me, and those pictures . . .

I scramble for my phone, heart sinking at the sight of the empty screen. Jamie hasn't texted me back.

I open my internet browser and search Kat's and Jesse's

names, but there haven't been any updates today. Searching Brenda Dean only nets one recent headline, from her show's live blog: TONIGHT: JUROR DISMISSED IN CASE OF "HOT CAR DAD," SPARKING MISTRIAL MURMURINGS

Good, I think. Lawrence Cowen, aka Hot Car Dad, is Brenda's topic of the moment, and a twist in the trial should give her enough red meat to gnaw on for a thirty-minute show. I might be safe. For tonight, at least.

I gnaw the inside of my lip, eyeballing the *watch live* link at the top of the *Hard Line on Crime* blog. I click it, log in through our cable provider, and dig through my nightstand drawer for earbuds.

The live broadcast begins in seven minutes. I mute the advertisements looping in the video window, unable to take the jingles for Walmart, the sight of B-list celebrities hawking life insurance.

Eight p.m. The video buffers; I disappear under the covers with my phone.

The sight of Brenda Dean's face behind her desk makes the pit in my gut widen. Recently, she dyed her short blond bob a sassy shade of red, a decision my mother and I discussed at length back when my friends weren't missing and we consumed other peoples' tragedies for entertainment.

I raise the volume on my phone so I can hear Brenda around the thrumming in my ears.

"Breaking news tonight: A juror in the Lawrence Cowen trial has been released due to tweeting about the case from a secret account." Brenda's lips, slick with pink gloss, form a snarl. "Defense attorneys are calling for a mistrial—will Baby Braden ever get justice?"

I turn onto my side and close my eyes, let her murmur in my ear about what a piece of shit Hot Car Dad is. Say a silent prayer of thanks that she's so obsessed with this guy, she's sidelined a story about a beautiful, young missing couple.

"When we return, bombshell new revelations in the Kat Marcotte and Jesse Salpietro disappearance."

My eyelids fly open just in time to see Brenda's coy stare at the camera before the commercial break.

I sit up, my heart battering my ribs. Of course, she wouldn't just let the story go because she couldn't get an interview with me. The look on Brenda's face said she doesn't care, she has a bigger fish on the line.

"If you're just joining us, we're on a video call with Paul Santangelo, a Good Samaritan."

Paul Santangelo cleaned up for his TV debut. The beard he was sporting in front of his house the other day is gone, and his hair is slicked to the side. He's wearing a forest-green pullover with a collared shirt underneath. He looks like someone who hands out flyers for Greenpeace—not someone with a Confederate flag sticker on his pickup truck.

In the frame on the right, Brenda folds her hands on the table and leans toward the camera. "Paul, I want to thank you for speaking with us. I understand it's been a whirlwind of a day for you."

"Yes, ma'am—ever since the *Daily News* published that article."

"You're referring to the *Daily News* story that falsely ties you to the disappearance of Kat Marcotte and Jesse Salpietro?"

Paul Santangelo licks his lips. "Yes, ma'am. There are also people calling me racist, due to a sticker I have on my truck that honors my family's heritage."

"Paul—you don't mind me calling you Paul, right? How did you come to be involved in this case?"

Santangelo's eyes flick to the side. "I wouldn't say I'm involved—"

Brenda Dean waves a ring-clad hand. "Of course. Why don't you tell us what you witnessed on Bobcat Mountain last Saturday afternoon?"

"All right, sure. Well, I camped at Poet's Lookout Friday night."

"For our viewers at home, Poet's Lookout is a point on

Bobcat Mountain, west of Devil's Peak, where Kat and Jesse were last seen, is it not?"

A crude graphic splits the screen with Brenda's face. Two large Xs are marked on the opposite sides of Bobcat Mountain, labeled Devil's Peak and Poet's Lookout. The implication is clear; Paul Santangelo was camping on the complete opposite side of the mountain from where our campsite was.

My spine straightens. I'm finally about to find out what Paul Santangelo saw or heard—along with the rest of Brenda Dean's viewers.

"Yes, ma'am." Paul Santangelo's face, stoic, replaces the graphic.

Brenda is back. "Paul, do you often do overnight hikes by yourself?"

"Sure do. I photograph the stars—last weekend was the first set of clear nights. Except, I saw some clouds rolling in Saturday at dusk, so I decided to pack up and head back down the mountain at maybe five, six p.m."

"And what did you see on your way down the mountain?"

"A girl. She was alone, and it looked like she was trying to make a phone call. There's no service on the mountain, so I asked if she was okay. She said yes; I asked if she needed help, and she said no, she was headed for the parking lot. I said I was too, and she could follow me if she was lost."

"Did she *seem* lost to you?"

"Well, yeah, it was obvious she didn't know where she was going. I knew we weren't far from where the Devil's Peak trail sorta forks off, and the trees don't have trail markers. If you're headed down from Devil's Peak and hit that fork and take the wrong path, you'll wind up at Poet's Lookout, which is pretty far from the parking lot."

"What did she say, when you offered help?"

"She said she was fine and waiting for someone." Paul Santangelo looks uncomfortable. "I continued on my way, but after a few minutes, when I didn't hear anyone behind me, something told me to go check on her. She didn't seem right—scared or upset, maybe. Looked like she'd been crying."

"And did you? Go check on her?"

"Yes, ma'am. Only, when I got back to the spot where I'd left her, she was gone."

"Now just to be clear, we're talking about Claire Keough." Brenda draws out my name; my brain seems to dissociate from my body, hearing my name on prime time television.

"I only just learned her name. I thought, I hope she knows what she's doing. When I heard a couple days later there were kids missing on the mountain, I thought it was her, so I rang the sheriff."

"So, you told Sheriff McAuliffe your story, only to be named by the *Daily News* as a possible *suspect* in a high-profile disappearance a few days later."

"Yes, ma'am. I'm having trouble wrapping my head around it all."

"And at no point while you were on the mountain did you encounter Jesse Salpietro or Kat Marcotte?"

"No, ma'am. Just Claire Keough." My name sounds forced coming out of Paul Santangelo's mouth. Brenda Dean must have encouraged him to use it, so her audience won't forget it.

"Why do you think Claire Keough claims you were at the Merry Mackerel at the same time she went in the restaurant asking for directions Friday evening?" Brenda props her elbows on the counter, knits her fingers together delicately. "Our sources tell us Claire claims you were watching her and eavesdropping on her, despite your having time-stamped photos on your camera that confirm you were at Poet's Lookout Friday evening."

"She mistook me for someone else, I guess," Paul Santangelo says. "I'd never in my life seen her before that day on the trail."

I've watched enough Brenda Dean to know she won't be content to leave it there. She won't stop until she draws blood.

"But why would she make statements to the Sunfish Creek

sheriff that you might have been involved in her friends' disappearance?"

Paul Santangelo hesitates. "I don't know, ma'am. Like I said, something didn't seem right."

His TV affect slips from his voice. *Summin' didn't seem right.*

Now the idea is in everyone's heads, if it wasn't already. Something isn't right about my story. I was alone, without my friends, when Paul Santangelo encountered me.

I am Brenda's new Lawrence Cowen.

Brenda looks right at the camera. "Thank you, Paul, and I'm very sorry to hear about the harassment you've been facing. When we return from the break—wild photos unearthed on social media spark even more questions about Claire Keough, best friend of missing lovebirds—"

I close the video window and yank my earbuds out. It doesn't matter what she has to say about the drunken pictures of me. Her viewers have heard the only thing that will ever matter about me again:

I am a liar.

I scramble out of bed; when I swing my door open my parents are already on the other side, faces ashen. They saw it too.

"I think," I say, "I need to talk to that lawyer."

CHAPTER THIRTEEN

NOW

The office of Michelle Yardley, attorney-at-law, is in a four-story building, wedged between a Wells Fargo Financial Advisors and a gynecology practice.

Mom insists this is just a consultation. I don't want to know how much Michelle Yardley is charging for an hour of legal advice, and thanks to the Ativan I popped before we left, I'm finding it hard to focus on anything coming out of her mouth. My gaze drifts from the framed degrees over her head—SUNY Binghamton for undergrad, Cardozo for law school—to the picture frame with Mickey Mouse ears on her desk.

In the photo, Michelle Yardley is posing with two vapid-eyed little girls in front of Cinderella's castle. It's obvious the photo was taken at least ten years and ten pounds ago because the Michelle Yardley in front of me is a busty older woman with neatly penciled eyebrows.

Mom pokes my arm from the seat next to me.

"Sorry, what?" I say.

"I said, I don't love that the FBI jumped all over the chance to interview you without counsel present. Or at the very least, your parents."

I don't dare look at my mother, because I don't want to

relitigate the issue. Of course, as she has pointed out fifty thousand times since I came clean to her last night about finding Kat's car keys, I should have called her the second I found them. I should have called her the second the goddamn FBI showed up at our front door.

But I didn't. I screwed up, in more ways than I can count, and that's why I'm here.

Michelle Yardley folds her hands together, studies me from behind her tortoiseshell Kate Spade frames. "But refusing to talk to them would have been problematic."

I swallow. "It wasn't a formal interview, I don't think. They didn't even write anything down."

"It doesn't really matter what it was. They left knowing your blood type."

"Why would they want to know her blood type?" Mom murmurs. "If they found blood, but no bodies, can they somehow prosecute—"

I dig my fingers into the skin on my thigh, below the hem of my shorts, still refusing to look at my mom. I hate her right now. I hate her for entertaining the idea that I could have done this, and for thinking, on some level, I should get away with it even if I did.

I watch Michelle Yardley, who hasn't looked up from studying the hospital papers in front of her. "If Kat's and Jesse's bodies are recovered from the base of Devil's Peak, it will be hard to argue someone of Claire's size could have overpowered both of them. If they don't recover the bodies, it will be an even harder sell that she somehow dragged both bodies and concealed them in a location the searchers still have not been able to uncover."

I let myself breathe a little. Of course, it makes no sense that I killed them. I wait for Michelle Yardley to point out the obvious: I had no *reason* to kill my friends—but she clicks her pen, circles something on one of my hospital forms.

"What about the car keys?" Mom puts her fingers to her lips. "What do we do with them?"

Michelle looks up at my mother, her forehead creasing. "You're going to call the FBI and tell them you have them."

When Mom opens her mouth to protest, Michelle holds up a hand, startling the Mickey Mouse frame on her desk. She sets it straight and looks right at me, as if Mom weren't in the room at all.

"You'll tell them exactly what you told me," Michelle says. "You found them while doing laundry. You don't know why you had them. Your position is you don't know anything because you don't remember what happened."

My *position*? I blink at Michelle Yardley. "I don't remember. It's the truth."

She shrugs. The truth is irrelevant to her. Her job is to keep me out of jail.

"Here's what I suggest you do," Michelle says, the razor edge gone from her voice. "Go dark. Absolutely no talking to the media until the frenzy dies down—and it will. If the FBI has further questions, tell them you've decided to retain my services in response to Brenda Dean's smear campaign and that all communication has to run through me."

"Won't that look suspicious?" I ask.

Michelle Yardley gives me a look as if she feels sorry for me. Like she wants to say that train has already left the station, but she doesn't want to miss out on the check in my mom's hand.

We're out the door and getting into the elevator, my mom staring straight ahead. She's probably wondering where she went wrong with me. Her one rule was that I always had to be honest with her, and I couldn't do it. I lied about where we were going last weekend and I ruined my life.

That's what's going on here, isn't it? Even if I had nothing to do with Kat's and Jesse's disappearance, I'm over. Done. Canceled. I accused an innocent man of being involved in my friends' disappearance.

People I don't even know hate me. My own parents can barely look at me.

Kat and Jesse are dead. Everyone is thinking it, because it's been over a week and there's still no sign of them.

Mom's cell begins to ring, nearly making me jump from my skin. The Who's "Who Are You" blasts from her phone. The two men in suits and a pregnant lady sharing the elevator look over at us. Heat fills my cheeks as Mom scrambles to dig her phone out of her bag.

"It's probably Dad," she mutters.

One of the men is still staring; I tear my eyes away. Has he seen the pictures of me in Anna Markey's kitchen? Does he know who I am and that this office shares a floor with a criminal defense attorney?

The elevator doors open to the parking garage; Mom and I let everyone else out first. She trails behind me, still unable to unearth her damn cell. It's stopped ringing, but now her voice mail tone is trilling.

"I think it's in the side pocket," I say.

Mom doesn't say thank you, just makes this strangled, sighing sound and slides her phone out of the pocket. I catch a glimpse of her screen and my thoughts go black.

Elizabeth Marcotte: (1) missed call

No. The word tears through my brain.

No, they cannot have found Kat's and Jesse's bodies. Even though Kat and Jesse being dead is the only outcome that makes sense, I refuse to accept it. Even if someone showed me their bodies I don't think I could believe it, like I'm one of those people who thinks the earth is flat or some other crazy bullshit.

Mom is just still sort of staring at the phone in her hand like the sight of it makes her sick. The words tumble out of me: "Listen to it."

"When we get to the car," Mom says.

Her Civic is parked on the other side of the garage from where the elevator drops us off. Somehow my legs carry me there; I get myself into the passenger seat without them collapsing under me.

Mom buckles her seat belt before pressing play on Mrs. Marcotte's message, holding her phone to her ear. I can't hear any of it over the sound of my heart in my ears.

When Mom sets her phone down, fingers trembling, I force myself to speak. "Did they find Kat and Jesse?"

"No." Mom pales. "It's Mr. Marcotte."

Christine, it's Beth—something's happened with Johnathan. There's been a terrible accident.

That's all Mrs. Marcotte said in her message. I made Mom play it on speaker for me twice because I couldn't believe what I was hearing.

When Mom calls back, Beth's number goes straight to voice mail. I move my hand to my pocket, the thought almost automatic. *I have to call Kat and see what happened.*

But my pocket is empty—Mom confiscated my phone yesterday—and even if I could call Kat, she wouldn't pick up.

"What's happening?" I say.

"I don't know." Mom starts the engine, her eyes still on the phone in her cup holder. "I don't know, Claire."

The FBI is holding a press conference at 3:00 p.m. CNN has been teasing it all afternoon, promising a major update in the search for Katherine Marcotte and Jesse Salpietro.

I put on the TV at two. I've been lying on the living room couch since we got home, eavesdropping on Mom as she calls every person in her contacts, trying to get more information about Beth Marcotte's cryptic message.

"Claire."

I open my eyes as Mom perches on the couch beside me. "I got ahold of Kat's aunt Erin," she says.

Erin Fornier, Amos's mother. My head feels too heavy to process the panic of my mother being one degree closer to Amos. I prop myself up on an elbow and look at Mom. Her eyelids shine with exhaustion and her hair is scraped into a stringy bun, as if she'd lived a thousand years since last night.

"What happened?" I ask.

"She only knows he was hit by a car in Sunfish Creek and airlifted to Columbia–Presbyterian for surgery. He's been under for hours." Mom's voice warbles. "It's not good."

Mom wraps her hand around mine, squeezes. Something has shifted between us since last night. I'm being given a pass on my outburst, because Kat and Jesse are missing and Mr. Marcotte might die and nothing matters anymore.

At ten after, the news breaks for a live broadcast inside the FBI's Long Island field office. Behind a podium flanked by an American flag and a justice department flag, a man—tall, thin, with mantis-like limbs—waits, eyes avoiding the cameras. Lined up beside the pea-soup-colored wall next to him are a bunch of interchangeable men and women in suits.

Among them are Agent Novak, his jaw stiff, as if he's trying to hide that he's got a piece of gum lodged there. Agent Cummings is next to him, hair blown out neatly to her shoulders, hoop earrings gone.

There is lots of shuffling, murmuring among the reporters off-screen, before the man—whom the chyron identifies as the head of the local FBI office—fusses with his tie and speaks. "Last night, at approximately 11:57 p.m., a suspect in the disappearance of Katherine Marcotte and Jesse Salpietro was killed while fleeing the scene of an automobile accident in Sunfish Creek, New York."

Dozens of camera shutters go off at once. *Suspect.* The word knifes through my gut. Next to me, my mother's hand moves to cover her mouth.

"Prior to the events of this accident, Johnathan Marcotte, Katherine's father, was critically injured in a confrontation with the driver. He was airlifted to the ICU at Columbia–Presbyterian Hospital. Further details about the individual will be released in the coming days. For now, to protect the integrity of the investigation, we will not be answering any questions about the events of the accident."

Noises of protest from the reporters; the director holds up a hand, like a teacher quieting an unruly class. Someone shouts: *Was Mr. Marcotte paying a ransom to the suspect?*

The word cuts off the oxygen to my brain. One thought rises to the surface: if they were kidnapped, they might still be alive.

The man goes red in the face. "I'm unable to comment on events preceding the accident. *If you'll let me finish—*"

The protests quiet, and the director clears his throat. "Our primary focus is recovering Katherine and Jesse. In light of GPS data recovered from the suspect's vehicle, we've shifted the focus of our search away from Bobcat Mountain."

My heartbeat stalls. If the FBI doesn't think their bodies are on the mountain, they had to have been kidnapped—they made it off the mountain *alive—*

A voice pipes up from the crowd—"Are you searching Blackstone Quarry?"

The floor seems to cave in beneath me. I grab the arm of the couch, a cold sweat pricking the back of my neck. *No. They didn't make it off that mountain alive just to be dumped into a quarry—*

Above the collar of his shirt, the FBI director's neck flashes red, as if he's going to pop a blood vessel at the punchline of his press conference being snatched from him. "Yes. We have shifted our focus to Blackstone Quarry, located three miles west of Bobcat Mountain."

At this, my mother takes my hand again. On the television,

a woman's voice echoes somewhere in the crowd. "Is it true an item belonging to Kat Marcotte was found in the quarry?"

Next to the director, Novak's nostrils flare. He shakes his head.

"We recovered an item of clothing." The FBI director wipes his forehead. "We're working to confirm if it belongs to Katherine."

"We'll take one more question," the director says.

Some shouting. The director points at someone off-screen.

A woman's voice. "Assuming Johnathan Marcotte was in that parking lot to pay the suspect a ransom for his daughter, why haven't you recovered Katherine or Jesse?"

The director swallows, his jaw set. "I'll have no further comment on that until our search of the quarry is complete. But I have to caution you: This is a recovery mission, not a rescue."

It's morning when the doorbell rings, pulling me out of my Ativan stupor. I don't know what time it is, or how I'm supposed to measure time now. The FBI director said a search of Blackstone Quarry is underway.

Blackstone Quarry is two hundred feet deep with zero visibility. According to the talking heads that appeared on CNN after the press conference, it could take the divers weeks to find anything at the bottom.

It could be weeks before we know for sure if Kat's and Jesse's bodies are in there.

My mother answers the door, because I haven't budged from my blanket cocoon on the couch since the press conference. Murmured voices in the hall, then Agent Cummings and Novak are in my living room and I still can't make myself move or speak.

Cummings takes the armchair while Novak stands in the

corner behind her. He's always standing, to the point where I wonder if he has a boil on his ass or something.

"Is there any word on Johnathan Marcotte?" Mom asks.

"He survived the first surgery and is scheduled for another today." Cummings's tone says there's nothing more to tell. "Mrs. Keough, could I trouble you for a cup of coffee?"

"Not at all." Mom's hand is at her throat, and she looks like she's on the verge of crying.

Something tells me Cummings asked for the coffee to get rid of my mother. Mom knows it too, because she watches from the kitchen archway.

Novak crosses his arms, studies me. "We hear you have an attorney, but I don't think it's necessary for her to be here for this."

I nod. Because I'm not a suspect; they have a suspect. A dead suspect.

"Who was the man who hit Mr. Marcotte?" I ask.

Cummings opens the folder in her lap and hands me a printed photo. A driver's license, or a mug shot, who can tell. The man's bright blue eyes and half smile are youthful, but his craggy face suggests otherwise.

"Have you ever seen him before?" Cummings asks.

"I don't recognize him." I drop the picture like it's on fire.

"His name is Michael Vincent Dorsey. It doesn't ring a bell?"

I shake my head. "Did he know Kat and Jesse?"

"We haven't been able to establish a connection," Cummings says. "Right now it looks like a crime of opportunity."

"But he kidnapped them?" The words stick in my throat. The FBI director had said they don't believe the suspect intended to return Kat and Jesse, which means he had them. He had them and now they're gone, which means they're dead.

My chest is stretched like a rubber band about to snap; I can't breathe. I try to focus on the words coming out of Agent Novak's mouth.

"We think the suspect went to the campsite looking for a robbery target," he says. "Once he found out who Kat was, he changed his mind."

"I don't understand," I say. "I was alone when Paul Santangelo saw me on the trail that evening. If we were attacked and Kat was kidnapped, why was I so calm when I saw Santangelo? Why didn't I tell him what happened?"

Cummings and Novak glance at each other.

"We don't know," Cummings finally says. "It's possible you'd already hit your head and lost your memory. The hiker said you seemed scared."

"It's also possible you didn't trust him," Novak says. "You might have wanted to get to the parking lot to call the police."

I swallow. "I found her car keys in my pocket. I think . . . she must have given them to me."

My voice trails off, drowned out by the sound of Kat's in my head. I know it's not real, because I don't remember, but I hear her. I know exactly what she would say, how she would plead for her life when she realized we were being robbed.

Please don't kill me. My grandmother has money—she'll pay.

She would have done anything to save us if she saw a gun. I close my eyes and I see her, slipping the car keys in my hand. Commanding me to run as she went with Michael Dorsey.

But why would Jesse stay behind?

Because he'd never let Kat go alone.

"Claire," Cummings says softly. "Maybe you could look at his picture again."

I swallow, nod. I don't think I can handle looking at his face but I owe it to Kat and Jesse, right? Because somehow, I got away.

I lift the picture. Michael Dorsey stares back at me, his expression blank and unthreatening. It seems impossible I could have looked into eyes that blue and not be able to remember them.

"Claire," Novak says, pulling my attention away from the

picture. "We tested the trees where you were found. We found some hair and skin cells."

It takes me a bit to figure out what this means. "Mine?"

"The DNA doesn't match Kat's or Jesse's, so we'll need to test yours to be sure. But your injury is consistent with your head being slammed into a tree."

It doesn't make me feel any better to hear him say it. I *was* attacked. I didn't hurt myself running away from something horrible I'd done. Something horrible happened to *us*.

"This Michael Dorsey guy," I say, voice quavering. "He attacked me?"

"We can't say for sure without you being able to identify him," Cummings says. "But we can loosely place him on Bobcat Mountain, and he had Kat's phone."

Why can't I remember him? I remembered Paul Santangelo—I remember feeling terrified of the hiker who was just trying to help me—but when I look at Mike Dorsey I feel nothing.

Was it too dark to see his face? Had he had his face covered when he smashed my head into that tree?

Or is my brain still trying to protect me after all, so that I don't have to see his face every night before I fall asleep?

I give the photo back to Cummings and bring my trembling hands together. "There was blood on my hands, in the emergency room."

"Dorsey had a stab wound on his shoulder when we recovered his body," Cummings says. "It was at least a few days old."

I lower my hands. "I had his blood on me. I had evidence it was him and now there's no way to know for sure—"

Cummings puts a hand on my knee. "Claire, victims unknowingly get rid of evidence all the time. You can't beat yourself up."

Victim. I resist the urge to find the tender spot at the back of my skull with my fingers.

But Michael Dorsey is dead. The idea is incomprehensible— the FBI *has* someone who could fill in the blanks in my memory, who could tell us what happened to Kat and Jesse—if only he were alive.

"I understand how you must be feeling," Cummings says as I'm wiping away a tear.

Anger rises up in me out of nowhere, the urge to lash out at someone as strong as my need to breathe. "How could you possibly understand?" I say.

Novak's eyes flick to his hands, knotted over his belly. "I'll go check on that coffee."

Cummings shifts on the couch, edging closer to me. "I know it was before your time, but you ever hear of that plane crash in Queens after September eleventh?"

I shake my head.

"My mother and aunt were on that flight," Cummings says. "On their way to visit our family in the Dominican Republic."

Thirty seconds ago, I wanted to die. Now, I want to die and have someone light my corpse on fire and flush my ashes down a toilet because it's what I deserve. "I'm so sorry. That's horrible."

"It was. I was only a few years younger than you are now when it happened," Cummings says. "It was twenty years ago, and some days I still don't want to get out of bed."

The knot in my chest tightens.

"How do you keep going?" I whisper.

Cummings glances at the kitchen entryway, where Novak disappeared through. On the other side, I hear my father murmuring words I can't make out. "You don't really have a choice. If you can't do it for yourself, you do it for the people who love you."

I rub the tears out of my eyes. Cummings opens the folder in her lap again, and my chest clenches.

"I know this is hard," Cummings says. "But take a look and tell me if you recognize what I'm about to show you."

I don't breathe; when Cummings sets a picture on the coffee table, a whimper lodges in my throat.

Kat's bandana, the pink one she wore to volleyball matches and used to tie back her wet hair that Friday night before.

A quick glance, and the grime on the fabric might be mud or dirt. But I look closer.

The stains aren't brown, they're a faded rust color, like a bloodstain left too long in the water.

I can't stop seeing it. Even after Cummings and Novak are gone, even after the three Ativan I sneak when Mom leaves me alone so I can take a bath, the blood on the bandana is there when I close my eyes.

It's there when I sink below the surface of the water in the tub. All my other senses dull, throwing the image of Kat's bandana into sharp relief.

How long do I have to stay under here, I think, *before it disappears?*

How long until I disappear too?

PART TWO

HOME

CHAPTER FOURTEEN

SIX MONTHS LATER
DECEMBER

The spring before sixth grade, when my parents told me that Mr. Marcotte had accepted a position at Aviano Air Base in Italy and Kat's family was moving with him, I shut myself in my room and refused to come out for anyone, especially Kat.

I knew I was being a giant brat about it, but we were about to start middle school. Kat and I had spent all summer making *plans*—we would both join the newspaper and maybe try out for the play and maybe finally sit with Anna Markey at lunch—and Kat was abandoning it all to move to *Italy*.

Starting middle school without her felt like a world-ending event. Mom implored me to imagine how Kat felt, having to start school in a country where she didn't know anyone, but I couldn't get over her leaving me behind.

I'd like to believe that if I'd known I would eventually lose her forever, I wouldn't have been such an ass about her moving away. But I think I acted the way I did because it's easier to live with anger at someone than to deal with the pain of missing them.

I miss her—I miss *them*—all the time, but I'm angry more often than I'd like to admit. I'll think of a stupid thing Jesse said to me, a pointless argument Kat and I had where I *knew* I was right but I just gave in because I couldn't win against her, and I get angry all over again.

It's easier to be angry. It's easier than wondering why I was the one who got away.

I've obviously had a lot of chances to discuss this in therapy. Mom found me a psychiatrist off campus who I take a twenty-minute bus ride to see every other week. There's also all the doctors I spoke to during my two-week stay at Twin Oaks, not long after the search for Kat's and Jesse's bodies started and I lost what was left of my shit.

Anyway, a lot of things have happened between then and now, but all that matters is I'm okay.

I have to be okay. Because for four weeks, I am going home.

I haven't been to Long Island since Thanksgiving; the drive from Geneseo is too long for spontaneous weekend trips, and to be honest, I'm not eager to spend a second longer in Brookport than I need to.

My father drives up two days before Christmas Eve to pick me up for winter break. I insisted I was fine to take the bus home, but Dad framed it as *I'm just excited to see you and want that extra six hours in the car with you!*

The real reason, obviously, is that my parents are probably skittish about me traveling alone. It's a miracle they even let me leave for school at all, considering I was barely a functioning human being for most of the summer.

I push the thoughts away and let the sound of Dad's audiobook lull me to sleep. We arrive home as it's getting dark; the sight of our Christmas tree, its rainbow lights reflecting off the bay window, makes my heart tug.

When we get inside, Mom is in the living room, guiltily straightening the pipe cleaner antlers on the reindeer ornament I made in kindergarten. "I'm sorry we didn't wait for you—Dad thought it might be nice if you got here and everything was all set up."

"Mom," I say. "I was at school, not—"

Missing.

"At war," I say, letting my backpack slide off my shoulder, but it's too late, Mom's smile droops a bit. She covers it up by planting a kiss on my forehead.

"Do you want Mama Lenora's or Panda Garden?" she asks, her eyes not meeting mine. "You're the deciding vote."

I'm suddenly not very hungry, but if I say so, she'll keep digging and find out I also told Dad I wasn't hungry when he asked if I wanted anything from the McDonald's at the rest stop on the drive home.

It is very hard to hide signs of depression when your mother is a therapist; I tried that once and it ended badly. Or it ended well, depending on how you look at it, since I am here, in my house, on winter break from college, and not still in Twin Oaks.

"Panda Garden," I say. "Can you get me my usual? I'm gonna start unpacking."

She nods, worry working her jaw muscle, but by the time I'm shut in my bedroom, she's on the phone with Panda Garden, her voice back to its normal, airy self.

I sit perched on the edge of my bed, my chest tight. I knew that coming home would be hard. What I did not expect was seeing our Christmas tree in that window—the same one we've had since I was in diapers—and barely recognizing it, as if it were an artifact from someone else's life.

I need to do something to anchor myself, quickly.

I unpack my laptop and I Google Mike Dorsey.

This is the first thing I do when I wake up and the last thing I do before I go to bed. Sometimes, I even sneak in a session or two between classes when I'm bored. The only person who knows about this little habit is my therapist at school.

He says indulging the urge to Google the man who killed my friends and almost killed me is like picking at a scab. Gratifying, maybe, but at the cost of healing.

I don't care enough about his stupid metaphor to argue with him about why it's wrong. Googling Mike Dorsey isn't gratifying, because I get nothing out of it.

There hasn't been an update about Kat and Jesse's case in months. The facts are out there, waiting for the necessary pieces to tie everything together: that definitively, conclusively prove that they're dead; that Mike Dorsey is the man who killed them.

No one knows for sure exactly what happened in that parking lot between Mike Dorsey and Johnathan Marcotte. The FBI is being tight-lipped—ask anyone and they'll say it's to protect their own asses, in light of how badly they fucked up. Because they were supposed to be close by during the ransom exchange, making sure no one got hurt.

And yet, somehow, Mike Dorsey figured out that Mr. Marcotte had told the FBI about the ransom demand, and they were waiting for him to leave with the money to catch him. In his panic, he tried to drive off. Mr. Marcotte jumped in front of the car, desperate to stop him.

Mike Dorsey dragged Kat's father's body three hundred feet with his Dodge Charger before he escaped long enough to make it to the top of the quarry, where he presumably shot Kat and Jesse before dumping their bodies into the water. He might have escaped if not for trying to speed away from the FBI agent waiting for him at the quarry entrance, and barreling his car straight into a passing tractor-trailer.

The FBI says that Kat's and Jesse's DNA was found in the trunk of Mike Dorsey's Dodge Charger. Tire tracks matching his car were found on the north side of Blackstone Quarry; an initial search of the water yielded Kat's bandana, some items from Jesse's wallet, and a camping knife that Elizabeth Marcotte identified as belonging to her husband. Not much biological evidence was left on the blade after the time it had spent in the water, but the FBI believes Mike Dorsey tossed the knife to cover up that his blood was all over it after I stabbed him in self-defense.

Marian Sullivan-Marcotte's hundred-thousand-dollar reward for Kat's return, dead or alive, still stands. After the authorities announced they were calling off the quarry search until the spring—the water was too deep, plagued by poor visibility and too many crevices to search for bodies safely—divers came flocking in from all over, desperate to be the ones to find Kat and Jesse and collect the money.

Once one of the divers got stuck in a narrow crevice and nearly drowned, the town of Sunfish Creek barred the public access to the quarry.

I know all of this, of course.

I know that Michael Vincent Dorsey, the man responsible for what happened on Bobcat Mountain, was born in Tampa, Florida, and moved to Sunfish Creek with his mother when he was fifteen. He was arrested twice in his twenty-five years—once for stealing cash from the register at his job at a pet store, and once for marijuana possession.

His Facebook profile is private, but posts he made that his friends leaked to the press reveal a man who loved cars, his mother, and their orange cat, Briscoe. He also ranted about how weed should be legal, how the series finale of *Game of Thrones* was bullshit, and how rich people are the scum of the earth and all-out class warfare is the only solution.

The people who were willing to admit they had once been friends with Mike Dorsey, in exchange for a thirty-second spot on the evening news, described him as mercenary, scheming, but above all, naïve. Mike Dorsey always had an idea of how he was going to make money, leave his life as a mechanic in Sunfish Creek behind. He wanted to live like the rappers and influencers he followed on his private Instagram account; in the absence of talent or brains he'd of course turned to crime.

Put all these pieces together, and it makes sense Michael Dorsey would murder the granddaughter of a wealthy congresswoman, along with her boyfriend, for one hundred thousand dollars.

It's enough for most people. But it's not enough for me.

It's an explanation, not an answer.

Outside my room, the doorbell rings, and Dad shouts that the food is here. I shut my laptop and push Mike Dorsey from my mind. If I let him linger there, I'll start to dwell on the question that will never, ever be answered.

How did he wind up at Devil's Peak that evening?

How did he find us in the last place we were supposed to be?

Serg called me while I was still studying for finals to ask if I'd be interested in working over my break, and I don't think I've ever said yes to anything so quickly in my life. I can tell my parents are disappointed I have to work Christmas Eve until I come home with a crisp hundred dollar bill in tips for covering waitress duties.

Tonight is New Year's Eve, one of the only nights we're busy enough to open up the dining room on the second floor. The bar gets so backed up that I'm pulled away from the hostess stand to run drinks upstairs.

I scan the room for the *crusty old dude and the woman who is too young for him* one of the waitresses instructed me to deliver two old-fashioneds to. My flats snag on the carpet and I almost swan-dive with a full tray of drinks because the woman in question is Ben fucking Filipoff's mother, Pam, and sure enough, Ben is sitting right next to her, across from said crusty old dude.

The man—slicked-back silver hair, clearly Brookport Old Money—flags me down. "Over here, sweetheart."

Ben's face turns the shade of a beet as I place one of the

old-fashioneds in front of the man. Pam Filipoff looks up from her chicken marsala and squeaks, "Claire! We didn't know you worked here!"

Kill me. I offer a full-teethed smile. "Happy New Year, everyone."

Mrs. Filipoff, nose and cheeks champagne pink, is not about to let me get away. She introduces me to Old-Fashioned, whose name is Frank and who is clearly unimpressed with having to make small talk with the help.

Ben bumps his hand against mine as I'm clearing the empty glasses on the table. "Where's the bathroom here?" he asks.

He knows it's downstairs; maybe he wants an excuse to talk to me or get away from Old-Fashioned, who is now whispering into his mother's ear.

"I'll show you," I say, balancing one end of the drink tray on my hip. Ben steps aside when we get to the stairs so I can head down first.

"You look good," he says, and I wish he wasn't behind me so I can see his face and determine if he means it.

"You too," I say. "Your mom's new boyfriend seems nice."

"He's a dick."

We're at the bottom of the stairs; the bathroom is to the right, the bar is to the left. Here is where we should part ways, but Ben blurts, "What are you doing later?"

My cheeks flush, because he asked, but also because the answer is embarrassing. My parents are at a party at their friends' house in Nassau County and won't be back until after midnight; I was planning on taking home meatball soup in a bread bowl and falling asleep before the ball drops.

"Nothing," I say.

"Same. My mom is going to Frank's tonight." Ben holds my gaze. "You know where to find me if you're bored."

I replay the invitation over in my head a dozen times over the next two hours. Around ten thirty, the chaos dies down.

The diners have been served the final courses of their prix-fixe menus, and I haven't had to seat a new table in over an hour. Serg relieves me of my hostess duties and I slip into the kitchen to retrieve my coat.

Carlos is sitting on the counter, prying open a bottle of Korbel. The cork flies out to cheers from the kitchen staff. He takes a swig and offers me the bottle.

I shake my head and he boos. "You better be coming to the tree lighting."

He's referring to the annual tradition in which he lights his Christmas tree on fire in his backyard and invites the whole staff to watch over cups of cheap champagne.

One of the waitresses whisks past me with a tray of crème brûlées and says: "She's meeting a guy at his house. I heard her on the stairs."

My cheeks burn while Carlos and the others whoop and holler.

"Get some, girl," Carlos shouts. "Maybe it'll loosen your ass up."

I give them the finger with both hands as I push my way out the back door with my shoulder. But when I'm out of sight, I touch the smile on my face, fingers stinging from the cold.

The smile is gone by the time I've pulled out of the parking lot. I have to see it every night when I leave work; the street sign for Idledale Road, home to Kat's empty house.

It doesn't seem right that everyone is going about their business just like last year, like nothing has changed. Like Kat and Jesse weren't here at all.

But you are, I think to myself. *You're still here.*

Ben and I are on his couch, eating the caramel corn his mom made this afternoon *in case he wanted to invite a friend over.* I don't think his ex-girlfriend was who she had in mind, but she's as casual about this stuff as my parents are.

When Ben gets up to get us some sodas, I text my mom that there was a change of plans and I'm hanging out with a friend.

She replies right away:

Which friend

Ben Filipoff

Claire, this is Dad. Your mother is quite drunk.
I see that you're with Ben Filipoff and I'd just like to remind you to be safe.

Blood surges to my face as I bang out a response.

O

M

F

G

WHY, DAD??

Because you're my little girl, that's why!

Ben comes into the living room, holding two Diet Cokes. "What's so funny?"

"The fact that my mother is wasted on New Year's Eve and I, a college student, am not," I answer.

He hands me a Diet Coke and we segue into the obligatory college talk. He tells me about UVA, how he's been thinking about transferring. The school is too big, it's too hard to make friends. Without sports he's not really sure where he fits in, especially when most of the people in his classes are smarter, wealthier, and laugh at his Long Island accent.

"I think what you're saying is you miss being popular," I say.

He laughs. "I think, Keough, you're right."

After a beat of nothing but the sound of our jaws working the popcorn, I take a sip of soda and ask, "What's the gang doing tonight?"

I can't help the note of bitterness in my voice, remembering how eager Noah and Shannon and Anna were to drag me when Kat and Jesse disappeared. How easy it was for Jamie to ghost me when she realized the tide was turning against me.

Ben flips the top on his soda. "Dunno. Haven't talked to most of them since we left for school."

"Really?" I realize sounding so surprised makes it sound like I care about who Ben is friends with, but I'm too curious to be embarrassed. "Why?"

"Because they're assholes."

Ben doesn't offer anything more; I'm trying not to do that only-child thing where I automatically assume everything is about me, but I wonder if this is about me. If maybe he saw the Facebook posts and told them they were being assholes; if maybe he finally chose me over them, even when it was too late for it to make a difference.

"So." Ben sinks into the couch, props his socked feet on the coffee table. "I texted you, after Mr. Marcotte's accident. I just wanted you to know it wasn't me—I didn't tell Noah or anyone at school you were there with them that weekend."

"I saw," I say. "And I believe you."

Ben didn't have a reason to lie to me, and there were three hundred people in our class alone who could have heard from anyone that Kat and Jesse didn't go on that trip by themselves. It doesn't matter who outed me, only that they did, and where I wound up because of it.

"I was going to respond to you." I glance sideways at Ben. "I just didn't get the chance."

There's no non-embarrassing way to admit to Ben why I didn't get the chance to text him back. My phone was confiscated for two weeks while I was checked into Twin Oaks. I wasn't allowed contact with anyone but my parents for the first few days while I was stabilized for major depression and suicidal thoughts.

My chest goes hollow at the memory: me, pleading, crying in the waiting room. *Don't make me do this. I don't belong here.*

"You probably heard the rumors about where I was," I say, keeping my voice even.

"I did," Ben says. "You don't have to tell me what really happened unless you want to."

It surprises me, but I realize that I do want to.

So I tell him everything: How after Mr. Marcotte got hurt and the FBI announced Mike Dorsey was dead, the media backed off me a bit.

And then, Brenda Dean. She was the first person to suggest that Mike Dorsey might not have been acting alone. She didn't use my name, but she didn't have to. One of her guests suggested that perhaps I had pointed a finger at Paul Santangelo to cover up my own involvement in the kidnapping.

Because how could a crime so heinous also be random? Mike Dorsey had to have known we would be there; murders are spontaneous, but kidnappings are planned.

I read every single Reddit thread about me. There were dozens, speculating that I'd helped Mike Dorsey, promising to split the ransom money with him.

People posted one-star reviews for my mom's therapy practice. *Says she helps people yet she raised a liar.*

Mom said it would pass, that people would find something else to get riled about, that we just had to ride out the storm. But I couldn't stop reading that shit. I became obsessed with Googling myself.

I hadn't slept in almost a week when my parents checked me into Twin Oaks.

When I finish, Ben doesn't say anything. I'm looking ahead, at the muted coverage of the ball drop, so I don't have to see Ben's face. Most people I tell about my stay at Twin Oaks, it takes them a second or two to wipe the pity from their face before they say something like *There's no shame in getting help.*

When I glance at Ben, he's watching me. I feel my lips part as he reaches, brushes a popcorn crumb stuck to the ends of my hair. He doesn't blink as he moves his hand higher so he's cupping one side of my face.

I climb onto Ben so I'm facing him. He pulls my face to his and kisses me like I am the only girl he's ever kissed, which I know isn't true because he's *better* at it than he was when we were together, so I can only assume he's had lots of practice on girls at college—

His hands move to my lower back and I press into him and when my fingers are on his belt loop he says into my ear, "Claire, this isn't why I asked you to come over."

I go still. "You don't want to?"

"Of course I do—I just don't have any condoms." Ben turns the shade of the cranberry couch.

The last thing I want is to look as disappointed as I feel; I stay where I am, my fingers still hooked over the waist of his pants. "Burned through them all last semester, huh?"

Ben's skin is hot on mine. "I've probably gotten one percent of the action you think I've gotten."

"That's still more than I've gotten." I snort. "Including tonight."

"That's hard to believe." Ben twirls a finger through the ends of my hair, dyed a lighter shade of brown than the rest. I've cut it to my shoulders, the shortest it's been in my life. "Your new hair is ridiculously hot."

I laugh, and he flips me over, pushing my shirt up to kiss my belly button.

He moves lower, and I close my eyes. My head goes blank;

for the first time in six months I don't have to remind myself that I'm still here. I just am.

My parents beat me home from their New Year's party, which is unfortunate because I would willingly go into witness protection if it got me out of questions about what Ben and I did this evening.

In the bay window, our Christmas tree is dark, but the living room lights are on.

Unease worms through me as I step through the door. Mom is on the couch, her face in her hands. She drops them to her lap. There's a smear of mascara on the side of her hand and her face is spotted with red.

"What's wrong?" I ask, and she shakes her head, unable to bring herself to speak.

Dad comes out of the kitchen, a glass of water in his hands. He halts when he sees me.

I force the words out. "What happened?"

Dad's voice is hoarse. "Mr. Marcotte is dead."

CHAPTER FIFTEEN

——

NOW

When I find my voice, it comes out warbled. "I don't understand. I thought he was stable."

Mr. Marcotte has been in the hospital since last June, when
Mike Dorsey mowed him down with his car. The last we heard,
he hadn't regained brain function. He hadn't spoken or used
his limbs since he woke up, and he likely never would again,
but he was alive.

Mom produces a crumpled tissue from her hands and uses
it to wipe the mascara pooling under her eyes. "Apparently
he's been on a ventilator since he got an infection last month.
Beth decided to remove him from it yesterday morning."

My throat goes tight. "You talked to Mrs. Marcotte?"

Dad looks uncomfortable. Oh. Of course they didn't.

The last thing Kat's mother ever said to us was over that
voice mail last June. *It's Johnathan. There's been a terrible accident.*

The memory of her voice, so small over the speaker of my
mother's phone, turns my stomach. In the fall, when Mr. Marcotte was transferred to a rehab facility in Westchester, twenty
minutes from Emma's boarding school, Beth immediately packed

up and moved with Elmo to be closer to both of them. We haven't heard a thing from the Marcottes since.

Not Marian. Not Amos.

Dad sits next to Mom on the couch, setting down the glass of water on the coffee table. He puts his other hand on Mom's knee. She grabs it.

"We heard at the party," Dad says quietly. "A good friend of one of the Sullivans got the call right before we left."

I turn this information over in my head until it feels real. Kat's father is dead.

I have to call her.

The urge is as reflexive as blinking. It stuns me, fills me with shame. Six months have gone by, and some part of me can't process that Kat is never picking up her phone again.

"Claire," Mom says. "Are you all right?"

There's fear radiating off her. She's wondering what this will do to me.

"Yeah," I say. "I'm just really tired. I need to get some sleep before work in the morning."

Mom glances at Dad, her grip on his hand tightening visibly. Dad is looking at me sadly, like maybe he understands I'm not crying or anything because I've been ready for something like this. There was never going to be a happy ending for Mr. Marcotte.

"I'm sure Serg would understand if you tell him you need to take a day," Mom says.

I blink at her. "No. I have to go to work."

I feel their gaze, hot on my back, as I head to my bedroom.

I'm about to shut myself inside when I turn, see them still on the couch, watching me.

"I love you," I say, meaning it quite possibly more than I ever have. "Good night."

———

Over the past six months, I've come to crave the first few moments of each morning. Those precious thirty seconds when I first wake up, and all I know is that I'm safe, in the comfort of my bed.

Nothing compares to those moments before reality sets in.

Mr. Marcotte is dead, but a quick scan of the news when I wake reveals that the rest of the world does not know yet. I shower Ben off my body and pin my hair into a bun on top of my head. Today's ensemble is a gray sweater dress and black boots and a fake smile because if someone posts on Yelp about how the hostess didn't smile at them, I'll hear about it from Serg's wife.

I'm not supposed to use my phone while working but I always leave it tucked behind the menus at the podium. Today I leave it in my purse in the kitchen because I don't know what Mr. Marcotte's death means for me.

It sounds disgustingly selfish, but I have to be this way to protect myself. When Kat's and Jesse's names pop up in the news, there's always the chance mine will appear next to them. Everyone will be reminded that I'm going to college, working, doing all the things Kat and Jesse will never get to do. They'll be reminded that I came back and maybe they still don't know how to feel about that.

I don't go into the kitchen much except to use the staff bathroom back there; when I do, Carlos and the waitstaff are so busy that they don't stop to harass me about going over to Ben's last night.

The day goes by fast. My shift ends at three.

I wander to my car, the midday sun warm on the back of my neck. I buckle myself in and dig my phone out of my purse, bypass the handful of texts waiting to be opened, and Google *Johnathan Marcotte*.

It's on every major news outlet in the country. I open an article from the Associated Press.

REPORT: FATHER OF MISSING TEEN KATHERINE MARCOTTE DIES

Johnathan Marcotte, 45, died after being removed from a ventilator at Columbia-Presbyterian Hospital. Sources close to the family say that Marcotte never regained consciousness after a hit-and-run accident in Sunfish Creek, where his daughter Katherine, 17, disappeared from Bobcat Mountain with her boyfriend, Jesse Salpietro, 18.

The driver of the vehicle, Michael Dorsey, was pronounced dead at the scene. Dorsey's 2003 Dodge Charger collided with a tractor-trailer while he was attempting to flee the scene of the accident that critically injured Marcotte.

This morning, the FBI issued a new statement: "The investigation into the disappearance of Kat Marcotte and Jesse Salpietro is still an open and active investigation, as is our inquiry regarding the death of a suspect in the case, Michael Dorsey. Anyone with information is urged to come forward. Our tip line continues to generate dozens of new leads every week."

A spokesperson for the family confirmed that Johnathan Marcotte died yesterday and asked for privacy.

I lean back in my seat, shut my eyes against the threat of tears. I wipe my eyes with the back of my sleeve, force myself to look out my windshield, find something to focus on. A technique one of the doctors at Twin Oaks taught me. Name five things you can see around you.

I get stuck at one. The sky, brilliant and cloudless. It's the type of New Year's Day designed to trick you into thinking maybe this year the earth will skip the whole winter thing.

But there's no fast-forwarding through a long winter; there's only waiting it out.

Mom and Dad have to go back to work the day after New Year's. I don't have to be at the restaurant for my dinner shift until a quarter to four. I'm not sure how I'm supposed to kill an entire day when I have no school work and no friends.

Mom is already gone, on her way to the office, when I drag myself out of bed at nine. I'm rifling through the junk drawer in the kitchen when Dad tracks me down, hands cupped around his travel mug.

"Have you seen my headphones?" I ask.

Dad's gaze travels to my sneakers. "Are you going for a *run*?"

"Not if I can't find my headphones."

"I think I saw Mom put them in your purse," Dad says. He watches me fish the headphones out of my bag, which is on the kitchen table. "Since when do you run?"

I slip one of the pods in my ear, avoiding Dad's eyes. "I started at school."

"Oh," he says, head tilted slightly. I've never once run voluntarily in my life, but the lie feels easier than saying I just decided to go for a run this morning.

If I say there's no reason for what I'm doing, Dad will be even more convinced there is a reason. This is how it's been since my friends died and I survived; everything I do has to have meaning.

"Where are you off to?" Dad asks, adjusting the collar of his shirt beneath his sweater. He's trying to sound casual, like he's just interested in my route, but I know the real reason. It must suck to be a parent, to have to watch your children head off into the world, knowing you have absolutely no control over whether they'll come back to you in one piece.

"Just into the village," I say. "I'll watch out for cars and ice."

Dad pours the dregs of the coffeepot into his mug, forehead creasing at how little is left. They haven't adjusted to my being home again. Can't remember to put an extra scoop into the coffee maker each morning. "You probably won't be back before I leave."

"Probably not." I brush my lips against Dad's cheek. "Have a good day."

I can feel him watching me from the window as I head down the driveway and make a right toward the village.

January is back to its normal dickish self. I pull my hood over my head to keep out the chill, but as I pick up my pace, sweat starts to collect on my spine and my blood flows hot into my face.

The music in my ears is one of the playlists Jesse made me in middle school. He used to burn them on CDs, because he didn't have an iPhone or an MP3 player. Some of the songs are his own; he always had lyrics written for them somewhere, but he never recorded himself singing because he was too shy about his voice.

I didn't intend for this playlist to be my running soundtrack. I'd hit shuffle; the universe has always had a way of sticking Jesse Salpietro in my face when I'm trying to forget him.

I tug the earbuds out, shove them in my pocket. I slow to a trot at the stop sign at the end of my road and make a left, and before I realize what I'm doing I'm setting my internal compass for Jesse's house.

Jesse's aunt and uncle live on Main Road, just before the sign dividing West Brookport from Brookport Village. I slow to a brisk walk as I come around the treacherous bend that's marked by a wooden cross and a decomposing teddy bear.

Cars zip past on my right, drowning out the thump of blood in my ears, as I slow to a crawl. *It's just a damn house. You can handle walking past his house.*

In the driveway is an old blue Thunderbird, the car Jesse's uncle Donald uses for his twice-daily pilgrimage for beer, cigarettes, and scratch-off lottery tickets from the 7-Eleven down the street. His aunt Andrea's car is missing, which means she's probably at work.

The sight of the empty carport along the side of the house twists my heart like a rag.

Jesse bought the Volkswagen Jetta at the end of junior year for two thousand dollars from some guy off Craigslist. I went with him to pick it up so he wouldn't get robbed or murdered. When he test-drove it around the parking lot, "Born to Run" was on the radio, so I jokingly named the car Bruce and it stuck.

Of course, his aunt and uncle got rid of Bruce rather than keep up with the insurance payments.

The realization makes the fire in my lungs worse. I can't linger here, because if Donald comes to the window, things will get weird. I inhale and start to jog again, this time toward Brookport Village.

Andrea works at Fast n' Fresh, the village grocery store. Jesse always hung out at my house; the last time I saw Andrea was the week before prom weekend, while buying a bag of Twizzlers on one of my work breaks.

I should have stopped in to see her before I left for college, but I chickened out. I told myself, if I were Andrea, I was the last person I would want to see. Because even if Jesse's aunt believed I didn't have anything to do with his disappearance, she wouldn't be able to look at me without thinking it: Why did I come back and he didn't?

That's what I told myself, but deep down, I know she would have liked to see me. The lie was more comfortable, though.

I just didn't have the balls to face her.

It seems appropriate, now, that I at least show my face.

It doesn't take long to track Andrea down. I can see her in the alley between the grocery store and the CVS—a petite woman in a blue grocer's uniform doing a terrible job of pretending she's not about to light up.

"Mrs. Kelly?" I ask. My breath, ragged from running, frosts in front of my face.

Andrea whips around. Blinks several times before recognition sets in. "Claire. Oh my goodness."

My voice is suddenly defective. Andrea stuffs her pack of cigarettes into her apron pocket and comes toward me. Her usual blunt bob has grown out to her shoulders, her hair glossy and black aside from the silver streaking her part.

I return Andrea's hug, stiff and awkward. When we break apart Andrea takes a step back. Her eyes, big and brown like Jesse's, glisten with tears. "You look so grown-up."

I fight off the sting of tears, made worse by the bite in the air. "I'm so sorry it's taken me this long."

"Stop. There's nothing to be sorry for." Andrea squeezes my hand, a quick pulse before she begins smoothing the front of her smock. Her fingers linger at the pocket where she stashed her cigarettes.

"You can smoke," I say. "I don't mind."

I can practically smell the relief on her as she slips a cigarette out of her pocket and lights it, a tremor in her thumb. "I was doing good with quitting, and then."

She doesn't say *and then what,* but it's clear that it's Jesse's absence driving her back to old habits. Maybe, like me, it's even more than the absence. The silence, maybe—the waiting for the phone call that never comes.

"Have you heard anything?" I ask. "From the FBI?"

I haven't spoken to Agent Cummings or Agent Novak in months. Cummings called me in the fall, while I was at school—when I realized she had no news, she just wanted to see how I was coping, I was so angry I made an excuse about losing reception in the dining hall just so I could end the call.

"Not in a while." Andrea takes a pull from her cigarette. "I used to call every day, but I can't even remember the last time I spoke to them."

Andrea tilts her head back, blows some smoke out. "It

sounds terrible. Like I don't even care." She glances at me as she says it. Wondering if I agree.

Andrea had always wanted children of her own. She and her husband, Donald, had spent years and what little money they had saved up trying, only for her little sister, Diana, to wind up pregnant in her last semester of college. Jesse was convinced this was the root of his aunt's coldness to him; even in pictures of his aunt holding him as a baby, he said, she looked at him as if he were a house guest who had overstayed his welcome.

Jesse complained to me that Andrea only cared about her useless asshole of a husband—she never stood up for Jesse when Donald yelled at him for playing his guitar too loud, or forgetting his shoes in the hall, or simply because Donald woke up angry and hurting and needing to take it out on someone.

The pain on Andrea's face right now, though—that can't be faked.

"It doesn't sound terrible," I say. "I know you care."

Andrea wipes the corner of her eye with a knuckle before flicking the ash from the tip of her cigarette. "I was so hard on him, and God knows his uncle—I don't know what I'm trying to say. I'm just glad he had a friend like you."

I don't think it's possible for me to feel like a bigger piece of crap right now. A friend wouldn't have left Kat and Jesse at that campsite to go back to the lake house; a friend would have known that Jesse's band broke up.

"We were kind of distant from each other the past year," I say. "I didn't realize—"

My words die on my lips. Andrea watches me, big brown eyes blinking against the cold, until I force it out: "The sheriff said that you thought Jesse was depressed."

Andrea drops her cigarette stub, grinds it with the heel of her sneaker. "I don't know if I used that word."

"I just—I wish I'd been paying closer attention."

There's something she's tiptoeing around. Andrea looks up,

174

studies me. Whatever she sees makes her let her guard down. "It was her," she says. "Kat."

"What do you mean?" I ask.

"I figured he'd have hid it from you too." Andrea looks over her shoulder. "They were on the phone at all hours, whispering, arguing. I told him no girl was worth being that miserable over, even one as pretty as her."

Humming, deep in my ears. I can't believe what I'm hearing—Andrea using words like *miserable* to describe Kat and Jesse's relationship. "What did he say?"

"That it wasn't her." Andrea shrugs. "He loved her."

For some reason, I think of the flyer we handed out. Kat's picture—just Kat's picture. The one of her beaming at Jesse from behind the counter at Dolce Vita. The clouds part in my brain.

"Her family," I say. "They didn't like him, did they?"

"Jesse wouldn't come out and say it, but I knew that's what was upsetting him." Andrea looks me up and down. "Remember the party in May? The one they had for the grandmother?"

The grandmother. As if Marian Sullivan-Marcotte is a species of her own. In a way, it feels accurate. I swallow. "I couldn't go. I was working. Did something happen at the party?"

"He wouldn't tell me. But he came home—" Andrea shakes her head. "He didn't come out of his room for two days after. He wouldn't talk to anyone, not even Kat."

"He didn't tell you what happened?"

Andrea shakes her head. "That morning—he snapped at me. I got him to admit he was nervous about meeting her father and grandmother for the first time. He even asked me to trim his hair, and you know he never asked me for anything."

Andrea looks at me, eyes glistening. "I guess her family wasn't impressed with what they saw."

I swallow to clear my throat. Neither Kat nor Jesse had said anything to me; when I'd asked Kat how the party went, she'd said *fine* and changed the subject to our upcoming AP English exam.

"Is that why you didn't want to stay at the lake house with us last June?" I ask Andrea.

Andrea's eyebrows meet. "Didn't want to? Kat's family never even asked. I had to pay for a motel in town."

I'm reaching for the words—*What? Why?*—when Andrea's gaze lands on something beyond me. A boy in a black hoodie shuffles past us, hugging the wall of the adjacent CVS, doing a poor job of trying not to be seen by Andrea.

"Third time late this week," she mutters, putting a hand on my shoulder. "I've gotta go handle this."

"Yeah. Sure." I'm still so stunned by Andrea's revelation that I don't even think to return the awkward hug she gives me before turning to the grocery store, telling me not to be a stranger again.

Thick gray clouds blot out the sun by the time I get back to the main road. I should head home before they unleash whatever they have brewing in them, but I can't bring myself to go back to an empty house.

During a pause in traffic, I cross South Country Road. Let my feet carry me away from home, and toward the heart of the village.

Marian lied to me; in the hospital, she'd said Jesse's aunt hadn't wanted to stay at the lake house. But according to Andrea, Marian had never even extended the offer.

A lie so pointless has to have a purpose. Marian probably didn't think I'd ever ask Andrea why she didn't stay at the lake house with Kat's family; Marian probably assumed, correctly, that I had no idea Kat's family's feelings toward Jesse were causing a rift in their relationship.

Marian not asking Andrea to stay at the lake house might not have anything to do with whatever Andrea thinks happened at the party last May; Kat's parents thought from the beginning that Jesse was involved. Maybe they couldn't stand the thought of Jesse's aunt under the same roof as them while they thought he was responsible for their daughter's death.

But the Marcotte family is about appearances; their name peppers the town's playgrounds, park benches, even a road named after Marian's late husband. Marian's foundation doles out millions in aid to children in need; wouldn't they want to do everything they could to appear generous and accommodating to Kat's boyfriend's family?

I slow to a walk at the corner of Idledale Road. When I was younger, I wished I lived here, with the other village kids. Anna, Ben. Kat.

I struggle for air, thinking of her house. The pool deck where I tripped and split my chin open when I was six; the backyard Kat wanted to get married in someday.

Through the thrumming in my head, I hear my name, garbled as if the person calling it were underwater. Tapping behind the glass of the house I'm in front of.

I look up in horror to see Ben Filipoff waving at me from the other side of his door. He's in gray sweatpants and a New York Giants T-shirt that matches the flag over his garage door.

He props open the front door. "Hey."

I command my body to move up the driveway, meet him by the door, because as weird as it is to be caught outside his house, it would be weirder to shout back that hey, I was actually headed for my dead best friend's house, and continue on my merry way.

"Hi." I'm wheezing as I reach the top of his front steps. I shove my hands into the front pocket of my hoodie. "I was out for a run."

Ben stares back at me, prompting me to pant, "What?"

"You never responded to me yesterday," he says. "Thought I was being ghosted again."

I have the texts memorized.

Hey . . . I'm sure you've heard by now about
Mr. Marcotte. Nuts. are u ok?

I know this is weird and inappropriate considering
everything . . . but I had fun last night

"Can we talk inside?" I ask.

Ben's mom's car is in the driveway, but she doesn't materialize
as Ben microwaves two mugs of hot chocolate and leads me
to his basement lair. I know from experience that Ben's mom
leaves him to his devices, mostly out of necessity. She works
nights as a NICU nurse and started picking up extra shifts
when Ben's dad left a few years ago.

I follow Ben down the stairs, waiting to see where we're
sitting. His bed is down here, as well as an old couch and two
bean bag chairs. I try not to think about the things we did on
each surface as Ben lowers himself onto one of the bean bags.

He extends a mug to me as I take the bean bag next to him.
"I should have texted you back," I say. "I'm sorry."

"It's cool. I figured you were processing the news." Ben
lifts his mug to his lips. "I can't believe it."

"Me neither."

"I can't imagine what her mom and sister are going through.
Her grandma."

I feel Ben's eyes on me. I lower my mug and adjust myself
on my bean bag so I can see him better. "I talked to Jesse's aunt
this morning. To see how she was doing."

Ben drops his eyes to his mug at Jesse's name. Long, dark
lashes blinking rapid-fire. "How is she?"

"I don't know. It was a weird conversation."

"Weird how?" Ben isn't looking at me; apparently, even
though he's gone, Jesse Salpietro will always be a conversa-
tional landmine. I tamp down the memory of Ben's face, hair

clinging to his forehead, wet from Anna's hot tub. The way he looked at Jesse, coming to my rescue, before shaking his head. *Of course.*

"In the hospital—Kat's grandma came to see me, and she lied when I asked if Jesse's aunt was staying at the lake house," I say. "She said Jesse's aunt didn't want to intrude, but today his aunt told me Kat's family never asked her to stay with them."

Ben is quiet. I watch the marshmallows at the surface of my hot chocolate melt, congeal until they form a single entity. I'm embarrassed I brought up the conversation with Andrea. I'm finding meaning in things because I'm desperate for meaning. Marian's lie *has* to have meaning because if not, there's nothing.

We were random targets of a robbery turned kidnapping. I got away because I was lucky.

Next to me, the sound of beans shifting under Ben's weight. "Claire—did you have another reason for talking to Jesse's aunt?"

"What—why would you ask that?"

"You told me you talked to her to *see how she was doing.*" A smile tugs at Ben's mouth. "You always overexplain yourself when you're lying."

Heat fills my cheeks as Ben brings his mug to his lips. I set the mug on the coffee table behind us. "Okay. So maybe I went to see her because I wanted to know if she heard from the FBI. If they were looking into a connection, maybe, between them and Mike Dorsey."

Ben tilts his head. "But the FBI said there was no connection."

"They said they haven't found a connection. Not that there isn't one." I draw in a breath. "I know this sounds insane . . . but I just have a feeling that Mike Dorsey knew we'd be at Devil's Peak, and he knew who we were."

There has to be an explanation. Even if it's something as simple as us stopping for gas in Sunfish Creek that morning, Mike Dorsey seeing Kat's Infiniti at the pump . . .

I pick up my mug, take a sip. "Kat's family had been going up to Sunfish Creek for years. Maybe Mike Dorsey had seen her before—seen her with her grandma. I don't know. I just . . . need to know."

Ben is quiet for a beat. "The thing with Jesse's aunt not staying at the lake house—"

I turn my head toward Ben in time for him to cut himself off. He shakes his head. "I don't know."

"No, what were you going to say?" I steel myself. I've heard all the judgmental comments about Jesse's family. I saw the comments on an interview Andrea did with a local news site on the six-month anniversary of Jesse's disappearance. *I know Andrea Kelly. She's a good woman who works hard.*

Yeah, someone had replied to the comment. *So her husband doesn't have to.*

That's why, when Ben inhales and then says, "Kat's family. They're weird," I sit up straight.

"What do you mean?" I ask.

"I don't know—everyone on this street is pretty close. The Marcottes lived here longer than any of us, though, and they were always kind of standoffish. Like they didn't want anyone involved in their business." Ben shrugs. "And Mr. Marcotte scared the shit out of me."

I think of the coffeepot slipping from Beth's hand, the way Mr. Marcotte made her jump from her skin with one look.

Ben glances over at me. "Didn't you ever notice anything off about him?"

"He was always nice to me. I knew he was kind of controlling," I say. Of course, I'd noticed it. Anyone who spent five minutes with Kat's dad could tell he was a military man: He demanded not only orderliness, but perfection.

But it didn't seem to bother Kat that her dad was up her ass about her grades, her volleyball serve. No one could be as hard on Kat as she was on herself.

"Even as a kid, if I saw him outside, something told me to be on my best behavior," Ben says. "And then when Kat went missing, seeing him crying on TV—I don't know. He became a different person for the cameras. It didn't seem real."

I turn the idea over in my head: Mr. Marcotte, the distraught father, was all an act for the cameras.

The sip of hot chocolate I take is too big; it scalds my throat. "You think Kat's dad is hiding something?"

"I don't know—there's just something off about everything." Ben's fingers go still around the handle of his mug. "The night Mr. Marcotte got hit by the kidnapper—something weird happened at their house."

"What?" I ask. "What happened?"

"The security alarm went off at Kat's house," he says, and shifts in the bean bag so he's sitting straighter. "No one was home, so my mom went outside to talk to the village police that showed up."

My pulse accelerates. "Someone broke into the Marcottes' house?"

"No, that's the weird thing. The cops said all the doors were locked. There weren't any strange cars in the area so they told my mom one of the window sensors might have gotten triggered by the wind. It was probably nothing." Ben shrugs. "Just weird, you know?"

"Yeah," I say. "Probably nothing."

By the time Ben walks me upstairs, a light snow is falling outside. He insists on driving me home, and I let him, because I've decided running is the fucking worst.

And, I think, as I climb into his car, I'm not ready to close the door on whatever *this* is with Ben. Even if there are only a few weeks left before we go back to school and the door eventually slams shut, Brookport feels slightly more survivable with him next to me.

Ben pulls into my driveway, coasting to a stop. I could be

imagining it, hoping for it, but it feels like the five-minute drive took much longer, and maybe Ben wasn't driving so slow because of the dusting of snow on the road.

He cuts his engine and turns to me. "So—"

"I usually get off work around ten," I say.

"Okay." He blinks at me. "Text me?"

I answer by brushing my lips over his. This is probably a bad idea, considering how he hurt me, how little time we have before whatever this is has to end—but the urgency in Ben's body as he kisses me back makes it clear. This time, things will be on my terms.

I am tired of letting things happen to me.

Judging by all the empty tables in Stellato's on Sunday night, everyone is keeping their New Year's resolutions to eat healthy. I sold dozens of gift cards last week but I'm guessing no one will be in to use them until they've dropped the holiday pounds.

As a result, Serg lets me go at nine. I draw my peacoat tight to my body as I navigate the icy parking lot, the wind nearly blowing my keys from my hand as I unlock my car.

I give in to a full-body shiver, start my engine, and blast the heat. Something stops me from reaching for my phone to text Ben.

My heartbeat picks up. I lower the force of the heat blasting in my face. Creep out of the Stellato's parking lot, and make a right toward Idledale Road.

I drive past Ben's, keep going until I reach Kat's house. I make a right and park next to the privacy shrubs lining the side of the property. I kill my engine and lights, hands trembling.

I don't know what I'm doing here.

I know exactly what I'm doing here.

The only reason I haven't left my car is because I'm waiting for someone's voice to pop in my head and talk me out of this.

My therapist's, maybe, asking me how I feel every time I go internet-diving for answers and come up empty-handed.

Angry.

I'm angry because there must be answers locked in my brain somewhere, memories I still can't access after six months. The answer, the rest of the story, could still be in there.

I know what my therapist would say: I need more to the story because the one I've been given sucks. Kat was kidnapped because her grandma was rich; she and Jesse were killed for no reason. How am I supposed to accept that the worst thing to ever happen to me has no meaning?

The sound of barking jolts me in my seat. *Elmo,* I think, before remembering it can't be Elmo; he's in Westchester with Beth and Emma.

Two summers ago, Kat's family went to a Sullivan-Marcotte reunion for the weekend in Montauk. Elmo was not welcome at the hotel, so Kat's mom paid me forty bucks a day to feed and walk him. She gave me a key to the house, told me to be mindful of the alarm. She wrote the code on a note on the fridge in case I forgot how to disable it: 11/13, Kat's birthday.

I'd forgotten to give the key back, and Kat's mom must have forgotten too, because she'd never asked for it. It's been sitting in my glove compartment ever since. When Ben told me about the alarm going off, I remembered my key.

Anyone the Marcottes trusted enough to give a key to their home would have had the code for the alarm system too. Maybe the village cop was right, and the alarm had been triggered accidentally.

I reach over and rifle through the debris in the glove compartment until my fingers meet cold metal. I fold my hand around the key, my pulse in my ears. I can get in—I have the key, and the alarm code.

I slip out of the driver's side and close the door gently, afraid the sound will draw the attention of the neighbors, even though their windows are dark, shades drawn. I pull my coat over my face to block the cold and slip through the Marcotte's back gate.

The pool is covered, the patio furniture packed away. The hedges lining the backyard fence are neatly trimmed, even though no one has lived here for months. Even empty, abandoned, the Marcottes' backyard is still magical. The wooden arch gate, the artfully arranged stones Kat and I used to play hopscotch on.

She said, if she ever got married, it would be in this backyard. And soon, it will belong to someone else.

I swallow as I wiggle the key into the back door, slip inside the kitchen, and fumble in the dark for the keypad beside the door before realizing it's too quiet. No warning sound emanating from the keypad prompting me to input the code.

The alarm has been disabled. Probably for the realtors.

Even in the dull glow of the half-moon coming through the window, the house looks the same as the last time I was here. It's only when I stop to take everything in that I notice the missing pieces. No more dog bed in the corner, no shoes stacked neatly on the rack by the back door. And the temperature. Fifty degrees, according to the thermostat in the hallway.

I head down the hallway, trying to make myself as weightless as possible. The house is old—like, nineteenth-century-farmhouse old—and every step, every opened door elicits a creak or a groan.

I'm here hunting memories. Not just of Kat and me, crawling into the attic, declaring it our clubhouse, or of us dressing Elmo up with whatever doll hats he would tolerate. I'm hoping this house has some trace of her—her smell, a glimpse of *something*—that might send signals to that damaged piece of brain where my memories of June 23 are hiding.

I push Kat's bedroom door open. I shut my eyes, breathe in. Step across the threshold.

The sight sucks the breath out of me, even though I knew it was a possibility.

Kat is gone from this room. Her desk has been replaced with a chair artfully decorated with throw pillows. Her closet, empty. The room has been staged to sell; all trace of the girl who inhabited it is gone, anything that screams *Kat Marcotte was here!* a liability for skittish buyers.

I glance under Kat's bed, but there's nothing but carpet, and the heating vent on the far wall.

My body goes still at the sight of the vent. A flash of eight-year-old Kat, pencil to her chin, as we wrote in our diaries, side by side on her bed. I carried mine around because when your mother is a therapist you don't have secrets; she always disappeared under her bed when it was time to hide her diary.

I shimmy so I'm flush with the carpet, stick my arm under Kat's bed. Reach until I make contact with the grate; I stick my hand through the slats, feeling around on the floor. My fingertips make contact with cold plastic.

I grit my teeth and shove my hand between the grate. Curse under my breath—I've pushed the object out of reach. When I pull my hand out, I take the whole grate off with it.

My heartbeat accelerates. That shouldn't have happened—unless the grate wasn't screwed on.

I reach back in the empty space, fumbling for whatever is hidden there. *Got it.*

I wipe the dust from my fingertips on my pants, turn over the object in my hand. It's a flip phone, no bigger than a credit card. It's ancient, and I don't recognize it as one Kat ever owned.

I flip the phone open and hold the power button down.

The phone comes to life and blinks, alerting me that it has 10 percent battery left. In the bottom corner, a (1) hovers over the text inbox. I wipe a slick of sweat from my thumb and open the message.

screw you answer my calls

CHAPTER SIXTEEN

NOW

Mom and Dad are in their bedroom when I get home, door closed, the laugh track of a sitcom the only indication they're even awake. I'm still shaking when I shut myself in my room.

I powered the phone down to conserve its battery on the drive home.

Kat's phone. Kat's *secret* phone.

I sit at my desk and power the phone back on. The whole drive home I had practically convinced myself I had imagined the text, but here it is, right in front of my eyes in the bright lights of my room.

> screw you answer my calls

Sent on May 19, last year. Just a month before prom weekend.

Even though it has a local 631 area code, I don't recognize the number, and there are no contacts saved to the phone, no names. But there are dozens of incoming and outgoing calls in the log, dating back to over a year ago.

I switch back to the text inbox, peruse the rest of the messages with the *screw you* person. The thread began April 24 last year, when the 631 number texted Kat:

yoooo you there???

yeah, sorry man. at my gf's house

Girlfriend. The idea of Kat Marcotte having a secret girlfriend is even wilder than Kat having a secret cell phone. Too wild to be true, even.

Which means it wasn't Kat texting from this phone—maybe it wasn't her phone at all. I read on, my heartbeat quickening.

Can u meet at brookport marina in ten?

lol Yuppyville in broad daylight?? R u serious?

I'll be with my gf and her dog.
No one will think anything of it.

I set the phone down on my bed, my palms slick with sweat. This wasn't Kat's phone; she was simply hiding it.

For him.

With a wave of nausea, I see Jesse, hand-in-hand with Kat. She's tugging at Elmo's leash, dragging him away from the edge of the dock, muttering *No, we're not swimming now!*

Why would Jesse have a secret cell phone? I mean, there's a pretty obvious explanation for why someone would be using a burner phone to meet up with people, but this is *Jesse Salpietro*.

He wasn't a fucking *drug dealer*.

Jesse, who could frost a perfect buttercream rose, who could play "Sweet Child o' Mine" on the guitar, who carried around a picture of his mother in his wallet—he wasn't a drug dealer.

The phone chirps at me, alerting me there's now 3 percent battery left. My heart climbs into my throat. I pull up the call log and take a picture of the screen with my own phone. Three, four, five shots capture every call this phone made or received.

I cross to my desk, rifle through the contents of my top

drawer until I find Agent Cummings's business card. I input her cell number into my phone.

Two rings, three rings—I'm about to hang up when a breathy voice fills the line. "Agent Cummings. Who is this?"

"Um, it's Claire Keough. I'm not sure you remember me—it's been a while."

"Claire, hey. Is everything all right?"

I pinch the bridge of my nose. "I'm not sure. I'm really sorry to call this late, but I found something and I don't know. I think you should know about it."

"Where are you? Are you safe?" Cummings sounds wide-awake, despite the fact that it's almost ten-thirty.

"Yeah, of course. I'm home. Is there somewhere I can meet you so I can give it to you? I'm sorry, I know it's crazy late."

"I don't care what time it is. It's just that I'm out of town for a few days." A rustling sound, as if she's unfolding a receipt or a piece of paper. "Hold on. I'm going to call Novak and see if he can meet you, okay?"

"What if he's asleep?" I ask.

"Then I'll wake his old ass up. He lives ten minutes from you."

"Wait." I glance at my door, imagining my parents across the hall, having their sitcom interrupted by an FBI agent knocking at our door. "Could we not meet at my house? If he's around."

Cummings pauses. "Let me call you back."

It's almost eleven when I get to the McDonald's on Montauk Highway. I told my parents I left my wallet at Stellato's and needed to go back out and get it. Mom told me to be more careful and I said *okay* and ran out to my car before she could climb out of bed and see that my wallet was in my hand.

Novak is seated at a two-person table, a cup of coffee in front of him. His eyebrows lift when he sees me. I slide into the seat across from him, hands shoved in my coat pockets.

Novak pops a Rolaid and replaces the roll in his jacket pocket. "So, Ms. Keough. To what do I owe the pleasure?"

I set the phone on the table. "I found this in Kat's room."

"Kat Marcotte?" he asks.

I stare at him. "Yes?"

Novak peers at the phone resting between us. I wedge my trembling hands between my thighs as he picks it up and flips it open. His brow creases as his fingers work the keys.

He looks at me over the top of the phone. "It's got no juice."

"I know."

Novak's face is impassive. "Can I ask *when* you found this in Kat's room?"

"Earlier tonight."

"And how did you get in the Marcottes' house?"

"I had a key." I swallow. "There's a vent under her bed. The phone was hidden there."

I think Jesse was dealing drugs.

"All right," Novak says.

That's it? *All right?* I stare at Novak. "I broke into their house."

"I can arrest you, if it would make you feel better."

"Are you—" I chew the inside of my cheek. "Will you check the phone out? If she was hiding it, there might be something important on there. . . ."

"We'll check it out." Novak isn't looking at the phone, which is now resting on the table. He folds his hands together over the belly of his fisherman's cable sweater, eyes locked on me. "How are you, Claire?"

It feels so weird, Novak asking me about my feelings, like I'm an actual human being, that I blurt: "What do you mean?"

Novak's eyebrows lift. "Are you *okay*?"

Someone who is okay wouldn't break into their dead best friend's house. My fingers tighten around the edge of the table. *No, I am not okay. I needed there to be a reason for what happened to us and now that I've potentially found one, I can't handle it.*

I wipe away a tear with the back of my hand.

Novak grabs a napkin and extends it to me. When I refuse to take it, he rests it on the table between us. "Claire, you're not always going to feel this way."

"Yes, I will, until I know for sure what happened to them."

Novak blinks. "Can I say something?"

I finally reach for the napkin resting between us. When I'm done dabbing my eyes, Novak says, "I think that even if I had the answers you're looking for, if I could tell you the who and the what and the *why* right now, it wouldn't make you feel a damn bit better."

I crush the napkin in my fist. "That sounds like bullshit."

Novak shrugs, his whole body moving with his shoulders, as if he's not made up of individual parts. There's no way he's not retired army or something. "Maybe it is, I don't know you. But I do know that I've seen people wait years to find out what happened to their loved ones, and when they finally do, the answers aren't enough. The emptiness is still there. Sometimes it's even worse."

"So I should be grateful that I barely remember anything? That you still haven't found their bodies?"

"I didn't say that. But it sounds like you've convinced yourself that having an answer will bring you peace, when it might do the opposite."

I return his stare, probing his face for some sort of clue there's a hidden message in what he's saying. Of course, Agent Novak knows more than everyone else does. Even in their absence, the FBI has more access to my friends' lives than I ever did. If there's a connection between what's on that phone and what happened on June 23, he must know about it already.

In any case, I'm tired of being a step behind everyone else in knowing what happened to me on that mountain. It ignites something in me. "Please, tell me something that hasn't been made public. Anything."

Novak studies me for a beat, a rare expression of pity crossing his face. "Like what?"

"I don't know. Anything. Did you find anything else in the quarry besides Jesse's wallet and Kat's bandana?" I knit my trembling hands together on the table. "What happened to his phone? Was it in the tent?"

"You know I can't give you that kind of information, Claire."

"What about other people who might have been on the mountain around that weekend?" I say, suddenly desperate to keep Novak's ass in that chair. "Anyone else who was camping or hiking who might have seen Mike Dorsey scoping the mountain out—maybe the sheriff kept it quiet like he did the robbery that happened the summer before."

Novak's eyebrows knit together. "Who told you there was a robbery on Bobcat Mountain?"

"Kat's cousin, Amos. A local told him about it while Amos was passing out Kat's flyer."

Novak frowns. "There's no record of a robbery occurring on Bobcat Mountain."

"There wouldn't be, if the sheriff didn't want anyone to know about it."

"Maybe." Novak's lips part as if he's going to say something; instead, he heaves himself off the chair, says, "Take care of yourself, Claire."

He puts a hand on my shoulder, almost as an afterthought. "And for the love of God, no more burgling."

As soon as I get home, I strip out of my work clothes and change into pajamas, burrow under my comforter with my laptop. I may have turned the phone from Kat's room in to the FBI, but thanks to the pictures I took, I know every number Jesse ever called from it.

I type each number into Google, hoping to dig up some information about the owners. No luck: each search tells me the city where the cell phone number originated and not much else.

The area codes range from Boston to Westchester to Vermont. The owner either has a lot of friends in different cities or the calls also came from burner phones. I don't know, maybe I watch too many movies that I'm even thinking in terms like *burner phone*.

I'm Googling yet another number when something yanks me out of autopilot. The area code—it's the same as the pharmacy that kept calling me for months after my hospital visit, asking if I needed a painkiller refill—

A Google search confirms it. The number belongs to a cell phone user in Sunfish Creek, New York.

I comb over the call log again. Jesse and the person in Sunfish Creek called each other four times since August last year, before Kat and Jesse disappeared.

I need to know who this phone number belongs to. I work quickly, as if I'm trying to stem the blood flow on a gaping wound.

Several reverse phone number look-up sites are useless, unless I want to fork over my debit card information. I switch gears and Google *how to find out who a cell phone number is registered to* and get a hit for a forum of disgruntled people.

The top-rated comment reads: *You could always try searching the phone number on Facebook. If the person has their phone number linked to their account, you'll be able to find their profile that way.*

I fly off my bed like someone is chasing me and open my laptop. I haven't used Facebook since the summer when I deleted it. I reluctantly reactivate my account and gnaw away what's left of my torn thumbnail while the home page loads.

Please work. I type in the phone number and wait—there's no way this will actually work, will it?

The phone number matches with a profile.

The privacy settings don't allow me to see anything beyond his picture and his location. But I've visited this page before, hundreds of times, hoping that magically something has changed and I'll be able to see some glimpse of who he was and why he did what he did.

Michael V. Dorsey.

CHAPTER SEVENTEEN

NOW

Monday morning. Between the blinds in my window, slices of sky, gray and mottled with even darker clouds. My phone says it's almost seven thirty. I could go back to sleep, but if I let that happen, who knows when I'll get up, if I even bother to at all.

Ben. *Shit.*

I'd totally forgotten about him in the chaos that was last night.

> I'm so sorry about last night. Got out super late and came home and crashed

> What are you doing tonight?

I hit send, my thoughts immediately turning to the phone I turned in to Agent Novak last night. Whoever it belonged to had been in contact with Mike Dorsey since last February.

The kidnapping wasn't random. Mike Dorsey *knew* we would be there, because he knew either Kat or someone close to her who had the opportunity to stash that phone in Kat's room.

Someone other than Jesse. I am looking for evidence it

couldn't have been Jesse because I can't handle it if it *was* Jesse.

My stomach squirms. How did Mike Dorsey pull the kidnapping off without help? Without inside information?

There's no way Jesse was involved—Jesse would sooner die himself than risk Kat's life, even for a huge pile of Marcotte money. Besides, in the weeks following the incident at the quarry, the FBI confirmed that they recovered the ransom money from Mr. Marcotte's Highlander.

Without that money, Jesse wouldn't have been able to escape and somehow avoid detection for the past six months.

The other option is that Jesse had never spoken to Mike Dorsey before in his life. He didn't tell Mike Dorsey we would be camping at Devil's Peak that weekend—someone else close to Kat did.

I shut my eyes, the blood draining from my head. Agent Novak's voice returns around the hollow thud in my ears.

I think back to the question that has been bothering me for six months—how come, no matter how many times I've Googled it, I was never able to turn up any mention of a robbery on Bobcat Mountain? Not a single person came forward about an attempted attack on two girls, in the same place where two teenagers would later be kidnapped.

Who told you there was a robbery on Bobcat Mountain?

But why would Amos lie to me? Why would he invent a story about a robbery on the mountain?

My pulse moves to my fingertips. I open the picture folder on my phone, enlarge the photo I took of the text thread, the one that culminated in the threatening message: *Screw you call me back*

One text—sent by the owner of the phone in Kat's room—sticks out.

I'll be with my gf and her dog. No one will think anything of it

The time stamp says the message was sent on April 28 of last year, at 12:57 p.m.

I wouldn't know where to begin confirming where Jesse had been on a Saturday afternoon almost a year ago. He could have been working at the bakery, at band practice, or still in bed, for all I know.

Kat, though—her schedule was mapped out to the minute, especially during volleyball and lacrosse seasons. And April 28 was right in the middle of lacrosse season.

On my phone, I search *Brookport girls lacrosse games*. I refine the search results to display the game schedules for last spring.

At 1:00 p.m. on April 28, Brookport played a game against John Glenn High School. We won, and according to the website, Kat Marcotte scored two goals.

There's no way Kat could have been at the marina with Jesse and Elmo on the twenty-eighth within ten minutes of this message being sent. So unless Jesse had a secret girlfriend he was willing to be seen with in broad daylight, two blocks from his real girlfriend's house, this phone *definitely* wasn't his.

The back of my neck turns slick with sweat. I throw my comforter off my body, get up and cross to the window, press my forehead to the glass. What else had Amos said to me in the canoe?

I will his face, his words into focus, but the memory is nebulous, as if I'm viewing the scene from underwater. I'd insisted to Amos that Jesse would never hurt Kat; Amos had agreed.

Not just agreed—he'd said *I know*. A strange vote of confidence for his cousin's boyfriend, whom he barely knew.

There's an explanation for why Amos would both make up a bullshit story about a robbery on the mountain and so easily agree that Jesse wasn't responsible—Amos knew exactly who was responsible.

But how did Amos even know Mike Dorsey? Amos is a Long Island trust-fund kid; Mike Dorsey was an almost thirty-year-old petty criminal who worked at an auto body shop upstate. The FBI said that as far as they knew, Mike Dorsey had never even been to Long Island. Sunfish Creek is the only place his path might have crossed with Amos or the Marcotte family.

And there's only one logical reason Mike Dorsey's number would be on this phone. I remember the hard clench of my stomach last night when I realized what this phone was probably used for. All of those numbers with different area codes, none with a name attached. Calls at all hours, texts with times and locations.

According to the press, Mike Dorsey had been arrested for drug possession in Florida, where he was born. In an interview, one of his friends said Mike's mother sent him away to Sunfish Creek to clean up his act. It's not too crazy to think that maybe, while he was there, he met a rich kid who was in town for the summer . . . a rich kid who was dealing drugs.

I lower myself into my desk chair, legs trembling beneath me. I'm not sure if Amos makes more sense than Jesse or my mind is desperate for an answer that *isn't* Jesse. I haven't been able to trust my own mind in six months.

A surge of anger cuts through me, so powerful that I find myself gripping the edge of my desk. Anger at the thought that Amos knew, the whole time, exactly who was responsible. Whether he casually mentioned to Mike Dorsey that we would be in town that weekend, or if he'd helped plan the kidnapping himself, Amos is the connective tissue.

I bolt out of my chair, dig my phone out from under my comforter. The text thread with Amos from last June is sitting at the very bottom of my inbox. I pause, fingers hovering over the screen, studying the last message he sent me.

What'd I do?

He'd sent it right before he called me and said he hadn't been the one to speak to the *Daily News*. I haven't spoken to Amos since; he never reached out after the FBI announced what happened at the quarry.

Amos has no reason to suspect that I know anything—about the phone, his connection to Mike Dorsey, his lie about the robbery—and I can't give him one.

I settle on:

> Hey . . . are you in town?

I hit send, heartbeat quickening.

A beat later, an exclamation point appears next to my message.

Message undeliverable.

Amos didn't block my number. To be sure, I called twice more: once from our home phone, and once from the line in my mom's office she uses to talk to people calling the suicide prevention hotline she volunteers at.

No voice mail, no ringing, just an automated prompt saying that the number is not currently in service. Amos changed his number.

It could have been a totally innocent decision. Too many reporters calling him, maybe, in the wake of Kat's disappearance.

Or, maybe, there's another reason Amos doesn't want to talk to anyone.

During my Amos Fornier phase, the summer before sophomore year, I could have told you anything you wanted to know about Kat's cousin. I was an information scavenger, every conversation with Kat an opportunity to find out Amos's dating history or what he did after school.

The space behind my right eye begins to pulse. I've had to retrain the muscles of my brain not to think about Amos too much over the past six months. Even if he didn't realize what he was doing, he betrayed me when he told his grandmother that I remembered seeing Paul Santangelo, the hiker. Thanks to the Marcottes, I was not just Kat's best friend in the eyes of the world: I was the girl who accused a Good Samaritan of murder. I was the reason people were harassing Paul Santangelo, whose biggest crimes were trying to help a lost girl and having a Confederate flag decal on his truck.

I got caught in the boomerang—the backlash to the backlash. It was impossible to separate what was happening to me online from the reason it happened.

I'd trusted the wrong person. A person I *knew* I shouldn't trust.

There's no going back and undoing that mistake. There's only turning my anger into something useful—like trying to prove the phone I found in Kat's room belonged to Amos.

Attempting to place Amos at Brookport Marina on a Saturday afternoon feels impossible, though. At least as far as the internet is concerned, it's as if Amos doesn't exist. After poking around for fifteen minutes, all I find is a private Instagram account with the username *famousam0s*. The profile photo, a close-up of a tanned face partially obscured by Ray-Bans, could be any douchebag with a trust fund. But we have one mutual follower—Kat.

It's him. It's the only trace of him, and I can't access it. I can't find out if he had or has a girlfriend who has a dog, let alone where he was on a Saturday last June.

A capsizing feeling hits my stomach. All of Kat's family members were interviewed right away, and everyone had alibis.

Think, think. There must be someone in Amos's social circle who has posted clues about what he's been up to since Kat and Jesse disappeared. If Amos is the connective tissue between them and Mike Dorsey and what happened to us on Bobcat Mountain, how could he continue to face his family every day? If I find a picture of him, smiling over a game of flip cup at some college party, will I know by the look in his eyes that *he* is the missing piece?

Think, Claire. Amos had a best friend in high school, or

at least he did at the time of the party at his house. His name was Erik and earlier that evening, while I was on the couch with Amos, I'd seen Erik catch Amos's eye, gesture down to his phone. I peeked at Amos's screen while he read a text from Erik: *Your cousin is pretty hot.*

Amos stared back at Erik and mouthed, *Don't you fucking think about it.*

What was his last name? Erik . . . Erik Carlson. I tamp down mild disgust with myself that I remember the full name of Amos's high school best friend. If I dedicated that brain space to something important, maybe I could do math.

But the information is useful: Searching for Erik Carlson on Instagram turns up a profile. His bio says he attends Pepperdine University in Malibu. He's following the *famousam0s* profile, but Amos isn't in his pictures from the past six months.

All of Erik's shots are of the beach, or himself in a black convertible, dark wavy hair slicked away from his face. I keep scrolling back. And there he is—August, over a year ago.

Amos, Erik, and a golden-haired girl on the beach. The girl, in a race-car-red bikini, is kissing Amos on the cheek; his arm is draped over her shoulder. Erik has tagged her in the photo.

Her name is Zoe-Grace; her bio is a link to a blog.

I scroll down to her most recent Instagram photos. Zoe-Grace could not be more different from Erik Carlson—or at least according to the version of herself she's presenting to the internet.

Her photos are of people. A man on the Long Island Rail Road train platform in enormous headphones. A teenaged girl, posing outside Penn Station, in a dress as lurid yellow as a taxi cab. She has triangular hot-pink earrings and a matching fanny pack.

I keep scrolling. A boy on the sidewalk carrying two kittens, an elderly woman on her porch, oxygen tank at her feet. I'm several weeks deep into Zoe-Grace's feed before I find a single picture of her.

Her face is tilted downward, a choppy curtain of hair falling over her bare shoulder. She could be naked, for all I know; the sun streaming through the window in the photo creates a prism, bathing Zoe-Grace's face in rainbow light.

She's beautiful.

I can't stop scrolling through her photos, even though Amos isn't in any of them. My neck is stiff from being hunched over my phone by the time I've reached last summer on Zoe-Grace's feed.

And there he is. The sight of him on Zoe-Grace's feed feels like a violation, even though she's a complete stranger to me.

They're posed at the end of a dock. Both tanned, his arms wrapped around her bare middle. She's in denim shorts and a crocheted white crop-top. Her hair is salt-water curled below the backward baseball cap she's wearing.

Amos is in Ray-Bans and a turquoise T-shirt that pops against the brilliant sunset behind them. Sitting at their feet is a Boston terrier.

Zoe-Grace posted it at 7:37 p.m. on June 23.

The oxygen leaves my body.

I zoom in on the photo. The dock abruptly ends a foot away from where Zoe-Grace and Amos are standing; three algae-covered posts stick out of the water where the dock used to extend before a hurricane decimated it a couple years ago.

My pulse accelerates. This photo was taken at Brookport Bay; I used to walk down the dock with Kat and Elmo on my work breaks sometimes. Kat would gripe that she wished they'd fix the damn dock already, replace the railing so she wouldn't have to yank Elmo back from trying to leap into the bay.

Except, the village *had* fixed the dock. Almost a year and a half ago.

So, Zoe-Grace had posted a picture of her and Amos that was over a year old. No big deal—maybe it was their anniversary and she put up an old picture to honor it.

But that date. *June 23.*

I can't shake the feeling that there's another reason Amos's girlfriend posted a picture of them, together, on Long Island, on the same day Kat and Jesse went missing on a mountain two hundred miles away.

Cyber-stalking Zoe-Grace has taken up the better part of my day; it's a welcome distraction from the fact Ben still hasn't responded to my text from this morning. I've combed through Zoe-Grace's entire Instagram feed, and even though I wasn't able to find her last name, her oldest posts—the ones she made before her documentary-street-photographer phase—have a few clues. Three years ago she started at St. Genevieve's Academy, which means she'd be a senior now.

The first photos of her and Amos appear at the end of her sophomore year, when Amos would have been a senior. The word *boyfriend* never appears in Zoe-Grace's captions, but she went to his prom with him, posed on his arm, the Blake Lively to his Ryan Reynolds.

Zoe-Grace hasn't posted a picture of Amos since the dock photo from last June.

I switch to a new browser tab and pull up the bell schedule for St. Genevieve's. The day ends at 2:05.

I glance at the time on my phone. It's almost 1:30. If I leave now, I can be there in twenty-five minutes.

I feel like some sort of pervert parking at the curb outside St. Genevieve's Academy, scanning the throngs of girls flooding the front steps after the last bell. Most head for the student parking lot, which is filled with cars that are nicer than the ones in the staff lot. Some of them wander to the left, milling with the crowds leaving the building for the boys' school next door, where Amos graduated from two years ago.

I keep my gaze on the front doors. A girl with chin-length

blond hair bounds down the steps, one hand wrapping an oversize scarf around her neck. She comes to a halt at the curb and becomes immersed in her phone.

Despite the gray skirt and black tights peeking out from below her coat, she's different from the other St. Genevieve's girls, with their pin-straight hair and Tory Burch flats, Kate Spade purses hooked over their arms. Zoe-Grace is in worn-in leather boots, a black backpack slung over her shoulders.

She glances up every few seconds or so, her gaze passing over my car and the others idling at the curb. Waiting for a ride. My stomach clenches at the thought of Amos rolling up behind me in his BMW to pick up his girlfriend from school and noticing me sitting here like a stalker.

I inhale—the cold sharp in my nose—and kill my engine. I climb out of the car and shove my hands in my pockets.

Zoe-Grace looks up from her phone and does another scan of the curb. Her eyes don't settle on me until I'm a few feet away from her.

"Hi," I say, because I didn't really plan this out or really think about it.

"Hi?" Zoe-Grace's eyebrows, carefully groomed and a shade darker than her hair, knit together with confusion.

"Are you Zoe-Grace?" I ask.

She adjusts her scarf. "Yeah. Can I help you or something?"

"I was wondering if I could talk to you about Amos."

Her eyes flick to a trio of girls to our right who are obviously watching us, listening. A white Mercedes rolls up to the curb; the girls climb in, a flurry of black peacoats.

When Zoe-Grace looks back at me, her knuckles are white as she grips the bottom of her scarf. "Who are you? Who sent you here?"

"No one sent me—I just want to talk about Amos."

"I don't know where he is," Zoe-Grace says. She cranes her neck to look past me, plotting an escape route even though I'm not blocking her from anything. "I haven't seen him in months."

"Wait," I say, because she's turning away, heading back up the stairs into the school. "Did you tell everyone Amos was with you the night Kat Marcotte went missing?"

Zoe-Grace goes still. She puts a hand on the stair rail and turns to face me. She doesn't speak until the throng of girls moving out the doorway, down the stairs, are gone.

"I don't know who you are or what you think you're doing," she says, her voice even, "but stay the *hell* away from me."

CHAPTER EIGHTEEN

―――

NOW

I drum my fingers on the steering wheel, eyes glued to the bumper of the car in front of me that hasn't moved in ten minutes. An accident on Sunrise Highway.

I expected Zoe-Grace to be creeped out by my showing up outside her school. I expected her to be angry and defensive at me asking if she lied to give Amos an alibi. I expected her to tell me to fuck off—

But her fear. That was unexpected.

Who sent you here?

A paranoid statement from a clearly paranoid person. Yet when she made it, I hadn't even brought up the alibi, yet.

I don't know where he is. I haven't seen him in months.

An even weirder thing to say.

Zoe-Grace assumed I came to her looking *for* Amos, and her reaction suggested I'm not the first person to have done so. She's obviously scared of that person or people—it could be tied to the illicit activities Amos was conducting via that burner phone in Kat's room, or maybe Novak and Cummings are on to her about the fake alibi she gave.

My pulse hitches at the thought of the FBI homing in on Amos. At him having to answer for all the shady shit he did.

Leaking the story I told him about the guy I recognized, to make it look like there was a chance Kat and Jesse had been taken by a stranger.

And then, my heart plummets.

If Amos is involved, Marian will call in reinforcements to protect him: lawyers, PR, more leaked stories to the press to shift the suspicion elsewhere. For all I know, she already *is* protecting Amos.

But what motive would Amos possibly have for kidnapping his own cousin? It's no secret that Amos has a sizable trust fund waiting for him someday, as do Kat and her sister, Emma. Marian won't live forever, and she's worth nearly twenty million dollars.

There's no amount of money that Mr. Marcotte could wrangle in time for a ransom demand that would exceed what Amos is going to come into someday. So why the hell would he kidnap his own cousin?

Unless it wasn't about the money at all—and Amos saying that Kat is the only person in his family he doesn't hate was the biggest of all the lies he told me.

Two days, three days, turns into a week since my meeting with Agent Novak at McDonald's. The clock is running out on winter break, and leaving home with more questions than I returned with is almost unbearable.

Zoe-Grace made her Instagram private, but I have the link to her blog stored on my phone. I've studied every picture, every caption, as if one will hold a clue as to whether or not she gave Amos Fornier a fake alibi for Kat and Jesse's disappearance.

Thursday is my last shift at Stellato's before I have to head back to school sometime on Sunday. We're so dead that Serg lets me go at seven, holding my last paycheck hostage in exchange for my promise I'll be back to work in May when the semester is over.

The sky is black, starless. A figure waiting by my car door makes me yelp.

Ben Filipoff steps out into the glow from one of the parking lot lights, holding a box and a white takeout bag from Mama Leonora's. He lifts it up. "Pizza and knots."

I tighten the scarf around my neck. "What for?"

Ben smiles with only half his mouth. "I think you know."

"Still would be nice to hear you say it."

"I'm sorry." He scratches his neck, inside his own scarf. "I've never been good at saying that. To anyone."

I unlock my car, gesture for Ben to follow. I start the engine, blast the heat. Ben settles into the passenger seat, grabs a piece of pizza for himself, and passes the bag to me. I fish out a garlic knot, unspooling the soft, greasy dough spiral.

"I was working the night we were supposed to meet up," Ben finally says. "I got off the same time as you. I tried calling to you—I waved from across the street—but you didn't even see me."

My stomach sinks. He saw me leave work at nine; he waited two hours only for me to blow him off with a lie. A surge of panic—what if he was close behind as I drove to Kat's house?

I swallow. "I was just . . . working some shit out."

"You don't owe me an explanation," he says. "But I think maybe I owe you one."

"About what?"

Ben rests his head back against my passenger seat, tilts to face me. "When we were together, I wished all the time Jesse would just . . . go away. I knew I could never compete with him."

"I didn't even know you cared enough about me to be jealous of him."

"I messed a lot of things up with us. And I can't seem to stop," Ben says. "When you blew me off, I just assumed it was about Jesse. I thought the problem was always Jesse, when obviously it was me."

My throat is tight.

"Dear God, Keough, are you crying on me?"

"Shut up." I nudge away tears with the sleeve of my jacket, pop the rest of the garlic knot in my mouth. "I'm pissed at you."

Ben makes puppy dog eyes at me. "But I apologized. I brought you pizza."

"I'm pissed because you're making me like you when I have to leave this weekend."

Ben reaches out, puts a finger under my chin. Pulls me close, brushes his lips over mine. "I hope you still like me when you get back."

When I get home, the sting of the cold lingers in my bones, but I still feel Ben's mouth, warm on mine. I sit at my desk, dicking around on my laptop while I warm up enough to get in the shower.

I have a couple new emails, mostly "Hello, here's the stupidly expensive textbook you'll need for this semester" from my instructors. One from Facebook, saying I have one new Messenger notification.

No, no, no. Panic snakes around me. I don't have Facebook anymore; I am not supposed to be *findable*.

Then I remember. I reactivated my account last week. In the ensuing chaos of connecting that phone number to Mike Dorsey, I forgot to deactivate it again.

I need to chill the hell out. It's probably just someone from high school who noticed I reactivated and is reaching out to see how I am. Not a reporter, not a hater from Reddit.

I log in, open my inbox.

Message from Zoe-Grace Palermo,
Thursday, 1:37 a.m.
We need to talk.

CHAPTER NINETEEN

NOW

Zoe-Grace and I decide to meet at the Dunkin' Donuts on Main Street in Islip, a couple blocks from St. Genevieve's, when she gets out of school Friday afternoon.

I spend the day fussing with my hair and change my clothes three times, trying to distract myself from wondering why Zoe-Grace is suddenly willing to talk now.

I show up to Dunkin' early, sweating beneath my coat. The latte warming my hands isn't helping. At 2:40, ten minutes after our agreed meeting time, I unzip myself and strip off my scarf.

Maybe she chickened out.

I'm seated at a table by the window. Outside, some hollering draws my attention. A pack of boys in shorts and St. Genevieve's hoodies run past the Dunkin'. Probably winter track. I look away, feeling sort of pervy staring at their legs.

The entrance door swings open; Zoe-Grace steps inside at the moment one of the running boys shouts something at her. She shakes her head, snowflakes at the ends of her hair dissolving.

I raise my hand at the same time Zoe-Grace zeroes in on me. She says nothing as she slides into the chair across from me, dumping her backpack on the seat next to her.

"Sorry." She removes her knitted beanie and runs a hand

through her hair. "I had to stay and talk to my photography teacher."

"It's fine." I study the patches on her backpack. There's a compass embroidered with the words NOT ALL WHO WANDER ARE LOST.

"I like that patch," I say. "Tolkien."

"What?" Zoe-Grace tucks one side of her angular bob behind her ear, revealing a silver hoop pierced through her cartilage.

"It's from a book," I say.

"Oh. I just liked the saying." Zoe-Grace glances at the counter, as if she's considering ordering something. Hesitates for a moment before turning her attention back to me. Deciding against it. Wanting to get this over with probably.

"Okay, first, if you repeat any of this to anyone, I'll deny it all. Cool?"

I nod, because even though Zoe-Grace barely clears five feet, she scares me a little. It's hard to believe she's in high school.

"The other day," she says, "You freaked me out when you mentioned Amos. Then later I realized where I recognized you from."

"I just want to know what happened to them," I say. "And to me, I guess."

Sympathy flickers in Zoe-Grace's eyes. "I swear, I don't know anything about *that*."

"But Amos wasn't with you that day," I say quietly.

"No, he wasn't," she says. "But he asked me to say he spent the night at my house. I thought maybe the police or someone sent you to talk to me because I told them he was with me when he wasn't."

"Do you know where he actually was?"

"No idea. I swear. We broke up in the winter, but at the beginning of June, he was back in town and we started hanging out again." Zoe-Grace looks embarrassed. "Obviously I should have known by then that Amos only shows up when he needs something."

My thoughts flicker to Amos at the table at the lake house.

I'd assumed he'd shown up to support his family, but what if he just wanted to see for himself what I remembered?

"Did he say why he needed you to say he was at your place?" I ask Zoe-Grace.

Her eyes flick to her hands. *Please don't lie,* I think. *Not now.*

"He was in trouble," she says, her voice low. "He wouldn't get into it but he said he owed someone a lot of money and he was scared. He said he needed me to post a picture of us together in Brookport so the guy who was looking for him would think he was on Long Island."

"So he *wasn't* on Long Island June twenty-third?"

"I don't know where the hell he was. I assumed he'd gone back to Vermont."

"Why would he go back to school if the semester was over?"

"For business reasons." Zoe-Grace snorts. "He hadn't been going to classes since the winter. He got kicked out of school."

"What?" I ask. Kat hadn't mentioned to me that her cousin got kicked out of college. But, then, she had no reason to. We avoided discussing Amos, out of some sort of mutual embarrassment. Me, at what happened at his house the night of his party, and Kat, because Amos symbolized everything she didn't want people to think she was. An entitled rich kid coasting by on his grandmother's name.

"He got caught dealing on campus." Zoe-Grace drops her voice to a hush. "It was a shitshow. His family intervened and got them not to press charges, but the school kicked him out. His grandma lost her *mind* and cut his ass out of her will."

"She disowned him because he was kicked out of college? That's intense, even for Marian."

"It was the final straw after what happened upstate the summer before."

"Upstate," I say. "You mean in Sunfish Creek?"

Zoe-Grace nods. "Amos took me to the lake house—we met some of his friends from school there. He went out on a beer

211

run and came back flipping out. The whole front end of his car was smashed in. He said he hit a deer, but he'd been smoking, so who knows what happened.

"Anyway, he had his mom wire him cash so he could get his car fixed at a place nearby the lake house. His grandma found out anyway.

"Everyone screws up sometimes, but when he told me he got busted for dealing, I ended things. Honestly, I should have told him to fuck off when he wanted to get back together at the beginning of June, but he legit seemed scared, and I don't know." Zoe-Grace kneads the knuckle underneath her silver thumb ring. "You can't just convince yourself not to care about someone when they were a huge part of your life."

"If he wasn't with you, he doesn't have an alibi for when Kat and Jesse disappeared," I say.

"I know." Zoe-Grace looks at her hands miserably. "But I said he was with me because I honestly thought there was *no way* he had anything to do with what happened to his cousin. He always said she was the only person in his family who wasn't a piece of shit, and then his uncle got hurt and they said they *had* the guy who took Kat, and he was dead . . . I thought I was the only person who would get in trouble if I admitted that I lied for Amos."

I believe Zoe-Grace, and not just because it means Amos not only has no alibi for that weekend, he also had a reason to kidnap Kat: He needed money badly, and what better way to get back at Marian for cutting him out of her will?

I believe her not just because Amos being behind what happened to us is an answer. I believe her because I can guess the damage Amos has done to her.

"You said he got his car fixed at a place near the lake house," I say. "Do you remember the name?"

"No," she says. "But it wouldn't be hard to find. There's only one car repair place in town."

I don't know why I asked, when I already know the answer.

Amos must have gotten his car fixed at Sunfish Creek Auto Body, the same place where he met Mike Dorsey.

It's a few minutes past ten; the house is quiet save for the whistle of hot air moving through the heating vent in my bedroom floor. I can't sleep, because how can I, now that I know for sure?

Amos is the only thing that connects Mike Dorsey and Kat and Jesse and me. Amos doesn't have an alibi for that Saturday night, and he may have even been on the mountain with Mike Dorsey.

Novak was right: Having an answer isn't enough for me. I don't feel a damn bit better; how can I, knowing that Amos has gotten away with lying for the past six months?

The FBI has the phone; they have all the pieces and every resource at their disposal to put them together. They'll arrive at the same answer, *Amos,* and there's nothing I can do but wait.

And then what? If they find and arrest Amos, will it be enough then? If he leads the FBI to Kat's and Jesse's bodies, will that be enough for me to accept that they're gone?

Or will nothing ever be enough as long as I can't remember what happened in those hours I was hiding like a coward while Kat and Jesse were kidnapped and murdered?

I'm turning on my side, wishing I still had an Ativan stash, when my phone vibrates. I have a text from a number I don't recognize.

hey can you call me?

this is Zo btw

Before we left Dunkin' Donuts, I put my number in Zoe-Grace's phone and told her to text me if she heard from Amos. My heart flip-flops as I select her number, hit call.

She answers the phone with, "Sorry, this was too long to text."

I keep my voice hovering around a whisper, even though there's no way my parents will hear me down the hall, if they're even awake. "Don't be sorry. What's going on?"

"This is going to sound super weird, but a few times a week, I check my blog traffic," Zoe-Grace says. "There's this weird IP address that's been visiting my site literally every day for months."

My pulse quickens. "You can track who visits your website?"

"Yeah, I've been checking to see if anyone from the schools I applied to were checking out my work," Zoe-Grace says. "I thought it was kind of weird this cell phone user in New York was visiting every day but then I talked to you . . . and I don't know, I think it might be Amos?"

"Where in New York?"

"I looked the town up and it's literally right on the border with Vermont."

"Did the IP address give you any other information?"

"Yeah. An actual address." Zoe-Grace is quiet for a beat. "Do you want it?"

"Yes. Please."

"It's Three Fifty-Two Townline Road, Timsbury, New York," she says. "Are you going to call the FBI?"

"I don't know. I mean, we don't know if that IP *is* Amos's, or if they're even looking for him."

If Amos is a suspect, the FBI hasn't made that information public yet. If he's not, they'll probably take the tip about the IP address in Timsbury as seriously as they do the whack jobs calling to say they spotted Kat and Jesse in Costa Rica.

"I messed up big-time," Zoe-Grace says. "I never should have said he was with me. What if everything that happened to Kat's dad is my fault?"

"Don't do that to yourself. I've been there, and it's just . . ."

I don't know how to say it, or maybe I'm just afraid of it sounding stupid. But I know how dangerous it is to fixate on one small action, one wrong decision. You eventually start to think you have more control than you do.

"I could get into a shit ton of trouble for lying to the police," Zoe-Grace says.

"Maybe," I say. "I honestly don't know."

"Hey, Claire," Zoe-Grace says, her voice trailing off. "Everything I told you . . . I know I need to own up. I just need to be ready."

I nod, even though she can't see me. "I won't tell anyone."

"Thanks," she says quietly.

We end the call and I immediately Google 352 Townline Road in Timsbury and follow a link to a listing on a vacation home rental site.

We're sorry. This property is no longer available.

According to the listing, 352 Townline Road is a three-bedroom, one-and-a-half-bath house. The pictures of it have been taken down, but there's a phone number for the owner.

I input it into my phone, my heartbeat picking up with each ring. After four, a man picks up.

"Hello?"

"Hi—I was calling about your rental property in Timsbury?"

"What? Do you know what time it is—and how'd you get this number?"

"From VacationRentals-dot-com. I'm a representative for the site. I was calling to see if you wanted me to update the listing."

The man shushes a dog barking in the background. "That house hasn't been available since the summer."

"Has the same person been renting it since then?" I ask.

The man goes quiet. "I don't see how that's anybody's business but mine."

"It's just for our records, sir. Would you like me to take down the listing?"

"Yeah, and get rid of my number as well," the man says.

Then the line goes dead.

Saturday morning. In the kitchen, my dad is facing the wall, still as a statue with one hand hooked behind his neck. It takes me a beat to see what he's looking at: two swipes of orange paint, brushed over the yellow my mother has been wanting to change for months.

"What are you doing?" I ask.

Dad turns. Blinks at me. "Trying to decide between these two colors."

"They look exactly the same."

"One is Pumpkin Pie, and one is Harvest Moon." He says this as if the difference should be obvious to me.

"I like Harvest Moon," I say and drop myself into a chair, then add, "I think I should drive myself back to school."

Dad turns to me. "That's a long drive to do alone."

"It's a long drive for you to do when you can be painting the kitchen," I point out.

Dad takes off his reading glasses and peers at me. "I don't know, Claire. You should understand why I'm skittish about you traveling alone."

"That's not very feminist of you."

"And *that* is manipulative of you," Dad says. "Why don't you want me to drive you?"

"It's not that. If I have my car up there, I can actually do stuff off campus. Like find a job."

"I don't know . . ." Dad sighs. I can sense him cracking. Mom was always the one who pushed the free-range-parenting thing.

"Dad," I say. "You can't protect me from everything because of what happened to my friends."

I reach for his hand. He grabs it back, brings it to his lips. He closes his eyes for a beat, then says, "I'll change your oil and put air in your tires today."

I leave Sunday morning.

I have an audiobook to help pass the time—one of the titles on the syllabus for my contemporary fiction class this semester—but I turn it off after an hour when I realize I haven't followed a single word of it.

My GPS is set for 352 Townline Road, Timsbury, New York. I mapped it out, and it'll take me five hours to get there, as long as it takes to get to Geneseo.

It'll take me another four hours to get to campus from Timsbury. It's a ton of driving, a ton of wasted gas money, but I have to know if Amos is there.

The sky is the color of a bruise by the time I reach the New York–Vermont border. The GPS says I have half an hour left. I pull over at the last rest stop on the freeway and buy an overpriced coffee I don't really want before I get back on the road.

By the time the coffee cools, the GPS is directing me to make a right onto Townline Road. There is no WELCOME TO TIMSBURY sign; the only indication I'm in the right town is the decreasing time left on my GPS. I pass a country store and a church. The latter has a sign that says HONK IF YOU LOVE JESUS / TEXT AND DRIVE IF YOU WANT TO MEET HIM!

The closest house to 352 Townline Road is a mile away. I slow to a crawl as I get closer.

The house is set up on a hill. The driveway is empty. I pass the house, keep driving as the GPS recalculates, alerting me I've passed my destination, prompting me to turn around.

Heart jackhammering, I back off the gas pedal, slow to a creep. A light snow has begun to fall. I flick my wipers on.

I pass by the house two, three more times before my heart

starts to sink. I head back into town and park in the lot of the local post office.

It has been five and a half hours since I left home. I call my mother and get her voice mail.

"Hey." I swallow, trying to blot the disappointment from my voice. "I'm here. Guess I'll talk to you guys tomorrow."

I end the call and set my GPS for Geneseo. It was foolish to come here; did I expect to find Amos Fornier on the front porch, eager to invite me in and admit how he got away with kidnapping and murder?

On the way out of the post office lot, I increase the speed on my wipers as the snow picks up. But instead of following the GPS and making a right, I make a left back toward Town-line Road.

The farmhouse is still dark.

I shake my head and start a three-point turn to head back to the freeway.

I'm changing gears when my car lurches forward. My forehead knocks into the steering wheel.

I lift my hand to my brow in a daze. Someone rear-ended me; I'll have to get out of the car and call the cops, who will report this to insurance and how the *hell* am I going to explain to my parents what I was doing here—

As I reach for my seat belt, my car lurches forward again. In the rear mirror I see a silver car ramming mine from behind—

A command breaks through the chaos in my brain. *This is not an accident. Get out of here.*

I hit the gas but it's too late; I'm off the road. Someone yanks my door open. I fumble for the handle to slam it shut at the same moment a man, face obscured by the hood of his sweatshirt, pries the door open.

A scream catches in my throat as Amos Fornier pulls me from the car and throws me to the ground, my spine numbing as it hits snow and ice. I see the shovel in his hands at the same moment he brings it down on my head.

PART THREE

THE OTHER SIDE

CHAPTER TWENTY

KAT

LAST YEAR
JUNE 23

I woke to golden light spilling through the blinds of the lake house master bedroom. I sat up straight, propelled by my sense of disorientation. Something was different. Aside from not being in my own bed, in my own home, I couldn't shake the feeling that I had forgotten something.

Beside me, Jesse stirred. He propped himself up on his hand, his elbow sinking into the mattress. "Is everything okay?"

I sank back down into the pillows, heart racing. The dream. That's what was different—I hadn't had the dream last night.

I'd been having the same dream for years, ever since we moved home from Italy. I'm watching the plane take off, and I know they're on it. My mother and father and Emma are *always* on the plane, and I'm not.

I don't know where I'm watching from, but when the plane explodes into a ball of fire and smoke I *know* they're on it and there's nothing I can do to stop it.

Last night, though, there was only darkness, peace. Jesse's arms. *Is everything okay?*

"Yes," I said, curling back into Jesse.

Everything was more than okay. Everything was perfect.

Because by the end of the weekend, I would be dead.

Everyone will want to know why. How could this happen—*why* would this happen—to Kat Marcotte, the girl who had everything?

I know that's what people thought of me secretly, bitterly. First chair in the clarinet section in band, volleyball captain, National Merit Scholarship, lead role in the fifth-grade play. My entire life, one long scorecard of wins.

In the locker room after volleyball practice in the fall, I overheard Shannon DiClemente and Anna Markey discussing the battle for valedictorian. Jamie Liu and me, fighting over it like a wishbone. It would come down to less than a point.

"I hope it's Jamie," Shannon said, toweling off her face, her neck. She didn't have to say more; it was obvious what she was thinking. Shannon, who was technically better than me on the court, but always arguing with Coach, too hotheaded to be appointed captain.

Kat gets everything.

Anna and Shannon hadn't seen me leaving Coach's office while they were talking, massaging the tendons in my wrist. It had been acting up, and I couldn't hide my discomfort anymore, not during serving drills, at least. Coach was worried, made me promise to see a doctor. Anna and Shannon didn't realize I could hear them talking about valedictorian, their wish that it would go to someone other than me for no other reason than *I had everything*.

I slipped into the showers, pressing two fingers down on the spasming in my wrist.

She had everything, they'll say when I'm gone. *Everything, just thrown away.*

How could this happen? they'll ask, and the only thing that matters to me now is that that question is never answered.

But I'm getting ahead of myself.

CHAPTER TWENTY-ONE

Imagine New York City through the eyes of a little girl seeing it for the first time. The energy, the lights, the way the people who walk the streets seem like they just woke up one day and decided to be whoever the hell they wanted to be. You can be *anyone* and still, no one would look twice at you. Everyone in New York wants to be someone, but everyone is no one.

Imagine how that possibility felt to a little girl who had wanted—ever since she could remember—to disappear and be no one. After that little girl set foot in Manhattan the first time, mittened hand in her grandmother's, outside the Russian Tea Room, that's where she went whenever she wanted to disappear.

When the yelling started, spittle flying in her face, she imagined herself slipping through the subway doors. When she barricaded herself, and eventually, her younger sister alongside her, in her bedroom, she imagined living in an apartment in the Village no bigger than the closet they hid in.

Her father said New York City was dirty, filled with degenerates and broken people, but when she thought of escaping to New York City and letting it break *her,* it filled her with longing so powerful she felt like she would rather die than give up that dream.

Someday, she would slip away from him, from all of them, and become someone else in the city. She would make it happen; she just hadn't realized, then, that New York City was not far away enough.

Imagine that girl, just turned seventeen, the November of her senior year, her birthday several months behind most of her classmates. That's never stopped her from being smarter than them, better than them, according to her family.

She's on the cusp of getting everything she's spent the past several years working toward. Everything she deserves. Her father, who has been given everything, says no one deserves anything—but her grandmother, whose parents were born with nothing, feels differently.

Her grandmother tells the girl she is exceptional, that she deserves to go to one of the best colleges in the country. The same one she went to herself, almost fifty years ago. Boston College, five hours away from the grit and glitz of Manhattan, of those hippies at NYU. She's applied to Columbia too, of course, because it holds the respectability of being an Ivy League, something her family cannot deny. But NYU has been her dream school since the eighth grade.

Yet her grandmother is so intent on her going to Boston College, she makes an offer. She'll make some phone calls, ensure an interview happens, she'll even pay every last line item on the bill; but only if every other school is off the table.

Including NYU. *Especially* NYU.

She knows she has no choice. She's never had a choice: not what classes she takes; what sports she plays; not even the time she wakes up in the morning. She knows what happens when she defies him. She doesn't want to know what will happen if she defies the woman who made him who he is.

So she trades everything she loves for that spot at Boston College: her dream of going to NYU; a future with the boy she has, against all her better judgment, let into her life.

Parts of it. He doesn't know what goes on in her house because she hasn't told anyone, not even her best friend. He curls his body around hers in his bed, his warmth in the dead of winter, whispering in her ear about all the things they'll do together when she goes to school in the city, fifteen minutes away from the apartment he'll be renting with his bandmates in the fall. She promises it'll happen, even though she knows it's a fairy tale. He does not realize she has been lying to her family about them, downplaying how serious their relationship has gotten.

Only her mother has met him, only her mother knows how much time they actually spend together. Of course her father and grandmother will not approve of him—maybe they will even hate him because they hate everything that makes her happy.

So she lies to him, over and over. When the email arrives from NYU—*Congratulations!*—she deletes it and tells him she was rejected. As his face falls, she says she doesn't understand it either, how it could happen. Because they're both thinking it—she gets everything she puts her mind toward, and somehow, she didn't get into NYU.

The thing about lying is that if you do it enough, it becomes something you don't even have to think about. Just like breathing.

I would know. I've been doing it my whole life, for them.

My family.

CHAPTER TWENTY-TWO

KAT

LAST YEAR
MAY

It started—or ended, depending on how you look at it—two weeks before my grandmother's birthday. Marian was at our house for Sunday coffee, a weekly expectation she had sprung upon my mother when we moved into the home on Idledale Road, her stitches not yet healed from giving birth to me.

Marian watched me from over the rim of her cup, waiting for a lull in my mother's prattling about the upcoming celebration at the Brookport Country Club.

"Your mother says things are serious with this boy you've been spending time with."

My mother added some more creamer to her coffee, eyes cast down. The only reason they dared to speak of it now was because my father was ten thousand feet in the air somewhere.

I stared at my mother, my heart crawling into my throat. A stab of fear as I wondered what she had been saying to Marian about Jesse—and her reasons for waiting until now, when I only had a few months left before leaving for college, to tell Marian that we were serious.

Marian's expectant stare, as if I were a server who had brought her the wrong meal, ignited something in me.

"He's not just a boy I'm spending time with," I said icily. "I've been friends with him since the ninth grade."

Marian's lips pursed as if she tasted something sour. Any reminder of my public schooling had that effect. I had fought like hell to avoid being sent upstate to Barton, like Emma; I had lasted half a year at Amos's school, St. Genevieve's, affectionately dubbed "St. Druggies" by all who knew it.

"He's a very nice boy," my mother said, but like every sentence she'd ever deigned to utter in Marian's presence, it sounded more like a question.

My grandmother poured from the Royal Albert china coffeepot, the set she'd handed down to my mother, even though my aunt Erin had coveted it since she was a girl. "Don't you think it's time I met him?"

I poured some milk into the coffee, imagining saying no to my grandmother. The grandmother who was paying for my college education, who had showed up at my house days earlier driving my unnecessarily expensive graduation present.

No, I imagined saying. *You will never get within ten feet of him.*

Marian's eyes moved to my mother, as if I had vanished from the room. "What about the party? Surely we could fit another place at the table."

"He works every weekend," I said, a beat too quickly.

Marian sipped from her coffee cup, leaving a smear of nude-pink lipstick on the rim. Chanel Rouge Coco in Marie; as a child I would sneak into her bathroom and uncap the tube, twist the lipstick to its full height. I imagined writing terrible words on her mirror, words I'd only ever heard my father utter.

"The party is in two weeks," Marian said. "That's plenty of time for him to request an afternoon off."

The phone rang in the kitchen, prompting Marian's departure from the table. My mother glanced at me, panicked, and said under her breath: "Please make sure he wears a tie."

There was no way around it; my mother even mailed Jesse an invitation to the party. Maybe she anticipated that I wouldn't tell him about it. That I would continue to attempt to hide him from the rest of my family. Not only from Marian and my father but the rest of the Sullivan-Marcottes. The Sullivans disgusted me: Marian's side of the family; a bunch of braggarts, Brookport born and raised. They had all made something of themselves—lawyers, doctors, Wall Street suits—but none like US Congresswoman Marian Sullivan-Marcotte.

I couldn't stand them, couldn't stand watching them try to outdo one another, using their successful, beautiful children as props. I pictured Jesse driving up to the country club in Bruce, seeing a fleet of BMWs and Audis and vintage Corvettes. I cared less about what my family would think of *him* than what Jesse would think of me.

I'd spent our entire relationship trying to be someone else. Someone like Claire, who didn't stay up all night obsessing about whether or not she'd gotten one answer wrong on a math quiz. I'd fooled myself into thinking I could be someone who didn't constantly live in fear because Jesse made me feel safe.

Fear, now, so powerful I felt like I might vomit into the bowls of peonies at the center of the table. Fear because Jesse was fifteen minutes late to the country club; fear because my two worlds were about to collide.

I sucked down half a glass of Diet Coke before sneaking away from the table to the lobby, away from the sound of Sinatra crooning through the speakers. I took my phone out and texted Jesse, *where are you??*

He was coming after work, and even though he promised he would leave an hour early so he'd have time to go home and shower, he was still fifteen minutes late.

"Kat?"

I looked up, and there he was, lingering by the collage of photos my aunt Erin had put together to honor Marian's life. Jesse, hair still damp, in a blue button-down and khakis. He hadn't put on a tie, and I guess my face fell a bit, because he asked, "What is it? What's wrong?"

I said nothing and I gave him a quick peck on the lips. "Nothing. Ready to meet a bunch of rich douchebags?"

My voice slid up to a squeak, and my heartbeat moved to my fingers as I clutched Jesse's hand and led him into the dining room. I took inventory of the room: my father was congregated with a pack of his cousins at the bar at the far side of the room, mercifully out of our line of sight.

My grandmother held court at her table. She was wearing a tasteful floral wrap dress, her hair freshly blown out and swept into a French twist. The sound of my pulse flooded my ears as I walked Jesse over to her.

Marian spotted us and lowered her champagne glass, an inquisitive look on her face.

"Grandma," I said. "This is Jesse. My boyfriend."

Marian accepted his outstretched hand. Hers, lily white, blue veins peeking through the skin. His tanned and calloused from his guitar. "Jesse . . ."

"Salpietro," he said.

"What an interesting last name." Marian's eyebrows lifted. "Is it Italian?"

Jesse slipped his hands into the pockets of his khakis. *No, don't slouch,* I thought. *She hates that.*

"Yes," Jesse said. "My mother was Italian and Mexican American."

It was as fast as a streak of lightning, but we both saw it. My grandmother's face pinched. Not at the word *Italian,* obviously, because my grandfather had been Italian.

Mexican American.

I swallowed the sick feeling rising from my stomach as

Marian murmured, *Excuse me,* turning her back on Jesse and me to greet another well-wisher.

"Come speak to me again later, Katherine," she said, her smile faltering as her eyes rested on Jesse once more.

I guided him away; Jesse's eyes were still on my grandmother. When I gave his shoulder a squeeze, he mumbled about needing to use the bathroom and headed for the lobby.

Only, the bathrooms were the other way.

"Jesse." I caught him as he was advancing on the lobby doors.

He turned around, the saddest look on his face I'd ever seen.

"You're leaving?" I said.

"I don't think I should be here," he said.

I opened my mouth, then promptly closed it. There was no excuse for how she'd treated him.

"I'm so sorry," I whispered. "Please. Stay."

Jesse's eyes started to water. "Kat, I can't do this."

It felt like a hole had been punched through my lungs. "Are you breaking up with me?"

"No—I don't know, Kat, I just can't be here right now." He wiped a hand down his face.

"Because of my grandma? I know she's awful. They all are. It's why I tried to keep them from you." I grabbed his hands, squeezed. "You know I'm nothing like them, right?"

Jesse's hands trembled in mine. I squeezed harder. "Jesse. Do you seriously think this changes things between us?"

"I don't know. I need time to figure it out, okay?"

"What do you mean?"

Jesse pulled his hands out of my grasp and he looked around the room as if seeing it for the first time. The crystal chandeliers, marble floors, gloved servers.

"I just can't be here right now," he said. "We'll talk some other time, okay?"

And then, he was gone.

I needed a drink. I needed something *stronger* than a drink, and luckily, I knew exactly who I could get it from.

Amos was slumped back in a chair at our family's table, balancing a butter knife on his knuckles. It was probably taking up his entire reserve of self-control not to take out the cigarette lighter in his pocket and fiddle with it. I slipped into the empty chair next to him.

"What's up your ass?" he said.

I stared at my grandmother, who was leaning in to talk to an old friend, her hand touching the woman's wrist. For some reason, I thought about a trip to the Sunfish Creek cabin when we were young. Amos had found me sulking by the dock because Marian had reamed me out so badly over refusing to eat my brussels sprouts that I'd left the dinner table in tears.

Amos got that cat-who-swallowed-a-parakeet look on his face when I announced *Grandma is so mean*. When everyone was sleeping, he lured me out of my room with a package of bologna. I followed him as he strategically hid slices around the cabin, knowing by the time Marian went back to the lake house in the fall the stench would be unbearable.

Now, Amos studied me studying Marian, as if we were a puzzling math equation. After a beat, he gave up, scooped a flute of champagne off the table and knocked it back. "I fucking hate this family."

"Me too," I said.

Amos just looked at me and snorted. "Yeah. Okay, BC."

Of course, he'd found out Marian was paying my tuition. She'd refused to fund Amos's education, since the best school he got into was the University of Vermont. There are no secrets in our family.

"Hey," I said suddenly. "Want to leave?"

"You're joking." Amos glanced at my father. "Are you sure—"

I knew my father would go ballistic if we just *left*, if he and

Erin had two empty chairs to explain to the other guests. But suddenly, I didn't care.

"Not joking," I said. "Let's go."

We both shut off our phones; Amos let me drive his BMW. We wound up on the parkway to Jones Beach, nearly an hour west of Brookport, toward New York City. He smoked a joint, one arm out the window of the passenger side, while I kept my eyes split between the road ahead and the speedometer. Sixty, seventy, eighty miles an hour.

When we parked at the beach, Amos said, "What do you think they're doing right now?"

I stared straight ahead out the windshield. "Cutting the cake and pretending absolutely nothing is wrong."

After a beat, Amos said, "You know Marian cut me off completely, right?"

I knew he'd gotten into some sort of trouble at school, that he was "taking a semester off" to straighten his behavior out. But *cutting him off*? "Are you serious?"

"No trust fund, no inheritance, zip." Amos snapped his fingers.

"You're lucky," I say.

Amos let his hand fall to his lap. He craned his neck to face me and smirked. "Oh yeah? How's that?"

"Because at least she doesn't own you."

I had no choice but to go home. Where else would I go? I could show up at Claire's and get her parents involved, but no doubt that would turn ugly fast. My father has never liked Claire's mother; there is only room in his life for one strong woman, and that is his own mother. If Christine Keough tried to help me, citing child protection laws and her psychobabble bullshit, it would be war.

It doesn't matter what happened when I did go home. There was shouting, of course, accusations lobbed at me.

Humiliated our entire family—

—spoiled brats!

We almost called the police—

But this time I was too calm, which only pissed him off more—when I tried to sidestep him to head into my room, he grabbed my shoulder. "Katherine, don't you dare—"

"Get the fuck off me!" I screamed.

That made him snap. I knew it would and I didn't care. I let my body go limp as he threw me onto my bed. In the hall, my mother was screaming: *Johnathan, what are you doing—*

The world went black when my head smacked against the wall. For a moment I thought I might not come back, that I was dying—

When I woke to him shaking me, fear replacing the rage on his face, my mother in the doorway whimpering, *Oh God, Oh God,* I stared into his eyes.

I wish you'd killed me, I tried to say with my eyes. *Then maybe someone would finally stop you.*

In the morning, my father left for work like everything was normal. Three days he'd be gone—Newark to Ireland to the UK and back. It was a pattern I knew well. He'd lose control, run off to work, and come back all smiles and hugs, like he was Atticus Finch.

And yet, something felt different this time. My mother was barely eating and couldn't look at me without her eyes filling with tears.

My father had locked up my car keys as punishment for the party incident; Monday morning, my mother offered to drive me to school.

"I'll walk," I said coolly, before closing my bedroom door in her face.

I thought about texting Claire for a ride but I didn't want to explain why I was going to her and not Jesse. I wondered if he'd told her what happened at the party, although deep down I knew he wouldn't. *I* still didn't understand what had happened, how he could blame me for my grandmother's rudeness. How after all this time he still didn't understand I viewed my last name as a curse and not a privilege.

After the last bell, I was debating blowing off honor society and lacrosse practice when Jesse found me by my locker. Shadows under his eyes and on his jaw.

Good, I thought. *You walked out on me and you deserve to be as miserable as I am.*

"Hey." His voice was hoarse, his eyes not meeting mine. "Can we talk?"

I followed him to Bruce. Even in his car, with less than a foot of space between us, he couldn't look at me.

"Just finish dumping me properly so I can get to my honor society meeting on time," I said.

When I looked over at Jesse, his eyes were wet. "You think that's what I want? To dump you?"

"I don't know what you want, Jesse. For my family to be different? I've never once for one second thought you weren't good enough for me."

After a long moment, he said, "What if I'm just not right for you?"

Tears sprang to my eyes. "If you love me, then you're right for me."

Jesse leaned forward, balancing his elbows on the steering wheel. "I love you more than anything, Kat."

And that's when the dam burst.

I told Jesse what happened after Amos and I skipped the party. I told him about the trashed bedrooms when I was a kid, how I learned how to barricade myself in a closet at age seven. I told him how I really got the scar beneath my eyebrow and why my mother moved us home from Italy. How the second my head cracked against my bedroom wall Saturday night, I thought, *I'm about to die and I don't even care.*

He held me while I sobbed into his shoulder, soaking his favorite Led Zeppelin T-shirt with snot and tears.

"How can I help?" he pleaded. "Just tell me what to do. I'll call CPS, I'll—"

"You can't," I said, my heart sinking with the realization. I had no physical proof of what my father had done to me the other night; my mother would lie her ass off for him, and Emma would be too terrified to take my side. My father controlled *everything.*

The only person who could possibly control *him,* the only person who could help me was the last person I wanted to ask for help from.

My grandmother did not look surprised to see me when she answered the door that afternoon.

The placid expression on her face put a ball of rage in my throat; my face was raw and tearstained. I hadn't slept in days. And still, instead of asking if I was all right, she said, "I'm glad you finally decided to apologize for your behavior this weekend."

I followed her into the sitting room. She sat on the love seat while I took the armchair across the coffee table, and we just kind of stared at each other for a long beat until she said, "Do you know we were all worried *sick* about you and Amos?"

"Not worried enough to leave the party and look for us."

Marian pursed her lips; they were bare and pale and it occurred to me this was the first time in my entire life I'd seen my grandmother without makeup on. "How long have you been seeing that boy from the party?"

"His name is Jesse. Maybe you'd remember his name if you'd pretended not to be a miserable racist for five minutes and actually spoken to him."

I was trembling; I'd never disrespected my grandmother before.

"This nastiness," she said softly. "I don't know where it comes from."

"Maybe you should ask your son the next time he's slamming my head into a wall."

Marian blinked at me. "That's an incredibly serious accusation to make."

"Accusation? It *happened,* Grandma."

Marian raised her voice. "I know you, and I know your father, and I know whatever *happened* was the unfortunate result of two out-of-control tempers."

A laugh bubbled up in my chest. It was my fault, then. Sure, I'd made him angry. But somehow, I doubted this was even about me. Maybe Marian needed to believe it in order to live with herself, because what kind of woman raises a man who hurts women?

"I guess we have nothing more to talk about," I said.

As I stood from the couch, she said, "Katherine."

I stared back at her, tears hot in my eyes. "What?"

"You're going to one of the best colleges in the country. You don't need the distraction of a long-distance relationship."

"Yeah, well, I don't really need to be worried about coming home to an abusive father either."

"End it with that boy, Katherine."

My feet fused themselves to the carpet. Marian watched me, impassive, as if she'd told me to go get the taillight on my car fixed. Finally, I forced out a response. "No."

She crossed her legs and cocked her head at me. "No, what?"

"I'm not breaking up with Jesse."

"You *are,* or I'm calling Boston College and rescinding your acceptance."

It reminded me so much of my father. *If you don't pick up your toys, I'm giving them to someone else.* Emma and I had fought over something once. A Barbie RV. To settle the dispute, he had flung it into the wall.

"It's too late for me to go somewhere else," I said, truly scared for the first time. "You'd make me stay at home?"

"I'm not making you do anything," she said. "I'm giving you the choice."

That word—*choice*—made me snap like a twig. I had never been afforded an ounce of control over my own life, had never been given something without strings attached. *Enjoy all of these nice things and keep your mouth shut about what this family is really like.*

"You're just like my father!" I shouted. "You're *evil*. There's no way you don't know how he treats us. I cannot spend another minute—"

My voice broke off as her stare turned to ice. "Then I suggest you end that relationship as soon as possible."

"You have to go," Jesse said when I met him where he'd been waiting in the marina parking lot. "You have to get away from him, Kat, even if it means doing what she says."

"That's exactly why I'll never *get* away." I was crying so hard Jesse held my head to his chest. His heart thumped wildly under my ear. "She'll make me go home every summer and holidays, and the thought makes me want to kill myself—"

Jesse sat up so abruptly my brain rattled in my skull. "Kat. Don't ever say shit like that."

Jesse held me tight as I sobbed into his shoulder, soaking his T-shirt. "I don't know what to do. I can't go back to that house. I'm done. BC isn't worth it. I don't even want to go there."

My body trembled from the effort it took to keep breathing, but a sense of calm was returning to me. I'd said it. I didn't want to go to Boston College. I didn't want to be a lawyer; I didn't want to owe my grandmother for the rest of my life; I didn't want to be a Marcotte at all.

The feeling was back, the desperation to just end it, to cease to be. But I couldn't, wouldn't do that to Jesse.

"Do you trust me?" he whispered by my ear.

When I didn't respond, he lifted my chin to meet his gaze. His voice was more urgent this time: "Kat? Do you trust me?"

I nodded, head heavy, my body weak from the adrenaline crash.

"Run away with me," he said, taking my face in his hands. "There's nothing for me here except you."

"But your aunt—" I swallowed. "You have your job. You have Claire."

"They'll all survive without me. I can survive without *them*." He tilted his forehead to mine. "You are the only thing that matters to me."

I pretended it was actually an option. Running away with Jesse. Where would we go? Was there anywhere that my family couldn't find us?

"I'm not eighteen until November," I said. "My family— they'd say you kidnapped me or something. You'd get in a ton of trouble."

"So we won't get caught. I have enough money saved to get us out of the state." Jesse's voice was growing more urgent, as if it wasn't the first time he'd entertained the idea.

I couldn't command my brain to form the words. *We'd get caught. He'd kill us both if we got caught.*

"Please." Jesse moved his hands from my face to my lap. He took my hands in his, brought them to his mouth and kissed my knuckles. "Just say yes. We'll figure it out together. Nothing matters as long as we're together."

He pulled me closer to him, heart thumping wildly, but his body loosening around mine. As if he already knew what my answer would be. I would follow him anywhere, as long as it was far away.

I knew, even when I said yes, that nowhere would be far enough. No distance would be safe. Italy had proven that.

The thing that made my father snap was eggs. My mother had gone to the market in Aviano and brought home a dozen eggs, and when my father discovered one of them was cracked, I knew what the look in his eyes meant. I locked Emma in our bedroom and returned to the kitchen to make sure my mother was okay.

I was afraid he'd hurt her—I was always afraid he'd hurt her, even though he purposely missed whenever he threw things. Not because he didn't *want* to hurt us but because he couldn't control what would happen if he left proof.

He was still screaming about the eggs when I got back to her. He didn't see me rushing to my mother's side when he threw the plate at the wall, and a shard ricocheted and hit me right over the eye.

She booked our plane tickets home two days later. I thought maybe it meant she was done lying for him, that for once, she was doing what she needed to do to keep us safe.

And then, the week before we were due to leave, someone from family services at the air base stopped by the house. There had been concerns raised. Even though he wasn't home, my mother sat at the table, a small smile on her face, and denied that my father had a temper, denied that she felt unsafe, denied that the cut over my eye that needed four stitches was anything but a freak accident involving a dropped dinner plate.

We are a very loving family, she said, and I knew then that she was moving us home to protect *him,* not my sister and me.

Before we said goodbye, my father sat Emma and me down, pinned us with those steel-gray eyes that have haunted my dreams ever since.

"Everything I do is for you two," he'd said. "Everything I do is for my family."

And that's when I became scared of him in a way I'd never been before. Nothing is more terrifying than a villain who sees himself as a hero. He may have been letting my mother take us back to the States to save him from himself, but we were still his.

We were his family. He deserved us, he deserved his own happy family after the trauma of losing his father at a young age. We were his and no one would ever take us away from him.

It's why I could never escape. If I wanted to get away from my father I had to stop being Kat Marcotte.

It's why I—why *we*—had to die.

CHAPTER TWENTY-THREE

KAT

LAST YEAR
MAY

There was no way around it; if my family knew I'd run away with Jesse, they would move heaven and earth to find us and punish us. The idea of me being with Jesse was so distasteful that my grandmother had threatened to take away my education—what would she do to me if I threw my entire carefully planned future away to escape with him?

The only way to ensure that they stopped looking, eventually, was for everyone to think we were dead.

We spent the next several days planning our mysterious deaths. Obviously there would be no bodies, only the grimmest of discoveries that left little hope we'd ever be found. Jesse suggested pushing my car down an embankment, somewhere heavily wooded and far from home. Upstate New York, maybe, near my grandmother's lake house. How many people have crashed their cars and, unable to find cell service, wandered into the woods only to succumb to the elements?

But I wasn't comfortable hoping everyone would just forget about us, accept that Jesse and I were a pile of bones waiting to be uncovered in a few years by some backwoods morel hunter. Captain Johnathan Marcotte himself would comb every inch of every mile of the Catskill woods to find me until he brought me home to rest.

So, then, one of the only ways to truly disappear a human body: water.

My father, of all people, had given me the idea.

He'd brought my sister and me to Blackstone Quarry as children, on one of our family trips to the lake house. He'd bored us with the details about how many miles deep and wide it was. The punch line of his story? A couple of fool teenagers went cliff diving at the quarry when he was young; the water was too dark, too cold, too filled with crevices, and two of the kids drowned, their bodies lost to the quarry forever. Emma and I had better never acquire that taste for danger, lest we succumbed to a similar fate.

Kat Marcotte and her boyfriend jumping to their deaths at Blackstone Quarry would shock everyone who knew us, might even warrant a *People* magazine cover with WHY? splashed above our faces.

Marian and my father would know exactly why. They would know they were responsible for sending me to the bottom of the quarry; they would have to live with the fact that even the Marcotte money could not change that dredging Blackstone Quarry, searching every corner for our bodies, was an impossible task.

It was almost foolproof. Except for, of course, money.

Jesse and I had a combined twenty-five hundred dollars to our names. All of the cash Jesse had saved working over the years had gone to buying his piece of crap car.

I've had a bank account since I turned ten. All of my money—birthday checks, babysitting earnings—went right in so I could earn a pathetic interest rate and feel like a big girl.

But I wouldn't be able to withdraw it all, or even a large chunk, without setting off alarm bells. I imagined investigators jumping to check my bank account, maybe having a chuckle that Marian Sullivan-Marcotte's granddaughter had six hundred and sixty-seven dollars in her personal checking.

We needed money to escape. We'd need a car, for one thing, and a place to stay. We'd need enough cash in reserve to tide us over until it was safe enough to look for work as new people, in a town hundreds of miles from here.

The lack of money threatened to cripple the entire plan. And even if we had the money to buy a car off Craigslist, to find an apartment online, how could we do any of that without leaving a trail?

Maybe even more than money, we needed someone we could trust.

The next afternoon, a Saturday, Amos agreed to meet me outside the coffee and pastry shop in the village. Summer had arrived violently and without warning; most of the tables inside the air-conditioned café were filled. We opted for one of the patio tables out front.

I kept one eye trained on the sidewalk for any stragglers passing by who might overhear us. Amos listened to my plea, fingers steepled below his lips, ignoring the croissant and glass of iced tea in front of him.

"I could find a way to pay you back, eventually," I said, my voice faltering at the look on his face.

"I'd give you everything I had, if I could," Amos said. "But I'm completely broke."

"What?" There had been murmurings, of course, about Amos's father not sending my aunt Erin money once Amos turned eighteen. But despite her not working since Amos was born, she was still a *Marcotte*. "Are you serious? What about your mom?"

Amos sipped his iced tea. "The Audi is leased, her credit cards are maxed out, and Marian pays the mortgage."

My fingers found my lips, now prickly with panic. Amos, who was wearing a $250 pair of Ray-Bans, was telling me he was broke. "What about all the money you make, you know? Dealing."

"Kat, I've got a few hundred bucks under my mattress. And I owe a supplier a grand for some shit the village rent-a-cops confiscated from me when they pulled me over last month."

We fell quiet as a woman walking two boxers passed by. One tugged at its leash, sniffed the potted geranium in the planter by our table. When she was gone, Amos said, "How serious are you about this? You know how much it would hurt your mother? Emma?"

"I can't do it." I pulled my gauzy cardigan around my body. "You know Grandma won't just let me walk away from this family."

"How much do you hate her?"

"Even more than my father."

"Then," Amos said, squeezing the lemon perched at the rim of his iced tea glass, "I think I have an idea."

My pulse went still as he reached into his pocket. He pulled out a cell phone; on old Motorola flip phone that Amos Fornier wouldn't be caught dead using.

He covered the phone with his hand and pushed it toward me. "From here on, I'll contact you through this. Hide it well. There are people in this phone you don't ever want to be associated with."

I swallowed, looked up at Amos.

"What's your idea?" I asked.

Amos smiled; my heartbeat moved into my ears. I didn't dare breathe.

He took a sip from his iced tea, tilted his head back toward the late-day sun. "Cash in on what she owes us."

CHAPTER TWENTY-FOUR

KAT

LAST YEAR
THAT WEEKEND

It had been easy to convince Claire to come with us. She didn't want to spend prom weekend with Ben Filipoff's friends and *their* friends. Girls who pretend to like the taste of Bud Light, boys who will risk snapping their necks at the bottom of the prom house pool just to get a laugh. Of course, Marian's lake house was the more appealing option. Ben was tougher, at first, until he figured out the lake house was the only way he'd be able to have sex with Claire all weekend.

The Craigslist Camry was retrieved, stashed in a wooded area a quarter mile from Bobcat Mountain. Mike knew the area, and said no one would notice it for days, if not weeks. We only needed it to stay undetected for twenty-four hours.

There had been the hiccup with the car, of course, thanks to Ben Filipoff. (My whole life, my escape, threatened to be knocked off course by the idiot across the street!) While Claire and Ben were supposed to be at prom, Jesse and I were supposed to meet Mike Dorsey for the first time.

Amos had arranged for Mike to meet us in a Burger King parking lot down the road from Sunfish Creek Auto Body Friday afternoon. We would give Mike the money, and Mike would meet with the man selling the car later that evening.

But, thanks to Ben, we had Claire with us. And Claire could absolutely not see Mike Dorsey's face. At no point in the plan was Claire to see his face—Amos had made it clear that Mike's involvement was contingent upon that.

So, Jesse had to drop the money at Mike's work when he went to pick up the pizza. Problem solved. Everything was in place.

Everything was right, but something was still wrong.

Saturday morning Claire sat quiet in the front seat on the drive to Bobcat Mountain.

"Are you okay?" I finally asked after ten minutes of silence into the fifteen-minute drive. Everything was fine when we'd gone to sleep the night before.

"Fine," she snapped. "Just getting carsick."

I caught Jesse's eye in the rear mirror. He shrugged, as if to say *Hell if I know what her problem is*.

We parked at the edge of the lot, closest to the start of the trail. At the other corner of the lot was a pickup truck, a Confederate flag decal on the back window.

Someone else was on the mountain. I had considered the possibility, but I wasn't worried. No one else would be camping at Devil's Peak. That was why I'd picked it.

Claire paused by the trail map posted at the base of the mountain. "Are you sure we're taking the red trail?"

"That's the one that goes up to Devil's Peak," I said, buckling my pack straps beneath my chest.

"It says here that the green trail is for camping." Claire pointed to the marker for Poet's Lookout, several miles west of Devil's Peak. "Look. Designated camping area."

"I know," I said. "But I've been here before—Devil's Peak has a better view than Poet's Lookout."

And no people. There would be no other campers at Devil's Peak. No other witnesses.

"But it says we're not supposed to camp there." Claire

tugged at her pack straps that were digging into her shoulders around her ribbed tank top.

"It's fine," I said. "The ranger's office closes at four. They don't patrol the mountains at night or care where anyone camps."

"I don't want to get busted over this whole weekend because you wanted a better view." Claire yanked at her straps again, still not meeting my eyes.

My stomach turned inside out; this was not Claire. Agreeable, down-for-anything, think-about-the-consequences-later *Claire*. The only reason she could possibly have for resisting me, questioning the plan, was pure petulance.

I'd done something. But of course, I hadn't done anything to her.

Which meant—

Jesse came up next to me, struggling under the weight of his pack, loaded with our tent and water, the sleeping bag attached to the bottom thwacking against his back. "What's going on?"

"Nothing," I said, locking Claire's gaze down. Daring her to challenge me. "Here, let me fix your straps."

"I've got it," she started to say, cheeks blooming pink.

"Claire. Let me fix the fucking straps."

She stared at me, lips parted with disbelief. I rarely talked like that, especially not to her. I stepped toward her and tugged at the straps, loosening them so the weight of the pack rested on her hips.

She shrugged away from me the second my hands fell from her pack. Turned around, defiant, and started heading up the trail.

Next to me, Jesse was quiet.

"Did something happen this morning?" I said, softly enough so that ahead, Claire wouldn't be able to hear.

Jesse shook his head. "I don't know what her problem is."

Well, we need to find out. I thought about snapping it at him, letting him see, for once, how I got when I felt things slipping outside my control. I needed Claire to be Claire, to act the way she always had.

Stay in the tent. Do what I say.

Last night, Claire and I were best friends. Today, it felt like she couldn't stand breathing the same air as me.

What the hell had happened?

I tried to breathe around the crowding in my lungs as the elevation on the trail increased. The trees on each side thickened, blotting out the afternoon sun.

Last night.

I woke to Jesse climbing into bed; he said he'd gone to pee and apologized for waking me. But I could have sworn I saw the motion light in the backyard glow for a second before I turned over and went back to sleep.

There's no way Jesse said something to her last night. He knew what was at stake for me—for both of us.

But maybe he'd changed his mind since Wednesday night. He'd said it was fucked up to leave Claire, alone in her tent, without Ben.

I'd convinced him we needed her. He didn't know my grandmother—the depth of her cruelty—how far she'd go to protect what was hers. Her money, her blood.

She would not hand over that money unless she thought there was a good chance she'd get me back in return.

I resisted the urge to turn and look at Jesse; I gripped the straps on my pack and continued on, the sound of Jesse's and Claire's footsteps on the trail behind me.

By the time we reached Devil's Peak and finished setting up the campsite, the sun was bending toward the horizon, the air cooling around us.

Claire collapsed into the foldable chair by the firepit and drained half a bottle of water. "I thought you said there was an amazing view."

I bit back my irritation. "It's a few minutes from here. I didn't want us to drag all of our equipment there."

Once Jesse returned from the clearing of trees with a pile of branches for the fire, I said, "Let's go to the peak."

Behind me, Claire sighed. We hiked through the clearing, up a steep staircase of stones, and emerged at the peak.

"Wow," Jesse said, climbing up the boulder nestled into the rock ledge. His mouth hung open a bit, admiring the view.

Claire sank down until she was sitting butterfly-style, staring out at a point beyond the view, her mind elsewhere.

I dropped down next to her as Jesse pulled out his phone and began snapping pictures.

"Are you going to tell me what's wrong?" I asked. "I feel like you're mad at me."

"Nothing is wrong," she said, and took a sip from her water bottle. "For someone who calls me insecure, you seem pretty obsessed with what I think about you."

I bit down on the inside of my cheek, hard. "It's weird that you're my best friend and I want to know if we're okay?" I asked.

Her stare—angry, aimed away from me, but purposefully avoiding Jesse as well—did nothing to squash the paranoia swelling in me. I let my own gaze travel over to Jesse.

Did he say something to her? There's no way, with everything that's at stake—

"Claire," I said. "*Are* we okay?"

"I honestly don't know." Claire nudged a tear away with the back of her hand. And that's how I knew, Jesse hadn't told her about our escape.

He had done something—said something—to break her heart.

I let the silence balloon between us. I didn't know what to

say, and it was becoming difficult to form words around the pounding in my chest.

Claire straightened. "Do you remember that party we went to at Amos's house?"

I swallowed. We never really talked about that party, so why was she bringing it up now? Why was she bringing *Amos* up now?

Claire had begged me to go to his house, and even though I couldn't stand the thought of being around a bunch of St. Genevieve's kids, watching them puke into my aunt's crystal vases, I relented. I wound up getting drunk for the first time in my life. In the morning I could barely get out of Claire's bed and had to lie to her mother that I had a migraine even though she definitely knew we were both hungover.

"Did you say anything to Jesse?" Claire asked. "About what may have happened at that party with Amos and me?"

My heartbeat went still. "No. I mean, I don't think so? It was so long ago."

"Okay." Claire stood, tugged at the hem of her shorts. "I'm gonna go back to the campsite."

"Wait," I said.

Claire went still, a twig cracking under her sneaker. She crossed her arms over her chest as if she were cold. "Yeah?"

"I think Jesse asked how it was, and I said something like, the party was stupid but I think Claire and Amos had fun."

She nodded, her jaw set. "You didn't tell him I had sex with Amos?"

"Why would I say that?" I'd asked Claire what happened when she disappeared with Amos into his bedroom, and she said they just kissed.

Claire stared me down. "I can think of a reason."

Before I could fumble out a response, she was gone.

———

After his photo shoot was over, Jesse plopped down next to me, his head heavy on my shoulder. "Where'd Claire go?"

"She left her phone at the campsite," I lied, already scrambling to my feet. "I should make sure she got back there okay— the trail isn't marked clearly—"

Jesse tugged at my hand. "Want me to come with?"

"No. Stay. Enjoy the view." I planted a kiss on his cheek. "We'll be back in a couple minutes."

Jesse gripped my hand as I stood; I gripped back, slowly pulling away until only our fingertips were left touching, then let go.

At the campsite, I found Claire bent over my sister's sky-blue hiking pack. Cheeks red, sweat pooling at her brow.

"What are you doing?" I asked.

"I think I should go back to the house."

"What? Why?"

She straightened, one hand moving to her hip. "Why did you even ask me to come?"

"Because I wanted you to come?"

Claire snorted, crouched back down to her pack. "Why did you want Jesse to think I hooked up with your cousin?"

"What are you talking about?"

"That party we went to at Amos's house. You told Jesse that Amos and I hooked up. Why?"

"Because I thought you *did* hook up with him." I blinked at her. "Sorry I was a gossip over three years ago?"

"You don't gossip. Except when you get something out of it." Claire stared at me. "So what did you get? Jesse to think I was a slut with a thing for private-school guys?"

"Claire, this is insane." Something in me snapped. The words fell out: "I know it must be hard to see us together."

Claire's stare went cold. "How do you mean?"

I swallowed. "Because you and Ben broke up, and you're here alone—"

"No." She shook her head, her mouth twitching with a ghastly little laugh. "That's not what you meant. Just admit it. You already won, so there's no point in lying."

The comment leveled me; I lowered myself onto the log beside the firepit. Is that how she saw my entire relationship with Jesse? A prize she lost out on?

"We're adults now," I said, my voice trembling. "If you want to be pissed at me for something stupid that happened when we were fifteen, fine."

"It wasn't fucking stupid, Kat. Jesse changed toward me after that."

"He changed toward you after his mom died. You said it yourself, he was weird with you—"

"It wasn't that." She shook her head. "It was you. I hope it was worth it."

My heart rocketed into my throat as she grabbed the hiking pack. "Claire. You can't leave."

"What's the code to get inside the house?" she asked.

"This is ridiculous," I snapped.

"Fine, don't tell me. I'll sleep in one of the chairs on the dock."

"I'm sorry, okay? Will you stay now?"

Claire yanked the zipper on her pack closed. "What's the code, Kat?"

I glanced around the campsite. "You're just going to leave me and Jesse to hike back with all of this stuff—"

"Jesse had both our tents in his pack. I just had the food and water in mine. Whatever's left won't add more to your packs than what you carried up."

"What am I supposed to tell him?"

"I don't know—say I got my period or something."

"Please," I said. "Tell me what you need me to do to make you stay."

"Time." She gnawed her bottom lip. "I just need time to get over it."

I couldn't speak, couldn't move. I had completely lost control of her. She sighed at my silence and moved over to my hiking pack. "Which pocket are your car keys in?"

"Right one."

Claire fished them out, hooked her finger around the ring of my key chain. "Call when you want me to come get you guys tomorrow morning."

When Jesse came back to the campsite, probably wondering what was taking us so long, he found me alone by the firepit, fanning the smoking pile of kindling to coax out a flame.

He stopped in his tracks, surveyed the campsite.

"Where's Claire?"

I snapped a branch over my knee, arranged the pieces around the growing tent-shaped structure in the firepit. "She went back to the house."

"What? Why?"

The wind lifted, sending smoke into my face, toppling my meticulously crafted kindling structure. For some reason, that's what finally made me fall apart.

"Kat, what happened?" Jesse took a step toward me. Stopped himself.

"We had a fight." I wiped my eyes with the back of my hand. "She wanted to go back."

Jesse gaped at me. "And you just let her go?"

"What was I supposed to do? Tie her to a tree?"

Jesse sank to the ground next to me. "Why didn't you come get me? I could have talked to her—"

"It's done," I said. "She's already on her way down."

"It'll take her an hour and a half to hike back. We have to go after her—"

"And what, tell her she *has* to come back?" I dropped my

voice to a whisper. "Yeah, that won't seem suspicious at all a few hours before you and I are kidnapped at gunpoint."

"How can you say that when it was your idea to—" Jesse wiped a hand down his face, cutting himself short, but it was too late, it was out there.

It was my idea to involve Claire.

Neither of us said anything for a long beat, staring at my failed attempt at a campfire. Finally, Jesse put an arm around me, pulling me closer to him. An olive branch, for subtly accusing me of screwing everything up by fighting with Claire.

He was right, though—it *was* my idea to invite Claire, to have her be a witness. Now, if no one believed we were kidnapped, it would be my fault. If Marian didn't think the ransom call was credible, if she didn't come up with the money, it would be my fault.

"Maybe it's better this way." Jesse took his arm back from me. He folded his hands together, leaned forward and rested his forehead on his interlocked thumbs. "She gets to spend the night in a warm bed. If she doesn't realize something's wrong until we don't call to get picked up tomorrow, we'll have more of a head start."

I did not want the extra few hours to escape; I wanted my grandmother to have to fork over a hundred thousand in exchange for her precious granddaughter.

I wanted to see her face when she realized she'd lost the money *and* me.

We lay in the tent, Jesse's body curved behind mine, our hands folded together over my belly. The temperature on the mountain had cooled as the sky darkened, but it was still too hot to climb inside our sleeping bags.

It was quiet enough in the tent to hear our heartbeats; outside, the only sound was the occasional snap of a branch, the footsteps of a chipmunk foraging for the bits of trail mix I'd left out for him.

Jesse rolled over, checked the time on his phone. 11:12. *One minute too late to make a wish,* I thought.

"Shouldn't they be here by now?" Jesse said.

"My cousin's never been on time for anything in his life," I answered.

And Mike . . . I didn't know if Mike, last name unknown, was a punctual person. All I knew about Mike the Mechanic was that Amos trusted him.

Now, with the minutes ticking past, doubt closed in on me. What if they weren't coming? I knew Amos would sell out most of his friends to Satan for a corn chip, but I was his *family*. He was one of the only other people who knew the truth about my father, and he'd promised to help me.

Would he really screw me over for three thousand dollars?

Jesse sat up straight. I followed, and that's when I heard it: arguing.

I yanked open the zipper to the tent at the same moment Amos yelled: "What the *fuck* happened?"

My brain went into overdrive: *Amos wasn't supposed to speak, what if Claire recognized his voice—*

He must know she's not here.

"What's going on?" I said, holding up the lantern, casting a yellow glow over Amos's face.

The look in his eyes was so wild that I wondered if he was on drugs. I tried to imagine my cousin doing something more serious than slipping a Xanax or smoking a joint. Mike stood to his side.

"What was she doing camping out in the middle of the damn woods?" Amos barked.

"What?" The blood drained from my head.

Some rustling in the tent behind me. Jesse stumbled out, eyes locked on Amos. "What are you talking about? Claire went back to the lake house."

"She was supposed to be *here*," Mike said.

His voice—a throaty growl—sent a chill to the tips of my toes. He grunted as he wriggled out of his backpack. With the hand not holding his gun, he rooted around inside the backpack, emerged with a bottle of vodka.

Mike winced as he lifted the sleeve of his T-shirt, prompting a gasp from me. Blood poured from an angry slash on his shoulder. He used his mouth to twist the cap off the vodka, then proceeded to pour the contents of the bottle onto his wound.

"How did that happen?" I asked.

Mike's gaze landed on me. "Your friend fuckin' stabbed me."

Amos stepped back into the glow of the lantern, holding a utility knife by the handle; my father kept one hooked to the side of all our hiking packs.

"Oh my God." I sank to the ground. "Oh my God—"

"Where is she now?" Jesse took a step toward Amos, his voice quaking.

"The real question is, why the hell are we still standing here having a coffee klatch?" Amos said. "We need to go *now*."

"What *the fuck did you do to her*?" Jesse reached for the collar of Amos's shirt—a yelp escaped me as Mike snapped, "Easy."

A clicking sound. The safety being released on Mike's gun, the barrel lifting so it was level with Jesse's chest. Jesse let go of Amos and took a step back, face ashen.

"She's alive," Mike finally said, with a resentful glance at Amos.

"I think she heard us talking on the trail," Amos says. "There's a chance she'll recognize that it was my voice when she wakes up and remembers."

I finally allowed myself to look Amos in the eyes. The anger simmering in them scared me more than the sight of Mike's gun, still trained on Jesse.

"Why did you let her leave?" Amos said, staring back at me.

I felt all their eyes on me, demanding answers I didn't have. Finally, Amos broke my gaze. "You really fucked up, Kat."

Silent, all of us, on the trek down the mountain. Amos leading the way, lifting the lantern in search of the red trail markers that would lead us to the parking lot where the Craigslist Camry was waiting.

Mike, at our rear, gun trained on Jesse and me, was panting. "Hold up."

I paused, turned to see Mike crouched, examining the wound on his shoulder in the scant light of the moon through the trees. My bandana, a makeshift tourniquet, did little to stem the flow of the blood from the stab wound. I pictured Claire driving the blade of the utility knife through his skin, his veins, all that biological evidence.

We'd need to make the knife disappear. Mike had agreed to play the role of kidnapper under two conditions: a ten-thousand dollar cut of the ransom money and zero evidence that could be traced back to him.

"Kat"—Jesse's fingers were on my shoulder, his voice a whisper by my ear—"we can't just leave her."

My blood flowed to a halt, my panic threatening to level me. Not only because if we gave up now we'd never get away—not from my father, not from what we'd done—but because while Jesse was concerned about Claire, alone and hurt in the woods, I could only think of what had happened to her with a clinical detachment. Her injuries, evidence that threatened to ruin everything.

There was something seriously wrong with me. Even now, when my best friend's life depended on it, all I could think about was my escape. *Our* escape.

I turned to Jesse, forced myself to speak through the tightening in my throat. "We'll go to jail."

"If she's hurt bad and we leave her, she could *die*—" Jesse hissed.

"Hey." Amos whipped around, training the lantern on Jesse and me. "Care to share with the rest of the class?"

"We're not allowed to talk to each other?" Jesse said, blinking against the light streaming in our eyes.

The snap of a twig beneath feet behind us; Mike was standing, coming toward us.

"You." He nodded to me. "Walk with me."

"Why?"

Mike looked from me to Jesse. "Because I don't fuckin' trust *him*."

Jesse stared at me, pleading. Anger surged through me. What did he expect me to say? What was I supposed to do with a gun pointed at me?

Finally, Jesse turned away from me, continued on the trail, between Amos and me and Mike. I felt my entire being crack in half.

Even if this *worked,* even if Jesse and I got away, it wouldn't matter; I had already lost him.

Amos and Mike had left the Camry parked in an overlook half a mile from the parking lot. The chill in the mountain air nipped at my arms. The backseat of the Camry was filled with Walmart bags of essentials that I'd snuck into my cart while picking up camping supplies. Uncooked pasta, trail mix, toothbrushes, three-dollar packages of white men's T-shirts and underwear. A starter kit for our new life. Amos would be able to bring us more food and provisions under the guise of a trip to Vermont in a few weeks to visit friends.

The farmhouse was waiting for us; Amos had already made the trip to Timsbury to secure it. Almost all our money—Jesse's money, mostly—was already gone, spent on the shitty old car and one month's rent.

When Amos was close enough to hear me whisper, I said, "The ransom call is too risky. What if Claire saw Mike's face?"

Amos's jaw, dotted with golden stubble, set. "You think Mike's gonna be cool with it if I say 'Hey, just kidding about that ten grand I promised'?"

I knew Amos was thinking about his own cut of the money. Forty-five grand. Peanuts, in comparison with what he stood to inherit someday if he'd managed to *not* commit to pissing Marian off as if it were a full-time job.

"You might still get the money someday," I said softly. "Maybe if you apologized."

Amos snorted, shook his head. "She doesn't make fake threats, Kat. That's why we're here."

"Can we speed this up?" Mike said from his post as sentry at the back of the Camry.

Amos looked at me, maybe as if he were considering hugging me, even though we'd never hugged once in our lives. Instead, he nodded to Jesse, alone in the car, his forehead resting on the steering wheel.

"Be careful," Amos said.

"Of *Jesse*?" I asked. "Why?"

Amos considered this for a beat before shrugging. "Guy obviously loves being a hero."

We arrived at the farmhouse just before dawn. It would be weeks, maybe months, before it would be safe enough for Amos to come by with the burner phones and fake identification he promised.

The plan was to stay in Timsbury for a year, until it was safe for us to venture into the world as new people. Until Amos found convincing Canadian passports that would get us across the northern border.

That was the plan, until Amos turned up on the front porch

of the farmhouse, banging on the door like his life depended on it.

"Mike's dead," he shouted through the door. "I can't go home. They're gonna talk to the guys Mike worked with and figure out I brought my car in and *he knew me.*"

The next morning, we found out that the FBI was searching for our bodies.

Before Mike called my grandmother's house and met my father at the quarry, he'd tossed Jesse's wallet, my bloodied bandana, and the knife into Blackstone Quarry. When my father handed the money over to Mike Dorsey, Mike would tell him Jesse and I were at the quarry, tied to a tree.

We don't know where that part of the plan went wrong. Maybe Mike's answer wasn't good enough for my father; maybe he refused to turn over the money until he saw me, had confirmation I was alive. The FBI thinks my father jumped in front of Mike's car, banged on the windshield to stop him from driving off.

It didn't matter what happened. Mike was dead. My father was as good as dead.

And, almost everyone agreed, Jesse and I were probably dead as well.

I think about something I read about myself, often.

Kat Marcotte could do anything. A quote from my volleyball coach to *People* magazine, in a story they ran in the weeks after the quarry crash.

She's right, I thought, folding the magazine and replacing it on the shelf at the grocery store I ventured to once a week. *I did it. We did. I escaped.*

But even Kat Marcotte can't come back from the dead.

PART FOUR

THE BORDER

CHAPTER TWENTY-FIVE

CLAIRE

NOW

When I wake, I'm being carried up a set of stairs. My feet collide with the bannister as Amos pivots sharply. The sound of a door hinge squealing, and then I'm falling, hitting the firm surface of a mattress. My skull feels like it's been split open.

I roll onto my side, groaning.

"Don't try to get up," Amos says.

I follow his voice; Amos is at the end of the bed, the gun in his hand pointed at me. I *know* it's Amos. I'd never forget his voice, but he still doesn't look like Amos—a full beard covers his face, and his hair is in a greasy bun at the nape of his neck.

A voice, soft from the corner of the room: "You really hurt her."

A dark-haired woman steps into view. We stare at each other for a bit before she sits at the foot of the bed opposite Amos.

I know it's her, but my brain is telling me it can't possibly *be* her. This girl's face is leaner, her freckles faded. Her hair is cut in a blunt bob, the ends jagged as if she'd done it herself.

I don't know what to say—*I thought you were dead* doesn't even scratch the surface of what is going on in my mind right now.

"How did you know we were here?" Kat asks quietly.

How did you know we were here? As if I've shown up to a party uninvited, as if everyone hasn't spent the past six months thinking Kat Marcotte is dead.

I lie back, my skull pulsing on the pillow below it.

Kat scoots closer to me, the bed creaking beneath her weight.

"Amos," she says. "Go get her ice."

"What?" Amos asks.

"*Ice.* For her head."

Amos stands. The suddenness of the motion makes me flinch. He leaves the room, shutting the door behind him.

Kat sits at the edge of the bed. "Does anyone else know you're here?"

"My roommate," I lie.

"What's your roommate's name?"

"Alexis," I say. "I told her I was coming here."

We just stare at each other for a beat; I wait for the falling sensation, to be yanked out of the nightmare and wake up in my bed in a cold sweat, thinking, *What a wild-ass dream.*

"I thought you were dead," I whisper. "*Everyone* thinks you're dead."

Kat averts her eyes, says nothing. What is there to say?

Anger floods me, the past six months coming back in a gut punch. Everything I've lost—my privacy, my friends, my happiness—and everything I risked to find out what happened to her.

My life was torn apart while she was doing what? Playing house in the woods with her cousin?

Why? How?

And where the fuck is Jesse?

My voice trembles when I finally collect it and say, "Is Jesse alive?"

"Of course he is," Kat says. She stands, her expression

darkening. She moves to the other side of the doorway, her hand lingering on the knob.

"We both know he's the only reason you've come all this way," she says, slamming the door shut so hard my brain rattles inside my skull.

CHAPTER TWENTY-SIX

KAT

—

NOW

Obviously, I have been imagining a situation like this for months—everything grinding to a halt because someone has figured out we're alive. In my head, it's the woman who works at the country store, the one whose eyes linger on me sometimes as if there's something she'd like to ask me.

Six months—we made it *six months* without anyone finding us or recognizing us. I have worked my goddamn ass off so we can stay here undetected—I've memorized every business in town with a security camera so we can avoid having our likenesses captured.

How? How? How?

It obviously was not me, because I do not make mistakes.

It sounds arrogant, but it's not a quality I would wish on anyone. I don't make mistakes because I *can't*. Shoes left in the hall? I'd be hearing about my thoughtlessness for a week. Didn't hear my father when he said dinner was ready? My laptop would be thrown into the wall, the essay I'd been working on lost to the ether.

I did not make a mistake here. Yes, I let Claire turn around. But I never looked back—I left *nothing* behind to explain how she wound up in Timsbury, New York.

Amos is waiting in the hall, listening, obviously ignoring my directive to get Claire ice. I grab him by the arm and shove him through the doorway to his bedroom. "How did she find us?"

Amos scowls, crosses to his dresser. "Why are you asking me?"

"Because you screwed up," I snap.

"Bold of you to assume it was me." He swaps his gun for a half-drunk bottle of Jack Daniels from his dresser and unscrews the top.

"So you're saying it was either me or Jesse?"

"I'm saying I don't know what the fuck happened." Amos plops down on his bed. The room smells of wet skunk, an unwashed pile of clothes in the corner and a string of empty liquor bottles lined up on the windowsill.

Amos has been drinking more than usual the past few months. At first, I thought it was the guilt of what happened to Mike and my father driving him to numb himself. But then, he started disappearing for a day or two at a time, only to return with more cash and more booze. I shook him down and got him to admit he'd been making the trip to Burlington to sell to some of his old contacts.

He swore he was being careful, that none of them even knew his real name, that they were the type of people who would never talk to the police. Amos was known only as "Devin," the name on his fake driver's license. Thanks to Devin and his connections in Burlington, we have an assortment of fake IDs, and more cash flowing in, even if most of it goes to the liquor store in town.

I drag my hands down my face. "What are we going to do?"

"I mean, it's obvious," Amos says. "We have to kill her."

"Be serious, Amos," I snap.

Amos's eyebrows knit together. He frowns, not breaking my gaze. It makes my stomach drop.

"No," I say. "Absolutely not."

Amos's eyebrows shoot up. "Then we just let her go and wait for the cops to roll in?"

"I can try to talk to her," I say. "She doesn't know anything."

Amos lowers the bottle of booze from his mouth. "What do you mean?"

I sit on the edge of Amos's bed. "I never told her about my dad."

"Okay." Amos blinks at me. He opens his top drawer and begins to paw through the contents. "So let me get this straight. Mike almost killed her, you made her think you were dead, and she has no idea why. Yet you think if we let her go she's going to keep what happened here a *secret*?"

"*Nothing* would have happened if you hadn't hit her with a shovel."

"She'd already found us!" Amos drops his voice. "Do you want to go to prison? Because once we get caught and your teary *Dateline* special is over, we're going down for extorting Marian. Maybe manslaughter, if they can pin what happened to Mike and your father on us."

I drop my hands from my face and look at Amos. "What? We didn't make Mike run my dad over."

Amos snorts. "Felony murder rule, look it up."

The word *murder* sets off a snare of fear in me. With nothing to do over the past six months, I have had a lot of time to replay what happened on the mountain, to picture the aggrieved way Mike glanced at Amos when he said that Claire was alive.

I'd assumed Amos had been the one to convince Mike not to kill Claire after they encountered her on the trail; Amos had said Mike had panicked when he saw her cowering behind the rock, had decided to run after her after she took off, terrified and screaming.

But sometimes I wonder if the look Mike gave Amos was more reproachful; as if he'd had to convince Amos to leave

Claire alive. After all, Amos had been the one who sounded so worried that Claire might have recognized his voice—so worried, in fact, he made the completely dumbass move of going to the lake house to talk to Claire, to see for himself what she remembered—

"You're not touching her," I say.

From his dresser drawer, Amos produces something that looks like a nicotine patch. He holds it up for me between two fingers. "You know what this is?"

"I don't feel like playing guessing games, Amos."

"It's a fentanyl patch." Amos sticks it in my face. "Get some booze in her, slip this on while she's passed out, and *bam,* overdose."

I swallow, my eyes on the Saran Wrapped square of plastic. "No."

Amos's eyes, bloodshot, oscillate like he didn't even hear me. "We can ditch her car and body near her school. Who wouldn't believe she was so fucked up over what happened to her that she decided to, you know—"

"*No.*"

Amos slaps the fentanyl patch on the top of his dresser so hard that the mirror on the wall above it rattles. "Then what do we do, Kat? Keep her locked in that room forever like Elizabeth Smart or some shit?"

"*Amos.* I'll figure something out." That pulsing behind my eye is back, right below my eyebrow scar.

"You'd better figure it out before Jesse gets home," Amos says, before crossing through the doorway, leaving me alone in his room. "Once he knows she's here, he's gonna absolutely lose it."

CHAPTER TWENTY-SEVEN

CLAIRE

NOW

They are arguing outside my door. I catch a single phrase—*screwed up*—before their voices fade out of earshot.

Where are they going? Panic zips through me as I scramble off the bed. I pause, hand on the doorknob. There are two of them, plus a gun. My keys and phone are in my coat, which did not make it into the bedroom with me. I have no idea where they put my stuff or my boots. I could not outrun Kat Marcotte on a good day, let alone after a shovel whack to the skull.

A punch of disorientation nearly knocks me back onto the bed. It's *Kat* in the next room. Kat took my keys and phone and any means of escaping this house.

My best friend, who was always coming to my rescue when I was drunk and needed a ride home or on the verge of being picked last for kickball in gym. The girl in the next room is *not* Kat, and she is definitely not my friend right now.

Something primal rises in me, stomping out my instinct to survive, escape.

I ball my hand into a fist and bang on the wall separating me from Kat's and Amos's panicked murmuring. The voices on the other side quiet; I bang again, harder. "Kat!" I scream. "Don't fucking *hide from me—*"

The bedroom door slams open, jolting me backward.

"What the hell are you doing?" Amos shouts, bursting into the room.

I look at his empty hands. A single thought cracks through my brain: *no gun.*

I charge at him, knock him into the dresser. Amos's arms fly up, reaching for me. I'm stepping over him when Kat shouts my name.

She blocks my escape through the doorway. When she grabs my arm, something snaps in me.

I want to hurt her. I grab a handful of her hair and pull until she's struggling beneath me like a cat. Amos darts out of the room and I know I should run but I can't break my grip on Kat's hair—

"*Claire*— Ow, *stop!*"

She's clawing at me; I yank her hair until she falls to her knees, smashing her face into the edge of the dresser. Kat cries out in pain as Amos snarls: "Don't. Move."

The barrel of a gun is inches from my face.

"Now"—he pants at Kat—"can we restrain her?"

"What the hell is going on?"

The voice makes all the fight leave my body. I release Kat and stare at Jesse.

He doesn't cross the threshold into the bedroom. He stares at Kat, her bloody face, before his gaze sweeps downward, coming to rest on me.

His lips part. A tear leaks from my eye, but I don't move to wipe it away.

Jesse crouches at my side. "Hey. Are you okay?"

Hey? I shrug Jesse's hand off my shoulder. "Do I look okay?"

Jesse stares at Amos, murder in his eyes. "What is wrong with you? Put that *down.*"

Next to me, Kat speaks. "I think she broke my nose."

"I didn't break anything," I say.

Jesse gapes at Kat. "What the hell happened?"

Kat wipes a smear of blood from her upper lip with her thumb. "Can we talk about this not in front of her?"

"No. You can talk about it right here." My voice is adrenaline warbled.

"Claire, how did you find us?" Jesse asks.

Kat sits on the edge of the bed. She wipes her nose with the collar of her shirt. "Amos, I'm guessing."

"Yes," I say. "Amos."

From where he's leaning against the wall, Amos says, "I don't know what the fuck she's talking about."

The look on Jesse's face says he has a lot of things he would like to call Amos. Decides he'd better not as long as Amos is still holding the gun.

"Jesse, Amos," Kat says. "Can we please talk in private?"

Jesse is still looking at me. He hesitates before standing up. My gaze moves to the window.

"Hey." Amos points at me. "That's a thirty-foot drop. Don't get any stupid ideas."

"I'll be right back," Jesse says to me.

"And *what*?" I snap. "We can *catch up*?"

In the doorway, Kat is staring at me with a look I can't decipher. Once Jesse and Amos step around her, she closes the door, shutting me in.

I bolt after them, jangle the doorknob, and yell, "Jesse—don't do this."

When there's no response, I ball up my fist and bang. *"JESSE—"*

On the other side of the door, the gun goes off.

CHAPTER TWENTY-EIGHT

KAT

NOW

Amos stands over the hole he just put in the floor, the gun still smoking at his side.

Jesse's body is flush against the wall. His eyes are wild as they move from Amos to the bullet hole.

"What the *hell* is wrong with you?" I shout.

Amos shrugs. "She's quiet."

"You put a bullet hole in the floor!"

Amos clicks the safety on the gun back into place. "I'm not sure our security deposit is the highest order of concern right now."

I glance at Jesse. His face has taken on a ghastly hue and he's still practically hugging the wall.

I lick my lip. The taste of my blood, coupled with the pain behind my eyes, makes me gag. I step into the bathroom across the hall, listening to Jesse and Amos argue as I run the tap in the sink.

"What if someone heard the gunshot?" Jesse says.

Amos snorts. "Yeah, I'm sure the family of deer outside are calling the cops right now."

I open the vanity doors, root around for a washcloth. Amos is the only one who uses this bathroom. There are no towels or washcloths up here; I'm not surprised. Judging by the smell and look of him, the last time Amos showered was probably around New Year's. I close the vanity doors and turn the tap off.

I step back into the hall and nod at Amos's gun. "Give me the bullets."

"What? Why?" he says.

"So you don't use them, obviously."

There's something unsettling about the look Amos gives me. He's been drinking, yes, but he does that every day. It's not like there's much else for him to do around here.

For the first time, I can see that he doesn't trust me.

I drop my voice to a whisper. "We obviously don't agree on how to handle this situation. Until we figure it out, I'd rather you didn't go around shooting things. Claire doesn't need to know it's not loaded."

Amos holds my gaze as he raises the gun. Releases the clip of bullets and hands it to me.

I slip the clip in my pocket and head downstairs. On the last step, it occurs to me that Jesse still hasn't asked if I'm okay.

I'm holding a hand towel to my nose, the water in the sink running pink from the blood I've washed away. *I really should clean this sink,* I think.

My mother would gag at the sight of this bathroom. This whole house would make her skin crawl.

Our landlord is a busted-looking old man who only comes by once a month to collect his fifteen hundred dollars cash and complain about his arthritis. I hang out upstairs when he's here, because he gives me the creeps. Once, when Amos went to see friends in Burlington and didn't come back for nearly two days, Jesse had to greet him and give him the rent. But the landlord brags about not having cable—hasn't had it in twenty years—so I feel confident he has no idea who we are.

I rinse the hand towel again, run the tap until the water turns hot. I hold it to my nose and catch a glimpse of myself in the mirror. My eyebrow area is already turning brownish purple, and I am reminded of another big, *huge* problem.

I'm supposed to babysit the Dolan girls tonight.

The Dolans live in the nearest house; each morning I make the half-mile walk there before Mrs. Dolan leaves for work to give her two girls breakfast and put them on the school bus. At three p.m. I return to collect them and entertain them for forty-five minutes until Mrs. Dolan returns with a twenty-dollar bill for me. If you add in the time it takes me to walk to her house, I'm paid less than ten dollars an hour.

But, obviously, we need the money.

Tonight, Mrs. Dolan asked me to babysit from seven to ten, for fifty bucks. *I'm just grabbing dinner with a friend,* she'd said, which means she's going on a date.

Anyway, I almost had a stroke when she offered fifty bucks, thinking of the dwindling pile of cash in my suitcase in the farmhouse. Almost all the cash cobbled together before we left went to the car and the first month's rent.

We were *supposed* to have a hundred thousand dollars, split among us. Forty-five thousand each for me and Jesse, and Amos; ten thousand to Mike Dorsey. It would have been enough to hide out in the farmhouse for however long it took to get Canadian passports, and find a place to stay across the border.

Amos promised that he knew a guy who could deliver. He could get real passports, even—it would just cost several grand. Several grand it would take us months to save up, even with Jesse working now, driving a snowplow truck.

The point is, we need that fifty bucks. The money Jesse makes barely covers our expenses; I suspect that Amos is raking in a lot more during his trips to Burlington than his share of the rent that he dutifully forks over every month, but I can't come out and accuse him of holding out on us when he's not even supposed to *be* here with us. He was supposed to take his share of the ransom money and disappear on a yacht to the Caribbean or whatever.

The money hardly matters now, and in any case, I can't go babysit the Dolan girls and act like everything is normal while Jesse and Amos hold Claire prisoner here. I certainly can't do it with a black eye.

But if I cancel, lie that I'm sick, there's the chance Mrs. Dolan will drive by the house to spy on me. . . .

There's a grimy basket of old Mary Kay cosmetics under the sink, next to all the cleaning products and my tampons. I haven't dared throw away the makeup in case it belongs to our landlord's dead wife—his favorite topic of conversation, according to Amos. I paw through the detritus until I find a crusted tube of concealer.

I'm using my finger to dab the makeup over my bruise when I hear the bedroom door. I step out of the bathroom, heart hammering, as Jesse plops down on the edge of the bed. He hooks a hand over the back of his neck; we're the ones who are supposed to be dead, but he looked at Claire on the floor of that bedroom as if he'd seen a ghost.

I sit beside him, take his hand, and weave my fingers through his. He returns my tight grip.

"We have to leave," he says. "Find somewhere else, fast."

"We can't." The throbbing behind my eyes grows; I hold two fingers to my brow bone, picture the scar my hair still does not completely grow over. It's so small, but such an easy way to identify me. "We won't find somewhere new in time."

We'd had to be sure none of the communication could be traced to us, which meant Amos had to handle everything. He rotated between different libraries, coffee shops with internet. Always on a burner phone. It was much harder than I antici-pated to find an owner who was willing to forgo a background check.

We got lucky with this farmhouse, with the landlord who

doesn't ask questions and knocks a hundred bucks off the rent for all the work Amos and Jesse do to maintain the property.

I clutch Jesse's hand harder. "Even if we found a place to stay, *everyone* will be looking for us."

I study Jesse, watch his throat muscles tighten, his shoulders tense. "We can't go back."

Hearing him say it makes my insides go cold. What did I expect? For him to lie and say it'll all be okay if we turn ourselves in—that everyone will forgive the extortion thing, all those searchers whose lives we put at risk on the mountain will give us a pass if I cry and say that I did it because my father was an asshole and my grandmother made me break up with my boyfriend?

And what about what we've done to Claire? Amos just *assaulted* her, and I'm pretty sure we've crossed into unlawful imprisonment at this point. . . .

But he's gone.

My father is dead. My grandmother had been willing to pay to get me back; she would probably spend her entire fortune in lawyers if it meant she could get *both* her missing grandchildren back, to keep the Marcotte name from becoming a public disgrace.

He was the only thing she wouldn't, couldn't protect me from. And now he's gone.

Jesse extracts his hand from mine. Sighs and leans forward, face in his palms. "How did this happen?"

"Amos must have messed up," I say. "Maybe he talked to someone at home, or maybe he even went back there one of the times he said he was in Vermont."

Jesse is still hiding his face. An ugly thought rises to the surface of my brain: Maybe I am not the only one who has had doubts about our living arrangement. Maybe he's weak, and he slipped up. . . .

No, there's no way. Jesse has as much to lose as Amos and me if we get caught. He hated the idea of extorting Marian, but he agreed to let Amos and Mike go through with it because he knew we needed the cash.

Jesse is in this as deep as Amos and I are. There's *no way* he secretly reached out to Claire over the past six months or left some clue behind that led her here.

I move my hand from Jesse's back to his thigh, feeling him tense under my touch. Lately, it feels like this is his natural reaction to me.

Something is wrong. Beyond the obvious—that everything has gone horribly wrong, and our life here isn't what we pictured it would be. We are always tired, always stressed, wondering if we will ever save enough to get the Canadian passports and disappear north.

I knew our new life would not be a fairy tale, but it wasn't supposed to be like this. Anger builds in me, all the things I've wanted to say to Jesse the past few months rising up in my throat. I'm tired of making the decisions, of being the one in control. I need him to give me a sign, to say or do *something* that will convince me our life here is worth fighting for.

Worth *killing* for.

All I can manage is "Is this about Claire?"

"What are you talking about?" he asks.

"The reason you're holding back from me," I say.

I thought I was imagining it at first, the way Jesse's hands never seemed to move below my hips anymore. He was always too tired, too worried, until I eventually grew sick of how desperate I must have come across. Every night when he comes to bed, he curls up behind me, arms around my waist, pulling me to him like a life raft.

Like he needs me, but no longer wants me.

And now, I'm running out of time to find out why.

"Don't deny it," I whisper. "You've never let her go, have you?"

"It's not that." Jesse almost seems as surprised as I am by his answer. "It's not about Claire."

"Then what *is it*?"

Jesse looks at me. "If they'd never come between us, do you think we'd still be together?"

"What kind of question is that? Of course we would be—we talked about staying together when I left for college—"

"I know we talked about it, but how could you be sure? How could you know that once you got to college you wouldn't have met some guy you had more in common with? How do you know you wouldn't have changed your mind and left me behind?"

My stomach sinks. He'd said this wasn't about Claire, but it has to be. Jesse can only be thinking about what happened on the mountain. How I'd failed the most important test when everything had gone wrong.

Because even though Claire was hurt, lost, and alone, all I could think about was the plan, and what happened if everything had been ruined. About what it meant if I couldn't escape.

He wants to know if I'd do the same to him.

"Kat," he says. "How do you know?"

"I can't know," I whisper. "I never got the chance to find out. We could have turned into different people, for all I know."

"What do you mean?"

"That it's naïve to say you'll always love someone when you don't know what the future holds. People can change—"

"Yeah, but feelings don't." Jesse's face falls. "You're saying you're not one hundred percent sure your feelings for me will never change."

I stare back at him. "And you *are*?"

"Of course I am."

The look in his eyes does nothing to quiet the jackhammering in my chest. Months ago, I would have found such a declaration romantic. Now, there's only doubt. What is he trying to convince himself of? That he made the right choice when I told him not to go after Claire on the mountain? Does he need to know how sure I am about him because, if not, he'll wish he hadn't stayed with me at that campsite?

Amos's voice snakes its way back into my head, the thing he said to me at the quarry, before we got in the Camry and drove away from our lives. *Guy obviously loves being a hero.*

Every day for the past six months, I've puzzled over those words. I've had to wonder if Amos was right; if Jesse would do things differently if he got a second chance. If he'd save Claire instead of me. The only comfort was that I knew he wouldn't get the opportunity.

What happened on the mountain happened. We got away.

Jesse wasn't supposed to get a second chance to turn back.

CHAPTER TWENTY-NINE

CLAIRE

NOW

The bedroom door opens, making my heart ricochet from my chest to my throat. Amos wanders in, a bottle of Jack Daniels tucked under his arm. He's put on some weight in the past six months and lost some of his tan.

"Where's Kat?" I ask.

"In the shower," Amos says. "Washing away the shame of getting her ass kicked."

"I didn't kick her ass," I mutter.

Amos twists the cap off his Jack. "Oh, you totally did. It almost made me pop a boner."

My cheeks fill with heat. Amos takes a swig from the bottle and offers it to me.

If it weren't for the gun in his other hand, I would grab the bottle and break it over his head. "What the hell is wrong with you?"

Amos shrugs. "A combination of poor parenting and generational entitlement."

I wish it had been his face I'd slammed into the dresser. Amos sits on the squat wooden chest in the corner of the room, eyeing me over his bottle of Jack.

"All of that shit at the lake house—you being decent to me," I say. "You just wanted to find out what I knew. What I remembered."

Amos stands. I recoil as he steps toward me; he grabs a pillow from the bed and settles back onto the chest against the wall, stuffing the pillow behind his back. "Gotta hand it to you. It's impressive you found this place. I don't know why Kat thinks you're so stupid."

I swallow the sting of rage. "You were there. On the mountain."

"So you remember, then," Amos says, considering the label of his bottle. "That's impressive. I thought for sure you were done when Mike yeeted you into that tree."

I consider my options; if I tell the truth, that I still don't remember everything that happened, Amos might view me as less of a threat.

But pretending that I *do* remember might be my only chance at finding out, after all this time, what really went down on that mountain. And something tells me that no matter what, Amos is not going to let me leave this house.

I command my head into a weak nod. "Why did they want me there?" I ask.

"They wanted a witness." Amos wipes his mouth with the back of his hand. "If you told everyone a man with a gun took Kat away in the middle of the night, Marian might be more inclined to fork over the money to get her back. See, my grandmother may be a bitch, but she's as smart as she is cheap. We needed her to think from the beginning something bad had happened and Kat and Jesse hadn't just run away."

"You said *take Kat away*. What was supposed to happen to Jesse?"

"Jesse was going to be shot and thrown over the mountain during the kidnapping for trying to intercede," Amos says. "At least, *you* and your boyfriend were supposed to think that's what happened. Mike was gonna wave his gun around and demand you all stay in your tents. Jesse, of course, would ignore him and go to save Kat and then *bang*." Amos makes a gun out of his fingers.

I stare at Amos. "And you thought I would just believe all of it was real?"

Amos shrugs, his expression dark. "You'd know the gunshot was real."

A creak on the floorboards outside the bedroom makes Amos lower the bottle from his mouth. Jesse steps into the room.

"Get out, Amos," he says.

"Uh, no, *Jeremy*," Amos says.

Jesse sits at the edge of the bed. There's something different about him—beyond the short haircut and the bulk he's added to his arms. There's a forcefulness in his voice I've never heard before.

"I've got first watch," Amos says.

Jesse's face turns scarlet. "I'm not leaving you alone with her."

"Well, I'd be stupid to leave *you* alone with her," Amos says.

"Guess neither one of us is leaving, then," Jesse answers.

"Guess so."

Jesse and I stare at each other for a bit before I say, "I hate your haircut."

"I like yours," he says back.

I glare at him. "Why the hell did he call you Jeremy?"

Jesse's face flushes. Oh. That's the name he's been going by.

I turn on my side and draw the comforter up over me. Stare at the wall.

"Claire," Jesse says softly. "Please talk to me."

"I have nothing to say to you."

"Then think of something. Even if it's telling me how much you hate me."

I raise myself up just enough to support my weight on my elbow. "You really want to know what I'd like to say to you?"

Jesse swallows. "I'm sure I deserve whatever it is."

"I think your mother would be disgusted with you."

Jesse's jaw goes rigid. In the corner, Amos lets out a seal bark of a laugh and says, "Shit, that was cold."

I roll onto my other side, facing the wall, my heartbeat quadrupling in pace.

Jesse's voice is quiet when he finally speaks. "I'm sorry. For everything."

I yank the bedspread up to my chin, breathing through my mouth to avoid its musty smell. "Mike could have killed me."

"You weren't supposed to get hurt," Jesse says. "You weren't supposed to be there, on the trail, on the way down. We thought you made it back to the lake house."

I clench my jaw so tight it feels like my molars might shatter. "So it's my fault?"

"No—that's not what I meant, obviously." Jesse shifts on the bed next to me. "I don't know what Kat and Amos have told you, but we didn't do it for the money."

"I don't care why you did it," I say, even though it's a lie. I just want to use every tool I have to hurt Jesse.

"Her dad was abusive," Jesse finally says. "It got to a breaking point, and when Kat asked her grandma for help, she told her she wouldn't pay for her to go to BC unless she broke up with me."

The pounding between my eyes reaches a crescendo. I don't know if I'd be able to process what Jesse's saying even if Amos hadn't beamed me in the head with a shovel. "Back up," I say. "Her dad abused her?"

It's Amos who responds. "You really didn't have any idea?"

When I turn to face him, he's frowning, the Jack Daniels bottle wedged between his legs. The look on his face makes my mouth go dry.

"How did he abuse her?" I ask. "Like . . . sexually?"

"You watch too much TV," Amos says.

"Then what did he do to her?" I catch Jesse's eyes. I wonder if any answer will be good enough for me; if there's anything Kat's father could have done to her to justify any of this.

Jesse breaks my gaze. In the corner, Amos fiddles with something from his pocket: a cigarette lighter.

"Why wouldn't she tell me?" I demand, when their silence becomes too infuriating to sit with anymore. "If her father was abusive, why wouldn't she tell her best friend?"

"She never said anything to me either," Jesse says softly. "Not until she was forced to."

"No one had to tell me," Amos says. "I saw for myself."

I'm quiet as I rewind through thirteen years of memories of Mr. Marcotte. Yes, he was hard on Kat.

"Once when we were kids, we were fucking around, playing with her dad's stuff," Amos says, turning over the lighter in his hand. "He had this engraved cigar torch I was obsessed with. He caught me playing with it and picked me and Kat up by the backs of our shirts. Dragged us outside and held me over the deck railing. He stuck the flame right in my face. Kept saying, *You want to see what fire does to the body?*"

Amos sets his lighter down, looking at neither Jesse nor me.

My stomach turns over; if that's what Mr. Marcotte was willing to do to his nephew, what was Kat's punishment? "But if he was that bad, why didn't she tell anyone years ago?" I ask. "We could have gotten child protective services involved—"

Amos laughs. "Do you know how hard it is to get a kid taken away from their family? Especially when it's a family with money and everyone in it is either in denial, like my aunt Beth, or an extremely skilled liar, like my grandmother."

"She *knew*?" I stare at Amos. "She knew Kat was being abused and didn't do anything?"

Amos snorts. "My grandmother's been covering for his ass since he was in diapers. Why do you think no one knows the real reason Johnny left the air force?"

Real reason? "I thought he retired," I say.

"He was *forced* to retire. He was such a nightmare that his subordinates threatened to sue for harassment. They got rid of him quietly before it could become a whole thing."

I glance over at Jesse for confirmation. He's studying his hands, folded together, thumbs hugging, almost as if he's praying. A crush of fear hits me that's so powerful, it wipes my mind of everything: Mr. Marcotte, Marian, Kat, what they did to me.

I need to get the fuck out of here.

"What are you guys going to do with me?" I ask.

Amos lowers the bottle so it's resting on his kneecap. "We haven't decided yet."

"What are you waiting for? People could be looking for me."

"But they aren't," Amos says. "Not yet. I checked your phone—your parents think you're at school."

"Where is Kat?" I ask.

"She had to go do something," Amos says. "She'll be back soon."

"Are you sure about that?" I say.

This prompts Jesse to break his silence. "What do you mean?"

I shrug. "She obviously doesn't care who she screws over to get away."

I turn to face the wall, pulling the blanket over my body. Before I do, I see the worry flickering in Jesse's eyes.

They're watching me in shifts. I don't know what they think I'll do if I'm left alone up here; jump thirty feet out the window onto packed snow and ice, breaking every bone in my body?

Amos, Jesse, Amos, Jesse, Amos. I get the sense he never strays far from this room.

The sky is deep indigo and shot through with gray clouds when Jesse opens the door. He's holding a TV dinner, steam rising from the surface.

"'Bout time," Amos says. "I gotta piss."

Jesse's gaze doesn't move from me as Amos gets up, cracks his shoulder. He plods out of the room, across the hall, closing neither the bedroom door nor the bathroom door behind him. When Jesse finally speaks, it's over the rushing sound of Amos peeing.

"You hungry?"

"I'm not eating that."

"They're actually not bad," Jesse says. "We've kind of been living off them."

"I'm not worried about the taste."

"You think I did something to it?" Jesse gapes at me. "Come on, Claire."

"You left me for dead on that mountain."

"I wanted to go back for you. Make sure you were okay. Mike and Amos—" Jesse throws a glance over his shoulder. Across the hall, the toilet flushes. "He's out of his mind."

"You expect me to believe Amos is the ringleader here?"

"What's that supposed to mean?"

"Kat is the only one of you who's smart enough to pull all of this off."

Jesse looks down at his hands. "I know that."

I stare at him, anger rising higher in me with each second he spends staring at his goddamn hands. "You think what you did is okay, because it's what she wanted? What you did to *me* is okay?"

"It's not what she wanted—we didn't have a choice."

"That's bullshit." I sit up. "You could have waited until she turned eighteen and her family couldn't tell her what to do anymore."

"It wouldn't have mattered as long as her dad was in the picture." Jesse massages his eyelids with the heels of his hands. "Claire, you have no idea who he really was. The things he did."

Jesse's voice cracks. He lowers his hands, finally looks me

in the eye. "He was a monster, Claire. The world is better off without him."

"How do you know that's not all Kat ever wanted?" I ask. "To get rid of him and have his blood on someone else's hands?"

"That's not what she wanted," Jesse says.

"How do you know?"

"Because I know *her*."

The implication is clear: Jesse knows Kat, and I never did. And she's changed Jesse, or maybe I never knew him, either.

"Five years old," I say. "She and I have been friends since we were *five years old* and she was willing to let me die to get what she wanted. If you think she won't do the same to you, you're an idiot."

Jesse presses his fingers together, tents his hands over his mouth. Stares at the wall. "Then I guess I have to hope she never stops wanting me."

"I'm glad that's your answer," I say, rolling over to face the wall.

"Why?"

"Because now I can finally get over you."

CHAPTER THIRTY

KAT

NOW

The Dolans think that my name is Kaylee Brewer, which matches the name on the driver's license Amos got for me in Burlington. The New York State hologram is too detailed to be fake; I asked Amos where the real Kaylee Brewer is and whether she'll be missing her driver's license, and he snorted and said she was a friend of a friend who died of an overdose years ago.

Not that it matters. Mrs. Dolan and I never speak for more than five minutes at a time. She hasn't strayed from her favorite topics (how smart Ellie is, what a scumbag the girls' father is) long enough to inquire where I go to college, let alone ask to see my ID.

"You're a lifesaver," Mrs. Dolan says when she opens the door. "I can't thank you enough for doing this."

Her gaze moves from me to the girls, who are barreling toward me screaming *KayleeKayleeKaylee*. Maddy throws her arms around me, her hard little shoulder smushing against my still-tender nose until my eyes water.

Mrs. Dolan reaches into her wallet as I'm hanging my coat in the hall. "I'll leave you guys cash for pizza?"

The girls peel themselves off me and change their chant to *pizzapizzapizza!* Mrs. Dolan shouts that I can text her anytime and disappears so fast there's no doubt she's off to get laid.

I can do this, I think, letting Maddy tug my hand and guide me into the kitchen. It's just a few hours away. Amos will never do anything to Claire with Jesse around.

After dinner, I suggest a movie, because it might keep the girls quiet long enough for me to think of a way out of the situation with Claire. Ellie says she wants to watch *Toy Story,* which sends Maddy into a full-on meltdown because she doesn't want to watch *that*.

"What do you want to watch?" I ask, patience thinning.

She sniffles, wiping her nose with the collar of her Elsa pajamas. "I don't *know.*"

"There are more movies in the family room," Ellie says. "*Finding Nemo* is upstairs. She likes that one."

I feel a rush of gratitude for Ellie, followed by sadness. I see it every day, how adept she is at managing her sister. It's a role she didn't ask for, and one she'll be stuck with the rest of her life.

Pick up your toys, or Daddy will get mad. Don't interrupt him while he's on the phone. And don't ever, ever tell him not to yell at Mommy.

By the time I get upstairs to the family room, I'm shaking so violently from nerves that I have to sit. I collapse into the desk chair, bury my head in my lap.

I'm not a murderer. But if I go home, they'll call me one. For what happened to Mike, what happened to my father.

I will go to jail. Because now, Claire knows everything.

Downstairs, Maddy shrieks. It's a piercing, awful sound, like an animal in distress. And then: "Ellie, that's MY SODA!"

I sit up, blink away the bright spots swarming my vision.

"I'll be right there," I yell down to the girls, swiveling in the desk chair to face the computer.

Mrs. Dolan told me the password to the computer, in case I ever needed to use it. *EleanorNoelle,* in case she wasn't obvious enough about her feelings toward her kids.

I gnaw the inside of my cheek until I taste blood; when the internet browser finishes loading, I search, *fentanyl overdose.*

Mrs. Dolan promised she'd be back by ten, but it's a quarter after when the front door lock stirs. Maddy is asleep, her head on my lap, a finger hooked in her mouth. Ellie is curled into the opposite end of the living room couch, her chest rising and falling steadily under the shirt of her poop emoji pajamas.

Footsteps behind the couch; Mrs. Dolan comes into view, unbuttoning her coat. She surveys the scene in front of her and smiles, puts a hand to her chest. *Awww.*

I wriggle from under Maddy, laying her strawberry-blond head gently on the couch cushion, and follow Mrs. Dolan into the kitchen.

"Did you have a good time?" I whisper, because I don't have anything else to say to her.

"Oh, it was fine," she says, stripping off her coat. "Were they monsters?"

"They were great," I say.

Ellie and Maddie were so awful, I thought about calling and turning myself in to the FBI just to get away from them. But now, watching Mrs. Dolan shake the dusting of snow from her scarf, I feel a bone-deep sadness.

I will probably never see her and the girls again. I won't step through that door Monday morning and have Maddy come flying at me, chin covered with Lucky Charms grime, shrieking that she needs help finishing her homework before the bus comes.

"Won't you let me drive you home?" Mrs. Dolan looks me

up and down. I reach for my coat, breaking eye contact before her gaze can settle on the concealer botch-job over my eye. "I already texted my brother to pick me up. Thank you, though."

Mrs. Dolan spotted Amos once, leaving our driveway. I told her we're twins, and she asked if he shovels driveways. I only ever bring him up to get her to stop offering to drive me home.

She frowns and for a moment I think she's going to say something like *Is it just you and your brother in that house?* Instead, she opens her wallet and hands me a crisp fifty.

"Get home safely, Kaylee."

The lights in the farmhouse are off; the sight puts a pit in my stomach. I lock the front door behind me, stomp the snow off my shoes, and cringe at the skunky smell of marijuana.

Amos is seated at the dining room table. In front of him is a bottle of Diet Coke, a bottle of Jack Daniels, and two glasses.

"Are you expecting someone?" I ask.

Amos tilts his head back and blows out a smoke ring. "Have a drink with me, Katherine."

"Where are they?" I ask.

"Claire is asleep, or pretending to be. Jesse is stationed outside the door." Amos tosses something onto the dining room table as I sit across from him. Claire's phone.

"It's been quite illuminating," Amos says, pouring several inches of whiskey into one of the empty glasses. He knocks it back as I reach for the phone.

"She gave you her passcode?" I ask.

"She doesn't have one. Some people have no sense of self-preservation."

The pit in my stomach widens as Amos pours another glass of whiskey. Almost as an afterthought, he adds some to the glass next to it. He pushes it toward me. "She's been talking to my ex. They traced the IP address from the burner I've been using to look at Zoe's blog."

I can't speak. That he would do something so stupid—that he can sit here and tell me about it without a trace of shame—makes me want to grab the glass on the table and slam it against the wall.

I inhale deeply. "You told me you covered your tracks. Is there anything else I should know about?"

Amos sips his drink, his eyes never meeting mine. I shut my eyes, think of every step, every precaution we took. Amos had gotten rid of the burner he'd lent me—I was so paranoid about being seen ditching it, worried that even if I chucked the phone into the bay in the middle of the night, someone would see me—we planned for Amos to retrieve it from the heating vent in my house, under the guise of checking on the dog for my parents while they were in Sunfish Creek for the search.

My eyes fly open. "Amos. You got rid of the phone, right?"

He drains his glass, my insides frosting over. "*Amos.* Answer the question."

Amos sets the glass down. Watches me with bloodshot eyes, says, "I didn't get it in time. There were county police going through your room when I stopped by. I thought I had more time—but when Mike got killed I knew I had to get the fuck out of town. I went to your house to get the phone—I was all shaken up, and I forgot about the alarm. I put in the wrong code and the system flipped out at me."

"You told me you got it and destroyed it," I say, my vision blurring at the edges.

"Because I didn't want you to worry and do anything stupid like turn yourself in," Amos snaps.

"You were worried *I* would do something stupid?"

"I wasn't thinking clearly, okay? I fucked up. What does it matter now?"

Mistakes always matter.

"When Claire doesn't show up for class on Monday, people are going to notice something is wrong . . ." Amos sounds a bit mournful as he studies the rim of his glass. "You know we have to do it, Kat."

I don't say anything. Claire's dying would fix Amos's mistake.

"It'll be painless," Amos says, taking my silence as assent. "She won't even know what's happening."

"No one else is being killed because of us."

"I'm not going to jail, Kat." Amos's voice hardens, as if the thought of jail were worse than death. He shakes his head, refills his glass.

"What would you do if I tried to stop you?" I ask.

"You won't." Amos drains his glass, sets it down. "Because we're family."

CHAPTER THIRTY-ONE

CLAIRE

NOW

Footsteps on the snow outside. Kat, probably. My heart climbs up my throat as I move to the window, but there's nothing. No porch light, no streetlamps.

I sit back in bed, panic flooding through my veins. The nearest house is easily half a mile away.

I startle as Amos steps in the room, a half-drunk bottle of whiskey tucked under his arm. He assumes his spot on the chest in the corner, holding something out to me. A small square, shrink-wrapped, the size of a postage stamp.

"Pain patch," he says. "For your head."

"No thanks."

"Suit yourself." Amos slips the patch back in his pocket, lifts the bottle to his mouth.

"Kat's home," I say. "Where did she go?"

Amos swallows, considers the bottle in his hand. "I'll answer one question for every shot you take with me."

"I think you're overestimating how badly I want answers."

"I'm a little hurt, Claire. I thought you and I were growing close."

"You didn't leak the thing I told you about the hiker to the press, did you?"

"No." Amos takes another swig of whiskey. "The point was never for everyone to think you were involved. That was all Marian—she thought you were lying to protect Jesse. Everyone did. She thought if you started to get dragged, you couldn't handle the heat and you'd fess up."

"But you did tell your grandma what I told you out on the lake. That I remembered the guy from the trail and thought it was the same guy I saw at the bar."

"Only because I had to."

"Why?"

Amos tilts the bottle to me. I yank it from his hand, take a sip, my eyes on the wolfish grin spreading across his face.

"Marian is not a dumb woman," Amos says. "After a few days, when the searchers still hadn't found any bodies on the mountain, my aunt Beth raised the possibility that maybe they were kidnapped. That's when Marian sat me down and grilled me. She wanted to know what I knew about her fight with Kat a few weeks before they went missing."

"When she told Kat to break up with Jesse or she couldn't go to BC?"

Amos nods to the bottle, still in my hand. "Another question, another shot."

"It's not a new question. It's a clarification question."

Amos grabs the bottle back. "Yes. It hadn't escaped my grandmother that Kat mysteriously disappeared with her boyfriend after she gave her that ultimatum. I needed Marian off of my ass, so I fed her what you told me, plus that bullshit story about the hikers getting robbed. It had the intended effect. She actually started to believe that something bad had happened to Kat."

"You made up the story about those girls getting robbed on Bobcat Mountain?"

Amos shrugs. "Without you as a witness to the fake kidnapping, we needed a way to seed the idea Jesse and Kat were taken."

I pull my knees to my chest, against the steady drumbeat of my heart. They used me. They didn't care what happened to me, as long as they got away. I was collateral damage. Acceptable loss.

The door creaks open, and Kat's voice emerges from the dark in the hall. "Get out, Amos."

"I'm comfortable right here," Amos says as Kat steps into the room. The fire in her eyes from this afternoon is gone, as if whatever she was doing the past few hours sucked the life out of her.

When she sees the whiskey bottle in my hands, she goes still. "What are you doing?"

"What does it look like?" Amos says at the same moment Kat reaches out and snatches the bottle from me. Her hands tremble around the neck of the bottle. "Don't take anything he gives you."

The fear in Kat's eyes twists my gut, despite the fact that I'd kept a careful eye on Amos as he opened the whiskey and he's been drinking it too. I think of the pain patch he offered me, my heart picking up speed.

Kat turns on her heels, shoves the Jack Daniels back at Amos, remembering herself. "Jesse says you won't eat anything. You'll get sick if you keep drinking on an empty stomach."

"I love everyone's concern for my well-being right now," I say. "I don't think the shovel smack did any additional brain damage, by the way."

"Sorry," Amos says around another swig from the bottle.

Kat perches at the edge of the bed. "You really don't remember anything that happened on the mountain?"

I pull my knees up to my chest, which has gone hollow. It always does when I think about Bobcat Mountain, about those missing hours. Grim resignation spreads through me. What's the point of pretending anymore? If they're not going to let me go, I at least have to find out what really happened on the mountain. "I don't even remember waking up that day."

"So you don't know why you never made it back to the lake house?"

My throat muscles tighten. "I remember Paul Santangelo, the hiker who saw me. But I don't remember speaking to him or why I tried to get away from him."

I've had six months to puzzle over my actions. The only explanation is that I was scared. I was lost and alone, and I didn't trust a creepy man who offered to help me.

"I must have gotten even farther from the right trail when I tried to hide from him," I say. "When it got dark I probably gave up and waited for help."

But help never came. I squeeze my eyes shut against the pressure of tears, the full weight of their betrayal hitting me. I was alone and terrified and instead of helping me they let Mike Dorsey attack me and leave me for dead.

Agent Novak was right. Having an answer doesn't help.

Kat is still studying me when I'm done wiping my eyes. I struggle to find my voice. "Why did I leave the campsite?"

She thinks a beat. "You were pissed off at me."

"Why?"

Under the dull glow of the bedside lamp, Kat's cheeks redden. "Why does it matter?"

In the corner, Amos has gone still, the bottle raised halfway to his lips, listening. Kat must never have told him why I left the campsite.

She's ashamed of whatever she did, or said.

I swallow. "Did Jesse tell you he and I talked on the dock the night before?"

"No." The flatness in her tone suggests that she knows, anyway. Maybe she saw us, or maybe she realized in the morning that something had happened, when I couldn't look Jesse in the eye. Nothing gets by Kat Marcotte.

"Is Jesse the reason I was pissed off at you?"

"Yes."

Kat tilts her head back against the headboard and closes

her eyes. I'm jolted back through the past ten years, remembering the hundreds of times we've done this before, on her bed or mine. Quizzing each other the night before a bio exam, or deciding what movie to put on as background noise while we talked for hours about anything, everything.

All that time, I never knew what was going on in her head. Was our entire friendship a lie? Does it mean our friendship wasn't real if the whole time she was hiding things from me, making me more dependent on her, pushing me further away from Jesse?

"Why didn't you ever tell me about your dad?" I ask.

Kat opens her eyes. "Would you have believed it?"

"How can you even ask that?"

"Do you know how many people didn't believe it?" Kat's hand moves to the sliver of a white scar that bisects the corner of her eyebrow. "One of my teachers alerted the air force after she saw this. I was finally scared enough to admit that my father did it. They sent someone to the house to check on us, everything was perfect. My mom told them it was her fault, that she'd dropped a plate and it was a freak accident."

"Emma didn't back you up?"

"I'm the one who taught her to do what they said. Never argue with them, or their version of what happened, in our house." Kat picks at a pill of fleece on the blanket. "So many times, I wanted to tell you, just so someone *knew*. But I knew you wouldn't be able to keep it to yourself. You'd want to help and get your parents involved."

"You could have stayed with us," I say. "You know my parents would have taken you in a heartbeat."

"They would never, ever let me go without a fight. Even if my parents somehow accepted it, Marian wouldn't have."

"Does she know what he did to you?" I ask.

Kat's expression darkens. "Why do you think she pays for Emma to go to boarding school? She knows exactly who he was and she would have died herself to protect the truth."

I find myself glancing over at Amos for confirmation. He nods, somber.

I slump lower against the headboard, listening for Kat's breathing next to mine. "I'm trying really hard to understand why you felt like this was the only answer," I say.

Kat hugs her legs to her body, resting her chin on her knees. "You can't. Unless you had to get a dislocated shoulder popped back in at the ER on your seventh birthday, you'll never understand."

"You had other options. But you wanted everyone to think you were dead."

"Not everyone," she says, her voice a church-confessional whisper. "Just my family."

"What about me?" I ask. I hate how much I care about the answer—how desperately I need to know if the girl I thought was my friend is still in the body next to me. "Losing you guys made me lose my mind, Kat."

My throat seals with the memory of it. The shrinks, the medication adjustments, the sobbing in front of strangers in group therapy sessions—all because I thought I'd never have an answer.

And now that I do, of course it isn't good enough.

"I'm sorry for what we did to you." Kat's eyes are glassy. "But I'm not sorry for what I did to them. I'm happy they think I'm dead. I hope every day for the rest of their lives they wonder if it's their fault."

I don't know what she wants me to say. That I understand, even if I don't forgive her? That I'd do the same thing if I'd been in her shoes? I settle on: "I think this is the most honest I've ever seen you."

Kat shrugs. "Thanks, I guess."

"It's not a compliment." I pull the bedspread over me and face the wall. "I want you to leave."

"And I'm not leaving you alone with Amos," Kat says.

I keep my eyes trained on the wall, on the water stain

marring the textured paint. "I'd rather be alone with him the rest of the night than spend a single second longer with you."

I feel Kat stand up from the bed and hear the door open.

"That was cold," Amos says from the corner when the door clicks behind Kat.

"Whatever." I sit up. "Give it to me," I say, gesturing to the Jack.

Amos stands, comes toward me tentatively. I can tell by his gait how drunk he is, even though his voice is smooth, controlled.

Amos climbs onto the bed so he's sitting next to me. "I knew you and I would eventually wind up like this again, Claire."

"And why is that?" I ask.

"I can tell you're like me," Amos says. "You've got that sad puppy look in your eyes—afraid to be alone with your thoughts for one second because if you are, you'll remember how meaningless and shitty everything is."

"You've got me all figured out," I say.

"It's an only-child thing, I guess. The difference between me and you is that you think relationships are the answer." Amos takes a long draw of whiskey, smacks his lips. "I've figured out there's nothing that can make the loneliness go away. You can only numb it."

Maybe what happened on the mountain didn't change me. Maybe I'm the person I was always becoming.

Maybe Amos is right, and my future only holds more loneliness. Maybe all that's left to do is embrace it. Numb it.

When Amos is done with his long swig, he passes the bottle to me. I hesitate, my fingers around the neck, before I lift it to my lips and drink.

CHAPTER THIRTY-TWO

KAT

NOW

I'm pacing downstairs, cleaning. Disinfecting the countertops, combing every corner for strands of my hair, a hidden surface that one of us may have touched. A futile attempt to remove all traces of us from this house.

Futile because Claire did what the FBI, somehow, could not. She found the phone, she found Zoe-Grace. She found us.

If we leave this house, we will have to run forever.

I pause at the foot of the stairs. It's quiet in the second-story bedrooms.

Too quiet.

I drop my spray bottle and bound up the stairs, two steps at a time. Throw the door open at the same time Claire is yanking it from the other side—

I take in the scene before me.

Amos, on the bed, unmoving.

Claire, lower lip trembling, hair wild.

I swallow bile, look from her to Amos's body. *Body*.

"Is he—"

Claire stumbles past me, vomits on the hallway floor. I rush over to Amos, grab his wrist. He's still warm, but his veins are too quiet—

I turn to Claire, who is now watching me, a hand over her mouth.

"Go," I say. "Your keys and phone are on the kitchen counter."

"Kat—"

"*Claire.* You need to get out of here. Go."

Jesse's face is white as he gets into the driver's seat of the Camry. We are so far north we're practically at the Canadian border; thick flakes have covered the windshield in the few minutes I've been in the passenger seat.

I drove Amos's BMW, his body laid out in the backseat. Together, Jesse and I managed to get him behind the wheel of his car. I wiped frozen tears from my cheeks as Jesse put the car in neutral, pushed it down the embankment, toward the hidden lake that is exactly where the GPS promised.

I closed my eyes at the last minute, so I didn't see the BMW disappear. In my head, the crack of the lake's icy surface plays on a loop.

Next to me, Jesse says nothing, blinks away the flakes gathered on his eyelashes.

I grab his gloved hand. "Amos is dead. It's only his prints on his gun—we can say he was keeping us hostage—we could get out of this."

"And Claire?"

"She was never there."

Jesse grabs my hand back.

"Kat, your family's money is not going to save us from this."

I flinch; after everything, it's the first time he's brought up Marian's wealth.

"I can't go back there," Jesse says quietly.

"Why?" I ask. "Do you think I'll turn on you or something? I would never do that."

"It's not that." Jesse grips my hand. "If we go back, we can never be together."

I'm still grasping for the words when Jesse speaks again. His voice is flat. "That doesn't even matter to you anymore, does it?"

"Take whatever money we have left," I say. "It'll last longer if it's just you. You can get away, Jesse."

"That's really what you want?" Jesse's voice floods with emotion. "To never see me again?"

"If it's what we have to do to get away—" The look on his face stops me, my words frosting in the air between us. He knows, of course. He must have known for a while, that if I had an out, I would take it.

"Did you ever love me?" Jesse asks.

I squeeze my eyes shut against the sting of the cold. After a beat, Jesse rests a gloved hand on the side of my face. "Kat?"

Even if I gave him the honest answer—*Yes, as much as someone like me can love another person*—it wouldn't be enough for him. Because he gave up everything for me. Even if we stayed together, started a life somewhere, how do you ever repay someone who has already proven they would give you the world?

I lean into his hand, his glove cold against my cheek. "I'm sorry," I whisper. And I really mean it.

I'm in an overheated room at the Timsbury police precinct, a Styrofoam cup of tea on the table in front of me. It's too strong to drink, even though I'm still shivering. The police obeyed my wish not to go to the hospital. A paramedic came to take my blood pressure and pulse, and a female cop keeps checking in on me to dump vending machine snacks on the table and ask if I need more tea. I think she really just wants to gawk at me—Katherine Marcotte, alive, in her precinct!

I said I would only speak to the FBI, not the local police. The nearest FBI field office is in the Hudson Valley, four hours away, but I heard the officer on the phone say something about two agents driving up from Long Island.

If that's true, and I don't have to speak to anyone else until they get here, Jesse has more than enough time to retrieve his things and the money from the farmhouse, and get out of the state.

The clock over the door in my holding room says it has been six and a half hours since I arrived; the sound of voices outside the room makes my pulse go still. I recognize the voice of the officer who keeps checking on me, and two new voices.

A swift knock before the door cracks open, and a man steps in, flanked by a woman.

"Katherine?" the woman asks. Her head is cocked slightly as she takes me in, looking for evidence this is all a hoax.

I nod, silent.

"I'm Nicole Cummings, a special agent with the FBI," she says. "This is my partner, Bill Novak."

It takes me a moment to absorb this. She is young and black; he's older and white. She's tall and slim; he's squat and beefy. They're the type of people you'd see chatting next to each other on the bus and think, *I wonder if they have a single thing in common.*

"What's this about you not wanting to see your family?" Cummings asks, sliding into the chair across from me, setting a Dunkin' Donuts coffee cup on the table.

I prop my elbows on the table, rest my face in my hands. Shrug stubbornly, the ringleader of a food fight marched into the principal's office for questioning. Whatever it takes to stall.

Agent Cummings's gaze flicks to her partner.

"We just spoke to the medic who checked you out," Agent Novak says. "You sure you don't want a more thorough exam at the hospital?"

I shake my head. "I'm not hurt."

Agent Cummings strips off her suit jacket and drapes it over the back of her chair. "Can we get them to turn the heat down?" she says, as casually as if we're at the Olive Garden.

Novak sighs and steps outside, leaving me with Cummings.

There's a crescent of taupe lip gloss on the rim of her Dunkin' cup. She taps a smoothed, unpolished nail against the lid. "It might be a good idea to get checked out by a real doctor."

"I think I'm going to pass out," I say.

"Head between your legs," Cummings says. "Deep breaths."

I lower my head to my lap, just so I don't have to look at her. The tick of the clock overhead is the only sound in the room for a beat until the click of the door.

The man, Novak, is back. He shuts the door behind him and hovers next to Agent Cummings instead of taking a seat.

"We know you must be shaken up," he says. "But as you can imagine, we've got a lot of questions for you."

I nod. I have no plans to answer their questions.

Novak's brow furrows. "Why didn't you want the officers here to contact your family?"

I cast my eyes down at my hands.

"Katherine," Agent Cummings says, drawing my gaze up to her. "There are a lot of people who are going to be happy you're alive. But they're gonna want answers."

I say nothing. Maybe acting traumatized will buy me time. Buy Jesse more time, to disappear for good.

Cummings pushes her coffee cup aside and knits her hands together. "Where's Jesse, Kat?"

"I don't know," I say.

"Okay," Cummings sighs. "What about your cousin?"

"I don't know." I swallow to clear my throat, make room for the lies. "I last saw him yesterday morning. He went to Burlington to do a drug deal and never came back."

A knock at the door; before Cummings or Novak can reply to my claim, the gawking officer sticks her head in the room. "There's a woman here demanding to see Kat."

Mommy. The word streaks through my brain, even though I haven't called her that in years. I blink away the tears clouding my eyes, aware that Cummings and Novak are staring at me, watching for a reaction.

Movement in the doorway—the police officer is shunted aside as my grandmother steps into the room. When she sees me, her hand moves to her mouth. I stay still as she moves toward me, my heart sinking to my feet.

Marian stumbles on the last step before throwing her arms around me. It's not until I notice Cummings and Novak staring at me that I think to lift my arms and hug her back.

My hands go still; my grandmother's hair is in a perfect chignon at the nape of her neck. I think I even saw the smallest smudge of mascara at the corner of her eye. She got a call in the middle of the night that I was alive and safe and she *did her goddamn hair and makeup* before driving up here.

Over the past six months, I imagined her changing. Losing a son and a granddaughter had to have humbled her.

When Marian finally lets me go, she turns to the agents. "I'll be taking my granddaughter home now."

Novak folds his enormous arms across his chest. "I'm afraid it's not that simple, Mrs. Marcotte."

"Is she being charged with a crime?"

"No—"

"Then yes, it really is that simple: Katherine leaves with me."

Cummings stands; Novak puts a hand on her arm. "With all due respect, your granddaughter is an adult. It's her choice if she wants to stay and talk to us."

"Not until she's been examined by a proper doctor," Marian snaps. "If you have a problem with that, you can contact our family's attorney."

Marian grabs me by the elbow. Anger rises in me, white-hot, at the familiarity of it. I yank away from her. Compose myself in time to see Agent Cummings watching me, her perfectly shaped eyebrows bending toward each other.

"Katherine, this way." Marian is already on the other side of the door frame.

I follow her.

It's not until we're halfway down the hall—Cummings and

Novak out of earshot behind us—that my grandmother says: "I have a car waiting for us in the back lot. There will be reporters outside by now."

We are in the black SUV idling behind the police station. When Marian shuts the divider between us and our driver, I speak. "You should have let me talk to the FBI."

"Absolutely not." Marian lifts a hand to the crown of her head, winces. "You're not speaking with anyone until I speak to our attorney."

My stomach dips as the car begins to move. On some level, this was what I wanted—for Marian to rescue me from that shitty farmhouse, to take control and keep me safe—but now that I'm alone with her, I want to claw my way out of this car. The idea of the narrative of my kidnapping being in her hands, shaped by her PR pros and lawyers and money makes me feel like I'm suffocating. "I had everything under control—"

"Did you?" Marian snaps. "Because it sounded to me like you had no idea Jesse was apprehended trying to cross the Canadian border an hour ago."

The blood drains from my head. Jesse got caught. "Apprehended for what? He didn't do anything—"

"The FBI put out an APB for him as soon as you showed up at the police station." My grandmother reaches into her purse with trembling hands. She removes a bottle of Advil, pops the top. She swallows two, dry, her eyes closed. "You should have broken up with that boy when I told you to."

I want to scream at her, ask her if controlling my life was worth all of this, but my voice comes out in a whisper. "Why? Why do you hate him *so much*?"

"You really don't know, do you?" Her voice cracks slightly on the last two syllables.

It chills my blood. "What are you talking about?"

Marian pinches the skin between her eyes, as if a migraine is coming on. When she composes herself, she says, "His mother interned at my office while she was in college."

An unsettled feeling pools in my stomach. "What does Jesse's mom have to do with anything?"

"She had too much to drink at a fundraising event and made disgusting accusations against your father."

"That's why you hate Jesse?"

"I never said I hated him. I said *you can't be with him*."

The force in her voice seems to suck the air out of the car.

Jesse had been born when his mother was still in college; she'd left for a semester to have him.

I can't stitch the words swirling in my brain into a complete thought. "Did she say my father—is he Jesse's—"

Marian's eyes flutter shut. "You should have listened to me, Katherine."

"No," I whisper. "You're lying."

"I'm not, Katherine. As soon as I realized who he was, I told you to end things."

The party—she hadn't been horrified because Jesse said his mother was half Mexican. My grandmother was horrified because she recognized the last name Salpietro.

His dark brown eyes, the cleft in his chin just like the one my father had—

I bang on the window divider. "Excuse me? Please let me out."

"Katherine, don't be ridiculous." My grandmother snaps her head toward the front of the cab. "Please keep driving."

I bang on the window again. "I'm going to be sick—"

The car swerves off the road as if a train were barreling toward us. I stumble out and vomit onto the shoulder. When there's nothing left in me, I hunch over, arms around my middle, sobs rolling through my body.

All those nights that my father destroyed our house, that he screamed at me with spit flecks flying at my face, that I worried about him going downstairs to that gun safe and kill-ing us all, I would think, *At least if I'm dead I never have to go through this again.*

How I felt in those moments could never compare to how I feel right now. It's a thousand times worse.

I buckle over and vomit again as the driver hops out of the car and hurries over to me. "Miss, are you okay?"

"She's fine," my grandmother barks, hot on his heels. "Please get back in the car."

The driver looks from her to me. I really hope she made him sign an NDA before agreeing to drive us all the way to Long Island.

I stare back at her. "I don't believe you."

"For God's sake, Katherine." There are tears in her eyes. "Just look at the boy."

A cold sweat is spreading over me. She's lying—she'll do anything to keep us apart, even telling a horrendous lie.

But she would not lie about her son. Her darling Airman Marcotte.

She made disgusting accusations about your father.

Marian never reaches for me. The cars on the freeway whiz by. It seems unfair, that my entire world is falling apart as they're all searching for a decent radio station or debating where to stop for dinner.

"Now you know," Marian finally says. "I was only trying to protect you."

I wipe my eyes. "Protect me? You protected *him*. He should have gone to jail."

"It's easy for you to judge me. You couldn't possibly under-stand the position I was in. Until you have a child of your own you will never understand what you would do for them."

"What about my mother? You were just going to let her live with that *animal* for the rest of her life?"

Marian is breathing heavily. A lock of hair has escaped her chignon.

"I dated him for almost a year with no idea who he was," I whisper.

"If you hadn't hid him from us, I would have told you to break up with him much sooner."

"Who else knew?" I ask. "Besides you, and Jesse's mom?"

"Just us. My agreement with his mother was that she not tell him his real father's name."

"So, you paid Jesse's mother to go away?"

"No," she says. "I helped her with her medical bills and made sure the child would be taken care of once he turned twenty-one."

"You never even told my dad? How could you?" I say.

"How could *you*, Katherine?" She's finally raising her voice. "You've destroyed this family. You've probably destroyed that boy's life too."

That boy. She can't even say his name. Her own grandson.

I feel like I am going to vomit again, but I have nothing left. There is physically nothing left in me.

"I hate you," I say. "You are the worst person I have ever known in my entire life."

"Maybe you mean that," Marian finally says. "But where would you be now without me?"

CHAPTER THIRTY-THREE

KAT

FEBRUARY

They called it a *late Christmas miracle*. Kat Marcotte and Jesse Salpietro, found alive after six months. At first, everyone from Brenda Dean to Lester Holt wanted to interview us. The longer we stayed quiet, the more the public's appetite for answers grew.

The rumors began on the dark corners of the internet at first. Jesse and I couldn't be trusted—we had obviously run away together, maybe because I was pregnant. After Brenda Dean implied we were a teen Bonnie and Clyde, Marian started to get so many death threats that she, too, had to sell her Brookport house.

The FBI maintained a good poker face, saying they refused to comment on the case until the investigation was complete and any charges were announced. During that time, the tide began to shift. First, a story in the *Daily News* about the visits the social worker paid to our house in Italy, complete with quotes from subordinates of the captain, claiming he regularly threatened his employees with violence.

I have no doubt Marian was behind the leaks to the press. A carefully constructed narrative to support my own: I ran away to escape my father. The monster in a hero's uniform. My cousin was supposed to help me, but his own greed got in the way. Amos secured us a safe haven in the farmhouse; we were at the mercy of his drug money, and his gun, lest we thought about turning ourselves in. When Amos didn't come back from a drug drop, I decided it was finally time to go home and tell the truth.

I haven't seen or spoken to Jesse since I arrived at the police station. Marian, and my lawyers, have expressly forbidden it.

He deserves to know who he is. Who he really threw his life away for.

My mother is moving us to New Jersey, which, according to the people who believe in my guilt, might be a punishment worse than jail. Her family, my other grandparents, live in Princeton, in a gated retirement community. It had never occurred to me that my mother never saw her parents because the captain wouldn't let her.

Anyway, in the fall, I'll be enrolling in the local community college. Emma refused to move with us, refused to leave Barton for a Catholic high school in Princeton.

Our Brookport house sold. Over the past week, from the guest bedroom of my aunt Erin's house, I've seen the moving trucks pass by, carting our furniture off to Jersey. This morning my mother asked me if I wanted to say goodbye to the house before she left to hand the keys to the new owners at the closing. My stomach gave a violent twist at the thought of those empty rooms, the fist-shaped holes in the walls spackled over.

I close my eyes, picture my room, the heating grate. If Amos had just stayed calm and input the alarm code properly when he went to retrieve the phone, we would all still be in Timsbury. I would still be Kaylee Brewer, at least for a few more months.

The sound of an engine puttering outside startles my eyes open. I stand slowly and creep to the living room window.

The sedan parked across the street, oatmeal colored, paint chipping, belongs to Jesse's aunt Andrea.

My stomach catapults. His lawyers told him to stay away from me, and vice versa. He hasn't tried to reach out to me in the two months since we've been home.

He looks up. Sees me in the window.

I didn't think I'd be able to look him in the eye ever again. I never thought I'd even get the opportunity.

I slip on the shoes waiting by the door and hurry outside. He motions to undo his seat belt. I shake my head, freezing him to his seat. I open the passenger side door and slip into the car. "Sorry. No one can see you here."

Jesse nods, drumming his fingers on his knee. "I'm sorry. I shouldn't be here. I heard you were leaving and I needed to see you."

I look away from the hand on his knee, from the slight tremor in his fingers that suggests he's holding back from grabbing my hand, kissing the knuckles like he used to. I pinch the flab of skin between my thumb and forefinger, a move Marian always used to say could banish nausea.

"I heard the charges against you are coming soon," I say.

"Lying to investigators. My lawyer got the heads-up."

"I can't do this," I whisper. "I can't let you go to jail for me. I have to tell them the truth."

"Kat, you can't. That's what they want. If you contradict me, we'll probably both go to jail."

I swallow. "Are you? Going to go to jail?"

"I could get up to a year, but my lawyer thinks more likely it'll be a couple years' probation."

I have to put my head between my knees. Jesse rubs my back. "Hey. I'm lucky if that's all I get, after everything."

I look up at him. "You did it for me. *I'm* the one who deserves to go to jail."

"I did it for us." He moves his hand lower down my back. The warmth of his touch makes me recoil.

I jerk forward so his hand separates from my back. "You don't understand. There's a reason my grandmother wanted me to break up with you."

"Kat." His voice is gentle. "Don't."

"*No.* You deserve to know who my dad—"

"Kat. You don't have to say it. I already know."

My surroundings begin to blur. All the possibilities of how Jesse could have found out curdle in my stomach. If Jesse knows, it's only a matter of time before it's tabloid fodder.

I swallow against the nausea swelling up in me. "Did the FBI tell you?"

"No. They didn't." Jesse isn't looking at me.

"Jesse," I whisper. "How did you find out?"

"When my uncle said that thing to me last year—about what happened to my mom—I did one of those DNA tests. I just wanted to know his name." Jesse shuts his eyes. "He wasn't in the system, but I found out I had a distant cousin on Long Island. Their last name was Sullivan."

My blood frosts over. "When did you do the DNA test?"

"Last March—but, Kat, I didn't put everything together until your grandma's birthday party. The way she looked at me. She wasn't just disgusted, she was scared." Jesse wipes his eyes. "I got this horrible feeling that she *knew* me."

"So instead of saying something to me, you did what? You dug into my family and found out that we were *related*—"

"I needed to be sure before I said anything." Jesse's voice cracks. "I was going to tell you, but when you told me you were thinking of *killing yourself* it changed everything—"

"It didn't change anything!" I'm screaming—I've never once before screamed at Jesse.

I needed to escape a monster. Not run away with a different one.

I grab the door handle. Jesse motions to stop me—the voice that comes out of me is so frightening, it almost sounds like it can't be mine. "Don't touch me."

"Kat." He's full-on sobbing now.

He knew when he suggested running away together—it was the *reason* he suggested it—the reason why he didn't want to come home—

If we go back, we can never be together.

"No." I cover my mouth. "Oh my God. Oh my *God*."

"Kat," he pleads. "We didn't grow up together."

"Let me the fuck out of the car, Jesse."

He wipes away his tears with the back of his hand. The second the lock clicks, I stumble out of the car, slam the door shut behind me over the sound of his sobs.

CHAPTER THIRTY-FOUR

CLAIRE

———

MAY

The voice mail is brief.

"Claire, how ya doing? It's Bill Novak. Give me a call."

There's no mention of Amos, or his death, on the recording, or of a summons to testify in any upcoming proceedings that will decide Kat's and Jesse's fate. I'd been waiting for the latter ever since Agent Cummings personally called me to break the news that Kat and Jesse had been found alive.

I'd nodded along as she recounted what details she was allowed to give, even though Cummings couldn't see me.

Can't say for sure what is going on—

—going to be a complicated investigation—

—you could be called to testify about that weekend.

The weekend on Bobcat Mountain, I'd had to remind my-self. Not the weekend in Timsbury, New York, that never happened, as far as the FBI and police are concerned.

I'd thanked Cummings, told her to keep me posted. I went to my classes as if nothing had happened, watched the news of Kat's and Jesse's reappearance ripple through the student body for a day or two. I started and ended each day monitoring the news reports, waiting for the alert that Amos's body had been found.

It never came. Kat's and Jesse's arrest never came, despite Brenda Dean's nightly call for them to be charged with criminal conspiracy, the chorus of voices on Reddit backing her up.

I don't read the threads much anymore, but I know the debate rages on among people who still care.

She was the mastermind.

He was the mastermind.

They'd actually been kidnapped.

The FBI has only commented to say that the investigation is still ongoing and active, and that they haven't ruled out the possibility of charges being filed against the parties involved.

I took my last final yesterday morning. I drove straight home, no pit stops. Tonight, I worked my first shift at Stellato's since returning home for the summer; tomorrow, Ben comes home, and I don't know what will happen with that, but first, I have to finish burying her.

The girl in the mirror of the Sunfish Creek emergency room, bloodied and robbed of her memory. The girl in her dorm bathroom, sobbing under the steamy blast of the shower, praying that no one had seen her car fleeing that farmhouse in Timsbury or seen her arrive at the dorm building at four in the morning, a shivering mess.

I remind myself that I am here, in Brookport, behind the wheel of my car, parked outside Stellato's. I'm right back where I started but I'm not the same. And I'm not going to hide.

I play the voice mail again, ignoring the slick of sweat coming to my palms. When it's over, I call Novak back, wait for his grunt of a *hello*.

"Hi," I say brightly. "It's Claire Keough. You wanted to talk?"

He suggests meeting at a park not far from the FBI office, on his lunch break the following day. I find him on a bench, eating out of a Subway bag, not far from the entrance. Exactly where he said he'd be.

"Where's Agent Cummings?" I ask.

"On vacation." Novak dabs his mouth with a napkin. "She made sure to dump her paperwork on me first."

"Is that why I'm here? To help with paperwork?"

"No." Novak pops open a bag of Baked Lays chips, offers it to me. I shake my head. My insides have turned to solid rock, despite the fact that if Novak were about to arrest me for Amos Fornier's death, he probably wouldn't be stuffing potato chips in his mouth.

"Jesse's new attorney called the DA's office yesterday," Novak says, taking a pull from his soda. "He's talking."

I bite down on the inside of my cheek. "What is he saying?"

"That it was his and Amos's idea to stage the kidnapping. It was their grand plan to save Kat from Johnathan Marcotte." Cummings sighs. "Kat didn't know anything, and when everything went south, they convinced her she couldn't go home or she'd be implicated too."

A tingle in my hands. "And you believe that?"

"Of course I fucking don't."

I'm shocked to hear it come out of his mouth. I swallow. "Is Jesse facing any charges?"

"None that will hold up at trial. The only person we can put at the scene of the extortion is Mike Dorsey, and without Amos to testify that it was actually Kat's and Jesse's idea . . ." Novak shrugs. "I'm sorry, Claire. I know this is hard to hear, after what you went through."

Not as hard as you'd think. "A lot of people think they're guilty, though," I say.

"Perception can change. Or be bought." Novak's mouth forms a line. "In lieu of Amos answering for his role in what happened, his family has reached a settlement with the town of Sunfish Creek. Marian Sullivan-Marcotte will compensate the sheriff's department for expenses incurred during the search for Kat and Jesse."

I fiddle with the drawstring at the neck of my thin hoodie, desperate to steer the conversation away from Amos. "I just don't understand why she never told anyone about her father."

"There are loads of reasons why abuse victims stay quiet. None of which you or I can really understand." Novak crushes the empty bag of chips into a ball. "If new evidence emerges, we might be able to get them on lying to investigators. But putting an abused girl in front of a jury is a prosecutor's worst nightmare. *A lot* of people witnessed the abuse over the years. Kat's and Jesse's lawyers are the best of the best—they'll find anyone out there with a story to tell about Johnathan Marcotte and get them on the stand."

"I don't understand," I say. "I thought Jesse had some random public defender."

"He just retained Young and Associates, a criminal firm out of Manhattan."

There's no way Jesse could afford a fancy attorney without the Marcotte family's help. Amos was right; Marian Sullivan-Marcotte really would do anything to protect her family, even if it means buying off the boy she hated. The boy her family had been destroyed over.

I lean forward, rest my elbows on my knees to match Novak's stance. I bury my head in my hands and inhale.

"It's not over until we hear what Amos has to say," Novak says, mistaking my silence for disbelief. Despair, that they would get away with what they did, to their families, to me. "We'll keep looking, but my guess is he's on some yacht halfway around the world right now."

He shrugs, as if to say there are actual missing people who need to be found, who deserve all the FBI's attention.

"I've got to head to a deposition," Novak says. "If there's anything you need—you have my number, right?"

I nod, even though I know I will never see him again. There won't be a trial for what happened that weekend; I won't have to look Kat and Jesse in the eye as their lawyers call me a liar. I won't have to be a headline again.

It's a small comfort. I'll have to live with the truth living in me like a cancer.

I was surprised at how quickly the fentanyl patch worked on Amos. He'd already been on the verge of passing out from how much he'd had to drink. I almost didn't expect it to work, but I didn't think twice about slipping it out of his pocket, onto his skin when he climbed on top of me, all too eager to pick up where we left off in his room three years ago.

It was easy. The choice between my escape and Amos's life wasn't even a choice.

I wonder, wherever she is now, if that's how Kat felt when she decided to leave.

I don't think I'll ever know for sure. But as I'm finding out, there's a lot I can live with.

I feel a little lighter when I reach my car. I tilt my face to the sun. Summer is close by.

RESOURCES

While this is a work of fiction, emotional and physical abuse is a reality for many, regardless of age, gender, or socioeconomic status. If you or someone you know is experiencing abuse or domestic violence, you are not alone. Please contact the following hotlines:

CHILDHELP NATIONAL CHILD ABUSE HOTLINE
1-800-4-A-CHILD (1-800-422-4453)

NATIONAL DOMESTIC VIOLENCE HOTLINE
1-800-799-SAFE (1-800-799-7233)

ACKNOWLEDGMENTS

I have endless gratitude for my editor, Krista Marino, who always sees the trees even when I am so deeply lost in the forest.

Thank you to Suzie Townsend and the entire team at New Leaf Literary, especially Dani Segelbaum, Joanna Volpe, Veronica Grijalva, Victoria Henderson, Pouya Shahbazian, and Hilary Pecheone.

Thank you to Agent Extraordinaire Sarah Landis at Sterling Lord Literistic and all my other early champions of this book, especially Courtney Summers, Kit Frick, Karen McManus, Erin Craig, and Rachel Strolle. Many thanks to my film agent, Will Watkins at ICM, for your enthusiasm for this book.

Thank you to everyone at Random House Children's Books—Lydia Gregovic, Barbara Marcus, Beverly Horowitz, Elizabeth Ward, Kelly McGauley, Jenn Inzetta, Kate Keating, John Adamo, and Mary McCue. I am also eternally grateful to the art department for yet another beautiful cover.

Thank you to my supportive group of friends for their late-night brainstorming sessions and encouragement through multiple drafts of this book. Thank you to my family and everyone in my life who helped me keep a small human alive and entertained during said drafts.

And thank you to my readers. I hope this one was worth the wait.

CHAPTER ONE

Hell is a two-hour layover in Atlanta.

The woman to my right has been watching me since I sat down. I can tell she's one of those people who take the sheer fact that you're breathing as an invitation to start up a conversation.

No eye contact. I let the words repeat in my head as I dig around for my iPod. I always keep it on me, even though it's a model that Apple hasn't made for seven years and the screen is cracked.

Pressure builds behind my nose. The woman stirs next to me. *No eye contact. And definitely do not—*

I sneeze.

Damn it.

"Bless you, honey! Hot, isn't it?" The woman fans herself with her boarding pass. She reminds me of my gram: she's old, but more likely to be hanging around a Clinique counter than at the community center on bingo day. I give her a noncommittal nod.

She smiles and shifts in her seat so she's closer to my armrest. I try to see myself through her eyes: Greasy hair in a bun. Still in black pants and a black V-neck—my Chili's uniform. Backpack wedged between my feet. I guess I look like I need mothering.

"So where you from?" she asks.

It's a weird question for an airport. Don't most people ask each other where they're going?

I swallow to clear my throat. "Florida."

She's still fanning herself with the boarding pass, sending the smell of sweat and powder my way. "Oh, Florida. Wonderful."

Not really. Florida is where people move to die.

"There are worse places," I say.

I would know, because I'm headed to one of them.

• • •

I knew someone was dead when my manager told me I had a phone call. During the walk from the kitchen to her office, I convinced myself it was Gram. When I heard her voice on the other end, I thought I could float away with relief.

Then she said, "Tessa, it's your father."

Pancreatic cancer, she explained. Stage four. It wouldn't have made a difference if the prison doctors had caught it earlier.

It took the warden three days to track me down. My father's corrections officer called Gram's house collect when I was on my way to work.

Gram said he might not make it through the night. So she picked me up from Chili's, my backpack waiting for me on the passenger seat. She wanted to come with me, but there was no time to get clearance from her cardiologist to fly. And we both knew that the extra ticket would have been a waste of money anyway.

Glenn Lowell isn't her son. She's never even met the man.

I bought my ticket to Pittsburgh at the airport. It cost two hundred dollars more than it would have if I'd booked it in advance. I nearly said screw it. That's two hundred dollars I need for books in the fall.

You're probably wondering what kind of person would let her father die alone for two hundred dollars. But my father shot and nearly killed a convenience store owner for a lot less than that— and a carton of cigarettes.

So. It's not that I don't want to be there to say goodbye; it's just that my father's been dead to me ever since a judge sentenced him to life in prison ten years ago.